Amending the Shades of Pemberley

by

Award-Winning Author

Regina Jeffers

Amending

the Shades of Pemberley

Copyright © 2023 by Regina Jeffers

Cover Design: SelfPubBookCovers.com/Designsbypimpimol

All Rights Reserved

This is a work of fiction. Names, places, characters and incidents are either the product of the author's imagination or are used fictitiously, and any resemblance to any actual persons, living or dead, businesses, organizations, events or locales is entirely coincidental. All trademarks, service marks, registered trademarks, and registered service marks are the property of their respective owners and are used herein for identification purposes only. The publisher does not have any control over or assume any responsibility for author or third-party websites or their contents.

All rights Reserved under International and Pan-American Copyright Conventions. No part of this book may be used or reproduced, transmitted, downloaded, decompiled, reverse engineered, or stored in or introduced into any information storage and retrieval system, in any form or by any means whether electronic or mechanical, including photocopying, recording, etc., now known or hereinafter invented without the written permission from the author and copyright owner except in the case of brief quotation embodied in critical articles and reviews. Please purchase only authorized electronic editions and do not participate in or encourage electronic piracy of copyrighted materials. Your support of the author's rights is appreciated.

WARNING: The unauthorized reproduction or distribution of this copyrighted work is illegal. Criminal copyright infringement, including infringement without monetary gain, is investigated by the FBI and is punishable by up to 5 years in federal prison and a fine of $250,000. Anyone pirating ebooks will be prosecuted to the fullest extent of the law and may be liable for each individual download resulting there from.

ABOUT THE PRINT VERSION: If you purchased a print version of this book without a cover, you should be aware that the book is stolen property. It was reported as "unsold and destroyed" to the publisher, and neither the author nor the publisher has received any payment for this "stripped book."

Your support of the author's rights is greatly appreciated.

Chapter One

Early Autumn 1814

"How might I be of service, Sister Elizabeth?"

Elizabeth looked up to view the solemn face of Mr. Bingley. Today was the first time he had made an appearance at Longbourn since Jane's untimely passing. Sadness still marked the man's features, and Elizabeth reached out to take his hands in hers. "Thank you for coming. I know all this is difficult for you."

"No more so than it is for you and Miss Mary," he said kindly. "Have all the arrangements been made? What of you and your sister?"

"Mary will stay with Aunt and Uncle Gardiner. The Phillipses have offered me a home, but I could not remain in Meryton and view Longbourn in the hands of another," she admitted. "Aunt Gardiner's second eldest brother is a vicar in the north. Her eldest brother passed at the same time as her father. Mr. Ericks has agreed to take me in until I can claim a position as a governess or a teacher at a girls' school."

"There is no need for either you or Miss Mary to enter service. You are my sweet Jane's sisters. You will always have a home with me," he declared.

Elizabeth wrapped her arm through his. "You are wonderfully generous and caring, and Mary and I are honored by your kindness; yet, we cannot accept. First and foremost, you do not require a constant reminder of your loss. You must eventually begin again, for you owe it to your family name to do so. I know you cannot yet think of taking another to wife, but you must some day act accordingly, and such would be quite awkward if your late wife's sisters resided with you. No woman wishes to share her house with 'reminders' of another, especially a woman of Jane's angelic beauty and kindness."

Elizabeth knew Mr. Bingley's sisters would not approve of his attentions to Jane's family. Although Jane's being a gentleman's daughter had raised Mr. Bingley's status in society, Miss Bingley and Mrs. Hurst had never approved of their brother's marriage to the woman he loved and was dearly loved in return. The sisters wanted their own tickets into society, riding their brother's coattails into the *haut ton*.

"There must be something of significance I may do for you," he insisted.

Elizabeth led him to a small sitting room. She purposely avoided her mother's favorite drawing room. She and Mr. Bingley each had too many memories associated with the room. It was the room in which Bingley had proposed and in which her dear father had taken his last breath. "Would you like tea?" she asked. "Or something stronger?"

Mr. Bingley shook off the offer. "All I require is for you to speak to me honestly," he instructed.

Elizabeth heaved a weary sigh. "The news from Mr. Birkhead was worse than I initially thought," she began without looking directly into Mr. Bingley's eyes. "The area lost so many to the pox. Some saw whole families wiped out. Despite the passing of Lydia and Kitty and Mama, Papa was certain we could go on. I should not say this, but you will understand: Neither Mr. Bennet's thoughts nor mine were meant to be malicious. Yet, with Mr. Collins's passing and Charlotte delivering forth a daughter, Mr. Bennet believed he had been presented a reprieve. He could, assuredly, after a period of mourning, marry another and, perhaps, produce a son to keep the entailment alive."

"Who is to inherit now?" Mr. Bingley asked.

"If I understand it properly," she began, "the entail will end, but a thorough search will be conducted to learn if another can make a claim. There are no male heirs coming from Mr. Bennet's line, but perhaps that of another cousin."

"Could not you and Miss Mary inherit through some sort of common recovery? Or, perhaps, though not what you wish, even Mr. Collins's daughter? Was not Collins's claim through a female line some four generations removed?" Mr. Bingley asked.

"I am not as well versed in Mr. Collins's lineage as I should be, but Mr. Birkhead says otherwise. Moreover, I have spoken to Charlotte, and she will make no claim on the estate. In fact, it is my understanding, the gentleman who will replace Mr. Collins at Hunsford has requested to court Charlotte once Mrs. Collins's mourning period has ended. It seems Lady Catherine de Bourgh believes Charlotte would be a good influence on her ladyship's new rector."

"Then why cannot you and Miss Mary remain in Meryton?" Mr. Bingley asked.

Elizabeth swallowed hard. "There is not enough money."

"I could . . ." Mr. Bingley began.

However, she signaled for him to swallow his words. "It seems Mr. Bennet planned some sort of sweet revenge on Mr. Collins. As you may have concluded, my dear father greatly despised Mr. Collins' father. When Mr. Bennet thought he held no chance of seeing his own line succeed, my father mortgaged Longbourn in order to invest in a mine. If the mine succeeded, Papa meant to provide all his daughters with enticing dowries and simply enjoy his final years in some luxury. According to his correspondence with Mr. Birkhead, if the investment failed, it would be Collins's debt of honor. Unfortunately, when Mr.

Collins passed, along with Mrs. Bennet and my younger sisters, Mr. Bennet's prospects changed, but the gold mine vein was too weak to sustain the debt. My father's revenge on Mr. Collins turned its ugly head on its server. The realization of his gambling away his heritage was enough to drive Mr. Bennet into a fit of anger and a spasm with his heart, one strong enough to kill him."

"How much?" Mr. Bingley asked.

"Nearly ten thousand. Everything must be sold or else Mary and I will each inherit a debt we can never repay, no matter how many years we labor in service. Uncle Gardiner has offered to assist us, but neither of us can permit his family to suffer because of our father's messy revenge on another claiming his beloved Longbourn."

Mr. Bingley appeared not to agree with her assessment, but he said, "In your note, you asked for my assistance: If I am not to see you well settled elsewhere, then I must return to my initial question: How might I be of service?"

"Mary and I discussed it. We hoped you might organize some sort of auction of the household goods. Surely my father's books must be of interest to collectors. He has many first printings, and there is the china and artwork. I realize Longbourn is not a stylish house in Town, but, according to Mr. Birkhead, we should not simply walk away from all inside. The gentleman says we could greatly reduce the debt if we sold the household in 'parts,' rather than a whole. I thought with your import and export business . . ."

"Your uncle's business could serve you equally as well. Mayo's is larger than mine in that manner," Mr. Bingley argued.

"Uncle Gardiner already holds several such obligations for others," she explained. "Moreover, I thought it would be difficult for him to be required to see his youngest sister's belongings sold to another, especially if someone offered less than the true worth."

Mr. Bingley smiled comfortably. "I have viewed more than one 'heated disagreement' at an auction, but never between those overseeing the sale and those bidding." He sighed in regret. "Naturally, I will arrange it all. Leave it in my hands. It will be part of my debt to

Jane. I will bring my staff from Netherfield to assist Mr. and Mrs. Hill in preparing the rooms. Once we have a list of the furniture and goods, I will have adverts printed and posted along the roads between here and London and throughout the neighboring shires. You should know," he said in hesitation, "I have decided not to renew my lease at Netherfield. It is simply too hard." He broke off with a sigh of grief.

"I am greatly remorseful for not being in a position to offer you the necessary comfort you required with Jane's passing," she said in true sympathy.

"You had your own hardships," he returned. "All of Meryton had their own hardships."

"We all thought you and Jane would be together forever," she assured.

"So did I," he said as tears misted his eyes. "If I had known having a child would steal away the woman I so dearly loved . . ."

"Each of us thought when you sealed off Netherfield from the rest of the community all would be well. It was quite a task to keep Mama from visiting Jane, but once she, too, took sick, Mrs. Bennet praised her own sensibility in protecting your child."

Mr. Bingley said with renewed sadness, "In the end, all our protections proved worthless. The pox did not take my Jane, but, rather, the gift with which God had blessed us did the job. I lost both Jane and my first child in one fell swoop. I cannot think upon how empty Netherfield appears without her within."

"You should have come to us," Elizabeth declared, although, instinctively, she knew he could not, for Longbourn was in total chaos.

"You had too much sorrow of your own," he countered, "and I required time to permit my dear wife her leave-taking. I am not quite there yet, but, with God's grace, I have reached some peace. It will do me well to serve Jane's family." He reached across to her and caught Elizabeth's hand. "You must make me a promise, if your plans become too much for you as a genteel lady, you will send me word. I will come for you immediately. Inform Miss Mary of my offer. Anytime. No matter the circumstances. I will be your gallant."

Elizabeth pulled her cloak tightly about her and set off for Oakham Mount. Within a little over a fortnight, she must say farewell to her favorite walk. She had no idea how many times she had climbed the "hill" and looked down upon all of Meryton and the surrounding estates and farms. When she was young, she had pretended to be a queen or a princess looking out over the ramparts of her castle and upon all over which she ruled. It was here she came when her mother had chastised her for first one offense and then another. She came to the mount when she wished to daydream over the latest handsome young man who had caught her eye and who had briefly claimed her heart. She came to Oakham Mount to grieve when the same boy chose Jane over her. More than she would care to recall, she nursed her broken hopes of knowing love while looking out over the fallow fields of nearby farms. It was here she came when she wanted to practice the Greek and Latin phrases her father had taught her, although young ladies were not to study the subject domains of a gentleman.

"My heart is broken," she told the view spread out before her. "When I leave Longbourn, you will no longer be a part of my life. I do not know how to say farewell to you. I had always thought I would some day bring my children here and point out all the fabulous places below and teach them something of my dreams and of . . ." She wanted to say how other dreams could become true; yet, her dreams would never know fruition. She would never know children, at least none of her own.

"Farewell, Meryton!" she called and heard the slight sound of the echo she so dearly loved.

"Farewell, Netherfield!" she shouted to the view off to the right, where the rooftop of Mr. Bingley's estate could be seen beyond the tree line.

"Farewell, Elizabeth Bennet," she murmured, nearly in tears.

Turning to the left where several Longbourn fields could be seen, she called with less force. "Farewell, Papa! Mama! Jane! Kitty! Lydia!" Elizabeth swallowed hard. "Farewell, Mary Bennet, for soon we will be separated for the remainder of our days."

After several minutes consisting of a good cry and deep regrets, she turned to make her way down the mount to the road leading back to Longbourn. By the time she reached her home, she had composed her features to convey assurances for all who depended upon her. She had been required to serve notice to all the servants except Mr. and Mrs. Hill. Elizabeth had taken what funds remained in her father's safe and bestowed them upon the pair for their devotion to the Bennet family. Now, her days at Longbourn were numbered.

Finally, the day of the auction arrived. For the last sennight various neighbors and others from the shire and outside Hertfordshire had traipsed through Longbourn's rooms, sizing up what was worth their time. Mr. Bingley had brilliantly numbered each of the items and grouped them as "china" or "linens" or "paintings. He had arranged it so people moved back and forth between the rooms to create more purchases of items someone may have overlooked otherwise.

"What a lovely vase!" Elizabeth had heard him say to his staff. "Move it into the large drawing room."

Every item in the house had been valued and labeled and priced. Mr. Bingley had brought what must surely be all the flowers still standing in Netherfield's gardens and the conservatory to provide Longbourn the feeling of "life" and not the somberness they all carried about with them.

"Jane would be so proud of you," Elizabeth told him. "She loved you dearly, you know."

For the briefest of moments Mr. Bingley's eyes were veiled by sand-colored lashes, and he ducked his head to disguise his emotions. "Some days, I still talk to her. I told her all about what we had planned and why we were all going away, but we would always carry her essence with us."

"Pardon my intrusion into your private moment," a deep voice said, "am I too early for the auction?"

Elizabeth rose quickly to shake out the skirt of her day dress. "Certainly not, sir," she managed to say, forcing herself to meet his grey eyes with a steady gaze. "My brother in marriage and I were just speaking of last minute details." She curtsied. "I am Miss Bennet, and this is . . ."

However, Mr. Bingley said from beside her. "Darcy, is that you?" He crossed the room to extend his hand to the stranger. "My goodness, man, I have not seen you since you departed university. Your face is so tanned, but then I had heard you were in India."

The gentleman took Mr. Bingley's hand. "I had no idea you were in Hertfordshire, Bingley. You were still studying for your oral exams when we last parted." The man glanced around the foyer and the drawing room. "And you have married into the Bennet family?"

Mr. Bingley's cheerful expression fell. "I did, but many in the area have lost their loved ones. A pox claimed Mrs. Bennet and two of her youngest daughters. Mr. Bennet passed from some disturbance of his heart. My Jane avoided the pox, but she lost her life to childbirth. I will be leaving Hertfordshire soon, but, first, I serve my wife's family." A few more interested in the auction entered the open door. "Pardon me, I see a few of the people who have approached me regarding the china and several of the paintings, including the one by Reynolds. Hopefully, we will speak again, Darcy."

"I would enjoy that very much," the gentleman said.

As Mr. Bingley moved away to greet the new arrivals, Elizabeth asked, "How did you come to hear of the auction?"

"I noticed the flyer posted on the wall of an inn in St Albans. I have known your father for several years. He was a fine man and a strong influence on my life. I admired his quick mind and generous nature. I had hoped, when I returned to England, I would have the opportunity to call upon him personally."

"Although the name sounds vaguely familiar, I do not believe I ever heard my father mention anyone named 'Darcy.' How well did you know him?" Elizabeth asked suspiciously.

"We met several years back. Six in total. Since then, we have corresponded regularly, or as regularly as the mail between Hertfordshire and India allowed. The last letter I received from him was shortly after the first of the year."

"Elizabeth," Mr. Bingley said softly as he returned to where she conversed with Mr. Darcy. "I will require your assistance in greeting those who wish to know more of individual items. We both adore Mary's goodness, but she does not possess your ability to make strangers feel comfortable."

"Most assuredly," she said. "Pardon me, Mr. Darcy, while I see to the business of dispensing with my family's history. Was there something in particular you wished to view?"

"Your father's library," the man announced. "Yet, I am certain there are other items which will catch my eye."

"Mr. Bingley will direct you to the library. Thank you for your kind words regarding my father. They were very comforting." She curtsied and moved away, but, for the next few hours, every time she looked up, her eyes met the gentleman's. He watched her with such interest, she began to feel as if he intended to bid on her.

As she made herself enter her mother's favorite drawing room, Elizabeth noted quite a few of Mrs. Bennet's former friends sitting about the room and sipping the wine Mr. Bingley had furnished for the occasion. "Dearest Elizabeth," Mrs. Long said, "you have our heartfelt sympathy. Your sweet mother must be turning in her grave with outrage at this travesty."

"Then I am assured you will wish an item or two to commemorate your long-time friendship with Mrs. Bennet," she said knowingly. These women came to gloat—not mourn Frances Bennet's loss. Her mother had bested them again and again. Mrs. Bennet had not only managed to place her eldest daughter with the first eligible bachelor to move into the neighborhood in more than twenty years, but she herself had landed a country squire, whose estate made them all jealous. Mrs. Bennet's only failure in life had been Elizabeth and her sisters. Bless their souls! If Mrs. Bennet had delivered a son, neither she nor Mary would now be in this predicament.

As she made her way across the room to greet several more of her mother's long-time friends, Elizabeth had heard the whispers speaking of how far the Bennets had fallen. The idea people spoke against her father, who would gladly have presented any of them the last shilling he had in his purse, saddened her nearly as much as the idea she and Mary were now penniless orphans.

"Pardon me," she said to the group when they meant to corner her and gossip as they always did. "I should assist Mr. Bingley."

She swept through the crowd to join Bingley, who was touting the merits of a large porcelain vase sitting prominently on a table. "The vase was a gift to Mr. Bennet from a friend living in the East," Bingley shared.

The words her father had repeated when he had uncrated the vase rang clear in Elizabeth's mind. She repeated them, as best she could, in remembrance. "It is from one of the southernmost sites of the ancient Indus Valley civilization—from Lothal, where the world's first dry dock was located. People have also found ancient, polished ceramic there. I believe in what is called the Adichanallur and Brahmagiri regions. Is that not correct, Mr. Darcy?" she asked the gentleman, who appeared to be closer than she had expected, as if he meant to protect her somehow. The idea both amused and confounded her, for she had yet taken a full measure of the man.

"Yes," he said with confidence, "although neither Adichanallur nor Brahmagiri have been properly excavated. Legend says Brahmagiri is where the sage Gautama Maharishi and his wife Ahalya lived. He was one of seven known Hindu saints. As to the particular piece on display, it was discovered in the area of Rajputana along the Van Ki Asha River. If one knows anything of the pottery of India, he knows, in opposition to the red ceramic, grey pottery originated along the basin of the Ganges, and black pottery can be found in the area of Delhi."

"Mr. Darcy has quite recently arrived in England from India," Elizabeth told those gathered about. She nodded her gratitude to the man. He was still leaning casually against a door frame as she made her way from the room.

"You were quite knowledgeable," the gentleman said when he caught up to her in the passageway. "Such will serve you well. I suspect the man and his wife will bid high on the vase," he observed softly.

"No matter how much Mary and I gain from the sale of our parents' life story, it will never bring them back. My sister and I will never know peace and family again," she reminded him.

"Then do not accept a lower price for your family's history," he warned her.

"But many within were friends of my family. Surely, they cannot wish me ill," she argued, although she had thought otherwise only moments earlier when speaking to Mrs. Long.

"Not all we once considered to be our friends can be counted upon to act with honor when required," he stated with a touch of bitterness in his tone. "Take care who you choose to trust, Miss Bennet."

He turned then to walk into an adjoining room, and Elizabeth could not resist wondering who had betrayed him. Taking his advice, she found herself more aware of the negotiations Mr. Bingley conducted on behalf of her family. Long-time neighbors offered extremely low bids and then haggled with her brother-in-marriage when Mr. Bingley suggested more. She most assuredly could not have tolerated their insolence. More than likely, she would have ordered them all from Longbourn and simply accepted her poverty rather than to think of a favorite item from her past so openly devalued by former friends and acquaintances. Her eyes misted over as she looked upon much-loved pieces of her family's history on display for strangers to "paw." It felt as if she had betrayed her dear parents by sanctioning the removal of their family's history from Longbourn.

"All is going well, Sister Elizabeth," Mr. Bingley said as he handed her a glass of wine.

Elizabeth took a sip and sighed heavily. "You have been a godsend, Mr. Bingley."

"The actual bidding on the main items will begin in a quarter hour," he explained. "You should know Mr. Darcy means to bid on the paintings. The vases. Most of your father's books, as well as the furniture and the silver."

She nodded her understanding and took a larger gulp of the wine. "Can the man afford such expenditures?" she asked. "He warned me not to trust people simply because they are friends. Is it possible to trust him? The gentleman speaks of regularly corresponding with my father, but Mr. Bennet never once spoke of the man. However, I suspect it was he who sent the red vase to father."

Mr. Bingley lowered his voice further. "I cannot speak to all of his history, but I can say, at Cambridge, he was exceedingly kind to me and several others who were often the object of disdain because we were not from the gentry or the aristocracy. Some criticized him for what they called 'great pride,' but all I ever saw was the right to his pride, for Darcy was one who acted with principles. I doubt such has changed, for they appeared to be ingrained upon his very soul. As to the matter of finances, Darcy comes from a wealthy and aristocratic family. His mother was the younger sister of an earl. However, something occurred which forced Darcy's father to send him off. I cannot speak to the seriousness of the incident, but, at Cambridge, many said the elder Darcy provided his son five hundred pounds and told the man you met today to earn his own way in the world. There was a notice in the newspapers, perhaps eight to ten months prior, regarding the passing of Darcy's father, which means the 'Mr. Darcy' whose acquaintance you have taken inherits the family estate and all it entails. A very large estate from all I know of him. Likely twice or more than my income."

"And his mother?" Elizabeth asked, suddenly very curious about what "crime" a man could commit to force his father to send him away.

AMENDING THE SHADES OF PEMBERLEY

"Lady Anne Darcy passed after giving birth to Darcy's sister," Bingley supplied.

"A sister? Where is the girl now? How much younger is she than the gentleman?"

Mr. Bingley's features screwed up in calculations. "Darcy, if I recall correctly, is four years my senior. He should be thirty. His sister was eleven or twelve years his junior."

"Kitty's age. Eighteen. How very sad. The gentleman appears to have lost as much as I. As much as we two," she observed.

"I heard him mention a daughter to one of the other bidders when observing the nursery," Mr. Bingley explained.

"Children and likely a mate. Then I erred: He is richer than both of us," Elizabeth declared. "And I am not speaking of money." Mr. Bingley's face fell, and Elizabeth immediately regretted her observation. "I apologize. My words were poorly chosen. My mind is deeply entrenched in the sentimentality associated with today's venture. I did not mean to betray your loyalty to this family."

"No betrayal felt, but the loss of Jane rarely leaves me. I am hoping both you and I find peace soon," he said before moving off to answer yet one more question before the bidding began, but Elizabeth noted how Mr. Bingley's shoulders hung a bit lower, as did hers.

Within an hour and a half, it was over. She had been unable to look on as each item had been brought to notice. As the successful and unsuccessful bidders departed the manor, Mr. Bingley appeared again at her side. "I have the directions and the written promises of payment, along with the winning bids for each item. I will have the information carried to Mr. Birkhead, and he will collect the monies before anything leaves the house."

Elizabeth caught his hands in hers. "You have proven to be my family's champion. Mary and I are forever in your debt." She rose up on her toes and kissed his cheek. "Someday, we will meet again. Please know, I love you dearly. Jane earned the affection of the best of men."

17

Although exhausted, Elizabeth sent Mary upstairs for a rest and then turned her attention to gathering the glasses sitting about on every surface possible. They must be washed, dried, and boxed to return to Netherfield, and she would not permit Mr. and Mrs. Hill to be the only ones to labor in the effort to see Longbourn set to right again. "I must be satisfied to know work of any kind," she murmured as she reached to the mantel to remove two glasses to sit upon the tray.

"Permit me to assist you," a deep voice said from the door's portal.

Elizabeth clutched at her heart. "You frightened me, sir. I thought all had departed." Her eyes scanned the room. "Mr. Bingley tells me you purchased the majority of this room and several others. I offer you my deepest gratitude."

"The house is just as your father described it," the gentleman said. "Those images were to what I clung when I was at my lowest point."

Elizabeth would like to ask something of what Mr. Bingley had shared of Mr. Darcy's own family, but she swallowed her many questions. Rather, she said, "My father had an unusual sense of humor. He likely entertained you with tales of Mrs. Bennet chastising my sister Kitty for being in possession of a persistent cough, or something of my mother's many schemes to place each of her daughters in the path of eligible gentlemen."

He admitted, "There were a few such tales. Mostly, he spoke of books and something of politics, but the greater part of each letter spoke of you."

"Of me?" she protested. "Was I the source of Mr. Bennet's amusement?"

"Rarely," Mr. Darcy clarified. "In truth, you were the source of great pride."

"Thank you for sharing your observations, sir. The idea will sustain me as I must leave this all behind." She made a sweeping gesture with her arm.

"Do not leave it, then," he said softly.

"The choice is no longer mine."

"It could be," he argued.

"How?" she asked in frustration. Elizabeth did not understand the game he played nor did she want to do so. "You own it. I do not. Shall I set up a regular visitation on my half day off, assuming I am presented the opportunity for even a few hours to consider all I have lost."

"There is no need for you to prove yourself the martyr," he said in tones which irritated her further. "Do not permit your pride to destroy what may save you."

"I do not comprehend your meaning, sir."

"Simple. I will own all your family's memories. Join them in my house," he explained.

"If you are suggesting you wish me to serve as your mistress, sir, I would know great offense."

"I do not require a mistress in my bed. I do require someone to set my house to order—an order of 'my preference.' Moreover, I require someone who is educated, instinctive, and caring to attend my five-year-old daughter."

"What of the child's mother? Will she not object to your hiring a governess without her interviewing the lady?"

"The child has no mother," he said in hard tones, which had Elizabeth wondering whether such was the betrayal of which he had spoken earlier. "Both my daughter and I require an ally. Mr. Bennet continually assured me you could be that person."

"You expect me to take on the role of governess to your daughter in a bachelor household? My reputation will be ruined as it is because of Mr. Bennet's bankruptcy. It would not—could not—survive more scandal," she argued.

"Your pride again, Miss Bennet?" he charged.

"Your insane prejudice, Mr. Darcy," Elizabeth countered. "If I accepted your offer, and you later released me for not performing as you wished, I would never find another position."

"You have willfully misunderstood me, Miss Bennet. You have no worry of my releasing you, for I do not wish you to perform as a governess to my daughter, but rather as my wife and the mistress of my hereditary estate."

Chapter Two

Darcy had been enchanted from the first moment he had laid eyes upon Miss Elizabeth Bennet. She was exactly as her father had described her, except Darcy thought Mr. Bennet had not given her feminine form justice. Perhaps a father never considered his daughter's appeal to a young gentleman, but Darcy felt it nevertheless.

It had been a pure stroke of luck, although it was his luck hitching a ride on the back of the Bennet family's misfortune, that he had taken note of the advert for the auction. He had been in England less than a day when he had stopped in St Albans for refreshments for himself and Alice, before he made the last twenty miles or so to London to settle his father's affairs. If Darcy had had his choice, he would have immediately traveled to Pemberley and sent all involved in his banishment from his ancestral home to a place much hotter than the constant sun of India. Yet, once again, Thomas Bennet had extended his hand, only their roles had been reversed. Instead of calming Darcy's woes and offering friendship, this time Thomas Bennet, or rather his family, required a hand up. Somehow, the Bennet family had fallen on hard times, which Darcy did not fully understand, but he would eventually discover the truth of it. He owed Mr. Bennet his loyalty.

Therefore, he had taken a detour, not south to London, but rather north to a small village called "Meryton" to discover what had occurred.

"The pox kilt more than sixty," the innkeeper explained, "including quite a few from the militia."

"What of the Bennets?" he asked as casually as he could. "I am familiar with Mr. Bennet from a business endeavor."

"Only Mr. Bennet and two of the daughters survived. The youngest be quite friendly with Colonel Forster's young bride. The two ladies spent time together in Brighton when the militia removed for training late last spring. Miss Lydia was meant to marry herself a lieutenant, but the ladies and many of the soldiers carried the pox back to Meryton. Perhaps fifteen or twenty of the militia passed, as well as several townsfolk. Bennet, he survives, but had some kind of heart spasm. Gone quickly. Now, only Miss Elizabeth and Miss Mary survive."

Darcy had said a silent prayer of thanksgiving for God sparing Miss Elizabeth. He had promised himself he would someday take the lady's acquaintance; after all, Mr. Bennet had promised his daughter would put Darcy's steps on the right path, and what man could walk away from such a challenge.

Although he had spent most of his adult life avoiding overzealous society mamas, who had touted the assets of their marriageable daughters, it was rare to encounter a father who sang the praises of his daughter; yet, Mr. Bennet had done exactly that. Except, Mr. Bennet knew Darcy had essentially been disowned. "Even an impoverished gentleman's daughter would be superior to a man such as I. One who has fallen from grace," he had told Mr. Bennet. Yet, though the man knew Darcy struggled shoulder-to-shoulder with his hired men in the depths of a mine, attempting to earn his own fortune, Bennet spoke often of how he would like someday to view his Elizabeth on Darcy's arm.

Driven by his curiosity, he had called upon the estate and had been a bit surprised by how much it felt of home, despite his never having seen it. Longbourn was smaller than Pemberley, but, then again, most estates in England were, even those belonging to dukes and princes. In one letter, Mr. Bennet had told him, "Longbourn has been in my family since the Restoration."

It had made Darcy sad to think the Bennet line had lost everything and had come to an end. He feared the Darcy line would die with him, and so, his inquisitiveness had led him to call on Longbourn.

Unsurprisingly, he had not been disappointed. It was a well-lived in house, one superior to Pemberley in that manner. Pemberley had become a "showcase" after Lady Anne Darcy's death, but it was no longer a place Darcy wished to be, at least not under his father's terms.

Then he had stepped into the room to discover a woman he had never seen, but one he recognized immediately, that is, except for her hair. Mr. Bennet had described it as red, but it was actually more bronze than the red of the Irish or Scottish lass Darcy had been expecting, for he knew the woman had Scottish relations. In his opinion, the lady was absolutely stunning, and, like it or not, the idea of her had claimed a corner of his heart long before he had ever laid eyes on Elizabeth Bennet.

"You cannot expect to purchase me as if I am another of Mr. Bennet's treasured books!" she said incredulously.

"Would you have considered my plight if I had courted you for the last few months?" he asked in sharp tones.

Elizabeth swallowed the anger rushing to her lips. Instead, she said, "An acquaintance of more than a few hours would be preferable."

"Would such actually have provided us more stability in our relationship? Should I have walked you home from church and sat in your mother's drawing room for six weeks every Sunday? Asked you to dance at the local assembly? Would you prefer such displays to prove you are handsome enough to tempt me?" he countered.

Privately, Elizabeth wished, when she married,f her husband would find her both handsome and desirable: She had stood in Jane's shadow for more years than she cared to admit, and, despite her sensibilities, she could not resist wishing for someone to look upon her with affection in his eyes. "My father never spoke of you to me," she objected lamely.

"Mr. Bennet spoke often of you to me," he confided. "I would be happy to share his letters with you when the rest of my trunks arrive in

England. Your father swore I required a woman of your nature to set my world aright."

"Is your world so off kilter, sir?" she demanded.

"It has been so for some years, but I pray my fortune has changed. My family and I paid a heavy price for a spoken lie," he stated flatly.

"A lie spoken by you or another?" she questioned.

For a moment, Elizabeth thought the gentleman would respond, but, instead, he said, "It does not matter who spoke the lie, for the past cannot be changed. Only the future can be molded to suit our natures. Your father was fond of telling me there was no future in the past."

Elizabeth found herself swallowing hard against the sudden swell of tears rushing to her eyes. "It was Papa's favorite saying when Mama bewailed one suitor or another abandoning her girls."

"Mr. Bennet reminded me often of the necessity to plan for a future," the gentleman said softly.

Elizabeth wished her father had taken his own advice. "What you ask is out of the question."

"Do you object to my appearance? To my manners? I assure you, as the grandson of an earl and a relation to the Da'cre and Fitzwilliam families, doors will be open to you as my wife, as well as to our children."

"I do not question your lineage, sir," she said dutifully. "Mr. Bingley shared something similar earlier." Elizabeth did not address his appearance, for how could she admit she found him handsome, despite the scowl currently marking his brow.

"I am a gentleman. You are a gentleman's daughter. We are equals in the eyes of society," he summarized.

"I am the daughter of a disgraced gentleman," she corrected.

He smiled weakly. "I am the disgraced son of a noble gentleman. In my humble opinion, we remain equals."

"Is there not someone from your past you would prefer to pursue?" she asked. "You cannot possibly wish to strap yourself to a woman you barely know. You cannot be so very old and running out of time in order to court another properly. Not to know affection in your marriage," Elizabeth argued.

"I was recently thirty," he remarked with a small smile, which transformed his features into something quite remarkable. "And you are two and twenty."

"You know my birthday?" she asked, flabbergasted.

"Month and year," he admitted, "but not the day of the month. I also possess a miniature of you when you were sixteen."

"The one father customarily kept on his desk?" she asked. "Mr. Bennet said he lost it during one of his journeys to London, a journey he claimed to be the most agreeable of his business ventures."

"He did lose it," Mr. Darcy explained. "On the dock when he saw me off to India," the gentleman said with a sadness about his mouth. "It was the morning after the night we met. We talked throughout the dark hours. One of the sailors found it and presented it to me, for Mr. Bennet had already departed. In a letter to him, I offered to return it, but your father claimed your image would provide me hope. And so it did. However, I must say, upon taking your acquaintance, the painter did not do your eyes justice."

Like it or not, Elizabeth enjoyed the compliment. "I do not know what to say, Mr. Darcy. This is all so sudden."

He nodded his understanding. "I must travel to London to settle the estate matters and to make arrangements to move your father's possessions to my home. I will return at week's end to present Mr. Birkhead with my signed payment. You may provide me your answer then."

"What of your daughter?" she asked, curious regarding what he might say of the child.

He sighed heavily before responding. "Alice has been frightened since we departed India. She is with her *ayah* at this time, likely staring out the window of the inn in Meryton and awaiting my return."

"And your sister?" she asked.

"I have sent word to Georgiana of my return and have asked her to consider joining me at our ancestral home," he explained. "I assume Mr. Bingley told you of my sister?"

"He did," she confirmed.

"And of my fall from grace?" he questioned.

"Some, but I do not believe he knew what actually occurred," she admitted.

"Few do," he said in obvious resignation. "From what I have been told by my uncle, my sister only knows what my father told her, and I imagine George Darcy went to great lengths to protect his daughter from the truth. I do not know such with any certainty, but from what Georgiana did and did not say, her vision of what occurred is severely skewed."

"And you did not correct her opinion of you when you wrote to her? Is such not a high price to pay for your pride, sir?" Elizabeth asked.

He shrugged his response. "What was there to say? I could not in good conscience speak against her only parent. It would not be fair to ask Georgiana to choose between her father and her brother. My shoulders are wide enough to bear her disdain if such proves to be her choice."

Elizabeth wondered if anyone could withstand losing all of his family. She had come close to doing so, and, she would admit, if Mary, too, had succumbed to the pox, she would be quite soured upon the world. She thought Mr. Darcy's actions both admirable and foolish at the same time. "I pray Miss Darcy chooses to return to your care, sir."

"And I pray you will seriously consider my offer, Miss Bennet." With those words, he turned on his heels and exited not only the room, but the house. The silence was eerily frightening, and, although others would not approve, Elizabeth wished the gentleman had not withdrawn.

Despite not being certain she even liked the man, she did appreciate the frankness of his responses, as well as the manner in which he looked upon her in apparent appreciation.

"He offered you marriage?" Mary asked in awe. "And our father had written to him of you?"

"Such is what he claims," Elizabeth explained. "Mr. Darcy says Mr. Bennet often touted my 'admirable' qualities to the man. I just wish I had at the very least known of the man prior to today's auction. How am I to know what is best?"

"Could you not learn to care for the man?" Mary asked.

"You know my mind, Mary. I despise a question not resolved, and there are so many questions left unanswered."

"Perhaps it is just me, but would it not be possible to seek answers equally as well as Mrs. Darcy as it would be as Miss Elizabeth Bennet? The man has a history, but who does not? You have a history, and so do I. Ours, up until this last year, was commonplace, very much of the nature of all our neighbors, but, you must admit, no other house held a mistress quite like our mother when it came to gossip, nor a master even half as intelligent or as well read as our father. None held a daughter as beautiful and sweet-natured as our Jane, and Heaven forbid there is another Lydia in the world. How could so much exuberance be contained?"

Elizabeth smiled easily. "And, absolutely, there can be no other child who coughs just to 'irritate' her dear mother as Mama always claimed Kitty did."

"We were quite blessed and none of us realized it," Mary said softly.

Elizabeth caught her sister's hand. "I do not wish to leave you to your own devices. I shall agree to marry the gentleman if he will consent to your coming with me. If Mr. Darcy's daughter is to live with us, should not Mrs. Darcy's sister be extended the same privilege?"

"What if he refuses?" Mary asked in alarm.

"Then we continue on with our plans to enter service," Elizabeth declared, but the idea of being a governess no longer appealed to her. Without a tangible reason to do so, she thought being Mrs. Darcy's wife and mother to his child would definitely be preferable to being Miss Elizabeth Bennet, governess. As Mrs. Darcy, she would tend her own children. Watch them grow. See them marry and have children of their own.

"I shall say a prayer for your happiness," Mary told her, "and for God's hand to guide each of our steps."

Darcy had been eager to return to Longbourn, but he feared the lady's response, and, like it or not, he desired her agreement. For longer than he would care to admit, he had wanted Miss Elizabeth Bennet as his wife. However, her father always said the lady was often too stubborn for her own good, and so Darcy held his qualms regarding her response. Equally as tense in the way she held herself, Alice sat beside him on the bench.

"We be on this road before," she remarked.

"Yes, we will visit the house and the lady I spoke of earlier," he explained.

"Who'll stay with me? *Ayah* go home," she said in alarm.

Earlier in the week, he and the child had seen Alice's nursemaid's return to India. Darcy had found the woman passage on a British East India ship. "You will call upon Miss Elizabeth with me. I think the two of you will like each other greatly. She is the daughter of a friend and no longer has a mother or a father."

"No mother, like me," Alice observed.

"Would it not be good for us all to know each other better?"

"She'll like me?" Alice asked.

"Miss Elizabeth will adore you, just as I do."

AMENDING THE SHADES OF PEMBERLEY

His carriage turned onto the lane leading to Longbourn, and Darcy turned his head to study the scenery. Although it was not his beloved Derbyshire, he would agree with the late Thomas Bennet: Hertfordshire was a beautiful shire. Darcy had said a prayer each night he was in India to be permitted someday to return to England and begin again.

Not all his prayers were answered. True, he was in England and there was the hope of claiming Miss Elizabeth Bennet as his wife; yet, he had finally heard from Georgiana before he and Alice had left London. Although his sister had not agreed to return to Pemberley, she had promised to give the prospect serious consideration. *"You must be patient,"* he warned himself as his carriage rolled to a stop before Longbourn. *"England and, hopefully, Miss Elizabeth. Discard what cannot be unchanged and count the goals you can claim as success as you earn them. The goals achieved will eventually outweigh what you once thought important."*

"Mr. Darcy, Miss Elizabeth," Mrs. Hill announced as the gentleman was shown into the sitting room, which was nearly bare of its furnishings. His men had arrived several hours earlier to load the furniture and such onto flatbed wagons for their journey to his home. Elizabeth suddenly realized she had no idea where Mr. Darcy lived.

She curtsied more from habit than realizing she did so. "Your men arrived promptly, sir."

"I meant to appear earlier, for I imagined all this has been difficult for you, but I was delayed by my sister reaching out to me."

"I am so glad, sir. I know such was your wish," she said in all honesty.

"I told her of you," he said.

"Of me?" she gasped. "What have you to say of me?"

"Only that I have extended my hand to you, and I believe the two of you might go on well together," he explained. An awkward pause hung between them before he said, "If I am not being too presumptuous, might I bring my daughter inside? She is most desirous to know the lady whose house I visited earlier this week."

"Please tell me you did not promise the child I was to be her stepmother," Elizabeth begged. "I have not presented you my response, sir."

"I simply described you as the daughter of a friend," he assured. "I would not use my child as a pawn to have my way. If you agree to marry me, I pray you do so because you believe a future together is in our grasp."

"If all is as you described it, I would be pleased to greet the child," she said with the slightest hesitation.

"Pardon me a moment." With a quick bow, he disappeared while Elizabeth claimed the interruption to pat her hair in place. Yet, before she was thoroughly prepared, the gentleman reappeared. He looked quite awkward as he bent to hold the child's hand. He was tall, and the child appeared to be so very small, though, in reality, she had the build of Jane, when Jane was a child.

"Who do we have here, Mr. Darcy?" Elizabeth asked with a smile. The child looked down, and Elizabeth instinctively knelt before her—not bending over, but going down on one knee to be at the child's eye level. "How very beautiful you are." The girl gazed shyly at her as she and her father came to stand before Elizabeth. Mr. Darcy knelt also.

"Miss Elizabeth," he said formally while watching his daughter, "may I present Miss Alice Darcy?"

The child frowned. "Biss Alice Faith Anne Darcy, Papa," the child said precociously.

"I stand corrected, my love," he responded dutifully. "Miss Alice Faith Anne Darcy."

Elizabeth noted the faint violet shadows under the child's eyes, belying her liveliness. "Your father told me what a wonderful daughter you are."

The child looked up to Mr. Darcy. "He says I'm his fav-or-right girl."

AMENDING THE SHADES OF PEMBERLEY

Elizabeth, too, looked to the gentleman. "I can understand his preference, and may I also have the acquaintance of your doll?" The child clutched a fine china doll with a head of blonde hair and blue glass for eyes.

"This is Biss Cass Andra Darcy," the child proudly pronounced.

Elizabeth took the doll's porcelain hand and shook it. "I am honored by the acquaintance, Miss Cassandra."

Before the child could respond, a few notes of music could be heard from the adjoining room.

"What that?" the girl asked.

Elizabeth assured, "Such is my sister Mary practicing her music. Would you like to greet her also?"

The child looked to her father. "I likes music, Papa."

Mr. Darcy's features softened. "I know you do, love." He nodded his permission for Elizabeth to escort his child into the other room, stood, and reached down a hand for Elizabeth to assist her to stand. Like it or not, Elizabeth enjoyed the warmth of his hand as it encircled hers. It was the first time she had felt safe in many months.

The child released her father's hand and claimed Elizabeth's free one, which, like it or not, had Elizabeth yearning for her own children. By the time she had led Alice into the small parlor, Elizabeth realized although he had risen, Mr. Darcy had not followed her. "Good day, Mary," she said as the child slowed her pace. "We have a visitor."

Mary stopped her efforts to address the child. "My, I do not think I have ever had such a delightful audience. Do you like music?"

The child nodded her agreement, but did not step closer. Elizabeth knelt again. "Should we ask Mary to play for us again?"

"Peas," the child said softly.

Mary nodded her agreement and set her fingers to playing a children's chant. When she finished with a flourish, the child begged, "Again."

"I mean to please," Mary responded and set about playing the tune once more.

"Again," the child ordered with a smile, which immediately melted Elizabeth's heart.

"Only if you ask Elizabeth to sing," Mary countered.

"Peas, Biss Lizbet," the girl pleaded.

Elizabeth asked, "Do you not know the rhyme?"

The child shook her head in the negative.

"Then might I teach you?"

"Yes, peas."

"Very well. Listen first, and then we shall sing it together." She looked to her sister. "The first phrase, if you would, Mary." Elizabeth waited for Mary to finish playing before she sang, "Humpty Dumpty sat on a wall."

"Again," the child ordered.

"Humpty. Dumpty. Sat. On. A. Wall," Elizabeth said slowly. "Will you try it with me?" The child nodded unsurely. Elizabeth began again, saying each word slowly. A third and a fourth time had the child mumbling some words while managing others. "Let us add line two. I shall permit you time to repeat each line until you are assured of yourself."

The child smiled weakly, but she did not look away. Elizabeth sang the first line, and the child repeated the words she knew.

"Humpty Dumpty had a great fall." Elizabeth enunciated each word slowly just as she had done with the opening line.

Alice's eyes widened. "I fells down once, but Papa not mad I torn my dress."

"I am pleased to hear it. My father never was angry when I tore my good dress," Elizabeth shared.

"Mama was," Mary remarked before she realized what she said.

"I no have a mama," the child explained innocently.

"Then we three are all alike," Elizabeth assured. "Mary and I no longer have a mother either."

"Are you bonely?" the girl asked.

"Sometimes," Elizabeth admitted. "You are fortunate to have your Papa." After an awkward moment, she sang the whole rhyme. "Humpty Dumpty sat on a wall. Humpty Dumpty had a great fall. All the King's horses and all the King's men could not put Humpty together again."

"Why Umpty break?" the child asked in concern.

"Most people consider him to be an egg," Elizabeth said as she looked to Mary who shrugged her response. "An egg would surely break if it fell from a wall."

The child giggled. "Spat."

Elizabeth bit her lip to keep from correcting the girl. "Shall we sing the lines again?"

Alice nodded her agreement and began the song herself. "Umpty, dumpty sat on a . . . wall. Umpty, dumpty, have a gre. . . at fall." Unexpectedly, the child plopped down on the floor, but when she realized she still held her doll, she jumped up to carry the doll to her father. It was only then Elizabeth realized Mr. Darcy was standing in the open doorway. "Did you see me spat, Papa?"

Mr. Darcy's smile widened. "I did, sweetheart."

"Biss Lizbet say she fell when she a little girl like me," the child announced.

Elizabeth noted how tears misted Mr. Darcy's eyes. Therefore, she said, "Perhaps we might convince Mary to teach you the notes on the pianoforte while I speak to your father for a moment." She shot a pleading glance to Mary, but Elizabeth need not worry, for Mary had already stood to move the bench closer.

With Mary's assistance, the girl climbed readily onto the bench.

"I will be near, Alice," Mr. Darcy told the child.

"Leave Biss Cassie," the child instructed without looking to her father.

Elizabeth whispered her gratitude to Mary, but her sister was already leaning over the child to take the girl's finger to play the first note.

Mr. Darcy waited for Elizabeth so he might offer her his arm. "Let us walk in the garden," he suggested. "If I know anything of my daughter, Alice will be highly entertained for at least a half hour."

Elizabeth slipped her hand about his elbow and permitted him to lead her outside.

"Pray, it is not too chilly for you," he said. "I did not think of claiming your shawl or your cloak. In truth, it has been many years since I offered a lady my arm to walk about the garden."

"Not even your wife?" she asked. "Has she been long gone from your life?" Elizabeth would like to know more of Alice's mother and the woman he originally took to wife.

"The last time I saw Ruth was shortly after Alice was born," he said. Before Elizabeth could ask more of the late Mrs. Darcy, he commented, "I was quite impressed with how well you tolerated Alice's questions and her proclivities. I fear I tend to allow her too much latitude."

"I thought her delightful," Elizabeth admitted.

After her spoken observation, they walked in silence for several minutes, each caught up in his or her own thoughts.

At length, Elizabeth mustered the courage to speak. "I have considered your offer most seriously, Mr. Darcy."

He set their steps on a second sweep about the little wilderness her mother had called a "garden."

"Am I to be accepted or denied, Miss Bennet?" he asked without looking to her, as if he meant to shoulder her denial if it came.

"Before I provide you my response, I would like to ask a favor of you," she said cautiously.

"I am listening," he assured.

"You spoke previously of attempting to convince your sister to return to your family home."

"Do you object to the idea?" he asked as he halted their progress and turned towards her.

"I would not object to claiming another sister. After all, I am quite accustomed to sharing a home with a number of ladies and personalities." She paused and looked down at her scuffed half boots. "I would not feel right, sir, if I were sleeping in a comfortable bed and sharing a full meal with you at your table while knowing Mary was serving as a governess in another's household. I am not capable of abandoning her. As Miss Darcy and little Alice are all which remain from your years of banishment, along with me, Mary is the only one with whom I share Thomas Bennet's blood."

"I had not thought to separate you from your sister. Mr. Bennet warned me you would not wish to be far removed from your family. As my home is in the northern shires, I was concerned you may know a number of qualms regarding our joining and leaving Hertfordshire."

"In truth, I was not aware of your being in a northern shire, though from Mr. Bingley's mention of Cambridge, I should have made that assumption. You will think me a woman of no sensibility, as I have not asked of your home," she said with a flush of embarrassment marking her cheeks. "Which shire, may I ask?"

"Derbyshire. Do you know it?"

"Only by reputation," she admitted. "My Aunt Gardiner's brother is a vicar at a church near a place called 'Lambton.' A Mr. Ericks. The vicarage was to be my destination until I could locate a governess position."

"I know Lambton well. It is the nearest village to my estate," he explained. "I know of a Mr. Ericks who was a surgeon, but he and a son died in a terrible flood. I was just a boy when that occurred. The vicar's position was open when I departed for India."

"The surgeon was Aunt Gardiner's father," Elizabeth said with a bit of excitement to know she might meet Mr. Ericks again. Occasionally, the man joined in with his sister for celebrations.

"Then you will not be completely without family in the area," he said.

"And you will permit Mary to be a part of your household?" she asked.

"If your sister promises to assist you with Alice's care and setting my manor aright, I would consider her presence a blessing. I must warn you, though I will be surrounded by women with the presence of the Bennet sisters and Alice and, hopefully, Georgiana, my home has long been without a mistress. You will find a 'masculinity' about the estate, as well as it being quite dated. My mother lost her life nearly two decades past. She was its last mistress. I would like to see it brought into its former glory as one of England's finest homes."

"Your home and your child," Elizabeth summarized. "Nothing for you, sir?" she asked tentatively.

"Permitting me time to right my family legacy will be an answer to my prayers. As it is now, I expect to know long days working alongside my tenants for many months until Pemberley is again prosperous. I do not wish Alice to think I have abandoned her. She will be frightened when I leave early and return late. Such was so in India. I would not have the child suffer again. I believe with you to guide her, she will learn to love England and Derbyshire as much as I."

Elizabeth regarded the array of emotions crossing his features. She prayed she was not making a mistake. If she were, she must find a means to survive it. In any event, she would have a home and, perhaps, someday a family of her own. Many women of society knew satisfaction with such an arrangement. Although Elizabeth had always thought to marry for love, she would make herself a life carved out of the security Mr. Darcy offered her and Mary.

"Mr. Darcy," she said solemnly, "I accept your kind proposal."

Chapter Three

A small smile crossed his lips. "I am pleased you have agreed. I promise to do my best by you and your sister."

"And I promise to do likewise by you and Alice," she assured him.

"Thank you for not requiring me to pronounce what a great honor you have presented me," he said. "Or profess my deep affection."

In truth, Elizabeth would not have minded if he had made a declaration, if not of love, perhaps upon her "fine countenance." She had always thought when she married, she would hold the gentleman in affection, and he likewise with her.

"Should we shake hands to seal our agreement?" he asked, extending his hand to her. "I would like to think we will go through life holding hands, if not in solidarity, at a minimum, in shared companionship."

Reluctantly, Elizabeth placed her hand in his. "A bargain," she said weakly, attempting to hide her foolish disappointment. "And companionship."

Mr. Darcy closed his fingers about hers. "You possess a solid handshake," he said as he tugged her a bit closer. "And excessively soft skin." The fingers of his free hand brushed her cheek. He leaned in as if he meant to kiss her, and Elizabeth knew her breath caught in her throat. She had never been kissed before. A woman of her age should have known at least one serious suitor. Naturally, she had had her favorites, those with whom she danced at the local assemblies and who teased and flirted with her at a variety of entertainments, but never once had any of them asked her father if they might court her. None had thought to attempt to steal a kiss from her either.

Lydia had known numerous flirtations. In fact, it was her youngest sister's connection to one of the militia officers which had brought the pox into their home. More than two dozen of the soldiers had returned from Brighton with the disease, reportedly thanks to a night of gambling and drinking with the members of a Portuguese ship. Lydia had traveled to Brighton with her friend Harriet, who was Colonel Forster's new bride. Immediately upon return to Hertfordshire, Mr. Wickham had presented himself to Mr. Bennet as a suitor for Lydia, which had surprised Elizabeth, for, though Lydia "pursued" Mr. Wickham, he had not shown any favor to her sister beyond a flirtation. They were later to learn Lydia had succumbed to Mr. Wickham's charms and a quick marriage was to occur, but Lydia had taken ill before the last calling of the banns. Then Kitty, Lydia's closest sister, took ill, as did Captain Denny who meant to marry their Katherine.

Only she and Mary had not had a serious suitor. Only they had remained without a taste of love. Although they two had not known the disease, they had also not known affection. Now, Elizabeth had accepted a man of whom she essentially knew nothing, but who would offer her security.

Mr. Darcy gave her a gentle tug, and Elizabeth went willingly into his loose embrace. He said huskily, "Would you object if . . ."

She was certain he meant to ask to kiss her, however, before he could finish his question and know her response, Alice came racing out the front door. "Papa! Papa!"

Mr. Darcy released Elizabeth immediately and turned to his daughter. "What is it, child?" he asked in tones of concern.

The girl raced as fast as her legs would carry her to catch his hand. "Come!" She tugged him back in the direction of the house. He looked back to Elizabeth. "Join us, my dear," he said with a smile.

Elizabeth followed, but a bit more slowly than the others. Silly as it would sound to say the words aloud, she resented not being kissed.

AMENDING THE SHADES OF PEMBERLEY

Inside the parlor, she found Mr. Darcy kneeling beside his daughter. Alice was plucking out one note at a time and mumbling the words to the nursery rhyme. She managed the first line perfectly.

"Miss Mary," Mr. Darcy said, "you are a genius."

Mary smiled sweetly. She looked to Elizabeth, "Is it settled between you?"

Elizabeth wanted to protest it would not be settled until Mr. Darcy kissed her, but she placed her feelings aside and said softly, "It is."

Mary looked back to Mr. Darcy. "I would be happy, sir, to teach Miss Alice to play or to read or whatever you require of me."

"If you and your sister can provide Alice your attentions, I would consider my agreement with Miss Elizabeth an excellent one."

"What is saddled?" Alice demanded, looking first to her father and then to Elizabeth and then to Mary in turn.

Mr. Darcy caressed the child's cheek, much in the same manner he had done with Elizabeth not five minutes past. "Miss Elizabeth has agreed to be your mother and my wife. She and Miss Mary will be coming to live with us in our new house. Would you like that?"

The child looked to both her and Mary a second time. "They will tay with me?"

"Yes. When your papa must be out during the day, Elizabeth and Mary will be with you, and then papa will return to tuck you into bed each evening."

"We go to our new house now?" the child asked.

Mr. Darcy stood, "First, I must make Miss Elizabeth my wife." To Elizabeth he said, "I have purchased a special license. My godfather is the Archbishop and so his secretary agreed to the purchase," he explained. "Would you care to be married at Longbourn, your local church, or wait until we reach Pemberley?"

"How long will it be until we reach your home?" she asked.

"Likely three, perhaps four days, depending on the weather and our limited travel passage on the Sabbath."

"Elizabeth," Mary suggested softly, "you should marry at Longbourn. Our mother will be dancing in Heaven if you are married by special license in our home. You know it would be her dearest wish if she were still with us. Can you not hear her delight and envision her rushing about, both her nerves and her ever-present handkerchief aflutter?"

Elizabeth smiled at Mary and nodded her agreement. "It would please me, sir, if the service could be conducted at Longbourn. Thank you for providing me a choice."

Mr. Darcy smiled again. Elizabeth enjoyed the ease of his smile. "Alice, will you stay and assist Miss Elizabeth to dress for our wedding? I must fetch the . . ."

"Vicar," Elizabeth supplied. "Mr. Williamson."

"I must fetch Mr. Williamson to perform the ceremony."

"Come back?" the child asked.

"Always," he assured.

Mary suggested to the girl, "Would you like to join me in choosing some flowers for Elizabeth's hair, Miss Alice?"

The child looked curiously at Mary, but accepted the hand Mary had extended, but only after reclaiming Miss Cassandra. "Why fowers in Biss Lizbet's hair?"

Once they were gone, Elizabeth asked, "Would you do me the favor of also calling on Mr. Phillips in the village? He is my uncle and a solicitor. I would ask him to examine the marriage settlements of which I assumed you also have a draft, just as you had thought of the license. Also, please invite him and my mother's sister to the ceremony."

"Should the gentleman sign any settlements for you?" he asked.

"Am I not of age, sir?" she countered.

"You are," he said with a gentle nod of his head. "Yet, it is always best to speak to a man accustomed to such tasks and who would want the best for you."

Elizabeth warned, "It is not wise to attempt to placate your soon-to-be new wife, Mr. Darcy."

"So noted, my dear. I shan't be more than an hour, two at the most."

"I will send word to Mr. Bingley. Perhaps I nay convince him to give me away or stand as witness for you. We neither much have friends or family we might count on to support us, do we, sir?"

*

"Yes, sir," the servant said, "may I be of assistance?"

"Mr. Darcy to speak to Mr. Phillips. His niece, Miss Elizabeth, asked me to speak to him on a matter of importance."

"Step in, sir. I'll fetch Mr. Phillips."

Darcy waited in the foyer but a handful of moments before a middle-aged man, perhaps a few years older than Mr. Bennet, appeared. "Come in, sir. I recognized your name from my wife's tale of how much of her late sister's life you purchased at the auction. My office away from my actual office is just along this hall."

Darcy was a bit impressed by the size of Mr. Phillips's house. Many country solicitors lived well, but Mr. Phillips appeared to be doing quite well. When they entered the man's office, Phillips closed the door behind him. "Claim a seat, sir. The servant said you came on behalf of my niece Elizabeth."

"Miss Elizabeth asked me to call on you and secure your attendance at her wedding, rather, I should say 'our' wedding."

"Most assuredly, Mrs. Phillips and I will be happy to attend, although I admit Elizabeth could have given us the happy news when she and Mary arrived today to stay with us while things are settled with the estate. I would much prefer our girl knew a home of her own rather than the prospects of service."

Darcy recognized Elizabeth's honor would not permit her to become a "poor relation" instead of a servant in another's home. In that manner, he and she were much alike. He toiled alongside the men he had hired to work the mine, though they thought him a bit daft for doing so.

"When is the wedding?" Phillips asked.

"Today. In an hour when Mr. Williamson comes to Longbourn. I brought a special license with me today."

"A special license?" Phillips asked. "Those are reserved for the aristocracy. Should I be addressing you as 'my lord' rather than 'sir.'"

My late mother was the daughter of an earl." Darcy grinned. "The Archbishop is my godfather."

"Does Elizabeth know this?"

"I mentioned it when I explained about the special license; however, I do not think it completely registered with my betrothed, though I expect several questions on the subject when Miss Elizabeth has time to consider what I said. I believe, today, your niece was more concerned with whether I would accept Miss Mary into my household," Darcy explained.

"And you agreed?" Phillips asked suspiciously.

Darcy unwrapped the strings from the satchel he carried. "Mr. Bennet and I corresponded for the nearly six years. This is the copy of the marriage settlements we agreed upon a little over five years back." He placed the papers on the desk. "Before you ask, Miss Elizabeth knows nothing of these negotiations between her father and me. She does know Mr. Bennet and I held a friendship and her father thought she would make me a good wife."

"I knew something of Thomas Bennet's correspondence with a young fellow in India, but I did not know you two began negotiations for a marriage between you and Elizabeth. Bennet must have thought highly of you if he took it upon himself to make such an arrangement.

Elizabeth is of her grandmother's nature and was something of a favorite of Mr. Bennet's, but I assume you know all this. Yet, I must say, this arrangement is all quite odd," Phillips declared. He read the first few lines of the paper. "Mr. Bennet openly states you hold no obligation to act upon the agreement if you do not find Elizabeth to your liking." The man's eyebrow rose in question. "I assume you believe my niece acceptable."

Darcy cut through the series of questions. "Miss Elizabeth Bennet is handsome enough to tempt any number of men, and you may count me among them. However, more importantly, she possesses other qualities I admire and actually require in a wife. Your niece has demonstrated the care she takes with all she encounters. I watched her at the auction with Mr. Bingley and her neighbors, and even calculated her interactions with me, a complete stranger. Moreover, thanks to Mr. Bennet's letters, I know much about Miss Elizabeth's exemplary character and even some of her faults. My family legacy is in tatters, the estate, though grand, suffers, which means I must spend a great deal of time out of my house to set it aright. I have a five-year-old daughter who requires a strong woman with a caring heart to make a home for her, something my Alice has never known, for, in India, I was often away earning a living. Alice is frightened and requires a stable influence in her life, something other than her doll upon which clings for comfort. I also require a capable mistress for my estate, and, naturally, I will eventually require an heir for all my labors."

"And you can afford to keep Elizabeth as she deserves to be kept?" Phillips demanded.

"Before I departed England, the family estate easily brought in ten thousand a year. We will not be looking at such amounts for some time, but, within a few years, your niece will be one of England's most revered women. I made a fortune in India, which I will use to set it all aright. If you require more information, Mr. Bingley can speak to my family's position in society.

"Mr. Bennet's personal papers should have a copy of this agreement among them. I am certain you may read it more thoroughly among his will and so forth, at your leisure, and find it legally binding if Elizabeth and I wish it. Your niece is of age and can choose where she may. We both understand, I could demand Miss Elizabeth marry me, and she would have little recourse but to agree. Denying me could place her back in the ranks of poverty or even in debtor's prison. However, I would prefer she enter our marriage on her own stated conditions. It would serve neither of us well to be on contentious ground, for there is much to be done and little time to do it."

"Dearly beloved," Mr. Williamson pronounced. The vicar appeared confused by the request for her and Mr. Darcy to marry, but, when she promised it was her dearest wish, the vicar agreed to read the rites. Her uncle had been equally as concerned, though Mr. Phillips admitted to knowing something of her father's correspondence with Mr. Darcy, which both vexed Elizabeth, while allaying some of her fears at the same time.

"Thomas Bennet did keep up a steady stream of correspondence with your young man, Elizabeth, but is this what you truly wish?" her uncle asked in a private moment. It pleased her Mr. Phillips was concerned for her future, but it was also quite frustrating to hear him speak with caution when she truly had few choices in the matter. "Please tell me you have not chosen to accept Mr. Darcy's offer simply because the man has purchased large lots of the Bennet legacy and has promised to surround you with it."

"I am marrying the man because Mr. Darcy has offered me a life I no longer thought possible," she said in firm tones. "I shall be mistress of my own house—a house in which Mary will also be sheltered. I shall not want for food or a place to rest my head or for the hope of children. Such is for what most women wish when they marry. Mr. Darcy and I will walk into the future together hand-in-hand."

"If your mind is settled, then so be it, but promise me you will write regularly, and you will send word if you wish to return to Hertfordshire. I will come for you," her Uncle Phillips declared adamantly.

Her uncle's words had brought tears to Elizabeth's eyes, for she would never be at Longbourn again. As Mr. Williamson continued, she attempted to listen carefully to the words from the Book of Common Prayer and to say a private word of thanksgiving for God's great goodness in sending this man into her life when her spirits were the lowest she had ever known.

The vicar was saying, "I require and charge you as you will answer at the dreadful day of judgement when the secrets of all hearts shall be disclosed, if either of you do know any impediment why you may not be lawfully joined together in matrimony you confess it."

Elizabeth half expected Mr. Darcy to say something at this point about how they knew so little of each other. Likewise, she thought she should protest, but the moment was gone before she could form the words.

Mr. Williamson hearing no objections continued. "Fitzwilliam, will thou have this woman to thy wedded wife, to live together after God's ordinance in the holy estate of matrimony? Wilt thou love her, comfort her, honor and keep her, in sickness and in health, and forsaking all others keep only unto her, so long as you both shall live?"

"*Love her?*" Elizabeth nearly panicked as she and Mr. Darcy had never spoken of affection. Their arrangement was a business contract of sorts. She knew he was a man with a fine countenance, although he could stand to smile more often; yet, if he were as wealthy as he claimed and as both Mr. Bingley and Mr. Birkhead had confirmed, then why would he not want a wife with a sizable dowry, rather than to set his sights on her?

Although she had not heard the actual words, she knew Mr. Darcy had agreed to his Biblical charge to her, and Mr. Williamson was now asking the same of her. Elizabeth swallowed hard before saying, "I will."

"Who giveth this woman to be married unto this man?"

Her uncle said, "I do."

Mr. Williamson instructed Mr. Darcy, "Take her right hand from Mr. Phillips and repeat after me, "'I, Fitzwilliam, take thee Elizabeth to my wedded wife.'"

Mr. Darcy spoke each of those "forever" phrases as he held her hand. Meanwhile, Elizabeth considered the strength she found in his hold. His hand was large, and her hand, foolish as it would be to say aloud, felt nestled and protected in his. Had she found someone she could truly trust in this man's form? If so, she thought affection could easily follow and perhaps hope and a future.

Mr. Darcy dropped her hand to place the ring Mr. Bingley handed him on the Bible held by Mr. Williamson. The vicar held the ring high and then returned it to Mr. Darcy who, this time, caught her left hand and slid it on her third finger. As one who rarely wore jewelry, she thought the ring heavier than she had expected. Elizabeth did not recall repeating her vows, but surely she must have said the words, for Mr. Darcy was already saying, "With this ring, I thee wed. With my body I thee worship, and with all my worldly goods, I thee endow. In the name of the Father, and of the Son, and of the Holy Ghost. Amen."

Essentially the deed was done, but Mr. Darcy, thankfully, still held her hand. Mr. Williamson continued on with the remainder of the service, but Elizabeth stood lost in her thoughts. If what Mr. Darcy said of her father's correspondence proved true, Mr. Bennet had believed they would serve each other well. She made a silent promise to do her best by her husband and prove her father correct.

At length, she and the gentleman were signing the registry Mr. Williamson had brought with him from the local church.

"Fitzwilliam?" she said softly as she took up the pen to sign her new name. "Very distinguished."

"My mother's maiden name," he explained. "You may also call me 'William' if you wish."

Elizabeth smiled. "I shall likely say both. Naturally, not at the same time." She shook her head in embarrassment. "I remain a bit nervous." This time, she giggled. "My mother would be doubly happy today. I was married by special license and claimed to have a case of the 'nerves.' Mrs. Bennet was often plagued by her 'nerves' when vexed by my father. My mother always said I was too much of my father's nature to recognize how she suffered."

"Your mother was much then of the same nature as Mrs. Phillips?" He nodded to where her aunt sobbed because all of her dear sister's family would "soon be gone forever." The fact Mary and Elizabeth would have departed for London and the north of England to enter service within the next week would not stand in defense.

"The Gardiner sisters," Elizabeth spoke with the softness of memories. "They faithfully loved their gossip and each other. Thankfully, their brother, my Uncle Gardiner, is one of the most intelligent and reasonable men God placed on this earth." She shrugged her embarrassment. "So, your family sometimes calls you 'William'? My family predictably referred to me as 'Lizzy.'"

He shook off the idea. "We should begin with 'Fitzwilliam' and 'Elizabeth' and permit ourselves the time to become 'William' and 'Lizzy.'"

"What if I prefer 'Will' or 'Wills'?" she asked with a challenging lift of her brows.

He smiled easily. "One of my cousins called me 'Wills' when we were young. He is a colonel in the British Army. My mother, as I said was a 'Fitzwilliam.' Her elder brother is Lord Martin Fitzwilliam, the Earl of Matlock. His two sons are Roland Fitzwilliam, Lord Lindale, the heir to the earldom, and Colonel Edward Fitzwilliam, my best friend. With my father's passing, the colonel and I share the guardianship of my sister Georgiana. Those stipulations were not changed in my father's will. Nor was any other part of it, as far as I could tell."

Elizabeth was cognizant of the sadness in his tone, but she made no comment to the state of his family connections. Instead, she said, "I can understand the necessity of your being 'William' in a room full of 'Fitzwilliams.'" When he did not reply immediately, Elizabeth asked softly as a slight blush of embarrassment marked her cheeks. She was quite aware of the intimacy of her question. "If we should someday be blessed with a son, shall we call him 'Bennet' or would you prefer to name him after your father?"

"No!" he said harshly. "Not after George Darcy!"

"Elizabeth?" Mary called before Elizabeth could respond to her husband's outburst. She belatedly realized she had jumped back at the anger lacing Mr. Darcy's response.

"Yes, Mary," Elizabeth attempted to disguise the moment of fear she had experienced.

"Aunt and Uncle Phillips are prepared to depart, and Mr. Hill reports Mr. Darcy's coachman has brought his carriage around."

Elizabeth barely nodded to Mr. Darcy before joining her family in the foyer. She worked hard to disguise what had just transpired, but she noted her uncle's glare in Mr. Darcy's direction, but her husband simply picked up his daughter and was speaking his farewells to Mr. Bingley.

"You shall be happy shall you not, Lizzy?" her aunt was asking.

"As happy as God wishes me to be," she assured, but Elizabeth was already wondering if she had erred in her judgement.

༺༻

They waited another three-quarters of an hour before they departed Longbourn, for Mr. Bingley had insisted they make use of his small coach for more comfort and extra trunks. "There is no sense in squeezing all of you in Darcy's coach when I have no need of my small one at this time." Elizabeth knew the coach had been purchased for Jane's use, eventually to be used for the children and governesses when they traveled as a family. Most assuredly, she had graciously thanked him and sought a promise from him that he would come to them anytime he was near Mr. Darcy's estate. "You will always be family," Elizabeth said as she rose up on her toes to kiss Mr. Bingley's cheek in parting, only to turn to discover a scowl marking Mr. Darcy's features.

"I will ride with Alice in the small coach," her husband announced.

"There is no need," Mary offered. "I do not mind keeping the child company. It would be my pleasure."

Yet, Mr. Darcy would have none of it. "If you do not mind, Miss Bennet, I will decide what is best for my daughter."

"Mary did not mean . . ." Elizabeth began.

He waved off her excuses. "Alice will be frightened by all the changes she has encountered today, and, I must admit, I have come to depend upon her innocence to remind me the world is not set against me. I fear I treated you poorly earlier, for my anger at the betrayal of my father marked my response to you. I will use the time with Alice not only to allay her fears, but to remind myself my primitive manners are not appropriate on British soil."

༄

Holding hands and looking through the small window at the back of the carriage, Elizabeth and Mary huddled together as the coach crossed through Longbourn's gate.

"Longbourn served us well," Mary murmured as the coach rolled under the arch and turned in the direction of the road leading north.

"I feel as if we are abandoning them all. Who will place flowers on their graves? Even Jane is in the Bennet gravesite," Elizabeth said through tears.

"If Mr. Darcy permits it, even if the estate is sold to another, you could use a bit of your pin money to pay someone to tend the cemetery. Mr. Birkhead could arrange it. Neither of us are of Lydia's temperament, requiring ribbons and new bonnets. We could save what funds come our way. I plan to make myself useful to you and the child."

Mary and Elizabeth turned together to face forward. "If you do not mind my asking," her sister ventured, "What upset Mr. Darcy so at the house?"

Elizabeth sighed heavily. "I wish I knew more of what transpired between my husband and his father, but I must advise you to avoid any mention of the man. Such is my plan." Elizabeth sat straighter as if placing a bit of granite in her spine. "We were speaking of Mr. Darcy's Christian name of 'Fitzwilliam.' It is his mother's maiden name. He told me at a family gathering there is often some confusion because his uncle, as well as his uncle's sons are also Fitzwilliams, with his cousin, a Colonel Fitzwilliam being in the British Army and his best friend. They two share guardianship of Miss Darcy. As is typical of me when I am nervous, I foolishly asked if we would then name a son of ours in the same manner and call the boy 'Bennet.' I should have waited for his response, though there was a bit of a pause, and I thought I had offended him. Therefore, I asked if he would prefer his father's Christian name for the child.

"We were getting along well until then. For a moment, Mary, I feared him. I had never viewed such resentment in a person. Such hardness in anyone's heart."

"We must avoid upsetting Mr. Darcy," Mary stated the obvious. "I imagine a return to his former home will have him more than a bit on edge. He did recognize how his speech was not proper, though I feel his excuse of Miss Alice's fear was a ploy not to hear your apology, for he knew it was his fault."

Elizabeth nodded her acceptance of Mary's opinion. "I had prepared myself over the last few days to prove I could be a good mistress for Mr. Darcy's estate and perhaps earn a bit of his respect, if not his affections. After all, there has been no mistress in the household for some eighteen years. Naturally, there is, most assuredly, a highly efficient housekeeper, but I had envisioned assisting my husband to be accepted in society again by winning over his neighbors and family, but, I fear, Mr. Darcy's animosity will destroy my most resourceful enterprise. I pray my intentions to save our family has not placed us in a more tenuous situation."

Chapter Four

When they stopped for their first evening on the road, Elizabeth did not know what to expect. After all, she was married to a man with a mercurial nature. Mr. Darcy could claim his conjugal rights, but he came away from the conversation with the innkeeper sporting another frown upon his countenance. "Mr. Eubanks has passed during my absence from England, and the Eubanks family has sold the inn to a man with whom I hold no acquaintance. He has presented one of the two rooms I reserved to another traveler. All which remains is a small room at the back of the inn. I will take it if you could make Alice comfortable with you and your sister in the larger quarters."

"Are you assured, sir?" Elizabeth said with as much meekness as she could add to her tone. "Mary and I could take the smaller room. My sister and I do not wish to be a trouble to you."

Mr. Darcy's eyebrow rose in a gesture of skepticism, which matched his tone. "There is no need to placate me, Mrs. Darcy. I have apologized previously for my bad mood earlier. As a gentleman, I would not permit any of you to sleep in a room set away from the others. It is too dangerous."

Elizabeth nodded her acceptance. "As you wish, sir."

"What I wish, Mrs. Darcy, is for my wife to return to the young woman who challenged me with our first encounter."

"I did not initially offer you a challenge," she corrected. "You were a purchaser—a very important purchaser—at my family auction. I would not have dared to offend you. In fact, we did not argue until . . ." She caught herself before she said the words.

"Until I made you an offer, impossible for you to refuse," he finished for her.

"Papa!" Alice came running. "Bis Mary says the food has arrived." The child pulled on his trouser leg.

He bent to scoop his daughter into his arms. "You may lead, Mrs. Darcy. At least the new innkeeper reserved the small sitting room as I requested."

"All that means, sir," she said as she crossed before him to hurry to where Mary waited, "is the innkeeper caters to a clientele not of the upper classes."

*

He cursed himself as he crawled into the lumpy bed. "Some wedding night," he grumbled. "Although it is what you deserved. It was not as if you and Elizabeth could have been intimate with Alice in the room, but it would have been nice to hold your wife and to kiss her. Yet, you destroyed the moment when you lost your temper. Now, Elizabeth is frightened of you, and the only means around it is to sit her down and explain something of what occurred to have my father banishing me to India. Yet, dare I? Would she think poorly of me?"

Darcy rolled over and punched the already flat pillow into a rolled-up position. "It has been so long since I could trust someone. What will she say when she learns the depth of the deception I practiced? I pray Mr. Bennet's estimation of his daughter's strength of character was accurate. My return to society, Alice's future, and the glory of Pemberley all rest in Elizabeth's hands."

*

"Bis Lizbet," the child said from a place closer to the bed than Elizabeth had expected. Although she had not been asleep, Elizabeth had been lost in her thoughts of Mr. Darcy and her future. By nature, she was a planner, and she was planning how best to proceed in her marriage.

"Yes, Alice?" she said softly so as not to wake Mary, whose soft snore had been a comfortable reminder of what a long day they all had experience.

"Papa be alone," the child said in sad tones.

"Your father is well," Elizabeth assured as she shoved herself upward. "He gave us the larger room, but he still has a warm bed and will find his rest. We will see him in the morning."

"Still alone," the child argued.

Elizabeth did not know how to address Alice's concerns. Most assuredly, she could not go to the man and offer him comfort while claiming a bit of comfort of her own. "I promise you your father is already asleep. Would you like to join Mary and me in our bed?"

The child quickly nodded her agreement.

"Fetch your blanket then," she instructed as she stood. Earlier, they had made a small bed for the girl before the fire. Alice scrambled to catch up one of the blankets and her doll.

Elizabeth lifted the pair to the bed. "No kicking Mary," she warned. "You stay in the middle." She soothed back the child's hair, while making a silent promise to do well by Alice. Although she might never earn a corner of Mr. Darcy's heart, she could still earn his loyalty by seeing to Alice's fears and proving herself a competent mistress for his household. "Enough," she murmured under her breath. It would be enough: She had no other choices. She crawled beneath the blankets and tucked Alice into the curve of her body. "You hold Miss Cassandra, and I will hold you." She kissed the child's temple. "Soon, we will all be in a new home, and none of us will be alone ever again."

❧

They had spent two more nights upon the road with the same style of accommodations. She had been married three days and had yet to know even the smallest gesture of "affection" from her husband. It was not as if Mr. Darcy had been cruel to her, for he was attentive. When the two of them shared a carriage, he told her about the various towns and villages along the way. "While at Cambridge, I traveled these roads often. I enjoyed viewing some of the historical sites."

"My father was always a great one to reference the history of each of the shires surrounding Hertfordshire," she remarked. "Ironically, he despised London and traveled very little beyond the estate. I suppose his influence makes me curious regarding so many things in this world."

"Pemberley has a library built upon the efforts of many generations. I pray you will make use of it, and, naturally, once I can set the estate aright again, I would be proud to escort you through the Peak District or the lakes or Yorkshire's dales. We can see it all. I have sorely missed England, although I expect to know a definite chill after so long in India."

"Am I to expect snow in Derbyshire? My Aunt Gardiner has spoken often of the frequency of its snowfall," she explained.

"We will know our fair share," he assured. "I hope such does not make you regret your choice."

Elizabeth purposely ignored his comment about "choices." She was determined to keep the peace between them. Rather, she asked, "Are there places to walk? In Hertfordshire, I customarily started my day with a walk to Oakham Mount."

"Oakham Mount?" he questioned.

"Not a mountain in the sense I am certain as is the Peak District," she assured. "A large hill, really, but I was accustomed to climbing it regularly. From the top, one could view Meryton in the distance or the roof of Netherfield, where Mr. Bingley and my sister Jane lived. Since I was small child, I would tell all the rocks and the trees my secrets."

"Did you tell them of accepting my proposal?" he asked.

"There was no time, but I said my farewells to all the sights from the mount's top a day before we departed," she admitted. "Just as I did on the day after the auction."

AMENDING THE SHADES OF PEMBERLEY

They became quiet then, for the coach turned in at the gate of what must surely be Pemberley Woods. Mr. Darcy stiffened, as if he prepared for battle. He no longer stared out the side window, but rather at the road they had just traveled through the small rear window. Elizabeth wondered at his thoughts, but her spirits were in too high of a flutter for her to share her own wonder. No words could express either of their feelings in that moment.

The park was very large and contained a great variety of ground. They had entered it in one of the lowest points and drove for some time through a beautiful wood stretching over a wide extent. Elizabeth slid closer to the window for a better view, but Mr. Darcy sat in stone-like silence, making no comment or even turning his head to rest his eyes on her or on the passing scenery. He kept his eyes on the smaller carriage in which Mary and Alice traveled; yet, Elizabeth was not certain he really knew the carriage was behind them.

She did not necessarily object to the quiet, for her mind was too full for conversation, and she saw and admired every remarkable spot and point of view. The coach gradually ascended for a half mile, where they found themselves at the top of a considerable eminence, where the wood ceased, and the eye was instantly caught by Pemberley House, situated on the opposite side of the valley into which the road, with some abruptness wound. It was a large, handsome stone building, standing well on high ground and backed by a ridge of high woody hills, and, in front, a stream of some natural importance swelled into greater, but without any artificial appearance. Its banks were neither formal, nor falsely adorned.

Elizabeth realized she was holding her breath: She knew delight and honor. She had never seen a place for which nature had done more or where natural beauty had been so little counteracted by an awkward taste. At that moment, she felt to be mistress of Pemberley was truly a great honor, but she wondered if she was up to the task.

Before she could speak to her qualms and bring Mr. Darcy from his stupor, the coach began to descend the hill to cross the bridge and circle the drive to halt before the house's main door. The manor's mullioned windows sparkled in the sun. Steep gables soared upward.

Carved stone marked the doors, each sporting brass knockers. Immediately, a line of crispy-uniformed servants streamed from several doors to circle the drive.

"Mr. Darcy," Elizabeth whispered when he did not move. "Mr. Darcy," she repeated, reaching for his hand. "Your servants await. Jasper has climbed down from the bench and means to open the door. Mary and Alice have already disembarked."

He nodded his understanding but made no move to respond. Therefore, she motioned for the footman to release the door lock and set down the steps. "Thank you, Jasper," she said sweetly as the servant offered her his hand.

However, before she could accept Jasper's gallantry, her husband scooted across the seat to precede her to the ground. "I will assist my wife," he instructed, and the footman stepped back.

Mr. Darcy climbed down and turned to extend his hand. Yet, when she meant to place her hand in his, he reached instead for her waist and lifted her down to set her before him. "Welcome to your new home, Mrs. Darcy," he said with more emotion than she had expected.

They turned together as Alice and Mary joined them. A very proper butler was bowing to them. "Welcome home, sir."

"Thank you, Mr. Nathan. I have missed Derbyshire."

Elizabeth thought it odd Mr. Darcy did not say he had missed his family. Most assuredly, she would miss Longbourn, but any place could be home if her parents and sisters were present.

Her husband was saying, "Mr. Nathan. Mrs. Reynolds, this is your new mistress, Mrs. Elizabeth Darcy. Also traveling with us is Mrs. Darcy's sister, Miss Mary Bennet, and, naturally, my daughter, Alice."

Elizabeth noted the housekeeper's frown, but Mr. Darcy was striding away from her to shake the hand of a man of perhaps forty years of age. "Sheffield, my goodness, man, it is good to see you among those gathered before Pemberley. I have not sported a proper cravat or held an informed discussion on the Roman empire or dozens of other such subjects since I was required to leave you behind. I am glad Mr. Nathan reached you and you were available."

"I had not gone so far," the man explained. "Your father kept me on as Mr. O'Connell had previously presented his resignation."

Again, her husband frowned, but no comment was made.

"Are the quarters arranged as I indicated?" Mr. Darcy asked.

"Yes, sir," Mr. Nathan said before words could escape Mrs. Reynolds's lips. Once more, the lady worn a frown, indicating she had not approved of Mr. Darcy's request. Elizabeth could not quite understand what the issue might be, but she would discover it quickly enough. Her duty was to protect her husband, her sister, and Alice. Everything else remained insignificant. The housekeeper likely held her own opinions of what occurred under Pemberley's roof both before and after Mr. Darcy's banishment. If the lady proved more loyal to George Darcy's memory than Fitzwilliam Darcy's reign as the estate master, Elizabeth would be presenting the woman her walking papers, no matter how long the lady had been employed at the estate. "If you will follow Mrs. Reynolds, she will show you all to your quarters."

Mr. Darcy extended his arm to Elizabeth, which she accepted with a small smile of reassurance to allay her husband's sudden return to his earlier stiffness, as they entered the house.

The high-ceilinged foyer was filled with natural light, and Elizabeth imagined, even in the night's middle, the moon would provide a gentle glow to the area. The aroma of beeswax mixed well with the lovely fresh flowers in several large vases. Every piece of metal shone with the reflection of the natural light, and the furniture spoke of the care presented the pieces over the years.

"Cook has prepared a midday meal which might be delivered to your suite, Mr. Darcy," Mrs. Reynolds was saying.

"What do you prefer, Elizabeth?" he asked her.

"I see no reason the staff should be required to carry a full service of dishes to a sitting room. Is there not a small dining room more easily accessible?"

"The morning room, Mrs. Reynolds. Say, in a half hour. Would such be enough time, Mrs. Darcy?" her husband asked.

"I believe we all could manage a half hour," Elizabeth announced. "I realize you are likely of the nature to begin your work on this day, but I was hoping you would provide your daughter, Mary, and me a tour of the nearby grounds and something of the manor itself. I know Mrs. Reynolds could do the deed well, for she likely conducts tours upon request; yet, we would all feel more at ease with you near."

Mr. Darcy did not answer immediately, and Elizabeth briefly worried she had upset his plans, but, after a long pause, he said, "I would be honored. Perhaps after our meal."

"Such would be lovely, sir."

Entering the suite indicated, Elizabeth paused in awe. The broad corridor leading to this particular wing of the house had been lined with artwork from Sir Joshua Reynolds and Thomas Gainsborough and George Romney and others she did not recognize, but would study when the opportunity proved itself.

Mrs. Reynolds opened the door to a large sitting room. "This is your suite, Mrs. Darcy, with the sitting room to be shared with the master. I will have your trunk brought up. Mr. Darcy indicated you would require a lady's maid; therefore, I have taken the liberty to hire a girl from the village on a trial basis. You are under no obligation to retain her services if she does not please you."

While the woman bustled about the room, Elizabeth naturally gravitated to the large window, sporting a window seat and several pillows, which she knew would become one of her favorite places to look out upon the well-groomed lawns of the estate. "I am certain the girl will serve me well. I am not one to sit before a mirror for very long." She turned from the window to run her fingers across the backs of two straight-back upholstered chairs seated before a fireplace, which had been set for her pleasure. The material used on the chairs complemented the green, such as that found in a forest, of the drapes. A compact desk occupied one corner alongside two floor-to-ceiling book shelves. A low table and a settee were available for sharing tea, and upon the floor stood a cream and green rug, likely from China. "Mama would be speechless," she murmured.

"Pardon?" Mrs. Reynolds asked.

"Just ruminating on my mother's delight in such a room." Realizing Mary and the child still waited for the housekeeper, Elizabeth said, "I should add a few more pins to my hair while you show my sister and Miss Alice to their quarters."

"Certainly, Mrs. Darcy," Mrs. Reynolds said as she pulled herself up royally to finish the task. "Mr. Darcy's quarters are through the dressing room, ma'am." She nodded to Mary and the child to follow her.

Elizabeth stood looking at the door the housekeeper had indicated. Would this be the night Mr. Darcy finally claimed his husbandly duties? The idea both frightened and enticed her. "Pull yourself together, Elizabeth," she chastised. "What is to be will be. You made a bargain to save yourself and Mary. You weighed your options, and this one proved the best. The house is magnificent and your husband is wealthy. For what more could you wish? What if Mr. Darcy does not hold you in affection? You would be no different from half the female population of England in that manner. You only asked for a place where you and Mary would be safe. God granted your wish: Do not ask for more."

She was nearly finished with her hair when Alice, carrying her doll tucked under one arm, bounded through the still open door. "Bis Lizbeth, I've a bowteaful room too. You'll come to see it?"

"It is nearly time for your father to fetch us for our meal, but I promise to view both your and Mary's rooms when we see the rest of the house."

"Did I hear my name?" Mary asked as she came through the door.

"Alice wishes us to view her new quarters," Elizabeth explained. "I suggested we wait until after our meal and Mr. Darcy's tour of the house."

"I am rather hungry, are you not also, Alice?" Mary said perceptively before the child could lodge a protest.

"Will there be cakes?" Alice asked. "Biss Cassandra likes cakes."

Mr. Darcy appeared in the open doorway. "If my daughter wishes cakes, she will have them," he announced as he lifted the child to his arms.

"Yet, not before Miss Alice eats a proper meal," Elizabeth corrected. "Cake will not have you growing up, but rather out." She gestured with her hands, and the child giggled. "Lead on, Mr. Darcy," she instructed. Wrapping her arm through Mary's, Elizabeth added, "All your ladies are at your disposal." To Mary, she teasingly said, "We should steal a few of the bread rolls and leave a trail of bread crumbs to find our way back to our rooms."

Her husband said over his shoulder, "Despite the tale in *Kinder- und Hausmärchen*, your doing so will only earn one of the maids a good tongue-lashing from Mrs. Reynolds." He grinned at Elizabeth.

Elizabeth remarked, "You really should smile more often, sir. It pleases me to see you thusly."

"Other than Alice, I have not had a reason to smile in many years." His brows lifted in an apparent challenge.

Elizabeth gently tugged Mary closer. "Then, we three ladies must provide you more reasons to know happiness."

The gentleman did not respond, but he looked upon her in a serious manner until Alice tapped his cheek to reclaim his attention, but Elizabeth thought, if only for a brief moment, he approved of her response.

✦

The meal had been excessively satisfying. Alice had kept them all entertained with a litany of questions and observations. A special chair for Miss Cassandra had been placed beside the child, and Elizabeth realized she and Mary must ease the child's strong dependence on the doll.

AMENDING THE SHADES OF PEMBERLEY

Yet, what Elizabeth enjoyed most was Mr. Darcy's tour of the house and grounds, for he spoke with such pride, even Alice stood in awe of his voice. The gentleman knew about every painting in the portrait gallery and the history of each of his ancestors. He knew when each generation had added a treasured urn or suit of armor or a new roof or even a wing to the house. However, when they entered the gardens, the Mr. Darcy she had known from the first encounter returned. Where Elizabeth saw natural beauty in the bit of overgrown paths, her husband grumbled about how the walkways and the plants had been neglected.

"This display has me very worried regarding the care of the home farms in my absence," he declared with great emotion, which had even Alice hiding behind Mary's skirts.

"Was there not a land steward?" Elizabeth asked. "Surely an estate of this magnitude employs a competent steward."

"'Had' a competent steward," her husband gestured wildly. "A man my father trusted to do the necessary work."

"What happened to the him?" Elizabeth asked softly. She suspected what troubled her husband rested in what he viewed as a lack of care of his family's beloved estate. Somehow, what occurred to the manor and the land had begun with his banishment to India. Now he had returned to Derbyshire and the estate; however, the question begged, what could they expect? Happiness or forever walking on eggshells?

"Nothing happened to the man—or I should say to the man's son, for the competent land steward passed some years back. Nothing that God had not designed for him, and, I suppose, for me." He looked off in the distance as if seeing something Elizabeth did not.

"Papa, I'm cold," Alice said into the silence hanging in the air as if a fog surrounded them.

"I will take her back inside," Mary was quick to say. "You and Elizabeth deserve a few minutes of privacy. You have had very little time together since we departed Longbourn." She took the child's hand. "We should fetch Miss Cassandra and see about another cup of warm tea. I imagine Miss Cassandra is missing both of us," Mary said as she and Alice walked away together.

Elizabeth watched them go before saying, "I did not mean to upset you again. It seems I do not know how we move forward. You must assist me. What do you prescribe for our life together?"

"I suppose your bargain appears quite unreal now you must live with the terms of our agreement," he said with a tilt of his head obviously to study her.

"It is real enough. I am Mrs. Darcy, but I have yet to discover my role in your life."

"I pray, in the end, you do not regret your decision," he said softly.

"Others would say I have no reason for regret, but I do wonder if you know the emotion," she countered. "Surely, I have disappointed you."

"How could I know disappointment? We both received what we wanted. You and your sister have a future. Alice is delighted to possess both you and Miss Bennet in her life, and, in that manner, so am I. I have been too long without family."

"I do enjoy the child's company and her wonder at this new world she is living in," Elizabeth stated. "I easily admit, even if we had no agreement, I would be delighted by your daughter."

"Yes, Alice can enchant even the greatest curmudgeon," he chuckled. "Not that you fit such a description, although some think I do."

For a moment, Elizabeth wondered what it would be like to have married this man in affection, rather than in necessity. His countenance often appeared stern and aloof, but when he smiled, the gesture had a strange effect on her. With his grey eyes lit in amusement, she thought him the handsomest man she had ever encountered. Just standing at his side had her preparing for the growing power of a storm. Most assuredly, she had walked home from Oakham Mount on multiple occasions with a storm churning about her, but she had never feared its strength, not in the way it was with him. There was an element of excitement and danger in both a storm and the man standing before her, and she wondered if it would not be safer to know nature instead of him. However, she instinctively recognized, if presented the option, she would choose Fitzwilliam Darcy over all the riches of the world.

"We are not in love," he was saying when she left her musings behind.

"No, we are not, but I had hoped for something resembling affection," she admitted. "Loyalty, perhaps. Or respect."

"You will discover me very loyal to you," he countered. "I do not intend to disabuse our marriage vows. However, for now, all my attention must be on Pemberley and my daughter."

"You want no other children?" she asked in alarm.

"I will not force you into performing your wifely duties. In truth, in the beginning, I expect to be gone from the house from dawn to well past dusk. You will see very little of me for the near future. I am already months behind in preparing the land for next year's crop and repairing the mill and the homes of my tenants. As to our private quarters, I only arranged the joined suites to allow you to save face among the household staff. I originally thought to provide you a wing of the house for your use alone, but I would not have you embarrassed by my actions or lack thereof."

"However, you would see me as childless while I am expected to attend to another woman's daughter," she argued. "Did you love Alice's mother so dearly? Or do you find me reprehensible? Do you not require an heir for the estate?"

"I shan't discuss Ruth with you," he stated in harsh tones. "And I, most assuredly, do not find you reprehensible. To be honest, my fingers itch to run them through your hair and to take you in my arms, and, yes, I require an heir. Even so, we must not produce one tonight. That is, unless such is your wish." He paused but his words had left her somewhat dumbfounded, and Elizabeth could not think how to respond. "My interests during the early months of my return to my ancestral home, as I stated previously, are Alice's safety and happiness, and amending all which plagues the very roots of Pemberley.

"For now, you should know, there is a lock on the door between our adjoined dressing rooms. I set it as locked on your side of the door before I met you and the others for our meal. You have my word I will never set a foot into your quarters unless you ask me to do so by unlocking the door. My presence in your life must be at your invitation. Such was our bargain."

Chapter Five

Elizabeth had not unlocked the door. In fact, she had avoided her dressing room and the joint sitting room as if another pox could be found within. She went so far as to ask Hannah to set her bath before the fire in her bed chamber, claiming a chill caused by the difference in the temperatures between the southern shires and those in the north. While, in reality, it was the chill in her husband's heart which had Elizabeth avoiding the door separating them. Through a mostly sleepless night, she had decided it would be a cold day in purgatory before she would unlock the door. If Mr. Darcy desired her, it would be he who must do the wooing. "Such is a man's prerogative, is it not?"

Therefore, she remained in bed until she heard her husband speaking to his valet in the hall, before she turned over finally to claim a bit more sleep. It was still dark outside, but, a man of his word, Mr. Darcy was off to tend to what he truly loved—his ancestral estate. Even the presence of his child could not prevent him from his mission. Such was the reason Mr. Darcy had married Elizabeth: To educate and comfort his child while he was not at home. Eventually, he would require an heir for the estate he loved more than anything or anyone else in the world. Then, he would discover she meant for him to "work" to earn her approval, just as she meant to make herself indispensable and worthy of the man's attentions. In that manner, her late father's opinion of her meant more than did her husband's.

When she entered the morning room some two hours later, Mary and Alice had already broken their fasts.

"I told you Elizabeth was not ill, Alice," Mary said with a knowing look. Mary evidently thought Elizabeth and Mr. Darcy had finally consummated their marriage.

"It is difficult to sleep when one is in a new bed and has so many things which must be addressed on her mind," Elizabeth said as she sat across from the pair and permitted Mr. Nathan to pour her tea.

"May I prepare you a plate, ma'am?" he asked.

"Eggs and perhaps some toast," she instructed. "I will use the conserves on the table."

"Yes, ma'am," he said and stepped away to do her bidding.

Elizabeth spoke to her sister. "Mr. Darcy wishes us to see to Alice's education. I know you, better than I, can see to certain aspects of Alice's needs, such as music. Yet, if you do not mind, I would enjoy sharing father's unique way of teaching each of us to read. I want a part of our parents to survive within these walls. Unfortunately, at least for the first week or so, I shall be required to oversee what Mr. Darcy has spoken of as a change for Pemberley. I despise asking you to neglect your own needs for the time being, for I know you, too, are grieving as deeply as I, but I pray I may continue to count you willing to assist me."

"Most assuredly, you may depend upon me. We are sisters first and foremost."

Elizabeth nodded her gratitude, for she knew she had not always treated Mary as well as she should have been treated. Too often, she had ignored Mary's opinions and her sister's need for attention when they were still at Longbourn. "I promise to retrieve Alice this afternoon. I thought you and I," she said to the child, "might begin a study of the garden to learn what will and will not grow there. We might also attempt some drawings, if you wish."

Mary said to the child, "My fingers are more adept on the pianoforte, while Elizabeth is a fine artist."

"I daw a fower for Papa," Alice said around a mouthful of eggs.

Mary diplomatically explained, "Although children of Alice's age would, generally, be required to eat in the schoolroom, I took the liberty of permitting the child to eat with us. I did not think you would mind, for we acted as such on the road to Pemberley, but now that we are in this fine house, I was not assured whether I performed appropriately. If not, I apologize."

"As Mr. Darcy was confidently persuaded to allow you and me decisions over Alice's education and her care, the decisions are ours to make. Alice will remain with one or the other of us, as we see fit. If Mr. Darcy chooses otherwise, he must overrule our choices."

They were quiet for a few minutes before Elizabeth added, "I would like to call upon Mr. Ericks on Saturday, and, perhaps, attend services on Sunday. We must inform Aunt Gardiner's brother of our presence in Derbyshire, do you not think?"

"I suspect our aunt has written to him regarding our change of circumstance," Mary observed.

"All the more reason for our visit to the vicarage," Elizabeth declared. "What might he think of our poor manners if we did not call upon family? I will make arrangements for transportation and someone to accompany us."

A half hour later found her examining her third room on the second storey when Mrs. Reynolds caught up to her. Elizabeth had made a bet with herself it would be her fourth room before the housekeeper had learned of Elizabeth's activities and would come looking for her.

"May I be of assistance, Mrs. Darcy?" the lady asked.

"Not exactly," Elizabeth replied cryptically. "It is nice to recognize the staff's loyalty to you, Mrs. Reynolds, but please inform them I am not the enemy. Mr. Darcy has charged me with refreshing the rooms of his house more to his taste, rather than his father's. I pray you hold no objections."

"No, ma'am."

Elizabeth said, "Then might you fetch paper and pencil to keep a list and then explain to me why these small cracks near the upper right corner of this window have not been properly addressed by someone who performs plaster work? Is there damp wood behind the frame? And the drapeve has several small holes. I had thought to make this my sitting room, but I prefer a light shade of drapery to this deeper one. These might be used elsewhere in the house, depending on how quickly and efficiently the repairs might be corrected and new drapes cut and hemmed for these windows."

"The room has known little use," Mrs. Reynolds said in apologetic tones. "It was the late mistress's favorite, but since Lady Anne's passing, it has known no changes. The previous Mr. Darcy left it as a 'shrine' to his wife: He could often be found sitting in here in the dark."

Elizabeth thought the idea quite sad for all involved, but she said, "I shall seek Mr. Darcy's permission to make the changes and use it for my sanctuary, but, whether I employ the room for my use or not, repairs must be made. Perhaps my husband will wish it left undisturbed; yet, I cannot imagine he would wish it to remain in disrepair."

"You are correct, ma'am. I shall fetch paper and pencil, and we may view the rooms together."

"Just so you know, I mean to examine every room in this house, wing by wing. I shall prepare a list of recommendations to present to Mr. Darcy. Such was one of his charges to me as his wife and the mistress of this estate. He will likely choose to prioritize what to complete first. The choice will be his. Not mine."

"I did not mean to insinuate otherwise," Mrs. Reynolds said dutifully.

"I understand your loyalty to this family, Mrs. Reynolds, for Mr. and Mrs. Hill served the Bennet family from the time my father was at Eton, and I do not wish to be your adversary; yet, I have no problem serving thusly, if such is what is required."

"I have been housekeeper for more than five and twenty years," the lady said in her own defense, "and employed at the estate before Master Fitzwilliam was born."

"Master Fitzwilliam is the one who charged me with this duty, and, whether you approve or not, I shall see it done to the best of my abilities. To be clear, Mr. Darcy wishes to erase his father's stamp on the manor and the estate. Sentimentality will not prevail with him."

After her warning, Elizabeth had spent a quiet, but productive, morning with Mrs. Reynolds and Mr. Nathan, the butler added to the conversation purely by accident, or so she supposed. Either way, Elizabeth had appreciated the man's presence, as well as his knowledge of the estate.

After their midday meal, Elizabeth bundled Alice into a cloak and a hat and took her into the garden.

"It's cold, Biss Lizbet," the girl complained after only a few minutes.

"I thought you wished to draw a flower for your father," Elizabeth countered. "Must I take you back inside?"

The child dug the toe of her shoe in the soft earth. "Papa be happy with a fower." She sighed heavily. "My cloak won't stay cosed."

Elizabeth reached to straighten the garment. "You require several pence in the hem," she declared.

"Peese?" Alice questioned.

"No, pence. They are coins. Permit me to demonstrate." She knelt before the child and caught up the hem of her own cloak. "Here. Feel." The girl ran her finger along the hem. "Those are coins. My mother taught me and all my sisters this trick. You sew a row of coins in the hem of your cloak. They are heavy enough to assist in holding the cloak in place. Moreover, if you wish to purchase something, you have money hidden upon you to pay for it. Would you like me to ask the maid to put coins in your hem?"

"Lots," the child said with a nod of agreement.

"Just enough to keep the cloak in place, but not so many you cannot walk about properly." Elizabeth stood and pretended to stumble this way and that.

Alice burst into laughter. "Too many, Biss Lizbet."

Elizabeth cupped the child's chin in her gloved hand. "I do not mind you calling me 'Lizbet,' but try for 'miss,' not 'biss.' It sounds like 'm-m-m-m.'"

The child giggled. "Like eating cakes. 'M-m-m-m."

"Miss," Elizabeth instructed. "Now your turn."

Alice screwed her mouth about. "'M-m-m-miss."

"Excellent," Elizabeth affirmed. She would not harp on the pronunciation. Instead, she would correct the child gently over a period of time. "Now, should we choose a flower to draw for your father? As you say, it has already turned colder here than it was at home in Hertfordshire. We might be called upon to draw a pine cone instead."

"I kin count to five," the child announced without a mention of a flower.

"May I hear you?" Elizabeth asked.

Alice stopped and pulled off her glove to expose her fingers. "'One,'" she said and held up her thumb. "Two" came next, along with her index finger. "Tree" brought the middle finger, which she held in place with her other hand. "'Foe,'" she said, pushing her ring finger in place. "Five" was followed by a smile and the pinkie finger.

"Congratulations!" Elizabeth said as she presented the child a quick hug. "Your papa will be so proud of you."

"I could count to tree befoe," Alice confessed.

"It does not matter," Elizabeth assured. "You now can count to five. Wonderful work. Did Mary assist you?"

"Yes, and we paid music, and I learnt nother song and two notes, and we pacticed how to hold our tea cups poperly, and we paid games," the girl shared.

"My, you have had a busy day. Are you too well worn to draw?" Elizabeth teased.

"Papa needs a fower from me," the child declared.

"I imagine such would be a lovely ending for what shall likely be a busy day for him," Elizabeth assured.

Eventually, they decided on a dahlia, which, along with three other such blooms, was hiding along a wall and behind an overgrown bush. Elizabeth was beginning to view the garden in the same manner as had her husband. The child had liked the Michaelmas aster better than the dahlia, but Elizabeth knew Alice would not be able to replicate the thin spearlike petals as easily as she would with the thicker petals of the dahlia. She found a place where they could spread their blanket on the flattened ground of the path. Two wooden lap-style desks and a leather satchel were placed before them by the footman Jasper, who appeared to have been assigned duties to attend them. Elizabeth withdrew paper and pencils from the satchel and laid them out on the desks. Alice sat cross-legged and waited for Elizabeth to begin.

Placing the dahlia between them so they could both see it, she said, "We should practice with creating one petal first. Then we may create more. We will practice on this paper and use a clean sheet for your actual drawing."

The child looked up to her. "You first, Biss . . . I mean, m . . . Miss Lizbet."

Elizabeth nodded her approval of the child's efforts for the correct pronunciation. "Let us begin. It really is not so hard," she assured the girl. She reached across to adjust the angle of the child's paper. "You will notice there is a circle in the middle of the flower." She lightly drew her pencil around and around to show Alice what she wanted the girl to notice. "We must begin with a circle." She demonstrated first before saying, "It is your turn."

Alice held the pencil tightly and drew circles in the air before attempting to add one on the paper. It was more than a bit lopsided, but it was close to the correct shape.

Elizabeth said, "Very good," and went on with the next step. "The petals also look like a circle," she shared while again tracing the shape of the petal with her pencil braced only an inch or so above the flower. "Yet, they have a straight line where it touches the center. See."

Elizabeth removed one of the petals from the flower and placed it on Alice's paper.

The girl attempted a petal, but she bore down so hard she broke off the tip of the pencil. Elizabeth adjusted the child's grip on a new pencil she had removed from the satchel and handed the broken one to the footman to sharpen with a knife. She said as she smoothed the child's hair from her cheek, "Yours was a good first attempt. See this side of your petal is well done. Let us attempt it again. Relax your fingers on the pencil. Might I hold your hand and direct you?"

In apparent disappointment for not drawing the petal perfectly the first time, the child's eyes were misted over with tears, but she nodded her agreement. Elizabeth shifted behind the girl, where she might move the child's hand more easily. "Let us repeat our efforts together. Up at a slight angle and curve across the top and another gentle curve on the other side."

"I like it, Biss Lizbet," Alice said with a smile.

"We must repeat the image another five times. You will count with me."

With each attempt the child counted, and Elizabeth eased her grip on Alice's hand. "Should we do another five? For the final drawing for your father, we shall require eight petals."

"I kint count to eight," the child argued.

"As I am doing now, I will assist you," Elizabeth assured.

"I like when you holds my hand," the girl said sweetly.

"And I like when you hold mine," Elizabeth said with another caress of Alice's cheek. "Your hand fits nicely inside of mine." She nodded to the paper and instructed, "Another five. You will count for me again."

"One," Alice said with a sigh before drawing the first petal. "Two. Papa used to hold my hand when we slept. I'd be 'fraid and he'd tuck me side him and hold my hand. Three. He'd say he'd not be 'fraid with me near." The child looked up at Elizabeth. "Is Papa 'fraid in this house?"

AMENDING THE SHADES OF PEMBERLEY

Elizabeth assured, "This is where he lived as a boy. He is accustomed to it," she reasoned, but perhaps the child had landed on an idea which had not occurred to Elizabeth previously. "Let us claim a clean piece of paper and draw your papa a pretty flower. If you like, I will add some paint to give it color."

"Papa likes red. Like yer hair," the child observed, reminding Elizabeth of her husband's previous remark regarding her hair. "Told me it is like fire."

Elizabeth swallowed a rush of emotions. "A red dahlia it will be," she declared. Placing the clean paper before the child, she explained, "First, we require a circle. Should I guide your hand?"

"A dittle bit," Alice said in deep concentration.

With a smile on her lips and in her heart, Elizabeth gently nudged the girl's hand to form a lopsided circle. "Now we must make the petals. Let us start at the top." She assisted the child to place her pencil at the appropriate point and then left her hand in place, sheltering Alice's, but she did not guide the child's efforts. "Excellent," she praised, although, in truth, the lines were more than a bit squiggly, she knew Mr. Darcy would treasure Alice's efforts. Elizabeth remembered how her own father always made a great show of every rock and drawing she had presented him. "First, tell me how many petals have we drawn?"

"One," Alice said with a grin. "News you would not ferget."

Elizabeth returned the child's smile. "We are learning mathematics and art at the same time. Your father will think you the most intelligent child he has ever encountered." She doubted her husband had much interactions with the children of others, except perhaps those of his tenants. "Now, we will turn the paper and you will add another petal here." She pointed to the spot. "Permit me to demonstrate on my own paper." She retrieved her practice paper and drew two petals onto the circle in the middle of her page.

The child stuck her tongue out as she concentrated on her work. Elizabeth no longer held Alice's hand: She simply turned the paper at the correct angle and instructed the child to count.

When they finished with counting and drawing, the flower had five rather fat petals and three thinner ones, but it was obviously a flower, even without prompting, Mr. Darcy would recognize it as such. Elizabeth wished desperately to have a child of her own who would one day present her with a flower drawing to cherish, as had her father with hers and her sisters and as would Mr. Darcy later today.

After returning to the house, she added a bit of color to the drawing with some water and paint and then placed it to the side to dry before tucking Alice in for a nap. "You give my fower to Papa?" the child asked.

"Do you not wish to do so yourself?" Elizabeth asked as she bent to brush the child's blonde curls from her forehead and kiss her gently.

"Papa like it better if you do it," the girl said with a sigh.

Elizabeth doubted Alice's sentiments, but she said, "When the paint is dried, I will see the task is done."

Therefore, some time later, she found herself knocking on her husband's door—the outside door, not the one connecting their rooms.

"Mrs. Darcy," Mr. Sheffield said in surprise when he responded to her entreaty. "How may I assist you, ma'am?"

"I have several items to leave for my husband," Elizabeth responded, extending the stack of papers she held in her hands. "I have viewed all the rooms on the main level and part of the north wing. I require Mr. Dar . . ."

"Who is it, Sheffield," a familiar voice asked, and Elizabeth nearly groaned aloud. She had not thought her husband would arrive home so early.

"Mrs. Darcy, sir," the valet responded.

"See her in, man," her husband ordered.

Elizabeth held out the stack of papers a second time, but the valet made no move to accept them. "I did not mean to intrude," she said. "Mr. Darcy may review my notes and address any questions . . ."

"Please come in, Elizabeth," her husband said from close by. He stepped around the corner of the open door. He wore his trousers and an open-neck shirt and was rubbing his wet hair with a towel.

She had never seen any man in such a state of undress, although, she supposed, "undress" was not the correct word. Her father had strict rules for those working on the estate regarding exposing his daughters to their nakedness. This close, she could view the dark curls of hair upon her husband's chest, and, as foolish as it was to think so, she wished to reach out and touch him. "As I was telling Mr. Sheffield, I simply wished to provide you with my notes from today, as well as a drawing from Miss Alice."

He reached for the drawing. "Alice made this?" he asked as a smile claimed his lips.

"Yes, Mary worked with her on her numbers to five and taught her a few more musical phrases, as well as to recognize the notation for whole notes. After I finished my inspection of the rooms on the main floor, I worked with Alice on simple shapes and then we drew a flower," she rushed to say.

"And Alice knew success in all these matters?" he asked as he studied the drawing.

"Why would she not?" Elizabeth demanded.

"She often refused to follow her *ayah*'s instructions," he provided.

"Perhaps it is because both Mary and I practice with her, rather than assign her a task," Elizabeth said with a shrug. "The drawing is a 'dahlia,' so please call it by name when you speak of the child's efforts and permit her to count for you this evening."

Mr. Darcy smiled again. "I have never known a red dahlia, though I suppose they exist."

"Alice says you like the color red; she chose red for you," Elizabeth explained. "I did more of the painting than she did, for she was quite prepared for a nap by the time we were finished. The 'yawns' had arrived."

"I do prefer red, although it is not a color British men choose for themselves. Such is one of the reasons I found you so beguiling."

She was standing in the hall: He remained in his room. The man was proving to be nothing as she expected. She swallowed hard, despising the fact she was so attracted to him. "The other pages are my notes on each of the rooms I examined today. I have marked items I believe should be addressed immediately and others which might be delayed, depending on what you consider necessary. I have also included possible colors for the furniture pieces which require reupholstering and my recommendations for items to be replaced."

"Quite efficient," he remarked in a tone Elizabeth did not easily recognize. "I will read them over before supper, and you may address any questions I might have then."

Elizabeth stiffened with the change in his tone. "Is such not what you asked of me, sir?"

"It is," he said as his expression changed to one resembling regret. "I just did not expect . . ." he began. "It has been a very long time since I have known someone upon whose word I could count."

Elizabeth did not know what to say. In truth, she suspected many of her husband's wounds were self-inflicted; yet, she would require time to know so with any assurance. "I should dress for supper. A paint-stained apron would not portray me in a positive manner."

"With your permission," he said, "I will call for you at thirty past the hour."

"I shall be waiting."

⚘

Thankfully, Mr. Darcy had made a great show of praising Alice's efforts in the drawing and counting and even displaying the few notes she knew on the pianoforte.

"I should have your drawing framed, but, if you do not mind, my sweet girl, I would rather carry it with me each day in a place close to my heart."

"Yes, Papa," the child declared with a wide smile. "Did you hear, Biss Lizbet?"

She did not correct the child this time. "I did, sweetheart," Elizabeth responded. "I told you your father would be quite proud of you."

"Come, Alice," Mary said. "It is time you had your rest. We have another day tomorrow full of new things to learn about Derbyshire and Pemberley."

"Good night, love," Mr. Darcy said as he bent down to kiss his child's forehead. "I will come tuck you in in just a few minutes."

As Mary and the child walked away, he said to Elizabeth, "If you would indulge me, Mrs. Darcy, I wondered if you might point out the cracks in the plaster you mentioned in your examination of the front sitting room."

"I assure you, they are present, sir," Elizabeth said defensively.

"I have no doubt," he responded with a softness not always present in his tone, "but humor me. I must see them with my own eyes to know which of Pemberley's staff to assign the repair."

"I thought Mrs. Reynolds would speak to the repair," she said, wondering now if the housekeeper had ignored Elizabeth's wishes.

"Mrs. Reynolds did speak of it; yet, until I have a more competent staff in place, I fear it will be you and I who oversee much of the work."

Elizabeth nodded her agreement. She did not know why she was so defensive. One moment she felt as if she could lose her heart to her husband and the next, she considered her choice to align herself with the man her greatest folly. This constantly being off kilter was likely to have her running mad in Pemberley Woods.

⁂

For a moment, Darcy had known pure pleasure: His child was learning quickly and appeared satisfied, at last, and, from all reports, Elizabeth had performed in an exemplary manner on this day. After his wife left his quarters earlier, Sheffield had shared how even Mr. Nathan had become involved in what was likely to have been a test of wills between Pemberley's long-time housekeeper and its new mistress.

"At first, Mrs. Reynolds took offense," Sheffield explained. "You are well aware of how Mrs. Reynolds's pride can sometimes cause her to puff up when anyone questions her position. I thought Mr. Nathan would burst a button or two on his waistcoat, he was laughing so hard as he retold the story to the rest of us. Evidently, Mrs. Reynolds thought she had taught the new maids your father hired at you-know-who's recommendation how to tend the rooms to Pemberley's standards, but we all warned her the girls were too lazy to be so fastidious or devoted as are our long-time help. I fear Mrs. Reynolds's pride took a beating today, but, in the end, she admitted how impressed she was with the new Mrs. Darcy. You chose well, sir."

"The lady's father chose Mrs. Darcy for me," Darcy had confessed. "Mr. Bennet swore over and over again his daughter would change my stars."

Sheffield remarked with a slight lift of his eyebrows, "Your lady, sir, is likely to change all our stars."

Chapter Six

Elizabeth cut across the back lawn towards the stables. Mr. Darcy had departed some two hours prior for his day on the estate. Today, he had delayed his departure so they could take tea together. Dressed casually for work, she had found him even handsomer than he had been yesterday.

Earlier, she had checked on Mary and Alice. It was then another pressing idea occurred to her. Actually, two ideas.

Mr. Farrin stepped out of the carriage house to greet her. "Mrs. Darcy, may I be of service?"

"I most assuredly pray so, sir. I have two requests," she said as she suddenly felt a bit awkward. She was not accustomed to ordering those outside of the household staff about. "Perhaps there are more than two."

The man smiled upon her. "Let us take them one at a time."

Elizabeth laughed lightly at her nervousness. "First, I was hoping there was a gig or a phaeton I might have regular use of when I wish to drive into Lambton. Back in Hertfordshire, my sisters and I regularly walked into Meryton, but such was only a mile. I understand Lambton is five miles removed. I would not mind the walk, but it would be wrong of me to ask the same of my sister and the child and worse of me to leave them behind."

"I understand, ma'am."

"I would also wish to employ the vehicle to visit with many of Mr. Darcy's tenants. I think it important for me to support my husband in a variety of matters." She paused before saying, "The horse should be of a gentle nature."

"There are numerous gigs and carriages available in the carriage house. I would be pleased to show them to you if you wish to view them," the man suggested.

"Would you think it terrible of me if I admitted I do not care whether the gig or whatever it is you choose is flashy or even the latest style? I care whether it is safe for me, my sister, and the child. I care if the rigging and the reins are frayed or cracked. I care if the horse is not sure-footed and if it is easily frightened by a sudden storm or a rabbit darting across the road before him. With those considerations in mind, I shall leave the decision to you."

A bit of what appeared to be respect crossed the man's features. "Do you wish the transportation today? It may take me a bit of time to examine what is available and make certain it is an appropriate ride for your needs."

"Actually, I did not plan to employ it until Saturday. I hoped three days would be adequate. If not, I shall require you to drive my sister and me, and, naturally, the child into Lambton on Saturday. We will visit with the vicar, Mr. Ericks. He is my Aunt Gardiner's brother. Miss Bennet would like to offer her assistance with any church charities he oversees, and, I am certain, he will wish news of his family in London."

"I should have an appropriate carriage prepared for you by the time you wish to call on the vicar, but, if you will permit my presence, I would travel with you on your errands to view if I must make adjustments in the reins or choose a different horse. Each driver has his or her own unique way of handling the strings. Moreover, I know the area. I would not wish you to become lost."

"I suppose your suggestion is reasonable," she said. "I, most assuredly, would not wish to place either my sister or Miss Alice in danger."

"And your other requests, ma'am?" he asked with a nod of approval.

"I was thinking Miss Bennet and I would periodically enjoy riding out together, especially once the springtime arrives in the shire. Pemberley is so large there is no means for us to walk all of it, although, I would admit, before I am too old to claim some of the scenery I can currently view from the upper storeys of the manor, I hope to accept the challenge of a climb."

"You are correct. It might be best if you left the longer rides to spring, ma'am. The winters in Derbyshire arrive quicker than they do in the southern shires. One day it might be a bit chilly and the next you'll find yourself knee deep in snow," he warned. "Tell me: Do both you and Miss Bennet ride well?"

Elizabeth frowned. "More likely you would call it 'painfully' well. We did not ride often at Longbourn, for the horses were required on the estate. Neither of us has had much practice and saddles did not necessarily fit our style or seat."

"I see."

"Both Mary and I will require instruction to improve our handling of whatever horses you choose for us. Yet, I feel we must be prepared for all situations," she stated. "It would not be wise for either of us not to possess at least a working knowledge of riding and surviving in this area."

"I find your willingness to adapt to Derbyshire's many eccentricities and its society very intuitive, ma'am. I can think of several horses already in the stables which might be good matches. Unfortunately, we have only two sidesaddles available. Both belong to Miss Darcy. We could start with those and determine what is best for you and your sister. We will have a saddle made for each of you."

"And one for Miss Alice," Elizabeth added. "And a pony. I would like to see the child learn something of riding. To view her have more opportunities than did Mary or me. And another thing: I wish the cost of all the saddles purchased to come from my pin money."

"Mr. Darcy will stand the costs, ma'am," Mr. Farrin stated.

"Yet, I wish the saddles to be gifts from me. If you must, charge my saddle to Mr. Darcy's accounts, but the other two to me."

⁂

"What is all this?" Darcy asked as he turned his horse over to a waiting stable hand.

"Mrs. Darcy asked me for a gig or phaeton she might employ to run errands into Lambton or about the estate," Mr. Farrin said as he looked up from where he sanded the new wood he had added to the bench.

"Surely, another carriage would be more appropriate. More stylish," Darcy argued.

"Your lady wanted something more stable, sir, so she might assure the safety of her sister and the child," Farrin said with a grin. "Mrs. Darcy not be one for flash, sir, though I'll add a bit of paint tomorrow to spruce this one up some."

"Everyone appears to be discovering my wife's 'reasonableness,'" Darcy remarked, while thinking, *Everyone but me.*

"She also asked for horses for herself and Miss Bennet, as well as a pony for the child. All gentle in nature. Will also require new saddles." Farrin paused his work to say, "Mrs. Darcy gave specific orders for the new saddles to come from 'her' pin money."

"Do as she ordered," Darcy instructed. "My lady has never asked of her pin money nor of the marriage settlements," he said with a bit of irony.

"Sounds as if the lady has trusted you to do right by her, sir, just as she placed her trust in me to provide her a safe carriage for her and the child and her sister."

"Inform me when you choose the horses and the pony. I wish to be involved in teaching Alice to ride." As he walked away, Darcy considered all the examples of his wife's "reasonableness" to which he had stood witness since arriving at Pemberley. "Very remarkable," he told himself. "Perhaps Mr. Bennet truly understood my needs better than I did myself."

⁓

Elizabeth and Mr. Darcy had quickly fallen into a routine. Her husband delayed starting his day until she came down to the morning room, where they shared a cup of tea and a brief private conversation regarding what they hoped to achieve during their day. The conversation often felt stilted, but, as a couple just learning of each other, they pushed through them. Elizabeth did appreciate his efforts to include her in his schemes to make improvements to the estate; yet, she yearned for more. He had yet to kiss her and rarely took her hand except to place it on his arm.

At length, Saturday arrived. She had not spoken to her husband of her intentions to travel into Lambton, for Elizabeth held no doubt Mr. Farrin had shared their conversation with Mr. Darcy. What was important to her was her husband had not countered her orders with those of his own, a fact which had impressed her a bit, for she had easily recognized Mr. Darcy's need to control all within his sphere.

Only yesterday, Mr. Farrin had seated both her and Mary on the saddles belonging to Miss Georgiana and introduced them to the horses which would be theirs to ride whenever they chose.

"Imagine," Mary had whispered. "No more sharing the horse with the estate. I cannot believe our good fortune. God has protected us, Elizabeth."

Mary often said such remarks, reminding Elizabeth of why she had accepted Mr. Darcy's proposal. She suspected Mary recognized the tension often flaring up between Elizabeth and her husband. "It was a negotiation," she privately reminded herself several times each day. "It was never meant to be more than that."

Today, as they traveled into Lambton, Elizabeth was conscious of Mr. Farrin's presence at her side, although she was enjoying the feel of the ribbons and the fresh air on her face, as well as how the horse responded. Earlier, Mr. Farrin had presented her a pair of leather gloves. "I had the smithy design them for you. Hannah permitted us to use a pair of your gloves for the pattern."

"I am terribly honored," she said when the man first presented them to her. "Please speak my gratitude to the smith. It was all so very thoughtful of each of you." Perhaps Mr. Darcy would never hold her in esteem, but she could earn the respect of the gentleman's workers and tenants.

"Stay to the left at the fork," Mr. Farrin had directed.

Elizabeth followed his directions and sighed. Although she did not know Mr. Ericks well, she wished to sit at his table and, mayhap, hold his hand. She desperately missed the squeeze of the back of her hand by her father. "What shall you do while we visit with Mr. Ericks?" she asked. "I am certain you would be welcome within if you have no other plans." She privately cursed herself for not considering Mr. Farrin's comforts earlier.

"Mr. Darcy provided me a list of supplies he requires for the repairs for several of the tenant farms, and I have a sister in the village. I thought to visit with her for a bit."

"Excellent. I am glad you have the opportunity to do so. Miss Bennet and I are quite looking forward to visiting with our relation also." She adjusted her hands on the strings. "Were you at Pemberley while my husband was in India?" she asked, suddenly wishing to know more of what had sent Mr. Darcy from a place he so obviously adored.

"No. I refused to remain at Pemberley under the circumstances." Elizabeth wished to ask of those "circumstances," but before she could form the words, Mr. Farrin warned, "You should slow your pace. Lots of people in the village still do not understand they must share the streets with the mail coach and other carriages."

Elizabeth grinned at him. "I did not consider Lambton might be on a mail route. Thank you for your very diplomatic warning."

Mr. Farrin grinned also. "Mr. Ericks's cottage is on the other side of the village church," he explained.

AMENDING THE SHADES OF PEMBERLEY

"I cannot believe we are in the village where our aunt spent her days as a young girl. It is just as she described it," Mary said wistfully.

"I am glad we hold some connections to our new home," Elizabeth said in equal awe of coincidence.

"The vicarage is up ahead, Mrs. Darcy," Mr. Farrin instructed.

Elizabeth guided the horse to a section of wooden fence backed by shrubbery, along the front of the house. The dwelling was built of grey stone and surrounded by full trees displaying several autumn colors. A church styled with Romanesque rounded arches sat off in the distance in a circle of oaks, as if they were Norman soldiers protecting it from the elements. Mr. Farrin climbed down and came around to assist, first, Elizabeth, then Mary, and, finally, Alice to the ground.

He went ahead of them up the lane and knocked upon the door. Evidently, the housekeeper had seen them, for she opened the door immediately. "Mrs. Darcy, Miss Bennet, and Miss Darcy for Mr. Ericks," he announced.

"Please come in, ma'am. Miss. Little miss," the woman pronounced in tones of deference. "We had heard young Mr. Darcy had returned to the estate and had brought his new wife with him. Many wondered if you were from India," she said on a rush and quickly realized her *faux pas*. "Pardon, madam. I didn't mean an offense. Jist someone saw him in London with a child and a woman dressed in all them scarves they wear in India."

"The lady was Miss Darcy's *ayah*, what we might call a 'nursemaid,' but the woman has returned to India. She was employed by Mr. Darcy to tend the child. You will quite consciously correct any such rumors, will you not, Mrs. . . . ?"

"Mrs. Tibon, ma'am," the woman said with another quick bob of a curtsy. "I'll be glad to correct any misunderstanding."

"I would appreciate it," Elizabeth said with a straight face, although she wanted to laugh. "Might we be shown through to greet Mr. Ericks?"

The woman reminded Elizabeth of her mother in the manner in which she said, "Bless me, where be my manners? Come through to the parlor. I'll fetch the vicar."

Mr. Farrin still remained by the door. "Will two hours be enough, Mrs. Darcy?"

"I believe such would be quite adequate, sir."

Farrin closed the door behind her as Elizabeth motioned the housekeeper to lead. Once they were deposited in the parlor, the woman left them to tell Mr. Ericks of their presence in his house.

Mary said softly, "Evidently, Aunt Gardiner has not informed her brother of our change of circumstances."

"Or perhaps Mr. Ericks has permitted his housekeeper her misconceptions. Our aunt always said the man was much of the nature of our father. I could imagine Papa not correcting Mrs. Hill's gossiping just to view how far it would spread."

"Mrs. Dar . . ." a man of some thirty plus years of age entered the room and froze in place. "Do my eyes deceive me? Admittedly, it has been several years since I last viewed my sister Madeline's family, but I would recall you two anywhere. Yet, as Mrs. Darcy? Such would not have been my guess in a million years." He reached for Elizabeth's hands. "I expected you on my threshold so you might seek employment as a governess, but not as the grand lady of the area's largest estate. When I heard the name 'Miss Bennet,' I thought perhaps the new Mrs. Darcy had employed you to tend the child." He turned to look upon Mary. "You are Mary. I would know you anywhere. I fondly recall us spending an evening playing piquet and discussing Bible verses: We drove the other couple at the table to distraction."

"We did, sir," Mary said with a ready smile, which in Elizabeth's opinion softened her sister's features. Mary did not often receive praise for just being Mary Bennet. Elizabeth reminded herself not to overlook her sister's many fine qualities.

"Please sit," he gestured to a grouping of nearby chairs. "I must write Madeline and chastise her for not informing me of your presence in Derbyshire. How long have you been at Pemberley?"

"Only a few days," Elizabeth assured.

"Mrs. Tibon, fetch us tea and some of your cakes," he instructed the waiting housekeeper, who had just listened in on another piece of gossip to share with others. With the woman's withdrawal, he asked softly, "How did you come to marry Mr. Darcy? We in Lambton only heard of the young master's possible return a little over a fortnight removed."

Elizabeth said, "Obviously, Aunt Gardiner told you of our father passing and made arrangements for me to come to you."

Mr. Ericks nodded his head in acknowledgement of her words. "We in Derbyshire did not suffer as did the southern shires, but Madeline said parts of London knew many deaths. It grieved me to learn your father survived the epidemic but lost his life, nevertheless."

Elizabeth swallowed hard, for speaking of her father's passing was still very difficult for her. "I am not aware of all the circumstances of how or when my father took the younger Mr. Darcy's acquaintance, but, according to my husband, he and Mr. Bennet corresponded on a regular basis when Mr. Darcy was in India. Evidently, Mr. Darcy was on his way to London, having landed along the coast instead of stepping down along the Thames, to settle his father's papers when he discovered the notice of Mr. Bennet's passing through the advert for the auction of our household goods. He traveled from St Albans to Meryton to pay his respects and to purchase Mr. Bennet's library. During our discussions, Mr. Darcy revealed how Mr. Bennet often told the gentleman I would make him a good wife."

Mr. Ericks looked to where Mary entertained Alice with a wooden puzzle box. "And the former Mrs. Darcy?"

"We have not discussed the circumstances fully," Elizabeth said candidly, while making a silent promise to ask her husband how he wished her to respond, for she knew she would be asked the question repeatedly. "Mr. Darcy took my father's advice and extended his hand in marriage. I did not accept immediately," she was quick to say. "He brought Miss Alice to take my acquaintance, for I would be assuming the role of mother to the child. More importantly, for me, Mr. Darcy agreed to permit Mary to join us in Derbyshire. Our agreement led to us marrying by special license at Longbourn before Mary and I were required to leave it behind."

Mrs. Tibon returned with a tray. "Leave it," Ericks instructed. "I am certain either Mrs. Darcy or Miss Bennet will pour. I will ring if we require anything else."

Elizabeth filled the tea for each of them, presenting the child only a half cup. Meanwhile, Mary placed several cakes on a plate for the child and motioned for Alice to kneel down before the low table to eat.

"Lemon cakes," the girl said with a smile.

"Your favorite," Elizabeth responded in fondness.

"The child has the look of her mother," Mr. Ericks said. Yet, before Elizabeth could ask of the former Mrs. Darcy, they were interrupted by a young man in the coat of a clergyman.

"Pardon, sir," the man bowed to them, while they all stood. "I did not realize you had company, or I would not have interrupted."

"Come in, Harris, but, first, ring for Mrs. Tibon. We will require more tea and cakes." After the man pulled the bell cord, Mr. Ericks said, "Ladies, permit me to give you the acquaintance of a most estimable fellow, one of my fellow clergymen, Mr. Morgan Harris. Mr. Harris holds the curacy at Kympton, which is one of your husband's livings to present, my dear," he said to Elizabeth, as Harris bowed low. "Harris, these lovely ladies are my sister Madeline's nieces on Mr. Gardiner's side of the family. Permit me to present to you Mrs. Elizabeth Darcy and Miss Mary Bennet. The youngest of the ladies is Mr. Darcy's daughter, Miss Alice. We were enjoying tea and lemon cakes, were we not, Miss Alice?"

The child quickly swallowed the bite of cake she had held in her jaw. "Yes, sir."

"I would not wish to intrude," the man said.

"Come sit next to Miss Bennet," Ericks said. "I imagine she can keep up with your knowledge of the Bible. Nearly put me in my place several years back," he said in that tone Elizabeth recognized as an Ericks' family trait. Half tease and half the truth. Aunt Gardiner used it often when she addressed Mrs. Bennet's or Lydia's or Kitty's silliness.

"How delightful," the man said as he circled the settle to sit beside Mary. "It is not often our female sect devotes time to the study of our scriptures."

"Perhaps such is because their days are as equally filled with work as are men's," Elizabeth said with a challenging lift of her brows.

"Naturally," Mr. Harris said in a tone of dismissal, indicating he had not truly listened to her objection. "Yet, women often have time to take tea and other such pleasant exercises. Just as you are now."

Mary's eyebrow rose, fully expecting Elizabeth's retort. "May I ask, Mr. Harris, what time you rose this morning?"

The man frowned, but he provided the answer. "Around nine of the clock, ma'am. Why do you ask?"

It was Elizabeth's turn to ignore Mr. Harris. "And you began your day right away?"

"I do not believe I understand you, ma'am."

"The inquiry is quite simple, sir. Did you leave your bed shortly after you woke?" she clarified. "Or did you lie in bed for another quarter hour? I assume some woman prepared you a morning meal. I wonder what time the woman rose to cook your food. You did take time to eat I do imagine and likely also partook of your midday meal, as it is well after time for such an activity, and you, most assuredly, did not depend on Mr. Ericks to feed you. Did the same woman prepare your second meal of the day? Naturally, I am not familiar with what you accomplished between said breakfast and the midday meal, but I pray it was beneficial to your position. Then there was the journey here. Again, I am ignorant of how far it is to Kympton, but likely far enough you did not come on foot."

"And you, Mrs. Darcy?" Mr. Ericks said with a smile of understanding. "I recall you always being an early riser."

"I, generally, rise between half past five and six. As Mr. Darcy leaves the manor between a quarter after and half past six to meet with his tenants to address repairs and improvements to the land, I attempt to join him for a few minutes over breakfast. Then I meet with the staff to initiate repairs and refurbishing of the various rooms of the estate. My sister and Miss Alice also rise early. Mary tends to Alice's lessons in the morning and then has taken on the daunting task of organizing and documenting the extensive library at Pemberley, which has been enlarged recently when Mr. Darcy acquired our Bennet family library.

"If I finish my tasks early enough at the great house, I have begun to call on Mr. Darcy's tenants. As we have only been in attendance at Pemberley less than a week, I am certain this will become a larger role in my life as the days progress. In the afternoon, I oversee Miss Alice's lessons. Afterwards, I meet with each of the servants with directions for the following day's work. After supper, Mr. Darcy and I go over what has been accomplished on that particular day and set goals for the next. If it were not for Mr. Ericks being a relation, I would have waited until after church services tomorrow to introduce myself to him, for I am, at this moment, neglecting several pressing matters to be here today. Under these circumstances, first, I take umbrage at your comment indicating women have time to take tea and, I suppose, gossip. My day is quite full, and I take tea when I require a few minutes to recoup my energy. Secondly, your comment regarding women not studying their Bibles indicates such is the duty of men, which is ridiculous when one considers how both men and women, alike, toil in their daily lives. Therefore, I would implore you to provide a bit of compassion if both Mr. Darcy and I, as well as many of the tenants on Pemberley and citizens of Lambton, do not spend time memorizing and analyzing Biblical verses. I believe the Darcy estate has employed both you and Mr. Ericks to ease our way in that manner."

She turned to Mary. "My sweet sister here devoted much of her time in Hertfordshire to the welfare of those less fortunate than we were at Longbourn. I do not wish to make light of her accomplishments. I am quite proud of her altruistic character. Even so, Mary does not dally about all day and only practice her benevolence on Sundays. She truly 'lives' what she believes. Yet, even Miss Bennet finds time to see to duties at home, as well as duties to the community."

"Well said, Mrs. Darcy," Mr. Ericks said with a knowing smile. "I doubt Mr. Harris meant his remarks as they sounded to each of us. Even so, your words were a timely reminder God created men and women in his image and placed them on this earth to toil and make it a better place for all God's creatures. My compliment to Miss Bennet was meant in sincere respect, and I, most assuredly, did not mean to indicate either of you were less than perfect examples of daughters of the gentry. I have dined with you and yours and know the values taught to you by your parents. Obviously, Mr. Darcy's success means hundreds in the community are capable of placing food on the table and a roof over their heads. None of us works alone, even if we are not married."

Mary was quick to say, "All these compliments are greatly appreciated; yet, I came with Mrs. Darcy today to offer my services to any of the charities your church champions, sir. As you are well aware, I always assisted Mr. Williamson back in Hertfordshire."

"I am certain we can discover some place for your talents, Miss Bennet," Ericks said in a tone which had Elizabeth looking at the man oddly, for it sounded as if he was flirting with Mary. "I was hoping you would consider taking up the torch here in Lambton."

With a sigh of resignation, Elizabeth said, "I should have kept my opinions to myself. It was ill of me to speak so honestly in your home, sir. I see now, we should have sent a message around before we called upon you. It was foolish of us not to consider you would be busy with matters regarding your services tomorrow. Perhaps we should leave you to confer with Mr. Harris."

"Nonsense," Ericks said. "You are my family—though extended it may be. Moreover, Harris is here because several ladies from the church guild generally arrive to discuss their ideas for events and such. Harris has it in his mind to impress one or two of the ladies. Such is the reason his shirt points are crisp today, hey, Harris?"

"If you are certain we would not be intruding," Elizabeth said, while ignoring Mr. Harris, who had not impressed her in the least. "Mr. Farrin is not to call for us for another hour or so. I would not wish for him to cut short his visit with his sister and her children."

Ericks declared, "It would be an excellent opportunity for you and Miss Bennet to take the acquaintance of some of the prominent ladies in the village, and, more importantly," he said with a grin, "you will increase their estimation of me, for I will have bragging privileges: I have known the new Mrs. Darcy since she was but a young girl."

Chapter Seven

In the weeks which followed, the pattern of her life remained unchanged. Such was not to say there were not some changes, but not in her relationship with Mr. Darcy and both the physical, as well as emotional, door separating them. A few of the ladies with whom Elizabeth had become acquainted periodically called upon her, sharing tea and local gossip, a mainstay of country life. Not of the same nature as had been her dearly departed mother, Elizabeth did not even know some involved in the latest "on dits," such as the man who had been kicked by a cow or the woman whose daughter was meant to marry a young farmer in a neighboring shire; yet, she listened and enjoyed the company. In truth, she was terribly lonely in a house full of people.

Surprisingly, yet, perhaps, more likely unsurprisingly, once she had considered the vicar's poorly-disguised motives, Mr. Ericks began to call at the estate once per week and often, at Elizabeth's invitation, came to dine after church. On each of those occasions, the gentleman spent time with them all, but, eventually, he would single Mary out for a few minutes of conversation or a joint reading of the scriptures or he would turn the pages of the music while she played for him.

Quite a few of the older ladies and their daughters who had initially befriended Mary and her became less friendly when they took notice of Mr. Ericks's obvious interest in Mary, but, Mary herself appeared to be oblivious of the man's intentions. Her sister's only indication to what was happening was Mary had asked Hannah if the maid would consider styling Mary's hair in a less severe manner. Evidently, Mr. Ericks had approved of the gentle change for Hannah taught the maid assigned to assist Mary how to bring about the style.

Elizabeth was not certain how she felt about the difference in age between Ericks and Mary. Certainly, Mr. Darcy was a bit more than eight years Elizabeth's senior, but Mr. Ericks was some sixteen years older than Mary.

Predictably, Mr. Darcy appeared to be unconcerned with the growing affection between the two. Of late, her husband had become more and more withdrawn, despite the need for his constant supervision over the estate having become less and less necessary.

An answer to her questions arrived on a Wednesday afternoon when she was meant to call at the vicarage to fetch Mary from a group who were knitting mittens and hats for the needy children in the area as a Boxing Day gift.

Not required inside, Mr. Ericks came out of the vicarage to greet her. They were just exchanging welcomes when a movement from near the church stole her breath away. Her husband came around the back corner of the church with an attractive woman walking at his side. Although Elizabeth could not view the woman's features with any clarity, for the lady wore the hood of a royal blue cloak over her head, she could see the woman was young and blonde and a bit taller than was Elizabeth. The lady was cut along the lines of her elder sister Jane, who had been one of Hertfordshire's most beautiful women and in whose shadow Elizabeth had often stood—often taking second to Jane. Now, she was evidently to stand second to this stranger.

Mr. Darcy and the woman were deep in conversation, and he had not seen Elizabeth until the sweet voice of the child sitting beside her froze them all in a terrible tableau with a simple call of "Papa!"

Mr. Darcy's head snapped up in recognition, while the unknown lady's followed his response with interest. Elizabeth could not breathe. Could not move to dampen the child's enthusiasm in spotting her father in the middle of the afternoon.

The woman took several steps in their direction, until Mr. Darcy caught her arm and quickly pulled her from the scene, disappearing behind the church once again.

"Papa!" the child said dejectedly, while burying her face into Elizabeth's side. Sobs shook Alice's shoulders. Elizabeth wished there was someone she might turn to for comfort, but her only someone was enjoying another woman's company. Women of her station were supposed to swallow their pain in such circumstances; yet, one must be able actually to swallow, and, at the moment, the despair was too great.

"Was that not Mr. Darcy?" Mr. Ericks asked as he caught the horse's head to steady the gig as the animal shuffled with the sudden movement of Alice standing up beside Elizabeth.

"Unless my husband has a twin," she managed to say, turning her attention to Alice. "All is well, sweetheart," she cooed. "Your father likely did not hear you. Remember, he said he had several meetings today. I just did not realize one of those was in the village or we could have met him here."

The child sniffed against Elizabeth's sleeve. "You tink so?" Alice's speech quickly reverted to a more childlike version of the words, something the girl had not done since shortly after they all had arrived at Pemberley. Since coming to the family estate, Alice had been turned over to her and Mary's care, and they had decided not to praise the girl's speech unless it was proper. Today, though, Elizabeth made no comment to the girl using "tink," rather than "think." She quickly realized, in Alice's own defense, the child sought a time when her father catered to her every whim. Elizabeth understood: She desperately wished her father was present to provide her comfort for what surely must be a broken heart.

"Why do I not see Miss Bennet home after the ladies finish their projects today?" Mr. Ericks suggested. "In that manner, you may attend Miss Alice without interruption."

Elizabeth did not speak to the vicar's other motives, for they were the least of her worries today. Instead, she expressed her gratitude, adjusted the child's position on the bench, and permitted Mr. Ericks to walk the horse in a loose circle to set Elizabeth on the road to Pemberley. "I am assured your Papa will see you have something special this evening once he realizes he could have spent time with you," she said in comforting tones. She would call upon Cook when they returned to Pemberley and ask the dear lady to add a sweet cake for the child to make certain Mr. Darcy did not destroy his daughter's hopes as easily as he had destroyed his wife's.

○○○

Darcy wished to throttle all involved. God continued to punish him. He had promised Elizabeth he would not be found in the company of other women.

"Is that Alice?" the lady asked as he hustled her away. She pulled her arm from his grip. "I wish to view her."

He caught her arm again and pulled her further from the scene. "Our arrangement says otherwise," he hissed in anger and presenting her arm an angry shake.

"I have a right," she began, but Darcy grabbed her tighter. "You are hurting me, Fitzwilliam."

"Do not 'Fitzwilliam' me! We are not on familiar terms: We will never be 'familiar.' Now listen carefully. I have paid you all I am willing to give you. If you have spent what would have lasted any of God's sensible creatures a minimum of ten years, then you must discover another pawn willing to dance to the tune you offer. I no longer care whether you breathe or die."

"There was a time when you wished nothing more than to dance with me," she said as she rose on her toes as if to kiss him. However, Darcy stepped back.

"And I have paid dearly for those thoughts and desires. Because I once listened to lust, I was knocked from my lofty aspirations to my knees. To crawl in the dirt with the unwashed."

"Do not say you have won the heart of a more 'deserving' lady," she spat.

Darcy prayed with all his heart someday her taunt would be the truth in his life; yet, for now, he warned, "Take your so-called charms to London and convince some other man to turn himself inside out to please you. Just know, if you come near me or mine again, I will destroy you and enjoy every moment of your fall from grace. I will lead the round of applause from all those you have abused in the name of conceit."

◈

"Elizabeth! Elizabeth!" he had bellowed when he entered the house, but Elizabeth did not rise from her place before the mirror where Hannah styled her hair. In the reflection, the maid appeared concerned by the "urgency" in Mr. Darcy's tone, but all Elizabeth said was, "Continue." The maid added another pin to hold the chignon in place about the same time as Mr. Darcy burst into her room.

"Out!" he ordered her lady's maid.

"Stay, Hannah," Elizabeth countered. "Although he dares many things, Mr. Darcy would not dare to deny his wife her choice of a lady's maid. After all, he is the typical English gentleman." She did not turn to look upon him, but, through the mirror's reflection, she noted he had flinched, and, privately, Elizabeth celebrated the damage she had done to him. Her implication had found a target, and, most assuredly, his sins had left a larger hole in her heart than her words had executed against him. "I believe Mr. Sheffield has your things laid out and is waiting for you. Your business in the village has kept you overlong, and supper will be served soon."

"Such is the manner in which you wish to address these issues?" he asked in hard tones.

"What issues, Mr. Darcy?" she ground out the words, but she made herself not turn to look upon him. Instead, she studied her own image: It was one which had greatly failed in keeping her husband's interest. "Your proposal, the one defining our marriage, leaves no room for 'issues.'" She stood then. "Per our agreement, I told Alice her father did not hear her call out for him today, for he was too far away. I have asked Cook to prepare a special treat for the child. Please be certain to ask Mr. Nathan to bring it up and make your apologies to your daughter. You owe me no such words. I would ask, however, in the future, you would inform me if your meetings are to be held in the village, especially those held near the vicarage. Both Mary and I travel there several times per week. Although you have not appeared to notice, it is my belief Mr. Ericks means to extend his hand to my sister. I would not have Mary harmed due to your thoughtlessness."

"As you wish, madam," he said through tight lips. With a stiff bow, he turned crisply on his heels to make his exit, but rather than to leave through the door he had come through, he reached for the door separating their dressing rooms to cross to his quarters. When the latch turned in his grip, he stopped short. Without turning around, he demanded, "How long has this door been unlocked?"

"Since the first week of my arrival at Pemberley. You told me to unlock it when I wished your company," she said in warning tones. "However, I shan't forget to lock it again. Was such not your plan, sir? You asked for a mistress for your estate and a mother for your daughter in exchange for a respectable position in society and my sister's safety. Such was my promise to you and you to me."

❦

Claiming a headache, Elizabeth had retired early. Thankfully, Mr. Darcy agreed to tend the child and Alice's nighttime ritual. Therefore, Mary saw Elizabeth to her quarters. "Mr. Ericks explained what occurred this afternoon. Did Mr. Darcy not offer you an explanation?" her sister asked in concern.

"What is there to explain?" Elizabeth argued. "He met with a beautiful blonde-haired woman in the middle of the afternoon and in a secluded area. When he spotted his wife and his child, he darted away, guiding the lady from sight. If it was an innocent encounter, why did he not introduce me? If you had seen the look on his face when he realized he had been found out, you would understand."

"Perhaps he was planning a special surprise for you or Alice," Mary offered.

"When did you become my optimistic sister?" Elizabeth teased. "I swear, since meeting Mr. Ericks again, you have turned into Jane.

Where did my beloved Mary Bennet go? She would be reciting a 'Thou shalt not covet . . .' phrase or two from the Commandments."

Mary ignored Elizabeth's attempts to turn the conversation. "You must permit Mr. Darcy an explanation," Mary said as she stood. "If not, you two cannot move forward in this marriage. You are not built for the unknown; it eats away at your self-esteem. Although I do not think Mr. Darcy would betray his marriage vows, for I have viewed the manner in which he looks upon you when he thinks no one else will see; yet, even if he acted as you fear, you must hear his explanation and offer your forgiveness. Otherwise, you will regret this moment forever."

Although Elizabeth did not agree with Mary's estimation of Mr. Darcy's "interest" in her, for she had never confided in her sister the full extent of the terms of Elizabeth's agreement with the man, she knew Mary's advice appropriate. Elizabeth knew she was not one to stew over a confrontation. She would permit her husband an explanation, assuming he wished to make one.

Therefore, she waited until she heard him return to his quarters before she crossed through the sitting room they had yet to share to knock upon the door to his bedchamber. Mr. Sheffield opened it almost immediately, which was fortunate, for her courage had wavered in those few seconds. "I wish to speak to my husband."

She could see Mr. Darcy standing before the fire—his jacket removed and his waistcoat hanging open. "I will ring if I require you, Sheffield," he ordered his valet.

"As you wish, sir." The man stepped to the side to permit Elizabeth to enter her husband's chambers, then exited through the sitting room, closing the door behind him.

"To what do I owe this honor?" Mr. Darcy asked suspiciously.

Elizabeth locked her knees in place rather than to run away. "Mary reminded me I am not built for stratagems. If you are willing to confide one, I would like an explanation regarding what occurred today." She waited and waited, but when he did not respond, she teared up. "I see," she sobbed and turned immediately for the door. Yet, her husband was quicker. He moved around her to catch her up in his arms.

"Do not leave," he cooed as he stroked her hair from her face and kissed her cheeks.

"You do not want me here," she said as she fought to leave.

"Elizabeth," he said in demanding tones, while catching her shoulders in a sturdy grip, "I want you here. I want you all the time."

"But the woman today," she murmured through another round of sobs before collapsing against him in defeat.

"Was not an assignation," he enunciated each syllable with emphasis as he nestled her closer to him.

The tears rolled down her cheeks. "Yet you turned her and walked quickly away," she protested.

"I did not want her to have a close look at Alice," he said.

"I do not understand," she pleaded. "Is Alice in danger?"

He released her shoulders to scrub his face with his dry hands. "Not exactly. God, I hope not. I would know great shame if bringing my child home to England placed her in danger."

"Tell me what occurred. If I am to protect Alice, I must know what to expect, and we must protect Mary also, for she is often with the child."

He chuckled. "Now there is my favorite termagant. Have I ever told you how beautiful you are when your eyes spark with fire?"

His words had her stomach filling with heat, but she said, "You have yet to tell me who the woman was and why you do not want her near Alice."

"Would you not prefer my kissing you until we both cannot name where you end and I begin? The prospect interests me greatly." He again gathered her loosely into his embrace, before bending to kiss, first, her forehead, and then lightly brushing her temple with his lips, to be followed by a line of wet kisses across her cheek. Dragging his lips lower to nibble at the corner of her mouth, he finally claimed her lips.

The heat in her stomach spread to her chest, as well as her most private parts. When he broke for a breath, Elizabeth gasped, "I have never . . ."

"Like everything else since the day we met," he said as he explored her neck and ear, "we will figure it out together. All I know is, now that I have kissed you, all I want is to do it again and again."

"You must teach me to please you," Elizabeth said tentatively.

"Trust me, Elizabeth Darcy, there is little about you which does not please me."

<hr />

Elizabeth rolled over and stretched fully. She looked about the room. She was back in her own bed. For a second, she panicked, then she recalled how her husband had carried her into her quarters before daylight. "You may wish a hot bath this morning," he had said as he leaned over to kiss her again. "You will be sore."

"Do not grin, sir," she admonished, "as if yours was a great accomplishment."

"I wish I did not have a meeting with the land steward this morning," he whispered as he nibbled on her ear. "I would much rather spend the day with you in this wonderful bed."

"I require a bit of rest first," she said with a sleepy yawn.

"Rest then, my darling girl." For a second Elizabeth thought he might profess some sort of affection for her, but he simply kissed her gently. "I will attempt to return for the midday meal, but, if not, I will see you at the evening one."

With that, he was gone. Only after he had departed did she realize he had never explained about the woman in the village. "He will tell me," she told herself, but a glimmer of doubt had entered her chest and ruined the glow of love which had taken root during the night.

Over the weeks which followed, they often shared relations, and, more often than not, they shared the same bed. Elizabeth found she enjoyed snuggling into the curve of his body, for the nights were becoming colder—a cold to which she was not yet accustomed. More importantly, she adored how he groaned when she wiggled her backside against him and when he said, "You will be the death of me, Elizabeth Darcy," right before he rolled her to her back and draped himself across her to kiss her senseless.

She kept telling herself, "Surely, he could hold no interest in another. The encounter was so insignificant, it has slipped his mind. Such is why he made no explanation." Yet . . .

Instead of working exclusively on drawing with Alice, Elizabeth had started teaching the child something of the flowers and vegetation found upon the estate. "We began this survey late, but it will be glorious to see how the view changes outside our windows over the next few months. My own papa taught me to do this when I was a child about your age. I still have the book we created together."

"I see it?" Alice asked.

"It is locked away in one of the trunks, which have yet to arrive, but when it appears, I will be pleased to share it with you." Elizabeth wished some of her Longbourn trunks would be delivered soon, for she, most profoundly, missed her father and all they had shared together. "We will save a leaf of the common ash tree—one for each season, so we may learn the wonder of God's plan for this world. There is an ash on the other side of the garden. Follow me."

Elizabeth used the properly placed stepping stones to cross the brook separating parts of the garden, only to turn to find Alice standing on the other side, looking as if the brook was the Indian Ocean. "Are you afraid?" she asked the girl.

Alice nodded her head quickly in the affirmative. "Fell in water and Papa jumpt in to grad me."

"I see." Elizabeth crossed back over the stones to stand next to the girl. "Sometimes we think we are not big enough or strong enough to fight our fears."

"I not," Alice said looking up to Elizabeth in apprehension.

"First," Elizabeth said, "you must know I would never ever ask you to do something I did not think you could do. This water is the type of water in which we might find a frog, especially during the summer. Not dangerous like the water your father dived into to save you. I suppose sometimes it might be deeper, especially after a hard rain, but, you see," and she pointed to the stones, "someone put these stones here for a reason, and that reason is to cross the brook to the other side. See the big tree there?" Alice again bobbed her head in agreement. "We want to study it. However, if we do not cross the brook here, we must walk all the way back to the fountain and then take the path on the other side." She waited for Alice to think about what she said. "Do you think, if I held your hand, you could cross the stones with me?"

The child looked around as if searching for another solution, but, again, she bobbed her agreement.

"One step at a time," Elizabeth encouraged. "Take my hand." Elizabeth stepped from the first stone to the second. Fortunately, they were close enough together for her arm to reach Alice. "Now it is your turn. One long step and you will join me on this stone." A few tears formed in the child's eyes, but she did as Elizabeth asked. "Very good," she praised. "Now, for the next one. Permit me to lead again." She stepped to the third stone and coaxed Alice to follow. Elizabeth stepped to the edge of the fourth stone and dropped Alice's hand. For a few seconds, fear held the child immobile. "One step at a time. You can do this, and I will be here if you fall. You are safe. You are loved. Step for me, Alice."

The child hesitated, but she stepped across the fourth stone. "I did it, Lizbet."

"Yes you did, love. Now, one more step. This time I wish you to lead."

"What if I fall?" Alice questioned.

"You will have a wet shoe, but I do not think you will fall," Elizabeth assured. "You are magnificently brave, for you traveled from India to England. Surely a girl as brave as you can take one step without holding my hand. Miss Cassandra and your papa and Mary will all be so very proud of you. One step at a time, sweetheart."

Alice studied the stones, but she stood a bit taller. "One step, Lizbet."

"I shall be right behind you. You are the leader this time."

Without more coaxing required, Alice long stepped for the last stone, and Elizabeth reached a hand to prevent her fall, but there was no reason. The child wobbled, but quickly stood firmly on the stone. "Now up the bank, love, and to the ash tree. You were quite wonderful, you know." And it was done. A lesson in bravery.

Following Alice up the bank, she could hear her own father saying, "Well done, Elizabeth. You are a brave girl," just as he had done all those years ago when he taught her to walk along a stone wall without falling. "One step at a time, child."

Experiencing her own bit of pride for teaching the child necessary skills, Elizabeth led Alice forward to stand beneath the tree. She pulled down one of the branches. "Let us continue our study. See the leaves always align opposite each other. Some of the smaller branches have three leaves on each side. See. Let us count them." The child counted the pairs as Elizabeth pointed to each. Next, she reached for a longer branch. "The bigger branches have six leaves on each side. One. Two . . ." Alice finished counting to six.

"Look, Miss Lizbet. That one has three. One. Two. Three. And there is 'nother with six."

"Excellent. You may tell your Papa of these wonders this evening. Let us see what else we might tell him. First, the tree leaves follow the sun, even this winter sun."

The child's face screwed up in confusion.

AMENDING THE SHADES OF PEMBERLEY

"Permit me to show you." She led the child back to the brick path and a few feet away. "Look up." Alice did as she instructed. "See how the top of the tree appears as if it is leaning to the side."

"Like this." Alice bent at the waist to lean to the side.

Elizabeth smiled largely. "Many flowers and trees, and even people who travel, like on the silk roads in India, follow the sun. Have you not seen people pause to look up at the sun to enjoy the feel of it on their faces?"

"Not in India," the child said innocently.

Elizabeth chuckled. "No, I do not imagine the sun is so kind there, at least not to Englishmen."

"Papa worked hard in the sun," the child disclosed. "Would fall asleep before me."

Elizabeth did not comment, but she filed Alice's observation away with the other tidbits she had learned of her husband—another piece of the puzzle. Someday, she hoped the image would be complete.

"We will take a few leaves today. In the spring, we will find flowers on the branches. The twig, which is what we call a little branch—a 'child' branch, which has yet to grow to its full size, will have purple clusters close to the tip. Then the new leaves will appear. The flowers are sometimes purple and sometimes yellow. The new leaves will be a softer colored green, almost yellow in color."

She walked the child back towards the tree. "The bark, as you can see, is pale brown." She pointed to the bark, peeling back a small piece to add to their collection. "Some parts appear grey." She took Alice's hand to direct it to the bark to explore. "In winter, which is quickly approaching our new home, twigs appear almost black, but we can see new buds forming. Feel the little bumps under your fingers when you touch it."

"Bumps," the child declared with a grin.

"Like that of each thing that in season grows. Yet, for today, we will only take a few leaves, but we will come back again and again. Each time we will claim something new. In the spring, we will add some flowers to our study and mayhap a bud or two. In late summer or early autumn, the flower clusters will change into seed pods. My sisters and I referred to them as 'wings.' The seed pods will fall to the ground. See, there are a few here. and few more over there."

The child scrambled to gather several clusters of the pods to carry them back to Elizabeth.

She bent to share their find with Alice. "The birds pick them up and carry them to another place. They drop the seeds and often those seeds will take root and a new tree is born."

"God's plan?" the child asked.

"I would think so," Elizabeth admitted. "Just as I think it was God's plan that my father met your father years ago. Their friendship brought your papa to my door when I needed him most."

"And I need you and Miss Mary," the girl spoke honestly.

Elizabeth felt her eyes tearing up, so she simply said, "Exactly," as she turned to point to the ground beneath them. "Notice, this plant here is called a 'dog violet' and this one," she said as she pointed towards the other side of the tree, "is called 'wild garlic.' The 'wild' just means it grows outside of the planned garden Cook uses for our meals. It is not 'wild,' as if it cannot be tame. Mr. Farrin and the others in the stables have tamed the horses we ride, so they are no longer wild."

Alice's expression spoke of the question forming in her thoughts before she spoke it. "Is the dog biolet not 'wild' then, and why you call it a 'dog'?"

Elizabeth's laughter bubbled forth. "God was smart in permitting the tree and the plants to share the same place, but He might have made an error in permitting people to name the plants." She turned the child in the direction of where they left their box. Elizabeth leaned over to say, almost as if it were a secret, "As I understand it, 'dog' refers to the fact this violet has no scent. Most violets are sweet smelling, but the dog violet has no scent. There are also pig violets and horse violets and even snake violets, but I have never seen any of those, but I assume they also possess no scent." She nudged the child forward. "It is time for us to return to the house. Do you have your leaves and your 'wings' to share with your father after supper?"

"Yes, Lizbet."

Elizabeth took the larger items and placed them in a cloth sack, while Alice added the smaller ones to the wooden box. Once they were prepared to return to the house, she led Alice towards the manor. She said, "Did you know the wood from an ash tree is so strong, we make our carriages out of them? In Norway, which is another country, just as India is one and England is yet another, the Norwegians believe the ash tree is the Tree of Life, meaning it is where God made the first man."

"But forgot to tell the man what to call everything," the child pronounced with pride.

"Your father will enjoy your version of the tale of God making the first ash tree. I imagine it will delight him excessively."

✒

Darcy had listened carefully to his child's recitation regarding what she had learned on this particular day, but his mind was on the wonder of the moment. Not only did Alice share the facts of the ash tree, but his child proved, without a doubt, his decision to make Elizabeth Bennet his wife was a turn for the better in his life. His daughter was no longer frightened by her own shadow. She no longer clung to him in desperate pleas not to leave her.

Alice was enjoying claiming Elizabeth as her "mother," although the word still remained from the child's lips. In his opinion, such was true because in English households in India, the children were raised by an Indian *ayah*, not the mistress of the house. In England, Alice should be raised by a governess. If his daughter claimed Elizabeth as "mother," then Elizabeth might slip away from someone taking care of her to someone who supervised the caregiver. His arrangement with Elizabeth placed her as both "governess" and "mother," a much better situation for his child.

"The ash tree is related to olive trees," he commented.

"Do I like olive?" his child asked.

"I seriously doubt it, but perhaps some day you will," he responded with a grin. "Olives are not sweet like Cook's cakes."

Alice smiled up at him. "Cook's cakes make me happy."

"Like that of each thing in season grows," he remarked.

"Miss Lizbet say the same today," his daughter shared.

He looked up to Elizabeth to notice her smile. "Elizabeth and I often share similar thoughts." He prayed she would be willing to share his bed this evening. "The line comes from a famous English writer who you, too, will read some day. Today, Elizabeth was speaking of how the ash tree changes with each 'season.' You likely heard her say the words 'summer, autumn, winter, and spring.' Those are the seasons for growing and playing in the sun. As for me, I was considering the writer's purpose of the story."

"Do you believe it will take a year?" his wife asked. "For it, for us, to be as it was for Navarre and the princess in *Love's Labour's Lost*? As they were at the end?"

"I pray not," he admitted. "Would you not say we are more than halfway there already?"

Chapter Eight

"I have missed you," her husband said softly, as he knelt by her chair. He was prepared to begin his day, but he had, uncharacteristically, tarried to speak to her privately after motioning Mr. Nathan and the footman from the room.

"And I you," she said. Elizabeth caressed his cheek. "I thought you would fall asleep before you could tuck Alice in last evening. You are working yourself too hard."

"You are correct about my weariness," he said with a sigh. "Yet, I do not wish to neglect you. The estate is not more important to me than are you and the child."

Elizabeth's insides filled with warmth. "When I called upon the wives in the south section yesterday, they spoke of how hopeful their husbands were for the future. The men are thankful for your return."

He smiled on her. "I am glad to hear they wish to follow the dream I have crafted for Pemberley, but I was considering us, not the estate."

Elizabeth blushed. "When Mr. Bennet spoke of my boldness, I pray you did not think he meant in intimacies."

Her husband rose up to kiss her gently at first, and then more demanding. When they broke for air, he rested his forehead against hers. "You will sleep in my bed tonight? I prefer you next to me."

"If such is your wish," she said with a small smile of happiness.

"Trust me, Elizabeth, I wish for you often—more often than I should for my own sanity." He kissed her a second time. "Until this evening, my darling girl. Wear your hair down."

"I have begun to think you would have married any woman with red hair," she teased.

He shook off her assertion. "Remember, I possessed an image of young Miss Elizabeth Bennet. Have you not noticed it displayed on the mantle in my chambers? Thankfully, the miniature did not do you justice or I might have been driven to Bedlam before I could return to England."

She wished to remind him he was on his way to London for Pemberley business when he learned of her father's passing. He had not come to Hertfordshire for her. In truth, he might never have acted on her father's promise if not for Mr. Bennet's untimely death. Instead, she said, "What of Alice's mother?" Immediately she recognized she had ruined the moment of connection between them.

Her husband's features hardened, and his tone changed. "She was fair of face, but manipulative and self-centered."

Elizabeth wished him to tell her more, but, rather, she apologized. "Please forgive me for looking into the past. Mr. Bennet always said you can find no future while staring the past in the face." She leaned forward to kiss him, a kiss which quickly became quite heated. It was as if her husband wished to brand her as his. She did not mind being "branded," yet, a question lingered just the same. Why would a man of her husband's fine looks and lineage require such complete loyalty from all who he claimed as his?

"Until tonight, Mrs. Darcy," he said as his lips lingered over hers.

"Until tonight, Mr. Darcy."

After he departed for his duties to the estate, Elizabeth's mind was too full for conversation. She told Mr. Nathan, "Inform Miss Bennet I started my duties early. She should seek me out in the oldest wing of the house if she requires me."

"The former master's study and quarters?" the butler asked with a frown.

"Those are the only rooms I have yet to examine. Mr. Darcy and I cannot draft an appropriate plan for renovations and repairs until I do so. Do you hold an objection to my choice, Mr. Nathan?"

"No, ma'am." He uncharacteristically shuffled his feet. "Except, Mr. Darcy instructed the staff to leave the rooms untouched."

Elizabeth hesitated briefly, but this new information made her more curious. "I understand how your master may not wish to redecorate his father's former quarters and study, but it would be foolish for him to ignore any rot or plaster damage, even if the rooms never see regular usage again."

"As you wish, ma'am. Should I send Mrs. Reynolds to assist you?"

Elizabeth and the Pemberley housekeeper had come to an understanding of sorts. "If Mrs. Reynolds has time to join me, I would welcome her company. Otherwise, I shall make my way through things without her."

The study proved to be a large, well-proportioned room, handsomely fitted up. Elizabeth, after surveying it from the door's entrance, went to a window to enjoy the prospect. The hill, crowned with wood, which descended towards the house, was, as always, a beautiful view, especially with the increased abruptness from the distance. Every disposition of the ground was good, and she looked on the whole scene—the river, the trees scattered on its banks, and the winding of the valley, as far as she could trace it—with delight. "I have enjoyed these objects from different prospects and different rooms, but from every window, they remain the beauty of God's creation."

She pulled the drapes back to allow the light to enter the room more fully. The furniture proved suitable to the fortune of its former proprietor, although she considered much of it too gaudy for her personal taste. She and her husband tended to prefer more refined lines, with less splendor announcing its wealth and more elegance than the somewhat overuse of flashes of gold and silver in the fabrics and on the walls.

With a sigh of determination, she began to evaluate the drapes and windows, discovering a few tats which could be mended without much notice. The lock on the window, however, would require repair for security purposes, as well as to keep the cold air from seeping into the room. She turned again to examine the room as a whole. In her opinion, this room would better fit her husband's needs, for it possessed more book shelves and a small sitting area, as well as an impressive desk which would immediately intimidate any who dared to question his decisions. "With changes in the decor to better suit his demeanor, this room could truly speak to his reign as Pemberley's master. Much better than does the smaller office in the other wing," she said aloud. "It is a shame to leave this room empty, but it is his choice, not yours, my girl."

With a shrug of her shoulders in resignation, Elizabeth set about her task. She was on her knees examining the ornamental nails used by the upholsterer on a settee set before the fireplace when Mrs. Reynolds entered. "Mr. Nathan said you might require my assistance, Mrs. Darcy."

"I might first require a hand up," Elizabeth responded. "I feel a bit vertiginous."

The woman braced Elizabeth to her feet. "Sit." When she was seated, the housekeeper touched her forehead. "No fever." She lifted Elizabeth's chin. "You do appear a bit pale. Should I send someone to fetch the doctor?"

"No. I simply require a few minutes to allow my insides to rest."

"Why do you not lie back against the pillows? Did you eat something from the norm?" the lady asked in concerned tones. She placed a pillow behind Elizabeth's head and eased her down upon the settee.

"I fear I am a creature of habit when it comes to breaking my fast," Elizabeth assured. "I am rarely ill. My father always claimed I had his mother's constitution. Grandmother Bennet lived well into her seventies. More likely, I was leaning over too long and the blood rushed to my head."

"I will remain with you until you are right again," the housekeeper assured. Mrs. Reynolds knelt beside the settee.

"First, while you are near, please fetch my papers from underneath this furniture," Elizabeth instructed. When the woman placed the sheets of foolscap on a low table, Elizabeth pointed to the drapes. "Do you think our staff can mend those three small holes on the left-hand side near the middle? They appear to be tears rather than insect or time damage."

Mrs. Reynolds rose slowly to her feet to look for the tears. "Ah, you have excellent eyes, Mrs. Darcy. One is a bit large, but I believe Louise is up to the task. The woman is a wonder with a needle. She is working on those we noted in the south wing, but I shall add these to her tasks."

"And the lock?" Elizabeth asked.

Mrs. Reynolds's fingers brushed the latch gently, as she made her explanation. "The former Mr. Darcy broke it during his attempt to call Master William back. It would not open because of the dampness. Mr. George Darcy regretted his decision to send his son away nearly as quickly as he made it. He struck the lock to force it open to call for his son's return. Yet, the carriage had already reached the hill."

Elizabeth asked quietly, so as not to disturb the moment. She thought she might learn more of what drove her husband from his ancestral home. "Why did the late Mr. Darcy not send a rider after the carriage? Or do it himself? Most assuredly, a rider could have overtaken a carriage, even one with a head start. It was not as if your former master did not know his son's destination."

Mrs. Reynolds worked to secure the lock before answering, finally abandoning the task. Without turning around, she said, "Because he was encouraged not to do so."

Elizabeth sat up quickly, so quickly her stomach did another flip, but she managed to ask, "Who? Who set Mr. George Darcy against his son?"

"It is not for me to say," Mrs. Reynolds was quick to respond, too quick for Elizabeth's liking. Thankfully, she noticed how the woman shot a quick glance to the small seating area.

"Very well," Elizabeth assured. "I understand your loyalty to your late employer." She stood cautiously. "Let us see what else might be necessary to address."

"Before your arrival, Master Fitzwilliam sent word ahead to have the estate books and other such papers moved to the other wing. We should only be required to examine the furniture and drapes," Mrs. Reynolds explained.

"Then we should be about it. Afterwards, I would see the quarters belonging to your late master and Lady Anne," Elizabeth instructed. She purposely turned away from the seating area to examine the fireplace. "Has the flue been thoroughly cleaned since Mr. George Darcy passed?"

"Yes, Mrs. Darcy, but, if you like, I will ask Jimmy to check this room and the sleeping quarters once more. Though Lady Anne's room has not been used since her passing," Mrs. Reynolds shared.

"Are there no bird's nests or squirrels then?" Elizabeth asked casually. "We had several very persistent squirrels at Longbourn."

"I cannot speak to when all the chimneys were last inspected, but I shall ask to see the records and set men to checking before the snow arrives," the lady assured.

"Shall we have much snow?" Elizabeth inquired as she casually moved towards the closely arranged chairs and tables.

"More than my old bones care to know," Mrs. Reynolds declared. "I am a bit surprised we have not had a dusting or two by this time."

"I imagine Miss Alice is fascinated by the prospect," Elizabeth observed. "I always was as a child. My sisters and I would build a snowman, which, with five girls appeared more of the nature of a 'snowwoman,' what with all the ribbons and bits of lace we employed to decorate it. The year my mother carried our Lydia, Jane and I presented the 'snowwoman' a large stomach. Like our mother, we all thought Lydia would be a boy, for Mrs. Bennet had been larger than she was with Mary and Kitty."

"I was not aware you had other sisters beyond Miss Mary," Mrs. Reynolds said.

"There were five of us, but, in the last year, we lost Lydia and Katherine to some sort of pox which the local militia carried into the village. They were both being courted, you see, by two of the officers. Our mother also succumbed to the disease after having attended them. Our sweet Jane was lost to us during childbirth. She was married to an acquaintance of Mr. Darcy from Cambridge, a Mr. Charles Bingley. Our Papa, who was a friend with the current Mr. Darcy, was taken from us by a heart spasm. Mr. Bennet and my husband corresponded regularly for some years. Mr. Darcy even has a miniature of me at age sixteen."

"He does?" Mrs. Reynolds said with surprise.

"Yes, in his quarters. It is silly to say, I always feel a bit exposed when I view it. It is similar to those yonder." Elizabeth pointed to the grouping. "Is that one of Fitzwilliam?" She reached for the likeness. "How young he appears," she remarked as she studied his image. "Handsome, even then."

"I know of none so handsome," Mrs. Reynolds declared. "Naturally, you have viewed the larger and finer image of him in the gallery upstairs. These images were created about the same time as the portrait. Some ten years back. This room was my late master's favorite, and the miniatures are just as they have been for years. Mr. George Darcy was very fond of them." The housekeeper directed Elizabeth's attention to one of a young girl. "And this is Miss Darcy at about eight years of age. She has turned out to be as handsome as her brother, but she tends to favor Lady Anne Darcy, except in height. Lady Anne was more of your stature, ma'am. Miss Darcy is taller and quite slender, more of the nature of the Darcy clan than the Fitzwilliam faction. The current Mr. Darcy is Mr. George Darcy's father made over, though the Fitzwilliams claim he favors their side of the family. I suppose it would be proper to say the young master favors both. Yet, have you noticed Mr. Winslow Darcy's portrait in the gallery?"

"Not that I recall," Elizabeth admitted, "but I mean to seek it out later today. Perhaps I shall share it with Alice." Again, Elizabeth noted the slight snarl crossing Mrs. Reynolds's features. Although the woman was never cruel to the child, there was something about Alice of which the housekeeper disapproved, and the idea of anyone disliking such an adorable child kept Elizabeth from fully appreciating and trusting the Pemberley housekeeper.

Instead of addressing Elizabeth's comment, Mrs. Reynolds said, "Miss Darcy is the handsomest young lady ever to be beheld and so very accomplished. She plays and sings all day. The pianoforte used by Miss Bennet and the child were purchased for Miss Darcy at the suggestion of Master Fitzwilliam for his sister's pleasure. As you know, she has gone to stay with Lord and Lady Matlock, but I hope she returns to us soon."

"And the third one?" Elizabeth asked, instantly recognizing the man's features.

"A picture of a young gentleman attached to the family, the son of my late master's steward. He was brought up by Mr. George Darcy at his own expense. The late master stood as godfather to the man, who is named for him. I have heard since he departed Pemberley, about a year prior to Mr. George Darcy's death, he has gone into the army, but I am afraid he turned out very wild."

To the woman's surprise, Elizabeth said, "Lieutenant Wickham suffered alongside many of his fellow officers in the same pox outbreak I spoke of earlier. The militia located in our local village drew from those from Yorkshire and Derbyshire." She set the miniature back on the table beside the one of Miss Darcy, but Elizabeth held the one of her husband pressed tightly to her chest. She wondered if Mr. Darcy knew Lieutenant Wickham had been stationed in Hertfordshire when he arrived at Longbourn. Had her father mentioned Mr. Wickham to Mr. Darcy? Was Mr. Bennet aware of the lieutenant's connection to the Darcy family? Most assuredly, she had heard the lieutenant's tales of woe and had come to despise the Darcy family, chiefly the younger Mr. Darcy, who Mr. Wickham characterized as especially callous in his treatment of the lieutenant. He had claimed her husband a man jealous of Mr. Wickham's close relationship to the elder Mr. Darcy. Who had she misjudged? Lieutenant Wickham or her husband? Why had she not made the connection to the Darcy name when her husband introduced himself? More importantly, why did Mr. Wickham leave Pemberley for Hertfordshire? Coincidence or a purposeful endeavor?

"Mrs. Reynolds, I believe I must wait for another day to finish this task. I am feeling more poorly than I expected. Would you ask Hannah to bring me some tea and dry toast?" Elizabeth's nausea had returned, but was it dizziness or a sudden fear her world was again to tilt on its axis?

"Are you well enough to walk to your room? Permit me to fetch a maid or a footman to assist you," the housekeeper insisted.

Elizabeth nodded her agreement, but she reached for the woman's hand. "I know you mean to protect the Darcy family at all cost, but, if I am to lead Fitzwilliam to some sort of peace, I must know whether it was Mr. Wickham who prevented the elder Mr. Darcy from calling my husband back to the house on that fateful day."

Tears rolled down the woman's cheeks. "Mr. Wickham meant to replace Master Fitzwilliam as Mr. George Darcy's 'son.' When the late master realized the full impact of what he had done, the previous Mr. Darcy lost the will to live. He wrote to his son and apologized over and over again, but Master Fitzwilliam never responded. Not a single word. When Mr. George Darcy died, he begged me to tell his son of his regrets and his love, but Master Fitzwilliam will have none of my words. If you have any influence over him, you must assist your husband to forgiveness. He will never know the greatness he seeks until he can forgive the unforgivable."

⁂

"Elizabeth!" her husband burst into her room without even knocking on the door. "Are you unwell?"

She looked up from the letter she was writing to Mr. Bingley. She hoped he had some knowledge of what had transpired between her husband and Mr. Wickham. Back in Hertfordshire, Elizabeth had listened to Mr. Wickham's tales of woe and had believed every word, as had all of Meryton, but, after considering the situation, in hindsight, she realized Mr. Bennet had warned her often how people instinctively made themselves appear the "victim" when they were not, but she had ignored her father's advice.

Most assuredly, Mr. Bennet had not been happy to learn Mr. Wickham had ruined Lydia, but her father had permitted Mrs. Bennet her way and had allowed the pair to plan their quick marriage. At the time, Mr. Bennet had thought his investment in the mine would stand for a proper dowry for Lydia. As terrible as it was to consider, the pox had saved Mr. Bennet from owing Mr. Wickham a fortune following Lydia's untimely demise. The marriage settlements had never been signed by their father, for Lydia had passed before the banns could be read a final time, or the settlements would have been another debt for Elizabeth to have assumed.

"I was simply a bit queasy for a time period this morning, shortly after you departed," she assured. "Hannah insisted I return to bed for a bit. I am much better now."

"Thank the Lord!" he said in relief. He knelt beside her chair, and Elizabeth turned so he could not view what she had written to Mr. Bingley. "When Sheffield told me you had been ill, I feared . . ."

"You and I have taken on an enormous task," she was quick to say. "We have both known a great loss of late, and we are working hard to right our world. I fear it caught up to me, just as those three extra hours of sleep you claimed Sunday morning did you well, the additional two I commandeered today assisted in clearing my head."

"As long as you are well," he conceded.

She leaned down to kiss him. "Thank you for caring for my future," she murmured against his lips. "Go now and have your bath. Alice will be thrilled you returned early."

"Are you thrilled also, Mrs. Darcy?" he asked seductively. "You have been much on my mind today."

AMENDING THE SHADES OF PEMBERLEY

"As you have been on mine," she said with a grin. "See what I procured today." She motioned to where his miniature sat on her bedside table. "You own an image of a sixteen-year-old Elizabeth, and, now, I have one of a twenty-year-old Fitzwilliam. Do you think they would have liked each other?"

He ignored her question, offering her a frown of disapproval. "You were in my father's study today?"

"I told you I planned to examine 'all' the rooms at Pemberley," she countered. "I am glad I did: There were several tears in the drapes and loose nails in the upholstery of the settee, as well as the lock on the window no longer being operable."

"It is not like my father to ignore any of those," her husband said with a sad sigh of resignation.

"According to Mrs. Reynolds, your father broke it in an effort to prevent your leaving," Elizabeth disclosed.

"Such is ridiculous. It is just Mrs. Reynolds's loyalty to my father doing the talking," he declared. "She has always been blind to George Darcy's faults." He rose to look down upon her. "Why would she disclose these facts to you?"

"Evidently, the lady has attempted to speak to you of the matter since your return to Pemberley, but you have shunned her efforts," she said as she stood before him.

"What is there to say?" her husband asked.

"Your father's regrets," Elizabeth said softly as she caressed his cheek.

"What regrets?" he nearly spat the words. "Five years, nine months, and two days before I heard a word from Derbyshire. Without your father's encouragement to return no matter what conditions I found in England, I would have lived out my days in India."

She had not known her father had written such to Mr. Darcy, but that was a discussion for another day. Instead, she revealed, "Your father wrote to you on multiple occasions begging for your return—for your forgiveness."

He stormed away from her. "Such is a lie Mrs. Reynolds has concocted to reshape my father's image."

"I do not believe hers is the lie," she countered.

Her husband jammed his fingers into his hair. "Why are you doing this? Were we two not carving out a bit of happiness from this disaster?"

"We are. We have," she assured. "Tell me you do not want to hear my thoughts on the matter, and I will never mention them to you again."

He said stubbornly, "I do not want to hear your thoughts on the past."

"Then I will wait for your call so we may go down to supper together," Elizabeth said in calmer tones than she felt.

"Perfect," he half growled, turned on his heels, and was gone within a matter of seconds.

❦

Darcy entered his quarters in a huff. "That woman will be the death of me!" he hissed.

"As you say, sir." Sheffield gently guided Darcy into a chair and began to remove his boots. "Your bath is waiting, sir."

Ignoring his valet, Darcy argued, "You were here. In the same position you are now. Serving the master of Pemberley. You would know more than anyone if my father ever knew even one ounce of regret for banishing me to India." A bit of desperation entered his voice, "Did George Darcy . . ." He could not finish the question.

"Every day, sir," Sheffield assured. "George Darcy searched the multiple newsprints available for any mention of you or the company you started in India. The late Mr. Darcy celebrated your successes with phrases of 'The boy has something of my father in him' or of your challenges with 'My son will overcome this. He is the best of us, you know.' And I would tell him the student was often more intelligent than his tutor. Those were the only moments he would truly smile." The valet paused. "He invested in your mine, you know. He found out who were your bankers in London, and your father invested in the mine so you would know success."

"Order a couple more pots of hot water," Darcy instructed. "I must speak to Elizabeth again, to hear her thoughts."

"You could hear from Mrs. Darcy after your bath, sir," Sheffield began, but, with a heavy sigh, his man said, "or I could order more hot water brought up."

"You are a good man, Sheffield," Darcy pronounced before he rushed back to his wife's quarters to find Hannah assisting Elizabeth to undress. "I will attend my wife," he ordered.

"Yes, sir." The girl bobbed a curtsy and disappeared through the dressing room door.

"Have you changed your mind or do you have another reason to send Hannah away?" Elizabeth asked.

"Tell me your thoughts," he said reluctantly.

"Please bear with me," she began, "for what I must share begins in Hertfordshire. I told you there was a militia in Meryton, and they proved to be the source of the pox which killed so many."

"I do not understand what this has to do with my father," Darcy said in bewilderment.

"You will," his wife assured. "Those in the Meryton militia were, generally, from Yorkshire or Derbyshire. One of them was a man who told anyone who would listen of the abuses he had earned at the hands of the family for whom his father served as steward."

Darcy sank into the nearest chair and buried his head in his hands. "Continue."

"I was one of those who listened and believed the man. You see, I had never possessed a serious suitor, and, at first, I appeared to be the gentleman's favorite. However, my father warned me against deceitful people, and Mr. Bennet proved to be correct. The man soon abandoned my company for that of Miss Emily King. My pride knew great umbrage, but Mr. Bennet reminded me of how Miss King had recently been presented an inheritance of ten thousand pounds."

Elizabeth paused as if she expected her husband to respond and to learn whether she should continue. With his head still buried in his hands, he said without hope, "Go on."

"When Miss King's uncle removed her from the area, the gentleman returned to Longbourn, only this time his attentions were on my youngest sister, a girl barely seventeen years of age. A girl whose mother had filled her head with stories of gentlemen in red coats."

His wife sat beside him and pulled his hands away from his face to grip his fingers tightly. "Today, I realized the man knew something of your successes and failures. I do not know how exactly, but you have said previously you wrote to your father to beg to come home. I imagine you spoke of your efforts to make your fortune. I suspect this gentleman made certain the letters your father meant for you never made it into the mail, and the ones you sent to Mr. George Darcy were never seen by him. It is my belief the gentleman from Derbyshire came to Meryton, for he knew something of your successes in India. He thought the Bennets might one day be rich. I can only assume his attention to Miss King had something to do with what had proven to be his mounting debts. While the militia was in Brighton, a Portuguese ship carrying the pox landed at Brighton. Along with the others, my sister and this particular officer returned to Meryton and were to be quickly married with a calling of the banns. He had ruined her during her stay with Colonel Forster's young wife. Unfortunately, only days before their wedding, they both had taken ill. Lydia passed away, but the man survived."

Darcy growled, "The dastard has more lives than a cat."

His wife lifted his hands and kissed his knuckles. "The man, as you well know, was Mr. George Wickham, the one whose image is captured within a miniature in your father's study. After Mr. Bennet died, the lieutenant attempted to place a claim upon Lydia's dowry, but my father had delayed signing the marriage settlements until after he heard from his investments. He could not pay the amount promised without the business profits. Mr. Wickham's claim was denied by Lydia's quick death."

"Sheffield says my father was one of the investors in my mine," he disclosed. "He sought out the English bankers with whom I conducted business."

Elizabeth nodded her understanding before continuing her tale. "I am assuming the lieutenant's arrival in Meryton had something to do with whatever he learned from his godfather of you. Of your connections. I cannot speak with any assurance, but I doubt his choice of the Meryton militia was a coincidence. Now, I fully believe he had targeted me, just as he had pursued Lydia. Mrs. Reynolds said your father sought the simplest of news of you, and he wrote often to beg your forgiveness, and, I imagine, to plead for your return to Pemberley. Forgive my impertinence, but I suspect George Darcy has been doing a jig in heaven every day since his beloved son stepped down from his carriage before the estate's manor house."

"My father believed Mr. Wickham's account of what Ruth confessed to her father," he admitted. "I am not certain I would have forgiven him, even if I had received his letters, but, for all those years away from home, I, most assuredly, prayed to hear the words of his regrets."

Elizabeth wished to pursue the slip in her husband's confession about his late wife; yet, she ignored it for now. Convincing her husband to believe Mrs. Reynolds's tales and Elizabeth's assumptions was what Mr. Darcy required at the moment. "I am confident you would not have opened any of the first dozen or so letters," his wife declared. "You are the most stubborn man I know, but you are also the most reasonable man of my acquaintance, especially when you nudge your pride to the side. However, after the tenth or eleventh or twelfth or thirteenth letter, your curiosity would have won out. You would have read the first letter, for we both know you would not have done away with any of them. They would have been tied together with a string and hidden away in a drawer so you would not see them with any regularity. You would have initially dismissed that first appeal, but you would have returned to it again and again, analyzing each word and even the slant of the letters.

Each comma. Each unfinished sentence. Adding your own intonation to the words as they bounced around in your head. Until, at length, you responded, even if it were words of anger you wrote. Such would have opened the door. Just a crack." She squeezed his fingertips again. "I asked Mr. Nathan the date of your father taking to his his bed in a woeful melancholy. George Darcy's progressive decline coincided with Mr. Wickham's appearance in Meryton. The wheels had been set in motion long before the lieutenant conveniently joined his friend Captain Denny in Hertfordshire. It was planned. Mr. Wickham saw the writing on the wall at Pemberley, for George Darcy refused to replace you as his rightful heir. The information in your letters to your father provided Mr. Wickham another means to benefit from your banishment. When Mr. Bennet convinced me to look elsewhere for a suitor, Mr. Wickham purposely ruined our Lydia. If he could not replace you with your father, he could claim a 'brotherhood' of sorts if you and he were married to sisters."

Chapter Nine

His wife had been correct, for Darcy could not quite shake the knowledge of everything she had shared four days earlier. Therefore, when Mr. Ericks caught Darcy's arm and directed him a few steps away from the rest of the congregation, he had been taken unawares.

"I know it might be an imposition, sir, but could you spare me a few minutes of your time after your Sunday meal, which Mrs. Darcy has again asked me to share with your family."

Darcy glanced to where his wife chatted with several women married to his tenants, as well as a few of the shopkeepers' wives. He marveled at how easily she could converse with a variety of people without sounding toplofty. She was truly one of a kind.

"May I ask the nature of your request? A church project?" he inquired, while still admiring the woman who had haunted his dreams for years.

"Something more personal," the vicar disclosed.

Darcy turned his attention on the man. "Ah, it is as Mrs. Darcy suspected. You mean to propose to Miss Bennet." Briefly, Darcy wondered why he had not taken note of the budding romance between the vicar and Mary Bennet. Even when Elizabeth mentioned her suspicions, he had not presented the idea any credence, for Ericks was much older than Mary and was a relation, of sorts. Yet, as he considered it, Darcy realized it would be a good match for Elizabeth's sister, although he knew Alice would miss having Miss Mary around each day.

"Yes, such is my wish. However, I would understand if you thought my doing so was self-serving. After all, this living, although bestowed upon me by your father, is still one of those over which you the granter," the vicar explained.

"I am not so whimsical to think such is your motive," Darcy declared, although he would admit, and only to himself, his choice to offer his hand to Elizabeth Bennet had come more from instinct than forethought.

"No, sir," Ericks was quick to say. "Just know I wish to speak to you privately. You may choose whether my doing so is today or upon another occasion. My aspirations will remain unchanged."

They parted then: Ericks bid a variety of families farewell, while Darcy gathered his wife and daughter and Miss Bennet to escort them all to his waiting carriage. "Home, Mr. Farrin," he instructed.

"Aye, sir."

Within a matter of minutes, they were on their way to Pemberley. He purposely waited until they had turned into the gates of Pemberley before he interrupted the chatter between the Bennet sisters. "Mr. Ericks wishes to speak to me privately when he calls upon Pemberley today," he informed them.

Elizabeth immediately reached for her sister's hand. "And . . .?"

"The vicar also requested a private audience with our Mary."

Elizabeth smiled widely, while a slight whimper escaped Mary's lips and was recaptured. "You are certain, Fitzwilliam?" his wife demanded.

"Yes. Mr. Ericks stated his intentions and assured me they had nothing to do with his living being part of those I may bestow on worthy members of the clergy."

"And you will present him your blessings and give them something as a dowry?" she pleaded.

"I will do so, if necessary," he said with a lift of his brows in challenge. Darcy had come dearly to love Elizabeth's features when she meant to fight a wrong.

"What do you mean, 'if necessary'? You know both Mary and I depend upon your kindness," she argued. A frown marked her brows. "You are well aware of our father's debts. Without you, Mary and I would be destitute."

"Not entirely destitute," he said simply. "Your father's shares of the diamond mine, though not the vein he hoped, still showed a profit."

Elizabeth hissed, "I have previously told you Mr. Bennet received a letter from his partner in the endeavor which stated it had not known success." Realizing her tone, she shot a glance to Alice, who had thankfully fallen asleep on the seat beside her.

"I must correct you, my dear. You said nothing of Mr. Bennet receiving a letter from his partner, only that he did not receive what he thought he would." He sat forward to press his point. "Elizabeth, although we did not speak of it in so many words, I assumed you realized I was your father's partner in the mine along with two officers of the East India Company. I became the onsite superintendent. They all agreed to provide me fifty-five percent of the profits, for I was the one in the pit with the men every day, swinging a pick, clawing in the dirt and the slime with my bare hands. Digging with my nails into the walls of the mine. Setting the explosives. They each took fifteen percent. I was thankful for their generosity considering, in the beginning, I barely had four hundred pounds to put into the operation. Your father and the others stood me for a thousand pounds each. For the first two years, I kept only enough of the profits to sustain a living for Alice and me. The funds I allotted myself went to pay for her *ayah* and my daughter's care. Many days I did without a proper meal so Alice could thrive. When I departed India, Mr. Bennet's share of the profits was a little over nine thousand pounds when we sold the operation. I put in enough for him to claim ten thousand to divide among his daughters' dowries."

"Where is this fortune now?" she demanded. "Mr. Birkhead said nothing of a profit from the mine. That would have been enough for Mary and me to remain at Longbourn." His wife appeared bewildered.

Darcy leaned forward to claim her hands. "Sweetheart, it would have taken more than ten thousand to clear all the debts at Longbourn. I know you wished to save it as much as I wish to save Pemberley. Yet, it was not possible. Mr. Birkhead said nothing of the funds, for Mr. Bennet only had them on paper. It will likely be next summer before the funds are actually in the Bank of England. Commerce moves at a snail's pace in that manner, especially from such distances. I was not able to bring all of my shares with me when I returned. I, too, am waiting for the revenue to complete much of what I have planned for Pemberley. We have been prioritizing repairs and such for the manor, have we not? I thought you understood, or I would have explained it all to you. You had spoken of having read through all your father's business papers and consulted the solicitor."

"But I do not understand," Miss Bennet said when Elizabeth broke into tears.

Darcy tugged his wife to sit beside him on the bench where he might comfort her with his embrace.

Mary appeared to be as emotionally drained as was her sister; yet, she managed to verbalize her thoughts. "Our father died for no reason. Such is what Elizabeth means."

"Now it is I who does not understand," he said. "I was told Mr. Bennet passed from an episode with his heart."

Elizabeth clutched at his lapels. "A letter . . . from his . . . business partner in . . . India . . . stated the mine . . . proved a . . . complete loss. Papa . . . thought he had . . . lost everything," she hiccuped through her sobs.

"It was a loss for diamonds, but proved good for several veins of gold," he said, and, as I stated earlier, I was your father's partner. I did write to tell him of my father's passing and my being summoned home by the estate's man of business and others paid to oversee various Pemberley ventures. However, I was able to book passage shortly after the letter went on its way, which customarily takes as long or longer than actually sailing from India to England, for there are multiple stops in Europe. In my letter, I told him I was to leave for Derbyshire as quickly as passage could be secured. I described the manner which I took to secure his portion of the profits and made arrangements for their transfer first on paper and then the actual funds."

"I swear such was not . . . what the letter . . . held," his wife argued. "I read it, Fitzwilliam." Elizabeth collapsed against him once again.

"And you believe it was my script? You have read multiple papers written in my hand. You have even commented on how I slant my letters," he argued. "I would never practice such a falsehood on your father. He quite literally saved me. Mr. Bennet's advice on the night I departed for India kept me from jumping off the ship which carried me away from England and, quite literally, drowning my woes in the ocean. It was his advice which permitted me to save Alice. Over and over again, it was his words of encouragement I heard in my head when I required them the most. I would never have exacted any harm on him. In many ways, I loved him. He became 'my father' when I had no one else to whom to turn."

"Then who wrote such a letter?" Mary asked from her place on the bench. Her face also was crumpled in tears. "Who wanted to harm our dearest parent?"

✧

Darcy had seen Elizabeth to her quarters, assisted her to undress, removed his boots and jacket and crawled into bed to hold her. Her tears had done something strange to his heart, and, he, too, sobbed for the loss of her father, as well as his. She fell asleep in his arms, but he did not move a muscle until Sheffield lightly tapped on the dressing room door. Then Darcy eased his arm from beneath Elizabeth's body so he might answer the knock.

"Mr. Ericks is in your study, sir," the valet whispered.

"I will be there momentarily," he said. "Has the vicar spoken to Miss Bennet already?"

"Yes, sir."

"Send Hannah to assist Mrs. Darcy. She will want to support her sister's triumph. I will wake your mistress and don my jacket. Fetch me a pair of shoes. I have no desire to wrestle those boots on again."

"Yes, sir. I will set them by the door."

Darcy nodded his agreement, retrieved his jacket, slipped it on his shoulders, and, finally, placed a knee on the bed to lean over his ever-tempting wife. "Elizabeth, darling," he coaxed, caressing her cheek. "Mr. Ericks is here, love. You must wake."

She stretched, lifting her breasts upward and making him wish there was time for intimacies. She reached up and pulled him down to kiss him quite thoroughly. Although his wife did not shun his advances, she rarely initiated a kiss or a gesture of affection. "Thank you for your tender care," she whispered against his lips.

"I will stand between you and the worst the world throws at us," he declared, sincerely meaning every word.

"When you are willing to speak of it," she said as she brushed his hair from his forehead, "I would be a ready listener regarding what you suffered in India, as well as how you and my father came to be such intimate friends. Such would serve us both well in our healing."

Darcy was not certain he could ever speak to the indignities he suffered in India, but he could tell her something of her remarkable father, a man who, upon appearance, might be considered indolent, but who possessed a charitable spirit and a wicked sense of the ridiculous, often asking if Darcy was not excessively diverted.

"'For what do we live but to make sport for our neighbors and laugh at them in our turn,' or something of that nature," he often told me in his letters," Darcy said in sweet remembrance.

"One of Papa's favorite remarks," Elizabeth said with a sad smile.

"I will be willing to speak of your father," he assured. "Despite all the madness still surrounding us, I am excessively glad he placed you before my notice."

AMENDING THE SHADES OF PEMBERLEY

"As am I," his wife said before kissing him in a manner leaving Darcy craving more.

⁂

Elizabeth was about to enter the dressmaker's shop when a familiar voice called her name. "Mrs. Darcy." Elizabeth turned with some reluctance. She knew her husband would not approve of her speaking to Mr. Wickham. She belatedly realized she had not relayed to Mary how Mr. Wickham was connected to the Darcy family, and, although her husband had yet to discuss with her something of Mr. Wickham's role in displacing Mr. Darcy at the late Mr. Darcy's side, as well as the downward turn of the estate's prosperity, Elizabeth made a silent promise to warn her sister of the true character of Mr. Wickham. Elizabeth had heard enough from the likes of Mrs. Reynolds, who had been open, of late, since the day they shared Mr. George Darcy's study, but, generally, from the womenfolk of Mr. Darcy's tenants—women who openly expressed their contempt for the man now bowing before her.

She could easily recall her first impressions of the man. Along with her sisters, they were all struck with the stranger's air, all wondered who he could be. Mr. Denny had introduced his friend. At the time, Elizabeth had thought Mr. Wickham only wanted for regimentals to make him completely charming. His appearance was greatly in his favor. He had all the best part of beauty—a fine countenance, a good figure, and a very pleasing address. The man before her still wore a smile, though, now, a slightly crooked one. One side of his face was as smooth and as handsome as ever, but the other held the marks of the pox he had survived. There was some puckering along his chin line. In her opinion, even his waistline was thicker than previously and his complexion paler.

"Mr. Wickham," she said with a curtsy, more from habit than from deference. "I did not realize you had returned to Derbyshire." She would be reporting this change of situation to her husband as soon as she returned to the estate.

"It is my home, Mrs. Darcy," he was saying in his customary smoothness. "My heart longs to be here."

"Really?" Elizabeth asked with forced sweetness in her tone. "I recall a time when you could not think to return to the area. In Hertfordshire, you spoke often of your disdain of your 'home.'"

"I loved Derbyshire and this area when the elder Mr. Darcy remained alive. He was my godfather, if you recall," he said with a slight lift of his brows.

"I recall," she said in warning tones. "Only a few weeks past, I viewed a miniature of you in the late Mr. Darcy's study. And just yesterday, several of the tenants' wives bemoaned the condition of the land upon which their husbands toiled. They claimed Mr. George Darcy's placement of you as his steward, in your father's place, nearly ruined the land."

"I warned my godfather I was meant for the law," he argued, "but he insisted I had some of my father in me. We were just turning a profit when Mr. Darcy, the senior, took to his bed, and I was removed by the estate's man of business while Mr. Darcy languished. Such was when I came to Hertfordshire."

"Law?" she asked. "I thought you hoped to be ordained. Did you not mention the living at Kympton having been promised to you?" She stepped a bit closer to press her point. "Did you realize the curate at Kympton must pay tithes to the vicar in Lambton?"

"I suppose I did," he said with a slight frown. "I never approved of tithes being paid," he confessed. "A curate receives so little compensation as it is."

"Too little to interest you with earning your living thusly?"

"I do not understand your point, ma'am."

"I was just thinking of Mr. Harris, the current curate of Kympton. He is an estimable young man, very much cut from the same cloth as my cousin, Mr. Collins, and, although he can be a bit off-putting at times, he serves his parishioners well. They are quite satisfied with him, and such is all that matters. Even Mr. Ericks, the vicar, is pleased with Harris's attention to his congregation. Do you know Mr. Ericks?"

Mr. Wickham appeared a bit confused by their conversation, but he responded, nevertheless. "A local family. His father was a surgeon."

"Do you recall my Aunt Gardiner? You met her at one of Mrs. Bennet's entertainments."

"Certainly I recall your aunt. We spoke of Lambton," he said with a frown.

"Yes," Elizabeth announced with a twinge of triumph. "My Aunt Gardiner was from Lambton, and, before she married, she was an Ericks. The vicar is one of her brothers. It is too bad you never made the connection." She would not say her aunt knew something about the curacy at Kympton that Wickham did not, but Elizabeth allowed the implication to take root before she added. "Mr. Ericks is to be attached to the Darcy family soon. He has extended his hand in marriage to our Mary. In fact, I was just about to go inside and order three new dresses for my sister as a wedding gift."

"Please give Miss Mary my deepest congratulations," Wickham repeated dutifully.

"Why have you returned to Lambton, Mr. Wickham?" she asked. "You cannot expect a true welcome at Pemberley or in the area. I understand this is your home shire, but you have burned many bridges."

"Yet, not all of them," he said cryptically. "Good day, Miss Elizabeth."

"It is Mrs. Fitzwilliam Darcy, as you well know," she countered.

He did not turn to bow to her or to respond. All she received was a flick of his hand in farewell.

❧

"What a lovely surprise," her husband announced as he approached where she and Alice waited in the gig.

"We'd brought yer meal, Papa," the child shared with a big smile.

"Mr. Farrin was repairing the spokes on the coach, so Alice and I volunteered to bring the baskets, did we not, darling?"

"Miss Lizbet said I being good." Alice's head bobbed up and down in approval.

"I am pleased to hear it," Mr. Darcy said, as the child stood to hug his neck. "And what of you, Mrs. Darcy?" His voice took on a huskiness Elizabeth well recognized. "Are you being good also?"

Elizabeth's brow rose in challenge. "Only you would know, sir."

He barked a laugh before presenting Alice a kiss. "Mrs. Darcy brought our meals today," he called to the men who were repairing a barn used to store wool. "Come claim the sacks."

The half-dozen or so men swarmed around the gig, each snatching their wool caps from their heads in deference and speaking their "Good day, ma'am."

Elizabeth made it a point to call those she knew my name. "Good day, Mr. Thomas. Good to see your arm feels better." To the man on the left, she said, "Last week, I had a right hearty cup of potato soup while sitting at your table, Mr. Rufus. Warmed me up nicely."

"Mrs. Rufus be right proud to serve you agin, ma'am. Welcome any time."

Her husband instructed, "Thomas, might I employ you to show Miss Alice where we store the wool?"

"Yes, sir."

"Allow her to feel the underside," Mr. Darcy said with a chuckle. "Here, my girl." He handed his child a chunk of the cheese from the sack he had claimed from under the seat. "Eat it before you touch the wool," he warned. "Your hands will be dirty. I will clean them when you return. Do not touch your dress or coat."

"Yes, Papa," the child said as she took Mr. Thomas's hand and walked away towards the barn.

Her husband opened the flask Elizabeth handed him and took a swig of the beer inside. He climbed up to sit beside her on the bench.

"This is truly a delight," he said, "but I come to recognize that slightly distracted look upon your features as an omen."

"An omen?" she declared. "When did you decide strict honesty was the means to woo me?"

"From our first meeting, love," he declared, as he claimed a large bite of the ham and cheese wrapped in a pancake-style bread the Pemberley kitchens had cooked for each of the men.

"Am I truly your 'love'?" she asked, suddenly feeling very needy and more than a bit pensive.

Her husband paused before responding. "I, most assuredly, would not wish to lose you," he explained. "I have come to depend upon you—your kindness—your insights—your dedication to me, Alice, and Pemberley. I am not certain I have ever known romantic love, but I would like to think we are well on our way to a deep affection. Why do you ask?"

Elizabeth sighed heavily. "I encountered Mr. Wickham in the village today. I was chastising myself for ever having found him handsome."

Her husband snarled, "Most women do. Why was Mr. Wickham in the village? As much havoc as he has wreaked in the area, why would he think anyone would welcome his return?"

"I do not know," she admitted. "I said something similar to him. Perhaps he heard of our marriage and wondered if you claimed my father's 'supposed' fortune. He was not wearing his uniform. Do you think he walked away from his duty to the militia?"

"He walks away from anything even halfway honorable," Mr. Darcy said in contempt. "The thing is, there is really little the military will do to him. It is not as it would be if he were in the Regulars. Please avoid him," her husband warned. "I would not bet against Mr. Wickham concocting a plan to extort money from me."

"You think me in danger?" she asked. "What of Alice?"

They both turned to where Alice skipped ahead of Mr. Thomas on their return to the gig. "My weak points are you and my child," he reminded her. "Although I do not wish to restrict either of you, I would also ask you to practice caution. Take Jasper or Mr. Farrin with you when you decide to travel into the village. Mr. Wickham will not stay long in the area, but count on him, at some point, to act in desperation."

<hr/>

"Fitzwilliam," she said as he waited for her to locate her slippers to wear down to supper. She knew he had again made another call in the village today, for she could tell by the scent of smoke on his jacket. Her husband had been making inquiries into whether Mr. Wickham's was still present in the area. He would join the men at the inn, make conversation, including his questions regarding a sighting of Wickham, purchase a round of drinks for all within, and return home frustrated by no sightings of his former friend, while she took the news of Wickham's absence as a sign the man had discovered some other scheme to line his pockets. "We received an invitation today from a Sir Lawrence and Lady Rowan for a ball and supper. I do not recall having taken their acquaintance. I wished to bring it to your attention before I responded."

"I have not seen either Sir Lawrence or his lady for more years than I can recall. Long before I left for India. Sir Lawrence and my father were chums when they were young." He paused as if considering how to respond. "You should know, before I agree, I certainly have not the talent which some people possess of conversing easily with those I have never seen before. I cannot catch their tone of conversation or appear interested in their concerns, as I often see done."

Elizabeth studied him for a moment before saying, "Yet, I will be on your arm, and you well recognize I am capable of discussing many topics. In truth, I thought you might object, for we are both, strictly, still in mourning, although, other than the black ribbons on the servants' arms, the color of our clothing, and the knocker removed from the door, we have not discussed socializing with others beyond attending church. It has been more than six months since my father's passing. I have never asked when your father knew his last days."

"Nearly a year since his actual passing. I received the news in early July. Lord Matlock wrote to me of my father's passing, forwarding some of the necessary papers stating my succession as Pemberley's master. My uncle oversaw the legalities of the estate passage into my hands, but my father took to his bed long before he met his Maker. Lord Matlock had driven Mr. Wickham from the estate and the shire more than a year prior to George Darcy's passing. My uncle reported Mr. Wickham traveled to London."

"If I have recollected the dates accurately, such is where Mr. Wickham reconnected with Captain Denny, who convinced Wickham to purchase a lieutenancy in the militia," she observed. "Then again, perhaps he had heard of the Derbyshire men being stationed in Meryton and purposely contacted Captain Denny to make his true plans appear coincidental."

"Likely purchased the commission with money or goods he stole from the estate," her husband grumbled.

"I wish I had held an inkling of his duplicity," she said with a heavy sigh. "I doubt Captain Denny realized what havoc Mr. Wickham wreaked upon the citizens of Meryton."

Her husband said, "As for me, in regards to the Rowan invitation, I am perfectly satisfied at Pemberley. You and Alice and all who depend on the estate are here, but I am well aware it would be egregious of me not to permit you some form of society beyond the vicarage. I would not deny you either amusements or acquaintances. Neither would I have others thinking I am ashamed of my wife, when, in reality, it was my family which knew the scandal. Yours simply knew the tragedy of being struck by situations beyond your control."

"Then what should be my response?" she asked as he braced her balance so she might step into the shoes she had retrieved from under the bed.

"Would you enjoy attending?" he asked.

Elizabeth spread her hands over his lapels to straighten them. "Do I wish to be seen on the arm of Mr. Fitzwilliam Darcy?" she asked in a flirtatious tone.

137

"The very disgraced Fitzwilliam Darcy," he reminded her.

"The very distinguished-looking Fitzwilliam Darcy," she corrected as she smiled up at him. "We could scandalize all of Derbyshire by dancing together more than twice or walking in the garden and stealing a kiss or two." A frown claimed her forehead. "You do know how to dance, do you not, sir?"

"My parents made certain I held the customary skills of any gentleman," he responded, as he caressed her cheek and edged her closer.

"Do you think they might have approved of me? Your parents, that is," she asked, suddenly feeling uncertain of her own worth.

"They would likely have objected to the speed of our joining, although, obviously, I knew more of your nature than any female who had been paraded before me prior to my banishment. Yet, I sincerely believe they would have approved of how you have conducted yourself as the mistress of Pemberley. They may have initially questioned my choice, but you would have easily earned their loyalty."

"Thank you for the compliment," she said sincerely. "Your affirmation has been a gift I shall cherish. Now, kiss me before we must go below. Mr. Nathan has already rung the chime once."

Her husband smiled upon her. "Harp. Harp. Harp," he teased. "Such a demanding woman you have become."

"I am fortunate then that you are a willing participant in my manipulations," she countered.

"A very willing cohort, my dear."

He kissed her quite thoroughly, in fact. As they finally broke for air, the chime rang a second time. "We must go below," she whispered against his lips.

"Yet, you will permit me to continue a litany of my dedication to you when we return to our quarters?" he asked in husky tones.

"I would enjoy it," Elizabeth said, suddenly embarrassed by her boldness.

He released her to place her hand on his arm. "Come along, Mrs. Darcy. Cook becomes irritated if we do not sit as quickly as the dishes are ready to serve."

As they walked, she remarked, "Your cook is an excellent one."

"You no longer suffer the nausea from some of her dishes?" he asked. "Have you become accustomed to Derbyshire cuisine?"

"The weakness only lasted for a few weeks," she assured. "Mary, thankfully, reminded me of how I would claim one of the small loaves our Longbourn cook made in the evening for the morning meal. I often would wake in the night's middle and eat part of it. My hunger would actually wake me, and I would be quite weak. When I did the same here, things were better. My mother often said my late-night hunger was because I walked so much during the day—to Oakham Mount and Lucas Lodge to visit with Charlotte or into the village. All were activities she considered very unladylike and reeking of peasantry. I always became hungry before the rest of the family when meal times neared."

"As long as you are not ill," he said as his free hand came to rest comfortably over hers. "You may have all the rolls you wish. I have come to depend upon your goodness and your competent handling of my household." Although he did not speak of affection, Elizabeth knew satisfaction. She had no doubt her husband's estimation of her aligned nicely with hers of him.

Chapter Ten

She knocked on her husband's door, and Mr. Sheffield responded. "Is Mr. Darcy available and decent?" she asked. A few days prior she had not thought to knock before entering his quarters, only to discover Mr. Sheffield pouring a bucket of water over his master's head while Darcy was in his tub. Most assuredly, she had viewed her husband undressed, but not with an audience present to view her response.

"Permit her in," Darcy said with only a hint of amusement in his tone. "I have yet to dress completely, Elizabeth."

"You hide your humor poorly, sir," she warned.

He chuckled. "You must recall I spent some five years without a reason to smile."

"I am glad to be a source of your ple . . ."

She caught herself before she said "pleasure."

"A source of your entertainment."

His smile widened, saying he considered the words "pleasure" and "entertainment" interchangeable. "Do you have a request, love?"

She wondered whether the endearment would ever hold a special meaning for him. She prayed so. "I have sent our acceptance to Lady Rowan: However, none of the dresses I brought with me from Longbourn are appropriate for the entertainment. I thought to have the village seamstress make me an appropriate gown in a color of, perhaps, half mourning, but Mrs. Caren means to leave at the end of the week to spend the time up through Twelfth Night with her family in Northumberland. The ball is a week after Twelfth Night. Naturally, she volunteered to stay and complete the dress, but I refused. Family is more important than a gown for the mistress of Pemberley."

"Such was very kind of you," he said. "But what will you do?"

"I thought to purchase some lace and ribbon to make over one of my own dresses; yet, I truly do not wish to embarrass you before your family friends and your neighbors. Mrs. Reynolds has suggested there is a very competent dressmaker in Matlock, for the woman often serves your aunt and would be accustomed to the style one requires for a supper and a ball."

"And you wish to travel to Matlock?" he asked.

She knew he was calculating the risks to her traveling alone. "I thought if you could spare a day from the fields, we could all go together. I also wish to procure an appropriate dress for Mary to wear for her wedding. I ordered her several day dresses from Mrs. Caren, but I wish something worthy of her kindness. For years, my sister has done with hand-me-down gowns or dresses sewn for displays for the Meryton's dressmaker's shop. Mary deserves a special gown for her wedding. We could take Alice along. We might have a new dress or two made for the child, something more to the nature of the daughter of an English gentleman. The seamstresses at Pemberley could use the ones we purchase as patterns for others. You could call on your aunt and uncle, if you wish, or purchase a special fairing for your daughter for Christmas."

"Nothing for you?" he asked with a gentleness in his tone.

"I have everything I require at Pemberley," Elizabeth responded and meant every word.

"I still wish to speak to Georgiana. Something more personal than a letter can express," he said, musing aloud. "Introduce you and Alice to her."

Elizabeth held his gaze to convince him of her words. "I wish with all my heart to claim Miss Darcy as my sister, but, obviously, you two must first have your say regarding what occurred at Pemberley before and during your absence. You have been home in Derbyshire for three months and have not spoken a word of Miss Darcy or received news from her since the letter right before our marriage. It is time, Fitzwilliam, whether it is a welcomed occasion or continued estrangement."

Her husband sat heavily. "I know you are correct, but I do not wish to know her rejection."

"Mayhap the Matlocks have not returned to Derbyshire from his lordship's time in Parliament," she suggested, wishing desperately to ease the pain written upon her husband's features.

"My aunt always returns early to begin preparations for Christmastide," he confided.

"Such reminds me," Elizabeth shared, "I ordered the men to locate an appropriate yule log. Your father did not have one last year. I also instructed the servants to gather greenery and ribbons to decorate the main rooms. Alice has never experienced any of our English traditions."

"Elizabeth," he said, with a hint of frustration in his tone, "distracting me with your efficient planning will not resolve whether my sister will forgive me."

"There is truly nothing to forgive, Mr. Darcy," she corrected. "You held no choice in what occurred at Pemberley. Your sister must be made to understand you are as much a victim as was she."

"I pray you are correct, Elizabeth," he said in quiet contemplation.

"If I am wrong, we continue as we are now. You will have me and Alice and Mary and Mr. Ericks as family, and, perhaps, someday, our own children. We shall find a means to continue on, but, before we take that road, you must extend your hand to your sister and ask her to be a part of our family. This rift between you will haunt your days if you do not make an honest effort."

"Tomorrow then?" he asked half-heartedly.

"Tomorrow will be lovely." She bent to kiss his lips. "Thank you for being so reasonable. You have greatly delighted the three women who reside at Pemberley."

⁂

"May I have wace and rittons?" Alice asked as the coach slowed on the outskirts of a small town, which surely must be Matlock.

"Lace and ribbons," Mary corrected.

"Lace and ribbons," Alice repeated, before adding, "And yellow? And blue?"

Elizabeth smiled upon the child. "Yellow is more a color for summer, and if we choose blue, it must be a darker shade, for your Papa and I are still in mourning for our fathers who are now in Heaven with God. So, think on dark blue or purple or even a shade of brown. However, we will say 'yes' to the lace and ribbons."

"I swear," Mary observed with a happy smile. "Sometimes I believe our Lydia has claimed a bit of Miss Alice."

"Bedia?" the child asked.

"Lydia," Elizabeth enunciated. "Miss Mary's and my youngest sister. "She also lives in Heaven."

Mary cleared her throat and lifted her brows as if to say, "Perhaps not in Heaven."

"Everyone live in Heaven?" Alice asked.

Her husband chuckled but made no effort to assist Elizabeth in explaining Heaven to a child. "Heaven is a wonderful place," Elizabeth assured. "It is where the angels live."

"Can I be an angel?" the child asked in sincere tones.

This time Mr. Darcy cleared his throat to disguise the laugh rushing to his lips. He still made no effort to explain the unexplainable to his daughter. "Angels are excessively good," she warned. "My father always declared every angel God created was a masterpiece—each one possessing his or her own special intelligence and his or her own special beauty."

"Nicely done, Mrs. Darcy," her husband said with a nod of approval as the coach rolled to a halt. He sucked in a steadying breath. "I will see you into the shop and call for you in two hours," he instructed.

"Thank you, Fitzwilliam," she said softly and caressed his cheek.

He nodded his acceptance and waited for Jasper to set down the steps. Mr. Darcy climbed down and turned to reach a hand back to her. He did the same for, first, Mary, and then Alice, while Elizabeth shook out her skirts. Taking his proffered arm, Elizabeth lifted her chin, but before they could take a step together, the door to the shop opened and a British army officer rushed forward to catch her husband up in a very masculine embrace, slapping Mr. Darcy on the back several times before stepping back to look upon Fitzwilliam.

"Darcy, you old dog! Why did you not send word you would be coming to Matlock today?" the man demanded.

However, Mr. Darcy's gaze was locked on a young lady standing in the still open doorway. Although Elizabeth had not been officially introduced to the young woman, she instinctively knew the girl's identity: Miss Georgiana Darcy.

The man glanced several times between the pair before Elizabeth took control of the situation. She curtsied to the officer. "You will pardon my husband's suddenly poor manners. I am Mrs. Darcy, Mrs. Elizabeth Darcy. This is my sister, Miss Bennet, and Mr. Darcy's daughter, Alice, and you are . . ."

The man shot another glance to her husband before he bowed properly. "Colonel Fitzwilliam, ma'am."

"Colonel," she responded, "I have heard much of you. If I understand the situation correctly, you share guardianship of Miss Darcy with her brother." Another glance to her husband told Elizabeth how much he was hurting, for Miss Darcy glared at him in obvious contempt. "Perhaps you might facilitate a conversation between the siblings, who have each had the ability to speak stolen away. Meanwhile, my sister and I and Miss Alice will be inside."

The colonel scowled at the girl. "You promised you would write to Darcy," he accused.

"I did," the girl claimed.

Elizabeth paused as she stepped around the young lady. "Three months ago," she told the colonel, "and not a response since." To the girl she said, "Your brother has known great anguish, Miss Darcy. You must tell him how it was for you and then listen to how he also suffered. If not, you both lose again and again. Time is too short for such anguish to be felt by either of you."

⁂

Darcy wished to call Elizabeth back, for he had become quite accustomed to her as an ally, but he held himself in check, as was proper for an English gentleman. His cousin said, "Provide me a moment to inform the countess of where she might find us." Before Darcy could object, Fitzwilliam disappeared inside.

"You have grown into a lovely young lady," Darcy said lamely.

"No thanks to you," she snarled.

"You are correct. I was not at Pemberley when you required my protection," he admitted. "Yet, you were rarely from my thoughts."

"Would you have returned if you were not to inherit?" she accused. "George said you only wanted the money."

Before Darcy could respond, his cousin reappeared. "George?" The colonel scowled. "You mean George Wickham? You were foolish enough to listen to that rascal?"

"To who else was I to listen?" his sister said through the tears forming in her eyes. "You were with Wellington." She gestured with a wide sweep of her arm in the colonel's direction. "And you—" She pointed an accusing finger at Darcy. "You found that tart so appealing you were willing to accept our father's banishment."

The colonel claimed Georgiana's hand and placed it on his arm. "This is not the proper location for this conversation. Let us claim the private room at Sullivan's."

Darcy shot a longing look to the shadow of his wife inside the shop before he followed his cousin and Georgiana. Darcy should have known Wickham would insinuate himself into his sister's life. Yet, he had hoped their father would not have permitted the dastard near Georgiana.

Once they were settled at the inn, Fitzwilliam began, "I am grieved you think both your brother and I deserted you. Yet, Georgie, you cannot seriously believe either of us would choose to leave you alone in a house with George Wickham. The man epitomizes all I despise in the world. Moreover, you know as well as anyone, when Darcy left, Wickham was set to marry the Hartis girl. He was away from Pemberley, some thirty miles removed. Supposedly, he was only asked by Mr. Chapman to arrange a meeting between Chapman and your father. Neither of us would have knowledge of the weasel crawling back into Lambton to wreak havoc on the Darcy family."

"All I know is, for the last five years, Mr. Wickham was the only one who cared how I felt about my brother's abandonment. You did not write even one letter to me upon which I could hang my hopes," she accused.

"I did write to our father," Darcy assured. "I begged him to permit my return, especially after—" he stopped himself from uttering his most closely-guarded secret. "After the diamond mine I purchased showed a profit, I thought our father would permit me to return once I knew some success; yet, the first I heard of him was when I received Matlock's letter informing me of George Darcy's passing and ordering me home. I assumed, right or wrong, if our father would not respond to me, he would never permit his daughter to write to the unworthy."

"You purchased a diamond mine?" Fitzwilliam questioned. "I never knew of your endeavors. No one spoke of your life in India."

"In a region near Panna, in the central state of Madhya Pradesh, which was a princely state of British India. More central than along the coast," Darcy explained. "I not only purchased the mine, I worked it alongside a few dozen men I employed. Every day. All day. I dug in the hard soil so far under the ground we could not see the light of day. It was as if I was in my grave. Often, I wished I was. I did without so I would one day know success and my father would permit my return."

"And you say your father knew of your life in the East?" the colonel asked. Darcy realized Fitzwilliam wanted to bring Georgiana to a better understanding, but Darcy was not certain he wished to revisit these memories.

"I wrote to him with some regularity, at least such was true for the first few years. I told my father of Alice's birth, of the men who had invested in the mine. Of how long my days were, and how I hoped he could find some pride in my success. I heard not a word nor were any of my letters returned," Darcy explained more to his cousin than to his sister. It would likely be up to Fitzwilliam to convince the Matlocks and Georgiana of the truth of Darcy's confession, though Darcy was well aware Lord Matlock had kept some tabs on him, for several of the British officers in India would say they were to send word of Darcy's life back to their family to share with his lordship.

"Perhaps your father never received your letters," Fitzwilliam conjectured.

"Mr. Bennet, Elizabeth's father never failed to receive my letters," Darcy argued. "I could perhaps believe one in three were misdirected, but not all of them. At the beginning of the fourth year of my absence from England, I abandoned my hopes of a reconciliation and simply accepted the fact I was a disappointment to my father. I was as good as dead to him."

"Why would you write to Mr. Bennet?" the colonel asked, ignoring what Darcy had just shared. It was the way with Fitzwilliam to have all the facts before placing the blocks in a row to find a solution. "I have never heard you speak of him. I assume the man is related to your wife."

"Her father." Darcy smiled easily. "I did not have the man's acquaintance until the night before Ruth Chapman and I sailed for India. I was deep in my cups, debating on whether to jump overboard when we set sail the following morning. Ruth had claimed the room I had secured for her. Dejected, I lifted my cup to finish off the last of the ale inside when a hand pushed my arm down. Naturally, I protested, but Mr. Bennet was not to be swayed. He ordered strong coffee and a thick stew and sat beside me. With a hand upon my shoulder, he said, 'I have never heard a drunk quote Shakespeare as you do. You must permit me to offer you a hand. Whatever bothers you, I am your man,' he declared. We sat together all night, discussing literature, but mostly I told him of my father's edict and my despair at being so soundly disowned.

"Mr. Bennet presented me another hundred pounds and begged me to write to him regularly, for he considered me a man worth knowing. It was a statement I cherished; therefore, I did write, and he would, without fail, always write back. Even with the distance, we shared six to eight letters per year. Sometimes they overlapped by a matter of weeks. He spoke of his life in Hertfordshire, of his estate, of his daughters, of the books he read, and even some gossip regarding people I did not know, but surely wished to claim their acquaintance and be among them, even when they were foolishly engaged. Mr. Bennet meant to remind me for what I struggled."

The colonel swallowed hard. "Those are the best type of letters to receive when a man is away from his home and all he loves. Every soldier I have ever known lives for those moments."

Darcy nodded their shared acceptance of what mattered in the world. "When I told Mr. Bennet of the possibility of purchasing the mine, he insisted on finding a means to assist me. As I had heard nothing from my father, I accepted the man's offer. Bennet wrote of the endeavor to two of his acquaintances in Cambridgeshire, and those men contacted their sons with the East India Company. Those officers also invested in the mine. Each took fifteen percent of the profits for their thousand pounds. With Mr. Bennet's persuasion, I was presented fifty-five percent. After all, I was doing the actual labor. Success or failure rested, quite literally, on my shoulders."

"You?" his sister accused with a mixture of disbelief and horror.

"Me, Georgiana," Darcy insisted. "I was in the pit with the proverbial unwashed. Every day. Some days ten- to twelve-hours' shifts. When I received Matlock's summons home, I sold the mine. Each of my partners received ten thousand pounds for their one-thousand-pound investment. I received eight and thirty thousand."

And what of Miss Chapman?" Georgiana asked with an obvious snarl of disapproval."

"She abandoned me and the child." He would say no more of Ruth. His secrets would go to the grave with him, if Darcy had his say in the matter.

"And now you are married to Mr. Bennet's daughter?" Georgiana asked with a slight lift of her brows.

"We are. Mr. Bennet has passed, and it only felt proper to offer my hand to the lady. Her father always said a woman of Elizabeth Bennet's nature would set my feet on the right path, which she has. She has won over the servants with her dedication to the estate. My tenants praise her goodness, and the villagers find her approachable, while they still provide her with the necessary deference. I am quite satisfied with my choice."

"Do you not find it a considerable coincidence Mr. Bennet touted his daughter as an appropriate match for a rich man?" she questioned.

"No more so than did every society mama before my banishment," he countered. "The difference is I was no longer a rich man when Mr. Bennet suggested his daughter as a good mate for me. I was poor. Dust poor. Moreover, Mr. Bennet knew all my foibles and still thought his Elizabeth would be a good match for me. With our marriage, my dear wife also inherited my cloudy reputation, but she still has stood by me in an exemplary manner."

When neither the colonel nor Georgiana commented, Darcy added, "Here is something of which you are not likely to be aware, for I did not know of it until recently, miraculously, after father took to his bed and Matlock had sent him away, George Wickham left Derbyshire for Hertfordshire. Naturally, some may claim his doing so was the 'coincidence' you sought earlier, Georgiana, but I would beg to differ, for, you see, both Mrs. Reynolds and Mr. Nathan have reported seeing a half-dozen or more letters addressed in my hand to my father. Yet, you claim, Georgiana, none arrived from me.

"Ironically, Mr. Wickham ended up in the Meryton militia, a unit made up of men from Yorkshire and Derbyshire. At Captain Denny's invitation. You recall Mr. Denny, do you not, Colonel? Wickham purchased a lieutenancy in the Meryton militia. Meryton. The village less than a mile from the Bennet estate of Longbourn, and the first lady he made to court was none other than my Elizabeth."

"How in blazes did Wickham manage to purchase a lieutenancy? The dastard rarely has even two coins to rub together," Fitzwilliam declared.

"According to his account books, there is money missing from father's personal safe in his quarters," Darcy confided. "We both know, for a man to become a lieutenant in the militia, he would be required to hold land worth fifty pounds per year."

"He might have gotten in thanks to your father paying for his education," the colonel said in disgust. "Some militia units have lowered their standards, otherwise, they can find no junior officers. The Lord Lieutenant of the shire may have permitted Wickham in with Captain Denny's recommendation."

"You have no proof of your assertions," Georgiana declared.

"And neither do you of Mr. Wickham's innocence," the colonel reprimanded.

Darcy meant to finish his tale and be done with his explanations. "Assuming Mr. Wickham read my last letter, he would have known something of my efforts to turn the mine to a profit and the blessing of Mr. Bennet's essential investment. Likely, my old school chum thought Mr. Bennet quite wealthy, when, in reality, the man was a simple country squire attempting to earn enough to provide each of his daughters a proper dowry.

"I do not believe anything about Mr. Wickham's choice of Hertfordshire, and, specifically, of Meryton was left to chance. Neither do I believe Wickham's charms were turned upon Elizabeth by pure happenstance. He knew Mr. Bennet's great hope was that his second daughter and I would strike up a match. If Wickham wished only to pursue one of the Bennet sisters, Miss Jane Bennet, a woman of great beauty and pleasing disposition would have been more to his taste. Wickham has always preferred his women fair of head." Darcy eyed his sister with suspicion, but did not speak his fears aloud. "Gratefully," he continued, "neither could Mr. Wickham ignore one Miss Emily King, a girl who had inherited ten thousand pounds. You see, he had been in Meryton long enough to realize Mr. Bennet's five thousand pounds would be split five ways, for Bennet had five daughters. Miss King's ten thousand would surely tempt Mr. Wickham more than Elizabeth's one thousand. I have seen him lose nearly that much on a simple turn of a card."

Fitzwilliam added, "At university, Wickham always sought out first one and then another lady with a large dowry."

Darcy nodded his agreement, but continued his tale. "By the time Miss King's uncle removed his niece from the area, Elizabeth, thankfully, had listened to her father's advice. Therefore, Wickham turned his efforts on Mr. Bennet's youngest—a girl of seventeen, and, although supposedly quite pretty, one of little sense. According to Elizabeth, Miss Lydia Bennet was set on marrying a Redcoat.

"Last spring, the militia traveled to Brighton for training, and Miss Lydia dishonestly secured an invitation from the militia colonel's young wife to be the woman's guest at Brighton. The girl returned to Hertfordshire with a ruined reputation, but a willing bridegroom, for word had leaked out Mr. Bennet had earned a small fortune thanks to the mine. Unfortunately, the soldiers brought back more than high hopes from Brighton. You see, the soldiers spent an evening of drinks and cards and womanizing with a group of Portuguese sailors. Thanks to their foreign acquaintances, those young Englishmen brought back some sort of pox to Meryton. Elizabeth and her sister Mary lost their mother and their two youngest sisters. Five dozen more lost their lives in Hertfordshire, Brighton, and along the docks of London."

"And Mr. Wickham?" Georgiana asked in concern, signaling how deeply involved with the man his sister likely had been.

"He was to marry Miss Lydia Bennet, but before the ceremony could occur, the girl passed from the disease he and she assisted in carrying back to the community. I do not know how, but Mr. Wickham survived, although, it is my understanding one side of his face is badly scarred. You might warn the countess, Fitzwilliam, for Wickham is back in Derbyshire. He recently approached Elizabeth in Lambton, but I have found no word of his whereabouts since."

"Why would Lady Matlock have a care?" Georgiana demanded.

Fitzwilliam leaned forward to place emphasis on his response. "Because her ladyship's niece has an inflated opinion of a scoundrel. Heaven help you if the earl hears even the whisper of your communicating with Mr. Wickham. You could easily find yourself in a nunnery."

Darcy hid the smile rushing to his lips. "I will finish my tale and then leave you to your own devices. I am certain Alice has asked a thousand questions by now." He paused to gather his thoughts. "Mr. Wickham had negotiated a marriage settlement with Mr. Bennet, but as Miss Lydia passed before the banns could be read for the last time, nothing was paid to Wickham." Darcy would not tell either of them of the letter supposedly reporting the mine had been a failure. At first, he had thought Wickham had sent it, but the lieutenant would not have wished Mr. Bennet to think the mine unproductive: Wickham wanted Miss Lydia's share of Bennet's fortune, which would have been a respectable three thousand and a connection to Mr. Bingley's fortune. Darcy still had no idea who the culprit could be, but he meant to learn the person's identity and make them pay dearly for their stratagems.

He stood then. "I will leave you to your thoughts. Fitzwilliam you are always welcome in my home. Georgiana, as Pemberley is also your home, the door is forever open to your return." Darcy bowed, turned smartly, and exited the common room. He walked quickly, for he desperately required a smile from his wife. He was no longer certain his relationship with Georgiana could be repaired, and he desperately required Elizabeth's ability to summarize what should be done if such was so. In truth, he had never acted in the wrong, and, quite frankly, Darcy was exhausted from paying the piper for sins not his own.

Chapter Eleven

Elizabeth gave one last look at her husband's stiff spine as he walked away from the shop, following the colonel and Miss Darcy. She knew regret at having initiated this meeting today, though, in reality, the Darcy siblings' encounter was overdue, but, perhaps not with such a public accusation on Miss Darcy's lips.

"Ma'am, may I be of assistance?" a woman asked from somewhere behind Elizabeth.

She swallowed her worry, placed a smile on her lips, and turned to respond. "Yes, thank you for your ready welcome. I am Mrs. Darcy." She handed the woman one of her husband's cards. "My husband and I are newly joined, and I am still waiting for the majority of my gowns and other personal items to be sent forward. Even so, what my sister and I wore in Hertfordshire is not appropriate for Derbyshire's colder temperatures." She added an extra smile, "Yet, I must warn you, both Mr. Darcy and I are still in mourning for our fathers, and decorum requires we dress appropriately."

"I understand, Mrs. Darcy," the woman said with a nervous glance to the back of the store. "What did you have in mind?"

"My most pressing need is an evening dress, and, afterwards, two or three day dresses. My sister is to marry in late January, and I would see her looking her best. Moreover, I mean to present her a number of new day dresses and proper night clothes. She will be the vicar's wife and must present herself properly. Finally, the child will also require several dresses. Until recently, she has lived outside of England and requires a more appropriate wardrobe for both the weather and her new station."

"With mace and bittons, Lizbet," the child said.

"Thank you for the reminder, Alice." Elizabeth caressed the child's cheek. "Miss Alice would like lace and ribbons on her new attire."

The shop mistress nodded her understanding. "I fully comprehend, ma'am. Which of you should be fitted first?"

"See to Mrs. Darcy's sister and the child first, Mrs. Woodfine," a very regal voice instructed. "Mrs. Darcy and I will look at the samples of cloth you have available."

"Yes, your ladyship." The shop mistress motioned Mary and the child to follow her, leaving Elizabeth alone with a very imposing-looking woman. Elizabeth made herself slowly breathe through the intimidation threatening to choke her.

"Let us retire to the room at the back of the shop where Mrs. Woodfine keeps the stacks of cloth. She has a beautiful green satin which I believe would look spectacular on you. I had hoped it might do well for Miss Darcy, but it is too dark for my niece's coloring," the Countess of Matlock said with authority.

Elizabeth wished she could see the humor in this awkward situation, but, since her first encounter with Mr. Darcy, it had been one thing after another. Without comment, she followed Darcy's aunt into the room and waited. "Would you mind closing the door, Mrs. Darcy?"

"I would, your ladyship," Elizabeth said in the calmest tones she could muster. "Miss Alice becomes easily upset when she cannot find either her father or me, and, as Mr. Darcy is with his sister and your son, I prefer to examine the cloth with the door open."

Surprisingly, instead of knowing umbrage, the countess laughed. "You will do well for Darcy. The boy requires someone to amend his ways. My nephew is as stubborn as his father." She lowered her voice. "I assume the child is the one belonging to Miss Chapman."

Elizabeth realized she had never asked of Ruth's surname. "Ruth's child," she responded, suddenly feeling very exposed. "Mr. Darcy only speaks of Alice as being his."

"He would," her ladyship observed. "And how did Fitzwilliam come to seek your hand in marriage?"

"Mr. Darcy and my father developed a friendship. They corresponded often while Mr. Darcy was away."

"And your father?" Lady Matlock asked.

"A country gentleman from Hertfordshire. Neither of my parents are alive. We lost three of our family because of a pox carried to the shire though the local militia. Mary and I are all of which remains of our family."

"I see," the countess remarked. "We will learn more of each other soon. Come. Let us look at the cloth I mentioned."

"I would enjoy your guidance, your ladyship. Mr. Darcy and I hope to join Sir Lawrence and Lady Rowan at their upcoming entertainment, and I would not wish to embarrass my husband."

"I am assured Darcy would never think poorly of you. Although you are not quite the type he would customarily pursue, I can easily see the reason for his interest in you. I imagine you are the type who can also quote poetry and Shakespeare."

Elizabeth fingered the green satin. It was truly lovely. "I am quite a reader," she confessed, as she moved on to a bronze wool, which she thought would be toasty warm for the Derbyshire winters. "My father was a great reader also." She attempted to sound casual when she asked, "What type of woman did my husband pursue?"

The countess smiled. "Piqued your interest, did I?"

Rather than to deny the obvious, Elizabeth admitted, "I am the curious type."

"Trust me, Darcy was never one to chase after a light-skirt. As he was to inherit Pemberley, it was more of his staying two steps ahead of each society mama looking for a rich husband for her daughter.

Occasionally, he would slow his step, especially if the woman was tall and thin and blonde."

"In that case," Elizabeth said in disappointment. "Mr. Darcy should have married my eldest sister, Jane. I have the look of my paternal grandmother. She was formed much in alignment with her Scottish roots."

"Did Jane Bennet succumb to the pox also?"

"No. To childbirth. She was married to Mr. Charles Bingley, one of Mr. Darcy's acquaintances from their days together at Cambridge, though Mr. Bingley is several years younger than my husband." She paused to look at the royal blue cloth. "I think this will look well on the child."

"It was a color her mother often wore," the countess remarked.

A memory Elizabeth would prefer not to revisit rushed forward. The woman, tall and blonde. Her royal blue, hooded cloak disguising the look of her, as Mr. Darcy hustled her towards the back of the church. Elizabeth still did not know the woman's identity. Mr. Darcy had not offered her an explanation beyond he did not wish the lady to see Alice. For a few elongated seconds, Elizabeth could not breathe. Before she could form a coherent thought, Alice rushed into the room.

"Lizbet," the child called as she scampered across the room to stand before Elizabeth. "They beasured me."

"Measured," she instinctively corrected.

"M-measured," the child repeated.

With no more comment, Elizabeth instructed, "Then come tell me what you think of this blue."

The child darted around the end of the table to stand before the cloth. "It is bewti . . ." but she corrected herself, saying the word "Beautiful" slowly to enunciated each syllable. Alice fingered the cloth gingerly.

"What of the red?" Lady Matlock suggested.

Alice answered with confidence. "Lizbet say we must wear darker colors cause her papa and my papa's papa live in Heaven."

The countess hid her smile. "Forgive me. I should have thought of that." She reached her hand to the child. "Let us look for more cloth for you."

Alice looked to Elizabeth for permission. "This lady is your father's aunt. It would be acceptable to hold her hand. Her name is Lady Matlock."

"Bady . . ." Again, Alice corrected herself. "Lady Lock."

"Close enough," her ladyship said. "You know I have two sons. I have never purchased things for a little girl. This will be delightful."

Elizabeth returned to the green and bronze cloth. "A third color," she mused. She was considering the deep purple when Mary appeared at her side.

"So lovely," her sister said in a wistful manner, one Mary rarely used, for Elizabeth knew her sister feared disappointment as much as they all did, if not more.

"Then you should have it," Elizabeth declared. "For your wedding dress. White lace and sash. Mr. Ericks will be offering a series of prayers for the brilliance of his choice of brides."

"I would like for him to look at me as Mr. Darcy looks at you in those quiet moments when you are singing or when you are assisting Alice." Mary lowered her voice. "I know you married Mr. Darcy to save both of us, but I pray you never regret your choice."

"Once all this madness with his sister is settled, I believe we can learn affection for each other," Elizabeth assured, attempting to convince herself as well as Mary.

Her sister reached for another cloth, one which was a cross between a violet and a glossy grey. "This for a day dress."

"It would heighten the pale blue of your eyes."

"Mrs. Darcy, if you would join us so we might take your measurements?"

Elizabeth nodded to the shop mistress. "I wish the bronze and the darker green. Let me know if you see another appropriate color. Lady Matlock is showing Alice the lace and the ribbons."

Mary chuckled. "I will also have a look at the fashion plates."

"I shan't be long," Elizabeth assured.

※

Darcy slowed his pace as he approached the dress shop. He stepped to the side to consider his confrontation with Georgiana. He had attempted to warn his father of the dangers of trusting George Wickham, but Darcy's parent was certain all Mr. Wickham required was a steady hand on his shoulder.

Even Sheffield had risked his position to inform George Darcy something of Wickham's behavior at Cambridge. "I explained to the late Mr. Darcy of the vicious propensities and the want of principle Mr. Wickham exhibited while at university, but your father always held the highest opinion of his godson, saying young men must sow their seeds. I did not dare to remind him he had sent you away from Pemberley based on another claiming you had 'sown' your seeds also. Yet, your father's attachment to Mr. Wickham was to the last so very steady."

"Obviously, I was to be held to a higher standard than Wickham. My father believed I would lie with the likes of Ruth Chapman," Darcy could not hide the hiss of displeasure rushing to his lips as he pronounced the woman's name. "Such shows how little of my nature my father really knew. He thought me of the same nature as was he at my age."

"You did have a fascination for the lady when you were young," the valet reminded him. "That is until you realized how shallow a woman could be. Can you imagine attempting to read Shakespeare's 'Taming of the Shrew' with Miss Chapman as you did with Mrs. Darcy last week? I should not confide this, but all the servants gathered in the passageway to listen. You two were truly Petruchio and Katarina. I have rarely heard the play done with such skill. From what I could see through the partially opened door, neither of you actually had to look at the books you held."

"My wife was so full of life," Darcy whispered as he prepared to open the shop's door. "*As to Ruth Chapman,*" he thought, "*she would not be able to pronounce half the words on the pages.*"

"Papa!" He stepped inside the door to be greeted by an exceedingly excited Alice, who rushed into his arms. "Lady Lock bought me a tea-r-r-r."

"A tiara?" he asked.

Alice bobbed her head several times in quick succession in the affirmative.

He crossed to where his aunt stood smiling widely and bussed the cheek she offered with a quick kiss. "Do you not think a tiara is a bit much, Countess?" he questioned in mild disapproval.

"I have never had anyone for whom I might purchase a tiara," she argued. "Georgiana already had the ones from Lady Anne, and my sons have both avoided marriage as if it were the plague," the countess made her excuses.

"I know from experience there is no use in complaining when you have made up your mind." He set his daughter on her feet. "Where is Mrs. Darcy?"

"Finishing her measurements," his aunt confided. "On first acquaintance, I was very impressed, Darcy."

"Thank you, Aunt," he said dutifully.

"Which I translate to mean you are grateful for my approval while remaining hesitant," her ladyship summarized.

"Mr. Darcy trusts few," his wife announced.

He was glad to look upon her sweet features. "I trust you, Mrs. Darcy," he said with a lift of his brows in challenge.

"And I am blessed for it," Elizabeth said, diffusing any arguments he might offer.

"Elizabeth, look at this plate," Mary called. "You would be exquisite in such a gown."

His wife settled in beside her sister. "I have never worn anything so daring," Elizabeth said with a hint of longing.

Lady Matlock looked to the drawing. "You are a married woman. No more of those virginal white dresses we force upon young ladies in the shires and London ballrooms. The green we chose earlier with a bit of beading at the neckline and a satin sash would be perfect. Mrs. Woodfine, the greenish-blue beads you have under the counter with a dark blue sash, do you not think?"

"You always have an excellent eye, your ladyship," the shop mistress declared while motioning one of her assistants to fetch the cloth as Mrs. Woodfine drew the beading from beneath the glass to place them upon the fabric.

Darcy could view the desire on his wife's expression. "You would be magnificent in it," he whispered in her ear. She looked up to him, her eyes searching for the truth of his words. "Order the dress, Elizabeth." Tears misted her eyes, and, for a moment, Darcy thought she might go on her toes and kiss him before them all, but she caught herself at the last second. He half wished she followed her impulse. Darcy would not have objected to a show of her affection.

Rather, she said, "Thank you, Fitzwilliam." Turning her attentions to the fashion plates, she asked, "What of this one for your wedding, Mary?"

"Would it shock Mr. Ericks for his wife to appear in such a dress?" Mary asked with the same type of longing Elizabeth had displayed moments earlier.

"Mr. Ericks is still a man," he told her. "He is a vicar, not a friar."

Mary blushed thoroughly, but, unlike her sister, she rose up and presented him a quick hug. "You always know what to say. Thank you, sir." She rushed off to claim the fabric she wanted for the dress, returning moments later with two folded over cloths. "For the wedding," she announced for the purple, "and a day dress for the grey. I shall be satisfied with those two."

Before the remainder of the decisions could be made, Fitzwilliam returned with Georgiana. When his sister's gaze fell on Alice, dismay returned to her expression. Evidently, the countess also noted Georgiana's animosity, for she said, "We must depart." She bent to speak to Alice. "I have enjoyed our time together. Hopefully, your father will bring you to visit with me soon." She instructed Mrs. Woodfine, "Place the tiara, the lace, the gloves and scarf, as well as the muff for the child on my account."

"Yes, my lady."

As an obvious show of solidarity, the countess hugged both Elizabeth and Mary. "I hope to see you both at Matlock Manor soon."

"Farewell, my lady. Thank you for your kind advice and keen eye for color. I am honored," Elizabeth said.

His aunt kissed Darcy's cheek. "As I said earlier, you chose well, Darcy. Count yourself fortunate."

"I do so every day, my lady."

Without a farewell from his sister, Georgiana followed Lady Matlock from the shop. "I will have her seeing reason soon," the colonel announced. "You will hear from me. Count on it." A bow to all had Darcy's cousin following his mother to the waiting coach.

When they returned to Pemberley, the gardeners had brought in the greenery and nearly every servant was busy stringing together boughs of freshly cut pine and spruce and fir limbs to hang upon the staircase, as well as adding some to the mantels and table displays.

"Look, Lizbet!" the child said as she jumped up and down in happiness. "Smells wonderful."

"Go and have your maid change your clothes into something more serviceable," Elizabeth instructed, "and then you may assist us in adding ribbons and bows."

Mary caught Alice's hand. "I will assist you to change, but you must wait until both Elizabeth and I can join you. We would not wish you to prick your finger on a holly branch or some other sharp branch." To Elizabeth, her sister said, "Stop by my room when you, too, are prepared to come back down."

"Will you stay and assist us?" she had asked her husband. Mr. Darcy kept up his end of the conversation on their return, but Elizabeth knew him still quite distracted.

"If you hold no objections, I believe I will change and ride over to where the men were supposed to finish the barn today. I want it up by Christmas, and the Holy Day is a mere four days removed."

Elizabeth wished to argue with him, but she knew he would continue his protest until he had his way. "Do not be too long. It is coming up on dusk, and I would not wish to have harm come to you."

"I will be well, Elizabeth, but I am grateful for your concern," he had said before taking the stairs two at a time to reach his quarters quicker.

"Is something amiss?" Mrs. Reynolds asked.

"Mr. Darcy had an encounter with his sister today, and it did not go as well as he would like," Elizabeth shared. "You might warn the others to provide him a wide berth until he can process all which was said between them."

"As you say, mistress," the housekeeper looked after her young master.

"I shall return momentarily," she assured the housekeeper.

"We can . . ." Mrs. Reynolds began her protest.

Elizabeth held her hand up to stop the woman's objections. "It is not of the nature of either my sister or me to place all the work on the staff. Some of my favorite memories of Christmas and Twelfth Night involved sitting about with my sisters, drinking hot cider, and weaving evergreen branches together. I would like to bring some of my Bennet memories to Pemberley to share with Alice and, perhaps, with my and Mr. Darcy's children. Therefore, Miss Bennet, Alice, and I shall be joining the maids. I wish to present Miss Alice with wonderful memories of her first Christmas in England. The child has only viewed an English Christmas in some drawings. This will be another 'first step' for her—a chance to build memories to carry with her for each day of her life.

"Moreover, Miss Bennet wishes to create several displays for the Lambton church. My friends and sisters always designed boughs and such to display in Mr. Williamson's church in Hertfordshire. Mrs. Williamson taught us how to embellish her husband's sanctuary with tasteful, but meaningful, expressions of the Holy Days. Mary plans to do the same for Mr. Ericks, by leading through example."

Mrs. Reynolds said, "Miss Bennet is one of the kindest creatures on God's earth. She will make Mr. Ericks a fine wife. Make him a better man and a better vicar for all in Lambton. I have heard of her efforts with the church charities. She has made a strong impression on the community. Your sister, Mrs. Darcy, is not afraid to embrace her role in Mr. Ericks's life. She will be a model of all she learned in the Bennet household. You must be very proud of her."

Elizabeth knew none of the Bennets, including her, had ever provided Mary the credit her sister deserved, but Elizabeth meant to celebrate the fact Mary had carved her own path to happiness. Being a religious man's wife and being of service to her community and her beliefs would make Mary Bennet Ericks the best of Thomas and Frances Bennet's children. The very best of their family. Better than her, no matter how much money Mr. Darcy had: Unlike Mary and Ericks, hers and Mr. Darcy's was not a love match, and both of them would suffer for it.

"I initially worried for the difference in their ages, considered it might be too wide for them to find anything in common. However, I should have known Mary would outshine even the most beautiful woman paraded before the vicar. Ericks is a far-sighted man and had the good sense to look to Mary's soul and her most excellent heart, not the fact her vision requires spectacles to read. I was just considering how she was the best of the Bennet family and none of us appreciated her appropriately. I have promised God never to do so again."

"Bless ye and the master, Mrs. Darcy," Mrs. Whitson said as Mrs. Reynolds, Jasper, and several of the gardeners, assisted the woman with the basket of food stuffs and a bag of corn meal being presented to each of Mr. Darcy's cottagers.

Elizabeth privately steamed in anger, but she placed a smile on her lips as the next tenant family approached. Although this activity should have been conducted by them as a couple, Mr. Darcy had again made his excuses and departed early this morning, leaving Elizabeth to oversee the presentation of the "boxes," baskets, in reality, to acknowledge St. Stephen's Day. Since their return from Matlock, her husband had become more and more withdrawn, even when Alice begged him to allow her to show him the new music she had learned. In truth, Elizabeth did not know what to do, and she was to the point of no longer caring. Yes, he had suffered at the late George Darcy's hands, but it was not fair of the current Mr. Darcy to make the rest of the household suffer still. Mary highly respected him. Alice adored him, and she . . . Well, Elizabeth was afraid she had presented the gentleman her heart, although for what purpose, she had no idea. Mr. Darcy did not seem to care about anything other than the blow of disrespect his father had practiced against him.

"You are most welcome, Mrs. Whitson," she told the woman. "I placed a jar of liniment in your basket for your mother's rheumatism."

"Ye be a blessin', ma'am. The master find heself a jewel in you, mistress." The woman curtsied and walked away.

Mrs. Reynolds said under her breath, "If I may say so, Mrs. Darcy, Mrs. Whitson's estimation is correct: You have proved yourself time and time again since your arrival at Pemberley."

Elizabeth swallowed the words of hurt rushing to her lips. Instead, she turned to the tug on her skirt and Alice.

"I cold, Lizbet: May I have some tea?" The child rubbed her eyes in a sleepy manner. At least Alice had thought to stand beside her in this endeavor.

"You were up very late yesterday, were you not, sweetheart? Christmas was a fun day with all your new toys." She caressed the child's head. Alice wore the cap and mittens Elizabeth had knitted for the girl. Her needlework and embroidery was never of the quality of Jane's or Mary's, but, thankfully, her Aunt Gardiner had taught Elizabeth how to knit simple squares, which, in the beginning, she sewed together to create scarfs and small lap rugs. Now, she could create a variety of items.

In fact, for Christmas, she had presented Mary and Mr. Darcy both with an intricately-designed patterned scarf, while she had given Alice the round hat and matching mittens. Mary and the child had appeared most grateful for Elizabeth's thoughtfulness, but she had not been able to read Mr. Darcy's true reaction. She imagined he considered the act a utilitarian activity for those without enough money to purchase expensive items. He would likely look upon her efforts with society's prejudices, rather than to realize the activity not only served a necessary household function, but also provided Elizabeth a sense of solace and satisfaction after a very hectic day. He had appeared to have caressed it with his fingertips, but the moment passed quickly and he set it aside.

Her gift must have felt quite rustic to him, for he had presented her with a garnet pin to wear upon her gowns—gowns which she did not own nor would be able to wear to places they would never see together.

"Seepy," the child said, leaning heavily against Elizabeth's leg.

Elizabeth looked to the line of tenants still waiting their turns. "Can you wait a few more minutes or permit one of the maids to take you upstairs?"

"They no know the song," the child whined. "Only you and Mary."

Mary was in the village assisting Mr. Ericks with the village children.

"It will be well," Mrs. Reynolds assured. "I can manage."

"I do not like leaving without greeting each family personally," Elizabeth insisted.

"Then permit Jasper to carry the child to her quarters, while you walk the length of the line to make your excuses and to acknowledge Mr. Darcy's tenants. They will be satisfied you thought enough of them to speak your farewells. More importantly, they will admire your care of the child. Each of them would leave the line to tend their own children."

Elizabeth nodded her agreement. She bent to speak to Alice. "Permit Jasper to carry you to your quarters. I will follow in a moment. I must speak to your father's cottagers first."

The child's countenance screwed up in displeasure, but she wrapped her arms about Jasper's neck so he could carry her inside without more complaints.

Elizabeth stepped from the table and extended a hand to Mr. Shane. "I fear I have been called away to attend little Miss Darcy, but I wanted to thank each of you for your loyalty to my husband and the estate."

She said something similar to each of the remaining families in line. She shook hands, caressed the cheeks of children, presenting each with a small bag of sugar balls, and spoke her regrets for leaving before they were properly acknowledged. They all told her how honored they were and how the child should come first. Yet, in Elizabeth's opinion, the tenants were Mr. Darcy's responsibility, as was the child. She adored Alice and did not regret her promise to Mr. Darcy to tend to Alice, and she had graciously accepted each of the tenant families' acquaintance with pleasure; yet, Elizabeth could not quite shake the idea she and Mr. Darcy had struck a bargain; however, the terms of the agreement had changed.

When her husband arrived in the supper room, he bent to kiss Elizabeth's cheek. "I apologize, my dear. I did not expect to be so long away from the estate today." He had never explained the necessity of his doing so nor anything of his "business" for the day, which had harmed Elizabeth more than he would ever know. "Mrs. Reynolds and Mr. Nathan say your actions reminded them of my mother, but with your own unique touches."

Elizabeth accepted his affirmation, or rather the servants' affirmation of her conduct as Pemberley's mistress; yet, the fact her husband thought something else was more important than his family and the estate on this day displayed something of a fatal flaw. "I am pleased I met your mother's legacy. I know such was your wish when we married, although I imagine Mrs. Reynolds or her eventual successor will serve the estate as well as I."

"Nonsense," her husband announced. "I encountered Mr. Shane in the village on my return to the estate. He described how you shook his hand and apologized for being called away to tend Alice. He said he knew of no other great house's mistress who would extend her hand to shake that of a man who rarely was without dirt under his nails."

*

Elizabeth took another look at herself in the long mirror. Instinctively, her hand came to rest on her lower abdomen. Since she, Mary, and the child had made a second call on the dressmaker for final fittings for their new clothes, she had been more cognizant of her figure.

"I apologize, Mrs. Darcy," Mrs. Woodfine said a second time. "It appears both garments are too tight about the waist and bust. I will have the seamstress make the necessary adjustments, and my son will deliver them to Pemberley. There is no need for you to make another journey into Matlock. I do not know how this could have happened."

"As long as I have the gown the week of the ninth of January, I shall be content. The Rowan ball is not until the thirteenth," she told the woman, "and the seams appear wide enough for the adjustment." Elizabeth stepped from the gown. "I do so adore the beading. Lady Matlock's suggestion was exactly what the gown required to set off the color."

It was only later when Mary was teasing her regarding Elizabeth's latest preference for chocolate instead of tea did Elizabeth even consider a new reality.

"It seems since your bout with an uneasy stomach," Mary teased, "only the chocolate pleases you. You must take longer walks, sister dear, if you are to remain the fit young lady you were back in Hertfordshire." A large grin had claimed Mary's lips.

At the time, Elizabeth had "poohed" Mary's assertions, but later, when Elizabeth was alone, she had considered her time at the estate. "I had my monthlies during that first fortnight at Pemberley," she reasoned aloud, but such was before Mr. Darcy first shared my bed." She sat heavily, for the possibilities were so shocking. "Yet, not since then. Of course, when I was younger, they were not so orderly, but such was before I was sixteen or seventeen. Since then, . . ."

Elizabeth knew more of her monthlies than most young ladies. When she had considered herself abnormal and was distraught by the idea, her father had permitted her to read two well-supported essays by leading men of science on the subject which said most women become regular by the time they were eighteen, which she did.

"But until now, I have had my monthlies with some regularity," she whispered. "But nothing for more than two months, though not yet three." The air was snatched from her lungs as she collapsed back against the chair. "Could it be? A child of my own. Will Mr. Darcy approve?" Tears misted her eyes. It was for what she had been praying. "I cannot tell him until I know for certain." Elizabeth attempted to recall what Jane had told her when her sister first discovered she was with child—information relayed by the local midwife and greatly criticized by their mother. "Four months. Must be at least four months before the midwife could speak with any certainty. I must recall the actual dates and begin to count when I might know any assurances. I will not inform Mr. Darcy until then—until a promise may be fulfilled. My children will have all Mr. Darcy has presented to Alice. They will be provided opportunities I could never have imagined for them, and, if I deliver a son, he will inherit all of this—all of Pemberley. As much as I wish for Mr. Darcy's affections, no one will be able to deny my son—my children—this legacy. You have said it before, but this time it must stick: It is enough," she announced with force as she dashed away her tears with the palms of her hands. "More than enough. You do not also require his heart. It appears he loves his estate and his sister more than you. For some reason, we lost those first hopes of knowing true affection. You must settle for what most women of society accept as natural." Yet, even as she said the words aloud, a bit of despair still lingered, and it would not release its hold on her chest, no matter how much she wished it.

Chapter Twelve

January 1815

A fortnight had passed since Mr. Darcy left her alone to tend his tenants. Something in her tone that evening must have warned him of her displeasure, for he had again been quite attentive since, though not what she would call affectionate.

As promised, her gown for the ball and Mary's wedding dress arrived on Tuesday, and, despite knowing a ball was not always what people hoped it would be, anticipation rose, nevertheless, and Elizabeth quite literally, danced with first Alice and then Mary as they went about their duties. Elizabeth had attended only one ball, the one Mr. Bingley had given when the man was courting Jane, though she and all her sisters had been present for a variety of country assemblies since they were each but fifteen.

Friday proved to be a crisp day, but a sunny one, which lightened Elizabeth's nerves, as well as presented rise to her spirits. It was a cloudless sky, and she and Alice had spent more than an hour in the gardens, again examining the ash tree and collecting more flowers and greenery for their collection. The child had become more comfortable with her surroundings, as well as more daring. It was sometimes difficult to keep up with the girl, for, inevitably, if Elizabeth turned her head to choose another pencil or to fold a piece of paper into a sleeve to secure another specimen, Alice would dart off after a different flower or leaf she spotted.

"Alice. Alice, come back!" she called as she looked up to view the girl further along the path than expected. "Jasper, please, if you can catch Miss Alice, I would be most thankful," she instructed.

"Yes, ma'am."

The footman hustled away, but before she could follow, Alice yelped. Elizabeth dropped her pencils, hiked her skirts, and took off at a run, only to be brought up short by the image of the footman as he stumbled to his feet.

"What is amiss?" she demanded. "Jasper, did you fall?" Elizabeth reached for the man. "Permit me to assist you."

"A man hit Jasper," Alice declared.

"What man?" Elizabeth asked as she examined the back of the servant's head, where Jasper pressed his hand against it.

"Dark head man," Alice said, obviously suddenly frightened. "Marks on his face. Hiding behind the tree."

Elizabeth wished to comfort the child, but, first, she must claim assurances regarding Jasper's health. "Are you well enough to walk back to the house, Jasper?"

"Think so, ma'am. Just a bit dizzy."

"Let us take it slow. Alice, come along, sweetheart." She took the child's hand. "No going so far ahead of me," she warned.

"Yes, Lizbet," the child said with a pout.

"I am not angry with you," she said aloud, "but we have rules for a reason. You probably came across someone hunting rabbits," she reasoned, although Elizabeth knew more than a bit of fear herself.

"Yes, ma'am."

Jasper stumbled, and Elizabeth reached for him. "You should sit on the bench," she instructed. "Alice and I will fetch someone to assist you."

"Just need to know my feet be under me, ma'am," the footman protested.

"No harm in taking it lightly," Elizabeth assured. "You will not pass out while I am gone, will you?" she asked studying the man's eyes, which were clearer than Elizabeth expected.

"No, ma'am."

"Come, Alice."

"The pencils?" the child protested.

"We will send someone back for them," Elizabeth insisted. "We must hurry." Yet, as she rushed away to seek assistance for Mr. Darcy's servant, Elizabeth had the feeling someone watched her exit.

※

Her husband had arrived back at the manor later than Elizabeth had wished. She had wanted to discuss what had occurred earlier and the uneasiness which still lingered, but there had been no time. She could hear Mr. Darcy barking orders to Mr. Sheffield in his quarters.

"Papa is loud," Alice observed.

"Sometimes," Elizabeth shared as if it was a secret, "he does not realize it would be acceptable if he is a few minutes late. Not always, naturally, for doing so would be rude, but it would not make either of us love him less. Would it?"

"You love Papa too?" the child asked before Elizabeth could reword her assertion.

"Come, permit me to pink your cheeks?" she said instead. Alice scrambled to stand by Elizabeth's dressing table. "Close your eyes so the powder does not become lodged in your lashes." Elizabeth bent to touch a bit of powder to the child's cheeks. "There." She put the brush back on the metal plate. "Tell me what you think."

Alice rose on her toes in an attempt to view herself in the mirror, but was not tall enough to view more than the top of her head.

"I have her, Mrs. Darcy," Hannah volunteered, before boosting Alice upward for a quick peek at the bit of powder.

"Bew... tea... full," the girl exaggerated the word to match her smile.

"You are quite pretty," Elizabeth admitted and instantly wondered on the look of her own children.

"I never see a lady dress for a ball," Alice admitted.

Elizabeth confided, "This is only my second ball, but I am certain your father has attended many."

"Permit me to fasten the sash, Mrs. Darcy," Hannah said just as a knock came at the dressing room door.

"Come," Elizabeth called and waited for her husband's reaction. She knew what she hoped to view on Mr. Darcy's expression when she saw him. Now, she said a silent prayer to know fruition.

⁂

Darcy opened the door to find his daughter dashing towards him, and, although he instinctively bent to catch Alice, his eyes did not leave the image of his wife standing in the room's center in all her glory. She wore the dark green satin. No flounces, yet the skirt was a bit fuller to permit her to move freely. The sleeves set off shoulders and reached her elbows, met by the long white gloves she wore. Again, no pushed up puffs of fabric, just the elegance of Elizabeth's form. She was simply sleek and breathtakingly beautiful. The beading caught his eyes and drew his attention to the dip of material across her breasts.

"Lizbeth beautiful, Papa," Alice declared.

"She truly is, sweetheart," he responded. "I am a most fortunate man." He kissed his daughter and set her on her feet. "I brought two sets of jewels once belonging to my mother. I had hoped one of them would complement your dress. Lady Anne Darcy would be as awed and as proud as I to have you wear one of them." He took the first box, which Mr. Sheffield held. "These are the emeralds." He opened the satin-lined box to show Elizabeth the items.

"Oh, my," his wife whispered. "They are . . . are magnificent."

Darcy handed the box to Hannah to hold. "Perhaps you would prefer the turquoise instead. These pieces are not as, how should I say this?"

"Expensive," Elizabeth suggested.

"Emeralds are difficult to mine," he explained.

"I understand perfectly," his wife assured. "Would you be ashamed if I chose the turquoise?"

"I would not," he told her in all honesty. "I have long ago abandoned such trifling ideas."

"Have you?" Elizabeth challenged.

"What if we use the emerald pin against the blue sash?" Hannah suggested. "And the turquoise tiara in your hair? We could allow the gold toggle to hang down across your locks to draw attention to the golden strands in your hair."

"What will you wear at your neck?" he asked.

"My grandmother's gold chain. It is a series of interlocking knots of gold," she declared. "Would you fetch it so Mr. Darcy may view it, Hannah?"

"Yes, ma'am."

"Are you certain such is all you wish to claim from the sets?" he asked.

"If you are not ashamed of me, I care not whether others approve of my choices," Elizabeth assured. "I only require your approbation."

Hannah returned with the gold chain and quickly fastened it about Elizabeth's neck. Next, the maid made short work of the pin on the sash. "This may be more challenging, Mrs. Darcy," the maid said of the tiara. "Please sit on the bench."

While his wife finished her preparations, Darcy asked his daughter, "Did you have a good day with Elizabeth and Mary?"

Alice frowned. "Good, 'cept when the man hit Jasper."

Darcy's brows drew together in concern. "What man?" he asked his wife.

So as not to disturb Hannah's concentration, Elizabeth did not turn, but he was able to view her expression in the mirror. "We were unable to discover him," she explained. "Your staff all assumed he was a poacher who wandered too close to the manor. He struck Jasper with some sort of 'stick,' or so Alice has explained. I did not view the incident, just the aftermath. Jasper has a knot on the back of his head. I have excused him from his duties for a few days. Mr. Lucas will serve us this evening."

Darcy still possessed a dozen or more questions, but they would wait until he and Elizabeth were alone.

"What do you think, Mrs. Darcy?" Hannah held the hand mirror so it would reflect the back of Elizabeth's head in the larger mirror for her mistress's inspection.

"You are quite brilliant, Hannah," his wife spoke in tones of true praise.

"Move your head around to make certain we have enough pins to hold the chain in place. We would not wish it to fall out and bring the tiara with it."

Elizabeth moved her head from side-to-side several times. "Feels as if it will hold."

"Then let us be about it," Darcy announced. He kissed Alice's forehead. "You will behave for Mary. Elizabeth and I will return very late, which means we will wish to sleep later tomorrow. Understand?"

"Yes, Papa. May I sleep in my tea . . . tiara?" His daughter's speech was improving daily. Darcy had noted how both Elizabeth and Mary privately and softly corrected Alice's slurring some of her words. They did not berate the child, a fact Darcy greatly appreciated.

"I will leave the choice up to Mary, depending on how well you listen to your aunt," he instructed.

AMENDING THE SHADES OF PEMBERLEY

"I'll listen. Pomise." the child insisted.

"*So much for the better pronunciations*," he thought, but made no comment. Like everything else in his life, Alice's speech had improved with Elizabeth's accepting of his hand. Now, he prayed his wife would never discover all the duplicity he had practiced, and, to a certain extent, was still practicing.

※

Within a quarter hour, they climbed into the closed carriage. Her husband made a great show of providing her a lap rug and a blanket to drape over her to keep her warm.

"How long?" she asked.

"A bit over an hour. Although it has been cold, the days have been dry. I am hoping the roads are not full of ruts and narrowed berms."

Elizabeth nodded her understanding and sunk into the warmth of the blanket. Neither the leather seats of the carriage nor the satin of her gown provided warmth in such circumstances. She tugged her cape closer about her.

The shadows inside the coach did little to hide how handsome her husband was—classically handsome. No soft lines, like the ones found on the likes of men such as Mr. Wickham, especially as Wickham was when first presented to her. Most assuredly handsome. But a softness to his skin. No lines to sculpt the former lieutenant's face into something to hold one's eyes. There was a weakness there Elizabeth had never considered before. Whereas, Fitzwilliam Darcy's lineage was on full display. Patrician nose. Sharp angles of his cheeks. At all times, the depth of his character was clearly defined by his expression and the way he held himself to perfection.

He flicked his tailcoat to the side so as to reduce the wrinkles of sitting upon it. The white of his shirt and intricately tied cravat showed even as the day had turned to darkness. In one hand, he leisurely held his gloves.

Once they were rolling away from Pemberley, he instructed, "Tell me what you omitted earlier from the tale of the intruder."

In many ways, Elizabeth wished to speak of the intruder, but, in others, she would not have minded a day where they were not compelled to address yet another interruption. Would they never know a day of peace?

With a sigh, she said, "Alice and I were in the garden looking for other leaves and winter flowers to add to the child's collection. Before I could put the pencils away and make a paper sleeve for her latest specimen . . . I must tell you, Fitzwilliam, I am pleased with the child's progress and her enthusiasm for her studies, and her, how shall I say this, for she was once so very, very timid. Anyway, before I could make the paper sleeve, Alice wandered off. I turned to pick up a pencil I had dropped, and, in those few seconds, she was from sight."

"One of a parent's most frightening emotions," her husband sympathized.

Elizabeth did not speak of her suspicions regarding carrying his child. She simply nodded her acceptance of his remark. "I sent Jasper after Alice. It is because of me, he was attacked."

"You cannot blame yourself, Elizabeth. I treasure Jasper's service to me and mine, but I would not wish you to have confronted the man. Did you see him?" he asked.

"No, he was gone by the time I reached Jasper and Alice, but two things had me seriously considering if we require some sort of protection at Pemberley." She paused briefly to hear whether her husband would make an observation. When none came, Elizabeth continued. "I could not shake the feeling someone watched us as I rushed Alice back to the house."

"Such would be natural after an encounter of the sort you describe," her husband assured.

"Yet, when I asked Alice if she saw the man, she said he had dark hair and marks on his face," Elizabeth disclosed.

"You are thinking the intruder was Mr. Wickham?" he asked, suddenly more on alert.

"I asked Mr. Nathan to set men to watch each of the entrances," she admitted.

"Wickham would not dare enter Pemberley with me in residence," Mr. Darcy said in harsh tones.

"I know you are correct, but when I sent Mrs. Reynolds to fetch the samples Alice and I took today, she returned empty-handed. Not a piece of paper. Not a crushed flower or a leaf. Not a pencil or even the satchel holding our supplies. All gone."

⁂

The rest of the journey to Derby was executed in general silence. Not anger, but each of them was lost in his or her thoughts. Elizabeth attempted to garner conversation by asking of the villages through which they traveled, and her husband dutifully supplied ready information of the history of each and the points of interests; yet, neither of them had left their earlier conversation behind until the coach turned onto a lane leading to a stately early Georgian home.

"Will you be well this evening?" she asked. "Would you prefer to turn the carriage about and return to Pemberley?"

He shook off the idea. "It is time I reclaimed the family name in a means long denied me." With the muted lights of the lanterns marking the drive, she could tell her husband was smiling, which was a thankful discovery. "And I plan to do so with the most 'beawteaful,'" he said, replicating Alice's pronunciation of the word, "woman in the shire upon my arm."

Within a few minutes, Mr. Darcy handed her down. "Watch your step," he warned. "The stones may be a bit slippery."

"You will keep me upright," Elizabeth said with assurance.

He leaned down to whisper, "I would prefer to keep you in my bed, love, but I believe dancing a waltz or two will have you thinking likewise."

"The night is still young, Mr. Darcy," she declared. "Anything is possible."

"Be still my heart," he said with a grin just as Lady Rowan appeared to greet them.

"My boy, how wonderful to see you again. It has been too long, Darcy," her ladyship said in familiar tones. "And this must be your lovely bride."

Her husband bowed reverently to the woman. "Thank you for the invitation. Mrs. Darcy and I required an evening away from our responsibilities to Pemberley. I fear, with so much to do, I occasionally have neglected my beautiful partner, which is most egregious of me. Lady Rowan, may I present my wife, Elizabeth Darcy?"

"I can guarantee Darcy cannot keep his hands off you," Lady Rowan said with confidence. "You are exactly his type."

Elizabeth would not disagree with the woman, for doing so would be bad manners, but she knew Lady Rowan had erred on both her observations. "We are both quite honored by your notice, my lady."

"Nonsense," the woman assured. "It is I who is honored, for I can claim bragging rights by entertaining the new Mrs. Darcy before you receive invitations from all our neighbors. It has been nearly twenty years since there has been a Mrs. Darcy at Pemberley," Lady Rowan reminded them.

Elizabeth thought perhaps it may have been nearly two decades since there was a Mrs. Darcy at Pemberley, but not so long since there was another Mrs. Darcy at her husband's side; yet, once again, she swallowed her comment. She expected to hear something similar often and continued protests would prove her to be petty.

"We should leave you to your hosting duties," her husband said as several couples waited to greet the woman. "But we will speak more later."

"How lovely," Elizabeth said when they finally reached the room opened for the dancing, which had already begun by the time they had disposed of their outer wear and been greeted by Sir Lawrence and a few others of her husband's acquaintances. The musicians were situated on a raised dais at one end of the hall. "Someday, it would be grand for us to host a ball at Pemberley."

"The last ball held there was well before my mother's passing." He paused as if considering his next observation. "My father lost his reason for happiness with the absence of Lady Anne Darcy in his life. It was as if he lost his ability to enjoy the blessings still remaining: his daughter, his son, and his ancestral home." Mr. Darcy shook his head as if presenting himself a reprimand. "We will have no maudlin thoughts tonight. I possess the most interesting and handsome woman in the room on my arm—a woman who has promised to save me from mundane conversations that do not interest me." He smiled upon her.

"Come, my husband," Elizabeth said with a returning smile. "I believe there is a wall yonder desirous of our company."

"You are declaring me shallow. Foul, I call, lady wife."

As they circled the dance floor, they kept up their easy banter, quite ignoring many who thought to catch their eyes, although Elizabeth saw the number of nods meant to draw their attention, she honestly believed her husband had not. He was laughing at her latest quip when he came up short.

"Uncle," he said. "My lord." He led Elizabeth in a bow of respect. "I thought you had returned to London, sir, after Twelfth Night, or I would have called at Matlock."

"Parliament has finished all the business of any merit on the docket," the man said with an obvious sense of importance. "I am assuming this is your new lady. Her ladyship has been singing Mrs. Darcy's praises to all willing to listen."

Before he made the introduction, her husband said sadly, "I suppose such does not include Georgiana."

"Your sister will know reason, but it shan't come easily. The girl is as stubborn as both George Darcy and my sister," his lordship assured. "I will see to Miss Darcy's reckoning. Your father sheltered Georgiana too long. She requires several doses of honesty at its best to cure what troubles her." The earl nodded to Elizabeth. "The introduction, boy."

Mr. Darcy smiled at her. "I fear I have acted in much the same manner as I described my father not five minutes past. I ignored the best part of my days to dwell on something over which I have no control. My lord, permit me to give you the acquaintance of the woman who has saved me in more ways than I will ever be able to name: Mrs. Elizabeth Darcy."

Tears rushed to Elizabeth's eyes, but she managed another curtsy. "I am honored, my lord."

"Nonsense," his lordship declared and reached out a hand to steady her rise. "You brought our dear nephew back to his home. It is our honor to count you as family."

Elizabeth protested, "Mr. Darcy had already planned to return to Pemberley before he extended his hand to me."

"Yet, you have provided him a reason to rebuild Pemberley, which is a grand home, but, without a family, it is nothing more than brick and mortar."

Before Elizabeth could respond, they were joined by Lady Matlock. "There you are, my dears." Her ladyship leaned in to kiss Elizabeth's cheek. "My, I must say, the gown exceeds all our expectations. I must tell Mrs. Woodfine of your success. You have likely stolen away the breath of more than Mr. Darcy this evening."

"Several times this evening, I have said how handsome my Elizabeth is, but I am always willing to praise my wife," her husband said with a grin, "for her slight blush of embarrassment adds a bit of color to her cheeks." He bowed to his relations. "I do not wish to be rude; yet, if you will pardon us, I have promised my wife a waltz, and the musicians appear to be signaling one is meant for the next set."

"Certainly, Darcy," her ladyship declared with a smile. "It has been too long since we have viewed you with a future worth naming."

The musicians struck up the promised waltz, and her husband led her to the dance floor. He set her at a proper distance from him and then edged her an inch or so closer. Elizabeth was nervous, for she had never actually danced a waltz, other than the few times the local dance instructor had held classes her mother had insisted they all attend. A country waltz performed at an assembly was quite different from the waltz brought over from the Continent.

"I have you," her husband whispered. "Just follow my lead and enjoy the dance."

"I have only danced the waltz twice previously, although my sisters and I practiced it often," she admitted.

"You possess natural grace," Mr. Darcy declared. "You have nothing to fear. I shan't permit you to fall or to trip. Look into my eyes and follow the gentle pressure of my hand on your back and my grasp where your hand rests within mine."

The arm encircling her waist was firm, and his right was splayed upon the small of her back. Her husband guided her expertly, and Elizabeth began to relax, though not completely, but enough for exhilaration to fill her chest and for a smile to claim her lips. It was as if her feet floated above the floor as she permitted Mr. Darcy to guide her around first one couple and then another. They swirled, as if in perfect harmony, their bodies completely attuned. All too soon, at least for Elizabeth's liking, the music slowed, indicating the end. The moment softly slipped into the night, but not before becoming etched in her memory forever.

"Thank you, Fitzwilliam," she said with a large smile, which she could not contain.

"My pleasure, my dear. It was quite magical watching your enthusiasm."

"I know it is not quite the thing to say," she whispered, still a bit breathless. "Yet, would you mind if we claim a glass of wine before we return to the dance floor? It will sound foolish, but I would love a moment or two to savor this brief interlude."

Her husband leaned closer to say softly, "As I have never known a woman who appeared to appreciate me for more than my family's fortune, how may I refuse?"

"In the most unexpected moments, you make the most profound assertions, Mr. Darcy," she declared.

"As do you, Mrs. Darcy. I assume such will see us well, for we will forever be astounding each other," he added, and, for the first time in more than a fortnight, Elizabeth knew happiness.

"Wine, Mr. Darcy," she ordered.

"Yes, my dear." He placed her hand on his arm and led her into one of the rooms set aside for refreshments. He seated her at a small table. "Any preferences, love?"

"I shall permit you to surprise me," she instructed.

"I will attempt to prove myself your gallant," he claimed and walked away towards the table holding drinks and a variety of cakes and the like.

Elizabeth leisurely removed her gloves, while, with interest, she watched the others about the room. There were small knots of people, all laughing and appearing to enjoy themselves. She appraised the women and what they had chosen to wear and judged herself an equal to many in the room, permitting herself another moment of triumph. She had not embarrassed her husband with her choices.

A man in a Rowan livery, but not the full dress of a standard footman, started towards her, carrying a tray sporting several fluted glasses filled with champagne; however, when he saw her, he appeared to veer off in the direction of the servants' door. The movement was so jarring it immediately caught her attention. On some level, especially his quick retreat, said she had not truly "seen" him. She turned her head to locate her husband, who was on the other side of the room with his back to her.

Her gaze urgently returned to the servant; however, all she could claim as real was he felt familiar. Before he could reach the door, she thought his gait held a familiarity, with his identity becoming clearer with each step. Then he turned to glance back over his shoulder at her, and she knew certainty.

In alarm, she again looked for her husband, to find Darcy crossing the room to where she sat. Behind him, a footman easily managed a small tray supporting a variety of tempting dishes, but Elizabeth was no longer hungry.

"You appear to have seen a ghost," Mr. Darcy remarked as he seated himself beside her and waited for the servant to place the cakes before them.

"Perhaps," she murmured in distraction. Her eyes remained on the servants' entrance. To the man setting out her husband's choices of food, she asked, "Has Lady Rowan hired extra servants for this evening? I noted several footmen not in full Rowan colors."

"Such is common in the area, ma'am," the servant explained. "If a man does well at such an event, he can often earn himself a permanent position in one of the finer houses."

"Thank you," Elizabeth said with a small smile. "I am new to Derbyshire. I appreciate your explanation."

"Yes, ma'am. Enjoy your evening."

When the footman walked away, her husband asked, "What an odd question to ask. Should I be jealous of your taking notice of one of Sir Lawrence's footmen?"

"Only if you consider me to be interested in Mr. Wickham," she retorted.

Chapter Thirteen

"Wickham?" he hissed. "You must be mistaken. Sir Lawrence would never hire Mr. Wickham. He often spoke to my father of the foolhardiness of George Darcy supporting his godson in the manner he did."

"Would not Sir Lawrence's butler or his housekeeper been the one to hire the temporary staff, rather than the baronet himself?" Elizabeth argued. "Moreover, earlier when we spoke to Sir Lawrence, the man said he had not come across your father out in society for some eight years. Would it not be an equal amount of time or more for him to be in Mr. Wickham's company, if ever?"

Her husband's voice deepened in accusation. "Do you not think it queer how you have encountered Mr. Wickham three times, but no one else can claim him even in the neighborhood?"

"Of what do you accuse me?" Elizabeth growled under her breath while being cognizant of the fact they were in a crowded supper room.

"You chanced upon Mr. Wickham in the village. Afterwards, I spent an inordinate amount of time and money for men to search him out, but to no avail. Then you suspected he was hiding near the manor and struck Jasper. Finally, you believe the man I despise most in this world has taken a position as a temporary footman in the home of my father's long-time friend," he summarized.

"Believe what you wish, Fitzwilliam." Elizabeth tossed her serviette on the table. "I never saw Mr. Wickham in the garden. Such was your daughter, but Alice's description spoke of the former lieutenant. Tonight, the man I saw suspiciously turned away, taking a full tray of drinks into the servants' passage. Is his doing so not odd? Yet, it was not his face which identified him, for though I saw the fellow, I only caught a glimpse of him, but long enough to make me curious. It was that slight hobble step which alerted me. You know the one. Mr. Wickham always humorously claimed his right leg to be shorter than his left. Often saying, it was the price for being born on a hill."

When her husband simply stared at her in disbelief, Elizabeth said in defeat, "I feel a headache coming on. If you wish to stay, I will ask Lady Rowan for the use of her carriage."

"Do not be ridiculous," Mr. Darcy chastised. "We will make our excuses to Lady Rowan, and I will see you home."

"Thank you for our one dance. It was quite heavenly." Elizabeth dipped her head, not wishing him to view her tears. "I warrant I shan't speak of the 'ridiculous' in the future, sir. I shall keep my opinions and thoughts to myself and never bother you with them again."

"I never meant to censure you," he insisted.

However, before she could respond, a small group of young men and women appeared at their table. Her husband had risen, more likely out of habit rather than pleasure, for he look thunderously at the group. Elizabeth reluctantly followed him to her feet. She knew Mr. Darcy was already extremely irritated with her, and the group appeared set on some sort of mischief, for they all wore smirks on their lips.

"Are you returning to the dance floor, Darcy? If so, might I claim your partner's hand," the man at the front of the gathering said with a cheeky grin upon his lips. "You may have the 'pleasure' of my partner in exchange." He had emphasized the word 'pleasure' with a knowing nod to her husband, and Elizabeth felt quite queasy.

Although she knew her husband stiffened in anger, he checked himself rather than to create a row in a crowded supper room. She glanced to Mr. Darcy's face which held, in her opinion, both a bit of longing and a large dose of loathing at the same time. Somehow, through pure will, he schooled his expression to one of simple contempt for the man and a bit of anger for those in the fellow's small knot of companions. Mr. Darcy did his best to ignore the pretty blonde among those standing before them.

Yet, though they had never taken each other's acquaintance, Elizabeth recognized the woman. She had seen her previously, outside the Lambton church overseen by Mr. Ericks. Slim. Tall. Blonde. Piercing blue eyes. Just like her older sister Jane, but the woman's features showed nothing of the softness and caring often displayed on Jane's features. Fine countenance, though. A pale blue gown accented her body in a way Elizabeth would never be able to duplicate. She suddenly felt very dowdy, when earlier she had thought herself more than "presentable," as the mistress of Pemberley.

"Good evening, Fitzwilliam," the woman said in a melodious voice, which matched her appearance perfectly.

"I have never permitted you the familiarity of my Christian name," Mr. Darcy growled. "I will thank you to remember your place." With that, he said, "Come, Mrs. Darcy." Her husband presented the group what must surely be a direct cut, although, in truth, Elizabeth had never seen someone snub another in society. She certainly would not wish to be on the receiving end of Mr. Darcy's wrath. The group separated to permit their departure.

Her husband directed her across the room and through the door while the entire company within looked on in silence. No one else dared to move until Fitzwilliam Darcy made his exit.

In the passageway leading to the main foyer, they were quickly accosted by Lady Rowan. "I apologize, Darcy," the woman said in what appeared to be real regret. "I had no idea Mr. Benson meant to escort that . . ."

Mr. Darcy halted the woman's apology. "There is no need for self-chastisement, my lady. You are not responsible for a lack of manners on Benson's part. Before Benson's antics began, Mrs. Darcy and I were already debating on whether we should return home or not. We both miss our routines at Pemberley."

"Are you assured, Darcy? I will gladly send Benson on his way, if you wish to stay," Lady Rowan stated with another glance of disapproval in the direction of the supper room.

"I would never consider creating such a scandal," her husband insisted, and Elizabeth thought such was the first truth he had spoken since they had entered the refreshment room.

"I am deeply grieved over your leaving," Lady Rowan admitted. "I feel as if I have disappointed Lady Anne Darcy. She was a dear friend and taken from us too soon."

"All is well," Mr. Darcy said. "Perhaps we can dine together soon. Mrs. Darcy will send a card around."

Elizabeth did not appreciate being placed in the middle of this disaster, but she remained silent, for she feared the first words from her mouth would be a demand to know who the woman was, as well as the lady's connection to Mr. Darcy. Any fool, and Elizabeth did not consider herself a fool, could recognize the earlier staged encounter was staged for the woman to reinstate an earlier claim to Mr. Darcy's affections.

Lady Rowan gently squeezed Elizabeth's arm. "I have presented you great harm. Please know it was not intentional."

Elizabeth nodded her acceptance, but simply said, "Mr. Darcy, might we leave? I am truly unwell."

Her husband looked to her oddly, but he said, "Naturally, my dear."

They made their final farewells and walked away together, with neither of them speaking to others or even to each other. Eventually, their coach was brought around and cloaks retrieved. Inside the carriage, they remained silent, each lost in his or her thoughts.

Finally, her husband said, "I am deeply sorry to have our evening cut short. I had hoped—"

"As did I," she said into the silence lying heavily between them. The weight of her husband's guilt and her curiosity was unbearable. "Who is she, Fitzwilliam?" she asked at last. Elizabeth purposely used his given name to learn whether he would also deny her, as he had the woman on Mr. Benson's arm.

"Just a woman I once considered as a potential mate. I greatly overvalued her charms until I learned something more of her character." His tone held the same coldness as it did earlier.

"She is the same woman I saw with you at the church," Elizabeth accused.

"Must we return to this topic time and time again?" her husband demanded.

Elizabeth responded in equal testiness. "Of course I am expected to account why I have noted Mr. Wickham's appearance in Lambton and be accused of still holding the man in affection, but when I ask of someone from your past, I am told I should ignore not only the woman's identity, but also the unspoken connection you two hold. I am not blind to your continued secrecy, sir."

He warned in angry tones, "As your husband, I insist you abandon this line of questions."

Elizabeth recoiled, drawing her cloak tighter about her, even drawing up her legs onto the seat to make herself smaller. "As you wish. After all, you are the master of Pemberley and also of me as your wife. Forgive me, Mr. Darcy."

"Do not do this, Elizabeth," he said, but again his tone was harsh. There was no regret to be heard. "I simply do not wish to live in the past. I wish our future."

Elizabeth doubted they would ever have the future either of them had previously envisioned. A very real headache had arrived, and she closed her eyes to drive away her tears. Her husband meant to restrict her movements and her thoughts, and Elizabeth knew she was not of an obedient nature in such situations. In the past, when she went against her mother's edicts, Mr. Bennet was able to reason with his wife. Unfortunately, Mr. Bennet's influence over Mr. Darcy no longer existed. She was alone, and she must be more cognizant of that particular fact.

When they finally reached Pemberley, she had rushed past him as her husband had presented Mr. Farrin and Lucas instructions for the evening and tomorrow morning. From what little she heard, Mr. Darcy planned on carrying out some of his customary duties tomorrow, although he and she had originally thought to rest after an evening of entertainment.

"One waltz does not equal an evening of entertainment," Elizabeth murmured beneath her breath before ordering Mr. Nathan to send Hannah to her. She did not pause to remove her cloak or hand off her muff. Instead, she was halfway up the stairs before she heard the main door close behind her. She paused on one of the stairs, half expecting her husband to call her name, but no such entreaty came, so she proceeded on to her quarters, purposely pausing long enough to lock the connecting door between her quarters and those of Mr. Darcy.

Finally within her sanctuary, both her tears and her anger arrived. She flung her cloak into one of the corners, ripped the gloves from her arms and tossed them into the grate. The fabric caught fire immediately, sparks escaping up the flue. Even so, she knew no satisfaction. Next, she attacked the pins in her hair, wishing with all her heart to be rid of Lady Anne Darcy's jewels and any reminder of the failure of this evening. Her first outing as the mistress of Pemberley had been an absolute disaster, and she did not deserve the Pemberley jewels, neither did she want the dress she had created specially to look presentable upon her husband's arm. Still, she did not have the heart to rip it to shreds, for it would be destroying yet another piece of herself.

"Mrs. Darcy." Hannah rushed into the room to take control of Elizabeth's sobs. "Sit, ma'am. I shall have it down in a moment." Defeated, Elizabeth did as the maid instructed. Within less than a minute, Elizabeth's hair hung about her shoulders. "Do you wish me to brush it?"

"Just bed, Hannah," Elizabeth said with a heavy sigh of resignation.

The maid grabbed Elizabeth's night-rail. "Permit me to unlace you so I might remove the gown."

Elizabeth stood with lackluster effort, purposely avoiding her image in the mirror. She did not wish to view the woman she had become. "Return the jewels to Mr. Darcy when we finish." Thankfully, her words held no signs of the emotions coursing through her.

"The master indicated the jewels were for your use, ma'am," Hannah ventured.

"They belonged to the last mistress of Pemberley, a woman most beloved by all who knew her. I have yet to earn that sort of respect from the current master of Pemberley."

Hannah appeared as sad as Elizabeth felt, but she said, "As you wish, ma'am."

Finally in her night-rail, Elizabeth instructed, "Douse the lights when you have finished. I shall not require further services this evening."

"Yes, ma'am."

Elizabeth crawled across the bed and released the tie holding back the bed drapes, wishing to block out the memories of this evening.

It was not much later when she heard her husband's knock on the adjoining door, but she made no effort to answer or to unlock the door. She had had enough drama for one evening, and Elizabeth knew herself too exhausted to respond sensibly.

"Elizabeth, do not do this," he pleaded against the wood. The handle rattled again and again. "We must talk."

Yet, she refused to respond. After a few more attempts, Mr. Darcy abandoned his efforts. Ironically, although the main door to her chambers remained unlocked, she knew Mr. Darcy would not enter that particular door if the inner door was locked. Her husband would not wish a servant to view him being required to use the door leading to the main passageway, for his doing so would announce to one and all, she had locked him out of her quarters. His pride would not permit him to perform in such a manner, even if his denial cost them their marriage.

Pulling the blanket up and over her head, Elizabeth hid away from the world and attempted to identify her options in going forward in her marriage. Women of her class could not simply ask for a divorce without bringing shame to all her dear family, meaning Mary. Elizabeth would not act in a manner which would deny her sister a chance at the happiness she would likely never know for herself.

She had hoped her husband had been about his duties to the estate by the time she made an appearance in the morning room; yet, he had tarried, obviously realizing her motives. During the night, she had sworn she could not act until Mary was safely under Mr. Ericks's care and until Elizabeth knew whether or not she carried Mr. Darcy's child. She had thought to ask his permission to live in Town, not that she knew much of London life, but there was a Darcy townhouse available, but she knew her husband would never allow her to leave, even for the capital, if she carried his heir. He would want to watch over her care himself.

With a straightening of her shoulders, Elizabeth entered the morning room. "Good morning, Mary." She bent to kiss the top of her sister's head. "Good morning, Alice."

She purposely circled the table to sit across from Mary, rather than at her customary place at Mr. Darcy's right hand. The gentleman had risen at her entrance, and, although he frowned with her choice, he made no comment.

"Mr. Darcy was just saying you were one of the most strikingly handsome women at the ball," Mary said with a welcoming smile.

"Such is kind of Mr. Darcy," Elizabeth answered in the sweetest tones she could muster. "I was far from being among the most becoming in attendance. Certainly, some of my husband's former acquaintances held more Town polish than I. Yet, I am indebted by his loyalty."

Even without his spoken objection, Elizabeth felt her husband's anger hitch a notch higher. His posture had stiffened, and the grasp on his fork tightened.

Ignoring the tension between her and the man she had married, Elizabeth said with a smile to allay Mary's obvious concerns, "I had hoped we might finalize the plans for the wedding breakfast today. We still have a number of items to decide. If you hold no objections, I would go with you into Lambton today so Mr. Ericks may have some say in your special day. Would you like to visit the vicarage, Alice?" she asked, before adding, "I suppose I should have asked if you had other plans for today, sir. Initially, we planned to spend the day together at Pemberley."

"I decided to ride out for part of the day," he said through tight lips. "Please visit with the vicar. Alice seems to enjoy playing with some of the neighbor's children."

"Mrs. Tibon makes cakes?" the child asked with her most charming smile.

"I imagine she did," Elizabeth responded. If she was forced to depart Derbyshire, she would greatly miss the child who had become quite precious to her.

"I should be about my business for the day," Mr. Darcy announced as he rose. He came around the table to place a kiss on Alice's upturned forehead. "You are to listen carefully to Elizabeth and Miss Mary. No going beyond where they might view you."

"Yes, Papa," the child responded obediently.

Next, he leaned over to kiss Elizabeth's temple. "You were by far the most handsome woman at Lady Rowan's entertainment," he whispered. "I knew a great honor in being permitted to escort you."

Elizabeth wanted to turn and throw her arms about his neck and welcome his embrace. Instead, she said, "Please be safe today. We all depend upon you as Pemberley's master." She could tell her remark had found its target, for he winced as if she had struck him. She did not speak of him as her partner, but as her master, which is what, in a fit of temper, he had demanded only last evening.

"I know my duties," he said in apparent sadness. "George Darcy demanded his son always perform with honor." He bowed to her and then the others. "Good day, Miss Bennet. Please keep my family safe."

Elizabeth watched him go and drove the tears from her eyes. "*A man of honor would be honest with you*," her inner voice announced, while another voice said, "*But you love him.*"

※

Later that afternoon, in the guise of discussing the wedding breakfast with Mr. Ericks, Elizabeth accompanied her sister in calling upon the vicarage. When Mary took Alice to the kitchen to assist Mrs. Tibon in setting a tray for all of them, Elizabeth claimed the opportunity to speak to Mr. Ericks. "I wished a private moment with you," she explained.

"Certainly." Ericks gestured to a circle of chairs before the fire. "How may I be of service?"

"I am not asking for your approval of my actions, but, instead, to provide you a warning."

"This sounds ominous," he remarked, as his brows drew together in concern.

"First, you should know, I have not discussed any of this with Mary, or anyone else, for that matter. I beg you to keep my confidences."

His frown deepened. "Naturally, if you wish it to be so."

Elizabeth fought to keep the tears from her eyes as she began her tale. "Last evening, Mr. Darcy and I attended the entertainment hosted by Lady Rowan. During the evening, I noted a servant who I believe was George Wickham. When I reported the sighting to Mr. Darcy, my husband accused me of 'wishing' to encounter Mr. Wickham again and making the man a part of my future."

AMENDING THE SHADES OF PEMBERLEY

"How ridiculous!" Ericks said adamantly. "Mary has told me much of how Mr. Wickham performed in Hertfordshire. I wish I had known Wickham had gone to Herts; I would have sent Mr. Bennet a warning regarding the man's character. Mr. Darcy cannot truly believe you hold an interest in Mr. Wickham."

"Although Mr. Darcy did make the accusation of my being the only one to have seen Mr. Wickham on three different occasions, I do not think my husband honestly believes I hold an interest in Mr. Wickham beyond a curiosity regarding why he has returned to Derbyshire, especially as my husband has reclaimed his rightful inheritance."

"Most assuredly, Mr. Darcy comprehends, as Mr. Wickham was to be your late sister's husband, the Church of England would frown upon your joining with the man, even if you were free to do so," Ericks observed. "Why would Mr. Darcy, who is generally a reasonable man, make such an absurd observation?"

"Because, in one of Lady Rowan's refreshment rooms, a Mr. Benson and some of the man's friends cornered Mr. Darcy and me."

"Benson?" Mr. Ericks asked with a snarl of disapproval. "Certainly not an estimable young man. I understand his parents are prepared to disown him."

"Disowning appears to be a Derbyshire solution to family woes," Elizabeth observed. "I never heard of anyone in Hertfordshire so disgraced as to be disowned." She sighed heavily. "Anyway, Mr. Benson requested my hand for a dance set and offered his own partner to Mr. Darcy."

Mr. Ericks frowned. "How truly bizarre. I cannot imagine Mr. Benson's lady would approve. Who was she?"

This time Elizabeth could not hide her tears. "The lady addressed my husband by his Christian name, and he responded by offering all in Benson's party a direct cut, after first warning the woman against her familiarity. When I later asked who she was, Mr. Darcy said she was a woman he had once thought to court until he discovered some sort of flaw in her character. Afterwards, we argued, and he demanded I permit him his privacy. His accusation regarding Mr. Wickham was a diversion so he would not be required to provide me the truth of the relationship he shares with the woman. To me, such means Mr. Darcy likely held her in deep affection. The type of affection he does not hold for me," she admitted reluctantly.

"I cannot believe Mr. Darcy has not presented you a piece of his heart. He looks upon you with such longing," Mr. Ericks assured. "Do you know the woman's identity? Perhaps I can attest to the end of Mr. Darcy's affections for the lady."

"It was the same woman with whom we saw him at the church when I was waiting for Mary," Elizabeth admitted. "The one he was speaking to when Alice called his name."

"Miss Chapman?" Mr. Ericks asked. "I did not recognize her at first, but later noted her in the village. Most assuredly, Mr. Darcy wants nothing to do with that particular lady. She was the cause of all his misery."

For a few seconds, Elizabeth thought she might swoon, but Mary and Alice returned just as the blackness rushed in. She was forced to drive her emotions away as Alice hurried forward to present Elizabeth a tight hug. "For what do I owe this honor?" she asked the child. Elizabeth smoothed the curls from the girl's face. Alice's hair and features were so like "Miss Chapman's," Elizabeth wondered why she had not made the connection previously. *And Mr. Darcy did not want the lady to have a good look at Alice,* Elizabeth's mind announced.

"Miss Mary say she and all her sisters hugged their mama when they be happy," the child announced and hugged Elizabeth a second time.

Instinctively, Elizabeth accepted the child's offering and kissed Alice's forehead. "How very grand of Mary to share her memories of Mrs. Bennet with you." Elizabeth looked up to her sister to note Mary's look of worry. "Thank you, sister dear, for reminding me of our mother's essential goodness and teaching it to our sweet child." To Alice, she said, "You presented me a wonderful gift. One I will always cherish."

Normally, Elizabeth would have been thrilled for the child's sweet kindness. Yet, she was not Alice's mother, for Ruth Chapman was alive, not deceased, as Elizabeth had assumed. Had Mr. Darcy divorced the woman? And, if he had not, he and Elizabeth were not legally married, making the child Elizabeth suspected she carried a "bastard."

Chapter Fourteen

Before she had departed the vicarage, Elizabeth warned Mr. Ericks not to speak of what they had shared. She had added, "When all this comes to a head, and it will and soon, a chance exists Mr. Darcy will lash out at my family and those who support us."

"You are insinuating, as Mr. Darcy is my benefactor, he may choose to replace me, especially if I choose to marry your sister?" the man questioned.

"I am saying, I am not made to share my husband with another woman. I had hoped to delay our confrontation until after you make Mary your wife. Yet, if you do not wish to continue your commitment to Mary . . ."

"Do not speak nonsense," Ericks responded in harsh tones. "I have considered making Mary my wife for more years than I should admit. Why do you think my sister was to send you to me when we thought both you and Mary were set for employment as governesses. Madeline recognized my interest in Mary and did not think it appropriate for your sister to reside with me. From the beginning of our acquaintance, I presented Mary a place in my heart. The difference in our ages was more of an issue when she was fifteen, and I was one and thirty. Ironically, God has presented us another opportunity, and I do not intend to have it snatched away again. Many say the years grow closer together as do the couple. Therefore, if Mr. Darcy proves himself vindictive, then Mary and I will make our home elsewhere. I will protect her against all who would think to harm her. I believe such is the answer to your question."

"It is," Elizabeth admitted. "I did not want you to be unaware of the situation."

Satisfied Mary's future would be secure, Elizabeth set her mind to crafting a fabulous wedding breakfast for her sister. It would be the first time Pemberley had hosted such an event since Lady Anne Darcy's death, and Elizabeth meant to prove herself as equal to Mr. Darcy's mother in the role of mistress of Pemberley, even if her ways were not identical to an earl's daughter. Moreover, she wanted Mr. Darcy to regret having deceived her with Miss Ruth Chapman. Or was it Mrs. Ruth Darcy?

She wondered, but only briefly, if Mr. Shane would have known approval of Miss Chapman. Somehow, she doubted it, for Elizabeth's manners were more provincial and Miss Chapman's showed a preference for London society. Elizabeth meant to disguise any knowledge of her husband's traitorous heart. At least for now. She would do so until Mary was safely married to Mr. Ericks. It was only another three weeks until Mary's wedding. Then Mr. Darcy would know Elizabeth's wrath, or she would know his. Either way, she could not long continue on this course: She was not built for such stratagems.

※

"A Mr. Bingley, ma'am," Mr. Nathan announced.

Elizabeth immediately rose to her feet. "Show him in, Mr. Nathan, and send for my sister."

"Yes, ma'am."

While the butler brought in her guest, Elizabeth patted her hair into place and pinched her cheeks for color. Another sennight had passed and another still would see Mary married to Mr. Ericks. The strain was taking its toll on Elizabeth, but she was determined to see her sister wed before finally confronting Fitzwilliam regarding Miss Chapman.

AMENDING THE SHADES OF PEMBERLEY

Within seconds, Mr. Bingley, wearing his customary smile, entered the room. Gladdened to see him, Elizabeth rushed into his embrace and held him there for a few elongated seconds before saying, "I cannot believe you are here. In Derbyshire." She looked up to his comforting expression. "What a surprise! Thank you for coming. You have been sorely missed, sir."

"I am due to my sister Louisa tomorrow, but I was in Yorkshire yesterday looking for a possible estate, and I thought you would not mind a visit," Bingley said with a gentle kiss on Elizabeth's temple.

Although she disliked doing so, for Elizabeth, most assuredly, required his comfort, she released him to motion him to a nearby chair. "Tea and cakes, Mr. Nathan," she ordered the waiting servant.

"Yes, ma'am."

Elizabeth sat across from her late sister's husband. "You received my letter regarding Mary's upcoming nuptials?"

"I did," he said. "Such is one of the reasons for my call. Mrs. Gardiner asked me to deliver a letter to Mary and another to her brother. Mr. Gardiner means to send a small pianoforte for Mary's use. I understand our sister Mary wishes to give music lessons to the village children."

She was surprised to learn of Mary's aspirations, but Elizabeth did not comment. Her sister was permitted her secrets. She imagined Mary did not want Elizabeth to be aware of the wish for a pianoforte, for Elizabeth would have taken on the task of having Mr. Darcy secure an instrument for her. Mary was no fool: Elizabeth's sister was aware of the tension between Elizabeth and Mr. Darcy. The whole household was aware, but there was nothing Elizabeth could do for the time being. Evidently, Mr. Ericks took on the task of securing a pianoforte for his new bride.

"She will be thrilled and oh so pleased to see you, as well as to hear from Aunt Gardiner," Elizabeth assured.

"And you, Elizabeth," Mr. Bingley said softly. "Are you well? Happy?" There was concern in his question.

"A bit weary. It has been difficult for Mr. Darcy to reclaim his heritage," she responded.

"I did not ask of Darcy," he chastised. He leaned forward bracing his arms upon his thighs. "I asked of you. Although I adored your enthusiastic greeting, for it felt as if it were the first honest thing you have said to me since the auction. Even so, we both know it was uncharacteristic of you. Has Darcy mistreated you?"

Elizabeth knew she blushed. "My husband has not raised a hand to me. As ours was not a love match, as was yours and Jane's, we have experienced some adjustments in our expectations. Why do you ask?" She thought perhaps he had heard what had occurred at Lady Rowan's ball.

"I do not like to carry tales." Mr. Bingley leaned back in the chair, his posture very stiff. "Yet, I promised Jane I would see to the care of her sisters, and I cannot pretend what I viewed did not disturb me."

"Tell me what you wish to say before Mary joins us. I do not wish Mary to worry for my welfare," she instructed and braced herself for what Mr. Bingley would share. "I believe I am already half cognizant of your information."

He nodded his understanding and leaned forward once again and lowered his voice. "I stayed at an inn last evening upon the Yorkshire-Derbyshire border. I did not want to arrive on your doorstep too early, though I promised Mrs. Gardiner multiple times I would make certain all was going well for you and Mary. Anyway, I tarried in my room, wrote some letters, and, generally, went over my plans to move forward without Jane. I had my breakfast delivered to my room so I did not go down to the common room until mid-morning."

Elizabeth fought back the tears rushing to her eyes, for she knew what Mr. Bingley meant to share before he pronounced the words.

"There was a couple tucked away in the corner of the room. I could not initially view the gentleman, but the lady caught my eye."

Elizabeth whispered through the strain in her voice, "She reminded you of Jane."

"Just for a moment. Certainly not as beautiful as my Jane. You know the woman?" he demanded.

"By reputation," she admitted. "She and I encountered each other at Lady Rowan's recent entertainment. What did you observe?" Elizabeth asked with more calm than she thought possible.

"The smiling blonde reached across the table and caressed the man's cheek. It was when she called him 'Fitzwilliam' that I took a closer look. I first considered the man might be one of the Earl of Matlock's sons and the woman, Miss Darcy, although, in truth, the woman looked very . . . how do I say this, hard. I suppose that is the correct word. Hard. Naturally, I have not been in company with Darcy's sister since she was fifteen or sixteen, but I understood she was residing with the Matlocks. The man leaned forward to catch the woman's hand. His profile in the sunlight, rather than the shade, disclosed his identity."

Elizabeth attempted to swallow, but she could not.

Instantly, Mr. Bingley was kneeling before her. "Should I send for your maid?"

She managed to shake her head in the negative. "I do not want Mary to be aware of this," she rushed to say. "She must be married to Mr. Ericks. She must be safe."

He handed her a card. "My lease on Netherfield is not over until Michaelmas, some nine months, but I cannot live there any longer. I am returning to my father's house in Staffordshire, and I will keep the house in Town for when I must be in London for business. The directions are on the card if you have a need of me. I will come immediately. No questions asked."

She nodded her gratitude as he stood quickly to greet a jubilant Mary rushing into the room. Elizabeth managed to stand, though her legs wished to buckle. Slyly, she slipped Mr. Bingley's card into her pocket. She would not go to him unless she had no other choice, but it was good to know a choice existed.

While Bingley and Mary spoke of family, Elizabeth poured and served the tea, sandwiches, and cakes. Her sister was happier than

Elizabeth had ever viewed her, a blessing Elizabeth would always cherish—one well worth her own misery. Perhaps if she knew what Mr. Darcy planned to do with the woman by whom he had sired Alice, Elizabeth could learn to live with his betrayal. Yet, it was the not knowing which held her in a state of both immobility and misery.

Bingley was well on his way to the home of Mr. and Mrs. Hurst by the time Mr. Darcy arrived home. Elizabeth refused to dwell on the idea he and Ruth Chapman had shared intimacies and such was the reason for his late arrival at Pemberley. The idea would likely drive Elizabeth mad, and so she forced it away each time an image of the two together crept into her mind.

"How was your day, my dear?" her husband asked as he joined Elizabeth at the supper table.

"Very pleasant," she said, without looking up at him. "Mr. Bingley called and had a light meal with Mary and me."

"Why was Bingley so far north?" her husband asked as he picked up his soup spoon.

"He looked at an estate in Yorkshire," Mary explained. "With our sister Jane's passing, and Elizabeth and I departing the area, he has no family in Hertfordshire."

Mr. Darcy spoke to Mary, but he eyed Elizabeth oddly. "I would think Mr. Bingley would wish an estate closer to Town, as his shipping business is in London. Hertfordshire was ideal."

Mary assured, "There are not so many estates available, but, in truth, I do not believe Mr. Bingley is quite prepared for the life of a country gentleman. Such was a life he had planned to share with our sister Jane. Netherfield likely has too many memories of his short marriage to be comfortable, and, if he should choose to marry again, his future wife would not want the reminders of Jane all about her."

"Would it not have been more efficient if Mr. Bingley had returned to Hertfordshire from Yorkshire rather than Derbyshire?" Mr. Darcy asked.

Elizabeth continued to permit Mary to answer for them, but she watched Mr. Darcy carefully. She was beginning to wonder if Mr. Darcy had espied Mr. Bingley at the inn, although Mr. Bingley swore her husband did not.

"Mr. Bingley was promised to his elder sister for some family celebration," Mary shared. "The Hursts are somewhere west and south of us, are they not, Elizabeth?"

"I cannot recall," Elizabeth said, "the exact location of Mr. Hurst's estate. I do recall Miss Bingley often complaining how long it took to reach London and going near, but not through Oxford. I always assumed it was in Leicestershire, but I do not believe anyone said so." She paused to sip her wine. "I thought you might know of Mr. Bingley's home shire. As you were both at Cambridge at the same time, would he not have hailed from a northern shire?"

Her husband looked suspiciously at Elizabeth, and she returned his steady gaze. "Although such is often true, there are those from the southern shires who choose Cambridge over Oxford. Sometimes, in a man of Mr. Bingley's position, as a first-generation gentleman, the person chooses a focus conducive to his background. Oxford tends to bring literature to the fore, while mathematics is the focus of much of the instruction at Cambridge. Both emphasize creative thinking and searching for a definitive answer, but the path to reaching that answer is often swayed one way or another depending upon the school."

Mary shot a quick glance to Elizabeth, as if she wondered why Elizabeth did not respond, but when Elizabeth remained quiet, Mary continued her tale, "Mr. Bingley called to bring me a letter from Aunt Gardiner, who I soon shall be required to call 'sister,' instead of 'aunt.' Is that not odd?" she chuckled. "Mr. Bingley also brought a letter for Mr. Ericks, but, more importantly, at least for me, our brother Bingley brought word Uncle Gardiner has located a small pianoforte to fit in the sitting room at the vicarage. I have so much enjoyed teaching Alice to play, I thought I might teach some of the village children. Just a few pennies here and there so as not to make their parents believe I consider them charity cases; yet, enough for both the parents and the children to consider music as important to their children's education."

In that moment, Elizabeth knew great pride in her sister. Mary had aspirations she had previously hidden behind a veil of righteousness. Elizabeth wished her parents were alive to view the transformation of their middle daughter. In truth, Mary had a brighter future than did she, for Mr. Ericks held Mary in deep affection.

"I would gladly have provided you a pianoforte if I had known," Mr. Darcy said

"I have no doubt," Mary reassured. "Yet, it was Mr. Ericks who made the arrangements, not I. It is to be my wedding gift, and, as the instrument must be a particular size, my betrothed contacted my Uncle Gardiner. As our uncle owns one of the largest import and export businesses in England, Mr. Gardiner possesses contacts even you do not." Mary quickly added, "No insult intended, sir."

"None taken," Mr. Darcy said and appeared to mean it.

Elizabeth was half tempted to question him about his day, but she swallowed the words rushing to her lips, for she did not want him to know of Mr. Bingley's sharing confidences. Instead, she said, "Mr. Thacker sent a missive saying two of your trunks from India have been delivered to Darcy House. I had hoped you would order them sent on to Pemberley. It would do me well to read the various letters you exchanged with my father." She turned to Mary, "Would you wish to read them also?"

Mary shot a quick glance to Mr. Darcy. "Most assuredly, I would be eager to read Mr. Bennet's letters, that is, if they are not too personal for Mr. Darcy. I would not wish to embarrass you, sir. I imagine Mr. Bennet was often bitterly frank. My father possessed a caustic wit, and I know, from the occasional comment delivered my way, his barbs can sting."

"Oh, Mary," Elizabeth reached across the table to offer her sister a soothing hand. "Papa never meant to be cruel."

"I know," Mary admitted. "We all accept humor as the only socially-accepted form of criticism, though I do not think our father's barbs were be meant to act as disapproval. He spoke to the things he could not control, and our mother was difficult to control, even on the best of days. Mr. Bennet simply enjoyed twisting the King's English in a unique manner. It was his entertainment. That and his books.

"Our father was so much wiser than everyone he encountered in Meryton and outside of it, which is likely, from my limited observation, the reason he and Mr. Darcy struck up a friendship. It is also the reason Mr. Bennet recommended you, Elizabeth, to Mr. Darcy. You are, by far, one of the most intelligent and reasonable women God has placed on this Earth. What you do not already know, it takes you a mere matter of days for you to possess a working knowledge of the subject, enough to hold your own with the majority of men. Both Papa and Mr. Darcy are, you must forgive my observation, sir, for I speak with fondness, not criticism," she told Mr. Darcy. "Both you and Mr. Bennet are at your best in small gatherings of like-minded people."

Surprisingly, Mr. Darcy said in sincere tones, "I would agree, Miss Bennet. I confided something of my nature with your sister recently."

Mary suggested, "If the letters are available, sir, please share them with Elizabeth. Whether she will admit it or not, my dearest sister always depended upon our father for affirmation. She will not rest until she has it one more time."

⌘

"Hush little baby, don't say a word, papa's going to bring you a mockingbird," Elizabeth softly sang the familiar lyrics as Alice nodded off to sleep. This was the third time she had sung the song this evening. The lullaby had quickly become Alice's favorite. Elizabeth suspected it was because the lyrics spoke of what her father might bring her.

"Papa," the child whispered and reached out a hand. It was only then did Elizabeth realize Mr. Darcy stood in the open doorway.

"Good evening, sweetheart." He stepped inside and knelt beside the child's bed. A gentle hand brushed the hair from Alice's cheek. "It is good of Elizabeth to sing the lullaby so many times."

"One more," the child said rolling her eyes upward to meet Elizabeth's. "Peas."

"Last time," Elizabeth warned, not because she disliked being with the child, but because she wished to avoid her husband. She began again, "Hush, little baby, don't say a word. Papa's going to bring you a mockingbird. If that mockingbird doesn't sing, papa's going to bring you a diamond ring. If that diamond ring turns to brass, papa's going to bring you a looking glass. If that looking glass is broke, your papa will bring you a billy goat."

Thankfully, the child's thumb found her mouth, and Elizabeth was not required to finish the song.

The nursery maid slipped into the room where she would sleep nearby. "I'll douse the candle, sir," the girl whispered.

Mr. Darcy nodded his agreement. He rose, but tarried a moment to look upon his child with an expression of longing Elizabeth could not identify, before he extended his hand to her. She did not want to touch him, for Elizabeth knew herself too susceptible to him; yet, she accepted the heat of his palm as it encircled her closed fist. Gently, he interlaced their fingers and led her from the room. As they walked away, hand-in-hand, she could not completely swallow the whimper rushing to her lips.

Her husband paused, turning her to face him. "What bothers you so profoundly, love?" he asked as he reached to caress her cheek.

Elizabeth wished desperately for him to touch her in affection; however, she knew such would never occur. She managed to say, "The lullaby reminds me of my mother. She sang it to each of her children. I have both her and my father on my mind since the Holy Days. Like Alice, I always wondered when my papa would bring me each of the fairings."

"I have never heard the song before. Where did you learn it?" he asked, tucking her hand about his arm and directing their steps towards their quarters.

"From my Grandfather Gardiner. He was a tradesman, building what is now my Uncle Edward's import and export business. At that time, Grandfather Gardiner often traveled to exotic and not so exotic places. Once, he made his way to the American continent, for he had heard of a place a bit north of what now is the port of Charleston. There were artisans there who created hand-crafted furniture, which my grandfather thought would be popular with many in London, for it was sturdy and made of an odd wood with lines, that when polish was added to it, made for a bit of what he liked to call a 'masterpiece in wood and grit.'

"While he dealt with the fathers in a rudimentary village, GG heard a woman singing the song to her child. She had a Scottish accent."

"You called your grandfather 'GG'?" he asked with a large smile.

"No, Jane called him such, for she had difficulty saying 'Gardiner,'" she corrected. "For a bit he was 'Grandfather G.' By the time Mary came along, he was 'GG.'" She paused, "Should I continue to speak of the lullaby or should we discuss what you called your grandparents when you were young, and do not forget, Alice calls me 'Lizbet.'"

"My maternal grandparents were your lordship and your ladyship," he said with that boyish grin which made him appear ten years younger. "However, I wish to know more of the song, Mrs. Darcy."

"The settlement was full of Irish and Scottish residents. Evidently, they both had a version of the song, which they gladly taught to him. By the time he returned to England, he had mixed up some of what they told him, but he enjoyed singing the song for first one grandchild and then another. As Mrs. Frances Bennet was the youngest of GG's children, she heard it more often than her older brother and sister, and she shared it with us often."

"I like the idea Alice has a unique lullaby," he admitted. "Thank you for providing my daughter a future. Such was one of my promises to her as a babe in the cradle, but I have always feared I had tempted the Fates one too many times."

Elizabeth wished to ask what other promises he had made to Alice and why the Fates would wish to destroy something so sacred for a child, but she swallowed her curiosity once more.

"Sleep well, my dear," he said as he bent to kiss her tenderly.

"You as well, sir." Elizabeth wished to tarry. To kiss him again and maybe one more time. Yet, she knew she could not share her bed with a man who took his pleasure elsewhere. Therefore, she turned quickly and entered her room, refusing to look back at the man who she had once thought would appreciate her efforts to please him.

Darcy had not been happy to hear from Ruth. The woman was becoming bolder and bolder. Their agreement in India had said she would never come near him and his daughter again. Obviously, at the time of their arrangement, neither of them had thought ever to be allowed to return to England and, more importantly, be accepted into society. They had held few prospects.

Now, Ruth thought he would again pay her to disappear from his life. If he did not also have a need to protect Elizabeth and Alice, it would be easier for him to be rid of Ruth. He could confront her as he had done at Lady Rowan's ball. He could seek the assistance of the Matlocks and his cousin Fitzwilliam and even his Aunt Catherine, though she did not often go about in society. Between them, they would be able to silence the woman by appealing to her parents who sat on the edge of the upper crust, much as Mr. Bingley did. They could be made to take control of Ruth before it was too late, just as his father had done during the fiasco which ended with Darcy's banishment.

It had been his father's idea for Darcy and the woman to leave England together. Ruth had not considered such an edict from her father and his. Most assuredly, Darcy had fought his father's decision, despite, on some level, understanding it. However, word of Ruth's claim she was carrying his child had made its way into society and had forced everyone's hands.

Darcy suspected the carrier of those tales had been George Wickham, as well as Ruth herself. The lies multiplied and the opportunity to know a different ending decreased; that is, until Darcy encountered Mr. Thomas Bennet at an inn along the London docks. Mr. Bennet had provided Darcy wise advice regarding what to do with Ruth Chapman and his prospects.

"You must change your stars, boy," Mr. Bennet had said. "You must prove to the world you do not require your father's hand on your shoulder to make you a man worthy of your destiny. Do not forget, Darcy, even if your father chooses to disown you, he cannot prevent your inheriting the family estate. The entail can only be broken by your death. Simply do not die, boy, and your family home and the fortune attached to it is yours.

"I wish there was a means for me to break the entail on my property," Mr. Bennet lamented, "for the man who is to inherit Longbourn is only a notch above an imbecile. However, Mrs. Bennet is not likely to conceive again. I just worry for my girls, especially my Elizabeth. Here, let me show you my girl."

Darcy had expected everything but the image of a girl he could not readily drive from his mind as the woman she had become.

"The miniature was made recently. My Lizzy is but sixteen, but she is growing into her beauty. She is whip-smart. Could teach your children sums and literature and a bit of Latin and Greek and something of nature and a garden, but, more importantly, my Elizabeth is up to every challenge. She could make a young man like you into a great man."

At the time Darcy thought Mr. Bennet only wished his daughter to claim a rich husband, but as their correspondence continued, and he became more dependent upon Mr. Bennet's sound advice, the more Darcy had bought into the idea of Elizabeth Bennet being his partner in life.

He had thought after their initial awkwardness, they could eventually come to love each other. Then Ruth Chapman reappeared in his life, and Darcy was afraid he would be required to sacrifice his feelings for Elizabeth to protect Alice. Doing so would break his heart, but, when Alice took her first breath, he had made a promise to an innocent child. That promise had not changed simply because he had presented a large chunk of his heart to Elizabeth Darcy. As he blew out the candle to claim a few hours of sleep, he reached under his pillow to retrieve the scarf his wife had made for him with her own hands. He wrapped it about his arm, where it would remain until Elizabeth learned to forgive him for bringing such sadness into her world. As he closed his eyes, Darcy surmised the scarf would be about his arm when he took his last breath, for he was not certain his wife could forgive such a sin as he had committed.

Chapter Fifteen

The days leading up to Mary's wedding passed much in the same manner. Upon occasion, her husband had taken her in his arms and kissed her nearly senseless, but "nearly" was the operative word, for Elizabeth's senses were now working overtime. She had yet to have her monthlies, making her relatively certain she carried Mr. Darcy's child, but she was still not assured when the baby had taken. If she were counting from the first time they had shared intimacies, she would be four months along, but the child may have been planted inside her during those first weeks of bliss between them—before she realized Mr. Darcy had repeatedly lied to her, and he was sneaking about seeing another woman, who he admitted once to have preferred as a potential mate. Every once in a while, she found her hand instinctively caressing her abdomen, wondering when she would feel the child move beneath her fingers.

Each day, Mr. Darcy was gone from the house from early on to, sometimes, after supper had been served. Generally, Elizabeth attempted to convince herself the stories he told of persuading first one and then another tenant to plant cold season crops between the rows of fallow to nourish the soil instead of overusing the land, as his father had long permitted, were true.

Elizabeth understood most of what he had shared, for Mr. Bennet had instituted a four-crop rotation in the fields of Longbourn so as not to overwork the land; yet, she purposely limited her comments, not certain whether her husband would welcome them or not. "I would have known less self-imposed censure if I had accepted Mr. Collins's proposal all these years removed," she told the darkness in the privacy of her quarters. "Charlotte Lucas managed to claim her sitting room as her private sanctuary and had managed to tone down Mr. Collins's propensity for haughtiness and imbecilic observations. I would never have respected or held affection for Mr. Collins, but how is such different from what I have at Pemberley?"

Elizabeth never permitted herself a response, for she already knew the answer: She had allowed Fitzwilliam Darcy more than just a bit of her heart, and, in all manner, except his continued relationship with Miss Chapman, Elizabeth respected her husband for his dedication to both his daughter and his tenants.

"You are quite beautiful today," Elizabeth told her sister. It was the first Thursday in February and Mary's wedding day. "Mr. Ericks will be struck dumb with awe. Mama and Papa must be smiling down from heaven upon you. You have proven to be the best of the Bennet family."

"None of this would have been possible," Mary said with a slight tremble of her lips as if she might cry, "if you had not agreed to marry Mr. Darcy. Though for a time we thought our futures would never hold those things again, at Pemberley, we were safe and warm and well fed and permitted to think for ourselves." Mary took Elizabeth's hands in hers. "I owe you so much. Mr. Ericks and I owe you our deepest gratitude."

"Just be happy," Elizabeth said, rising up to kiss Mary's cheek. "I will be quite satisfied to know you are happy in your choice."

Mary insisted, "I wish you to be happy, as well."

However, before Elizabeth could comment on that particular possibility, a soft knock came at the door. "It is time, Elizabeth," Mr. Darcy announced from the other side of the door. He was to escort Mary on this day.

Picking up her cape, Elizabeth opened the door. "Provide Alice and me a quarter hour head start before you follow," she instructed.

He said with a gentle smile. "The small coach is stationed outside, and Alice is impatiently waiting in the foyer with Hannah. She is wearing her new muff and matching scarf, courtesy of the countess. Her ladyship and I convinced her it would not be appropriate to wear her tiara today, but my daughter wishes 'Lizbeth's' approval."

Elizabeth nodded her understanding. "Do not permit Mary to wrinkle her gown. Ask Hannah to assist my sister. I shall see you two at the church."

She started for the stairs, but her husband caught her hand and brought it to his lips before saying, "You are very beautiful today, Mrs. Darcy." She had chosen to wear the bronze wool, but had added a short ivory-laced spencer to dress it up. A bit flustered by his unexpected gesture, Elizabeth could only repeat her earlier instruction to wait a quarter hour before leaving for the church. With that, she rushed away.

※

Elizabeth laid awake in her bed, reliving the day. Pemberley had been filled with local families and the Matlocks, minus Miss Darcy, which had greatly affected her husband; yet, as always, he had carried off what was required of the situation. Elizabeth had been quite satisfied by the turn out and how the staff had performed.

"Mama would be beside herself," she had told Mr. Ericks, as the vicar had escorted her about the room, while Mr. Darcy danced a reel with Mary. The local music teacher and the man's star student provided the music. "Mrs. Bennet would not only be full of pride in knowing Mary had claimed your heart, she would be quite overwhelmed with the idea an earl and countess attended both the wedding and the breakfast."

Mr. Ericks paused to look upon his new wife. "Your sister is magnificent; yet, she is the most unassuming woman I have ever encountered—present company excluded," he added quickly.

"I take no umbrage with you praising my sister. Rather, I hope to hear such accolades rained down upon Mrs. Ericks's head with some regularity. Tell Mary often of your affection for her and how proud you are to name her as your wife, and you will earn my ready allegiance."

Mr. Ericks lowered his voice, "What of you and Mr. Darcy?"

Elizabeth noted how her husband skillfully led Mary into the final form, as the music came to an end. She could not recall a time Mary danced so often. It was a shame her sister had been ignored so long, for Mary had proved herself quite remarkable.

"In truth,' she said as the last refrain of the music was played, "I possess no idea how it will all end. I suppose the next couple of days will tell the tale. I do not plan to be one of those wives who shares her husband's affections with other women. Once our overnight guests depart, I plan to speak of my expectations in an honest manner with Mr. Darcy."

Frustrated with how she could not leave the chaos of the last several weeks behind nor forget all which had trespassed between her and Mr. Darcy of late, Elizabeth replayed in her head, for what was likely the hundredth time, what she wished to say to her husband. Angry with herself and all which had occurred, she punched her pillow. It was then she heard it: A shuffling of feet, as if someone rushed about in an emergency. That sound was followed by a squeal.

Other than the Matlocks and Colonel Fitzwilliam, there should be no one else in this wing of the house other than family. The Fitzwilliams were all in an adjoining hall, for her ladyship had assured Elizabeth she had no intention of rising earlier than usual and would appreciate not being disturbed.

Elizabeth threw the blankets aside and stood to check the clock. "Two in the morning," she told the empty room. Reaching for her discarded wool dress, she dropped it over her head and brought the loose laces around her waist to tie them off. She had no means to lace it properly. Slipping her feet into her half boots and catching up her shawl for warmth and to cover her exposed back, she used a large pin to fasten it in place about her neck and opened the door to the hall to peer out.

AMENDING THE SHADES OF PEMBERLEY

The hallway was eerily dark with candles muted in the sconces. At first, she thought what she had heard had to be a servant finishing his or her duties; yet, she had sent both Mr. Nathan and Mrs. Reynolds to bed some three hours earlier, and the pair would have seen all of the staff to bed before they claimed their own rest.

Elizabeth glanced to her husband's door, briefly considering beckoning his assistance. "Assistance with what?" she whispered. Yet, before she could wake Mr. Darcy, a light along the hallway towards the rooms used by Mary and Alice caught her eyes. It was brief, but distinct. She thought perhaps the maid tending to Alice meant to fetch the child warm milk or even a tonic, for Alice had devoured close to half-dozen lemon cakes before Elizabeth had put a stop to the child's sweet tooth. Alice had eaten so many cakes, she had ignored most of her supper.

Concerned, Elizabeth started towards the child's quarters, but before she could reach the door, it opened and a man stepped out of the dimly lit room carrying the child, who was kicking and crying.

"No!" Elizabeth screeched as she to stop what she could not fathom. "Fitzwilliam!" she called knocking over several vases to create a commotion as she ran. "Fitzwilliam!" she screeched as she launched herself at the man, set on reclaiming Alice at all costs. "Give her back!" She struck at him indiscriminately. Fists striking his arms. His cheeks. His body, as he fought her off with one hand and held Alice tightly to him with the other. "Give her back!" she yelled, in frustration. "You will kill him!" She knew her husband would die if something happened to Alice. "You will kill him!"

"Stop!" a familiar figure demanded as he knocked her backwards. Elizabeth crashed into the door frame, but also into something softer. Instinctively, she struck out at what proved to be the man's accomplice. An elbow to the person's midsection doubled the fellow over. She turned to present the person an uppercut, just as her Uncle Gardiner had taught her one time in London when a man in the nearby park had become too familiar with her and Jane and Gardiner's children. It was after she delivered the blow did she realized the person was a female.

221

Elizabeth froze just long enough for the man to grab the bag the woman had dropped and turn to run, carrying the child away. "No!" Elizabeth screeched and darted after him.

"Lizbeth!" the child called in desperation.

"Kick, Alice!" she shouted as she gave chase. "Kick! Kick!"

The child did as she instructed, kicking with all her little might, but the man held tight. Periodically, he reached out to knock over a vase or a valuable urn, but Elizabeth did not stop following, knowing the child was her husband's life. "Stop! Please stop!" she called as she followed the man down the servants' stairs leading to the small kitchen. "Stop!" she yelled as she reached the open door to watch him dart in the direction a waiting coach. Holding her side where a stitch of pain stole away her breath, she again gave pursuit.

Alice was still fighting the man as he jerked open the coach's door and tossed the child and the bag inside before bracing himself to crawl up. Such was when Elizabeth jumped on his back, slapping him with her right hand across his neck and cheeks and eyes, while holding on about his neck with her left. He attempted to toss her off, but somehow, she held on until he backed her up against the opening from the carriage door. Then she felt it—something hard against the back of her head, followed by the click of a hammer.

"I would advise you to cease your caterwauling," a cold female voice warned. "She almost was too much for you, George."

The man straightened, shaking Elizabeth free of her hold on him. "Even I am not the type to strike a woman," he declared as he turned to look at Elizabeth.

"Mr. Wickham," she gasped. "What are you doing at Pemberley?" She looked to where Alice was curled in a ball on the floor of the carriage: The child was sobbing. "Why are you stealing away with Alice?"

"For me," the woman announced. "Now, both of you climb into the carriage." The woman was the blonde Mr. Darcy had favored over her.

"Just give me the child and leave. I shan't tell anyone what occurred. Go!" she ordered. "Just go!"

"Not without my daughter," the woman declared.

Such was when Elizabeth heard him. Her husband was calling her name from an upstairs window.

"Give me the child!" Elizabeth reached past the woman to pull Alice closer to the door; yet, before she could reclaim the girl, Mr. Wickham lifted Elizabeth upward, and the blonde assisted in dragging her into the carriage, hurling her across the open space and causing Elizabeth to strike her head against the wooden part of the bench.

Within seconds, Mr. Wickham crawled across her, and the coach began to roll away from Pemberley. Elizabeth could still hear her husband calling her name—heard the profanity, but she could do no more than reach out to claim Alice's arm and pull the child closer. Although Elizabeth's head hurt something terrible, she cuddled the child close and cooed reassurances she did not believe possible. "Your papa will come for us," she whispered to the child. "He will not rest until you are safe in his arms again."

*

Darcy was not certain what had shaken him from his sleep. He remained lying on his back, staring up at the bed drape and listening for several elongated seconds. He wondered if he should go to Elizabeth and profess his affection for her. They could not go on as they had for the last few weeks.

Yet, before he could decide whether to approach his wife again, he heard the outer door to Elizabeth's quarters open and close. "What the devil?" he grumbled as he crawled from the bed and slipped his trousers over his small clothes and stepped into his slippers. "Is she ill? Sleep walking?" He paused to consider if something more nefarious was afoot, and so he quietly let himself through, first, his dressing room, then the sitting room to come to the door of her dressing room. "Is it still locked?" he asked himself.

His hand was on the latch when he heard someone running. Darcy jerked on the latch, but it did not give. "Demme!" he cursed as he hit the door with his shoulder; yet, it did not budge. Turning in anger, he turned towards the sitting room door, but stumbled when he struck his knee against the table at the side of the settee.

Then he heard her screaming. Elizabeth sounded to be in agony. Limping forward, he hurried to reach the door to the hallway. There was the sound of a ruckus going on. Jerking the door open, he heard Elizabeth scream, and his daughter's cries.

Fear took over when he rounded the corner to view Elizabeth running behind a man dressed in what appeared to be all black.

Darcy started after her, but his knee hobbled his progress until his anger took over. He chased them only to come up short when a maid stumbled into him. The girl screeched when he caught her shoulders. "What has happened?" he demanded, presenting the girl's shoulders a good shake. "Speak to me!" he ordered.

"Took Miss Alice," the girl sobbed.

"Who? Who took Alice?" he shook her a bit harder.

"Mr. Wickham," the girl wailed before breaking from Darcy's grasp and skittering away.

"What is amiss?" the colonel called as he rounded the corner.

"Catch the maid!" Darcy ordered. "Wickham has Alice!" He turned immediately to give chase once more. *"Wickham had Alice, but was Elizabeth involved?"* his mind questioned as he raced to catch them. God, he hoped not, for he would be required to destroy the woman he loved.

As he turned first one corner and then the next, the floors were covered in broken glass and pottery, but Darcy ignored the chaos to follow the pair. At the back of the house, he spotted Wickham running across the kitchen garden. "No!" he called, shoving the window open. "No!"

He began to run again, crisscrossing corridors, catching glimpses of a waiting coach. Then he saw Elizabeth. Running. Stumbling. "Elizabeth!" he screamed, again shoving a window open. "Elizabeth!"

He entered the servants' stairs. Half skipping. Half sliding down the narrow stairs to burst through the still open kitchen door to view Wickham boosting Elizabeth into the open carriage door and following her in. Alice was nowhere in sight. "In the coach," he whispered as fear filled his heart as the carriage edged forward. "No!" he cried in despair when it picked up speed. "No!" he whimpered as the cold night air sank into his soul and he sat heavily upon the garden wall.

"Darcy!" his cousin called, following him into the garden. "Have they escaped?"

"Yes," he said dejectedly. "But I must give pursuit. They have Alice."

"They?" the colonel questioned.

"Wickham and Elizabeth," he said. "I suppose I will be required to pay a ransom for the return of my daughter."

"And not your wife?" Fitzwilliam questioned.

"Elizabeth was running with Mr. Wickham. I saw them with my own eyes," Darcy said sadly.

"With or after?" his cousin asked. "Perhaps Mrs. Darcy was attempting to stop him."

"Wickham boosted her into the coach," Darcy said with resignation as he stood. "She was not fighting him. Wickham once courted her while in Hertfordshire, and Elizabeth favored his company. Moreover, she has encountered him multiple times of late. Only her."

"As you have encountered Ruth Chapman?" Fitzwilliam suggested. "Perhaps Mrs. Darcy believes she no longer knows your favor."

Darcy said angrily, though the anger was turned inward. "We are wasting time. Please order horses for each of us. I assume you mean to go with me."

"A chance to rearrange Wickham's face? I am in. Quarter hour."

His cousin trotted away to rouse those in the stables; yet, Darcy lingered. He had no doubt he would find Alice and bring the child home. It would cost him several thousand pounds, but Darcy knew with certainty Mr. Wickham had no use for a child. The dastard had abandoned more than a half-dozen over the years. The question which remained to be answered was whether he would also be required to ransom his wife or would she prefer to stay with Mr. Wickham?

Darcy made his way back to his quarters only to learn the colonel had roused out the earl and left his lordship to question the maid. Matlock then joined Darcy in Darcy's quarters. "Your maid has been consorting with Wickham since before your father's passing," his uncle explained as Darcy dressed more appropriately to conduct his pursuit. "I have turned her over to Mrs. Reynolds until you decide what you mean to do with her. I suggested you might consider a charge of kidnapping, which is a hanging offense."

"If something ill happens to Alice, I will see the girl drawn and quartered." Darcy stepped from behind his screen to grab his jacket and, without considering his choice, he tugged the scarf Elizabeth had made him from beneath his pillow and wrapped it about his neck. "Did you learn anything else of significance?" he asked, hoping his uncle would not ask of the scarf, for Darcy had no explanation for his choices. He prayed Elizabeth had not betrayed him while being cognizant of what he had viewed with his own eyes.

"Your wife punched the girl in the face," Matlock said with a smile.

Despite his despair, Darcy remarked, "Sounds of something your younger sister might do." Both pride and concern were found in his tone as he tucked the ends of the scarf into the lapels of his jacket.

"Sounds of something both Lady Anne and Lady Catherine might execute, though my older sister would have blamed her indiscretion on another, while your mother would have boasted of her accomplishment."

Darcy hoped Elizabeth acted with either excuse, but he had no time for memories or conjectures. "Anything else?"

"The girl was crying profusely, but she claimed Wickham's plan was to go inland, not in the direction of the coast or London," the earl confided.

Darcy paused in interest. "Odd? Is the girl assured?"

"She repeated the same three times."

Darcy loaded his gun and claimed a sack of coins from his room safe.

"Do you mean to pay Wickham?"

"If I can capture him, I will permit the law its justice. What Wickham does not yet understand is I have faced enough criticism since my banishment that I no longer care if someone gossips about me and mine. I simply wish to spend the remainder of my days with my wife, Alice, and the promise of more children."

"Are you prepared?" Fitzwilliam asked as he stepped into the room. "Mr. Nathan says the horses have been brought around."

The earl stood. "If my son has a clear shot at Wickham, do not argue that the colonel should reconsider."

"I will more likely be cheering him on." Darcy motioned for his cousin to lead. "Wickham has crossed the line one too many times."

Chapter Sixteen

Elizabeth knew when they rolled through Lambton. Even at such an early hour, there were a few lights on in the shops. She was glad Mary was behind one of those doors and was safe and loved. When the brief flashes of light disappeared, Mr. Wickham reached down to her. Elizabeth was stubborn enough to wish to ignore him, but, if she was going to escape, it would be more difficult to do so if she was on the floor of the carriage. She edged Alice from the death grip the child had on her. "Permit me to claim a seat on the bench, sweetheart," she whispered.

The child nodded and removed her arms from about Elizabeth's neck and halfway stood.

Grudgingly, Elizabeth accepted Mr. Wickham's hand to rise. She remained a bit dizzy, but she settled herself on the seat beside him. Immediately, Alice crawled back into Elizabeth's lap. Wickham reached down to claim Elizabeth's crumpled shawl. In reality, she was surprised to see the shawl had survived this encounter. She shook it out, released the pin's latch that had held it in place, and spread it across the child to keep Alice warmer.

"Why do you not join me, child?" Miss Chapman asked. "I have two lap rugs I am willing to share."

"Want Lizbet," Alice said as she snuggled deeper into Elizabeth's embrace.

"Why do you desire to claim Alice now?" Elizabeth asked, unable to curb her curiosity.

"A child should know her mother," the woman declared, but Miss Chapman's tone said the words had been rehearsed, and Elizabeth imagined the woman had said them to Mr. Darcy and, perhaps, others.

"After more than five years?" Elizabeth accused. "Nearly six."

"Nearly six years?" Miss Chapman declared. "Darcy has presented my child a different birthday. He thinks himself God."

"Always did," Wickham grumbled. "The Almighty Darcy!"

Miss Chapman giggled, but to Elizabeth's ears, the gesture sounded forced. She began to wonder if the woman had ever known even one genuine emotion. "You should have seen him in India, Wickham. Even covered in mud and sweat, Darcy demanded his due." The woman shrugged as if she did not understand anything of Mr. Darcy's nature. In many ways, Elizabeth realized, she knew Fitzwilliam Darcy better in four months than Ruth Chapman did, despite having lived together for years.

"You expect Mr. Darcy to pay for the return of his daughter?" Elizabeth questioned.

"Why should I not?" Miss Chapman declared. "He has done so prior."

"And what of Mr. Darcy's feelings in all this madness? And the child's, as well? Do you have no care for the damage you cause Alice? I have stood witness to Alice's fears and her sometimes riveted shyness."

"You managed well enough. According to Wickham's latest conquest, the maid who assisted him this evening, Alice no longer clings to the doll, 'Miss Cassandra' is it not?" the woman countered. She paused, and Elizabeth thought she meant to say more of the maid's duplicity, but, rather, Miss Chapman switched the subject from Alice to Elizabeth. "I imagine now Darcy has claimed you, he cannot keep his hands off you. Even a statue like Darcy has a warm heart upon occasion. Can you believe it, Wickham?"

"Makes me wish I did not settle on Mrs. Darcy's younger sister," Wickham remarked while lazily leaning his head back and closing his eyes. "Would have been something to behold to view Darcy's countenance when he called on Mr. Bennet to discover Miss Elizabeth as my bride."

"After this adventure, I doubt Mr. Darcy will have anything to do with me," Elizabeth confessed.

"No fears," Miss Chapman remarked with a flippant gesture of her hand. "You and Darcy will continue continuing on. He will dote on Alice, but he requires an heir for Pemberley. Yet, I am certain you are aware of all Mr. Darcy requires in his life and his mission to set his world aright, and he is, most assuredly, aware of all you have to offer him. Your father sang your praises often enough, and then there was the miniature of you which Mr. Bennet 'accidentally' left behind. Darcy carried it with him everywhere he went. Even when he was in the mine. Even when he waited for me to deliver Alice, he studied your image. He was half in love with you before he took your acquaintance, for, after all, you were the virtuous and intelligent lady he had always desired."

"Yet, after tonight, even if I am permitted to return to Pemberley, Mr. Darcy will never trust me again. He viewed me running after Mr. Wickham, a man who only I have encountered."

Miss Chapman kicked Wickham's boot. "I told you Darcy would be jealous."

Wickham did not open his eyes, but he murmured. "And I told you Mrs. Darcy would admit the encounters to her husband. Mrs. Darcy is brutally honest. She cannot help herself."

Elizabeth quickly realized she and Darcy had played into Mr. Wickham's and Miss Chapman's hands. Miss Chapman smiled in a mocking manner, causing Elizabeth's hopes to plummet.

Though her understanding had likely come too late to save her marriage, Elizabeth fully comprehended how she must take control of this situation, for no one would give a care for her fate. She must discover a means to free herself and Alice and return the child to Mr.

Darcy. Wickham and the woman did not require Elizabeth alive to "sell" Alice back to her father. She was the "glitch" in their plan, and neither of her captors appeared to care for anything other than the prospect of Mr. Darcy's money. They could abandon her along the road somewhere, but Mr. Wickham would know her not afraid of a long walk. If they left her behind, Elizabeth would not stop until she located them. Whatever it took. In that manner, she and Mr. Darcy were of one mind: Save Alice from a conniving and vindictive woman.

She had ruminated in the silence of the coach for perhaps another hour before the carriage pulled into an inn yard to change horses. Elizabeth attempted not to sit straighter so she might have a better look and perhaps call out for assistance, but she must have inadvertently signaled her intentions to Miss Chapman.

"Change your mind, Mrs. Darcy." The woman raised her hand and pointed the gun at Elizabeth, who had forgotten about the weapon until this very minute. "I hold no qualms regarding the idea of doing away with you. Everything between Fitzwilliam Darcy and me changed after he took your father's acquaintance. All our plans—plans designed by his father and mine—dissolved with each nautical mile we traveled. I could have walked about the deck naked, and Darcy would have looked upon me with contempt. I learned to despise both your father and you. With each breath I take, I do not regret Mr. Bennet's unexpected death nor will I shed a tear when you join him."

Elizabeth squeezed her eyes shut to drive away the complete devastation she felt. She wanted to demand what Miss Chapman knew of Thomas Bennet's passing, but she dared not, and, before she could determine what she might do instead, the carriage began to roll out of the coaching yard. Therefore, she swallowed her questions. In their place, she kissed the top of Alice's head and lightly began to sing, "Hush little baby . . ." She refused to consider her own fate. Most likely, Miss Chapman would choose to kill her. At the very least, they would lock her away in a deserted location. She possessed no means to right the wrong: No idea where they were or their destination. No opportunity to alert another to seek assistance. No one who encountered her would likely believe anything she said. She was wearing her nightrail and the bronze wool dress from earlier today, which she had not bothered to tie properly. Her hair was in a long braid, but still quite messy. She sported multiple bruises and raw knuckles and a good-sized lump on her forehead.

All Elizabeth could do, for now, was to comfort Alice and pray for an opportunity for the two of them to escape.

⁂

Although Darcy did not wish to stop, his cousin had insisted. In Lambton, they had been able to confirm the presence of a coach traveling "at a good clip" from Mr. Spindale, the village's blacksmith, who had been up early to make the necessary repairs on Mr. Dilworth's broken axle.

At the fork along the main road, they had, based on the information Lord Matlock had secured from the maid, taken the southern road towards Staffordshire. "Before we go too far south," Fitzwilliam reasoned, "we must confirm we are following the correct route. If Wickham and Mrs. Darcy mean to escape your fury, it would make more sense for them to travel in the direction of Liverpool's port or even north to Scotland, where your lady could apply for a divorce after six months."

Darcy's stomach soured with the possibility of Elizabeth having turned to George Wickham, for his wife would not be the first woman who had turned to Wickham for comfort, but he said, "Ask your questions. I will see the horses receive water and some oats."

"Do not forget, Darcy, Wickham promised to take the maid with him. Surely the dastard would not guarantee the girl riches and his affection if Wickham meant to abscond with Mrs. Darcy. Even Wickham pursues only one woman at a time. This whole scheme does not make sense. We know from his past, Wickham does not act without extensive planning. Even when desperation sets in, Wickham is no fool. He would know you will pay dearly for the child, but he cannot think you would do the same for a woman who betrayed you. Even if your old chum held Mrs. Darcy in affection, he would give her up for a good-sized purse on your part."

"Your conclusion makes sense, except Elizabeth Darcy would not abandon someone she loves, and I hold no idea whether my wife prefers Wickham over me," he announced before leading their horses away.

"May I be of service, sir?" a young man jumped up from his seat on a barrel as Darcy approached.

"Thought to give our horses a cup of oats and some water while my cousin conducts business inside."

"Certainly, sir. Right away." The man reached for the colonel's horse. "Fine animal. Mighty fine horseflesh, sir."

"They have been favorites for more years than I can recall. Took possession of the chestnut when he was little more than a foal."

Darcy claimed a towel from the top railing of a stall and began to rub down both horses. "Is there any chance a carriage came in for a change of horses, say, about four or half past four in the morning?"

"Two different ones comes in, sir." The fellow filled the narrow troughs from a bucket of water.

Darcy's heart hitched higher. "Did you take note of the occupants of either?" He stopped the rub down to study the man's expression when he responded.

"Only one went inside for food. They be an older couple. The driver for the other be insistent on finishing fast."

"Did they both head south?" he asked cautiously.

"Don't know of the older gent and his lady," the young man said. "I be called to chop more wood fer the fire by that time, but the smaller coach left on the south road."

Darcy asked, "Did you view the passengers in the coach traveling south?"

"Not a good look, the man admitted. "Mighty pretty lady sittin' close to the window."

Darcy's heart dropped to his stomach as a rush of bile all but choked him. "Could you . . . could you describe the woman?"

"Couldn't see much, sir. Her head be turned slight like. Pretty cheek and nose. Yellow hair."

It took Darcy a few extra seconds to realize what the man said. "Yellow hair? The woman had blonde hair?"

"Tucked under a jaunty hat. A man might like such hair on his woman, don't ye think, sir?"

Darcy sighed heavily. "There was a time I might have agreed, but, some time back, I chose a woman with hair the color of polished bronze, with bits of red and gold to catch a fellow's eye. I fear, since then, no other will do."

Before more could be said, the colonel stuck his head inside the stable door. "There you are, Darcy. I had the innkeeper make us a meal. Ham. Bacon. Cheese. Chicken. And the bread buttered on both sides." Fitzwilliam handed over the stacked bread and meat, wrapped in a clean cloth. "The innkeeper said only an elderly man and woman called inside in the last couple of hours."

"Another carriage simply changed horses," Darcy shared.

"Another carriage? Mr. Wickham?" the colonel asked.

"Cannot say for certain," Darcy confirmed. "This young man only caught a glimpse of one of the passengers. A woman. Pretty blonde or so he believes, although he only glanced at her."

"Blonde?" the colonel asked. "Then it cannot be the carriage we seek."

Darcy tossed a coin to the young man and then motioned his cousin back outside. When they were away from earshot, he said, "Could Wickham have a partner in this matter?"

"You are thinking Miss Chapman?" Fitzwilliam questioned.

"I have encountered her three times over the last five or six weeks, just as Elizabeth has reported seeing Wickham about the shire. I saw Ruth once in Lambton and then at the Rowan's ball, of which I am certain the countess has apprised you of what happened. The last time was at an inn near Yorkshire. At each encounter, Ruth has begged me to permit her to 'visit' with Alice."

"Why would Ruth Chapman want access to the child? Did she not abandon Alice the day after giving birth?" Fitzwilliam demanded.

"I have repeatedly asked her the same question, but she claims she wishes to know something of Alice. In my opinion, the woman has not one ounce of motherly instinct in her body. I have forbidden her requests, repeatedly reminding Ruth she agreed to leave Alice in my care and to relinquish her claim to the child. I paid her well in order to make Alice mine. I simply could not, in all good conscience, leave Alice with such a she-devil."

"I thought neither she nor Captain Meacham wanted anything to do with Alice. Meacham has his own family, and Miss Chapman wanted her freedom from you and the agreement forced upon both of you by her father and yours."

"Do you not think it too convenient that it was Wickham who brought Mr. Chapman's and Ruth's claims to my father's notice at the exact same time I was in London and could not refute them. After Wickham approached my father, George Darcy summoned me home, but such was more than a week between the time of learning of Ruth's claim and my appearance at Pemberley. By then, Mr. Wickham had whispered his and Ruth's lies in my father's ears. No reason could be found. I had once kissed Ruth, but nothing more. I found it all quite dissatisfying."

"Does Mrs. Darcy know the truth of all which transpired?" the colonel asked.

"How could I tell her of the deception I practiced? She would turn from me. I could not risk it."

The colonel's eyebrows rose in challenge. "And you do not wish Mrs. Darcy's disfavor?"

"I do not," Darcy admitted grudgingly. "Now, may we resume our pursuit?"

The colonel laughed easily. "You do not want to believe Mrs. Darcy has betrayed you because you hold her in affection." His cousin jovially slapped Darcy on the back. "Let us discover your wife and settle this matter between you so you may live out your days in contentment."

※

A rain had slowed their progress to the point where the driver stopped and came around to the door to speak to Miss Chapman. "Pardon, mistress," he said in a whisper while Elizabeth pretended to be asleep. "I knows you wished to carry on, but the roads be flooding. We should stop soon and permit the storm to pass. I fears of the horses' footing."

"Where are we?" Miss Chapman asked softly as Wickham stirred to life beside Elizabeth.

"'Bout two miles from Stafford, ma'am."

Elizabeth caught the gasp before it could escape: Mr. Bingley resided in Stafford.

Wickham said, "If we are required to stop, surely so will be Darcy. A few hours will do us all well. Have you slept, Ruth?" he asked softly.

"Too worried Darcy would overtake us," the woman admitted.

Although Elizabeth did not move a muscle or vary the slow even breaths sliding in and out of her lungs, she knew the pair had turned their heads to study her. At length, Miss Chapman instructed, "Choose an inn which is not too busy."

"Yes, miss." The driver closed the door, and, within seconds, the carriage shifted as he climbed up into the box once more.

Elizabeth remained as still as possible and maintained her hold on the child. They would stop: Such was all the information she required for the moment. There was a chance, slim though it may be, to escape, and, if so, she meant to claim it.

"Darcy," the colonel called. "We must hole up for awhile. The rain is so heavy. I cannot see my hand before my face."

Darcy knew his cousin correct, but he did not want to abandon the chase so soon. His sweet Alice was likely very frightened and wondering why her Papa had not come for her.

"Darcy!" his cousin called a second time. "There is a barn yonder. The horses require a rest."

Reluctantly, Darcy stopped and turned his mount. "Lead on," he ordered.

The colonel cut across a nearby field yet to be plowed for spring to rein in before the barn. Fitzwilliam dismounted quickly and lifted the wooden latch to open the barn door. Darcy rode through the opening, his heart as bleak as the weather surrounding them. Within seconds, the colonel followed and tugged the door partially closed, leaving it ajar so they might monitor the storm.

"Found a bucket. We'll set it outside to catch some rain water for the horses. See if you find some oats or meal for the animals," his cousin ordered.

Darcy did as he was told, but his mind was everywhere but this barn in the middle of the English countryside. "How long?" he asked as he passed his cousin, who hustled about the area to claim some rags hanging on a ladder.

Fitzwilliam began to rub down the horses and the saddles. "Just until the rain slackens."

Darcy halted his search and turned in despair. "Alice is frightened, Colonel," he said dejectedly.

"Mrs. Darcy will not permit the child to suffer. They two may be hungry and wet, but Mrs. Darcy is tending your daughter as best she can. She is, after all, the woman to whom you entrusted Alice's care. You must believe your judgement sound, Darcy. Stop second-guessing yourself. You knew when you married Elizabeth Bennet, she would stand by you. Do not gauge Mrs. Darcy by that conniving . . ." His cousin sighed heavily. "I should not say the word, but you know my thoughts about women of Ruth Chapman's nature. Do not judge your wife under the same magnifying glass you might use on Miss Chapman. They are not cut from the same cloth. In fact, the countess believes Mrs. Darcy was the wisest decision you have made in years. So much so, she is again urging both Roland and me to claim a wife."

Darcy shook his head wearily. "I know what you say makes sense, but I have spent six years attacked on all sides. How do I permit my defense to fall low enough to claim what Elizabeth offers?"

The colonel stood perfectly still to emphasize his words of advice. "Listen to Mrs. Darcy's explanation. Do not name her as guilty until you view her true deception for yourself. I still think your lady was attempting to prevent Wickham's escape and the dastard only took her with him because he knew you were close to catching up with them. By your own words, you have declared Mrs. Darcy the type of woman who will follow her heart, no matter the size of the man's purse. Has she demanded extravagances since your marriage?"

Darcy shook his head in denial. "Yet, what if I have misjudged her?" He found himself rubbing his chest where the scarf still protected him from the cold and dampness, but was unable to allay his deepest fears—that of being too vile for a woman of Elizabeth's nature to love.

"Lord, Darcy you are your own worst enemy. You have pined for this woman for years. You know more of her personality and her character than you ever did of Ruth Chapman's. Through her father's letters, you have laughed at her young girl awkwardness and marveled at the woman she became. For years, you have desired to know more of her heart. Am I not correct?"

"What if her father's tales only glorified her finer qualities?" he demanded.

"You are a hopeless fool if, when we discover her, you do not catch your wife up in your embrace and tell her you adore her. Anything less will leave you guessing for the remainder of your days."

Chapter Seventeen

When they reached the chosen inn, a man came out with an oiled cloth to hold over Miss Chapman's head to protect her from the rain. Next, Mr. Wickham jumped down from the coach and followed the lady. If Elizabeth had any feeling in her legs, she might have jumped down and run away into the darkness. However, before she could move, the coachman appeared in the open door. "Come on, miss. It be miserable out here." He reached for Alice who squealed in fright.

"Go," Elizabeth said harshly. "I will carry the child."

"Then, you come," the man demanded.

Elizabeth scooted across the seat and tested her legs before climbing down the steps, but her first step on "solid ground" sent her to her knees, water soaking her gown thoroughly.

"Get up, girl." The man caught her arm and jerked her upward, while the brim of his hat directed water down her front. "Go!" he ordered. "I'll see to the child!" He shoved Elizabeth towards the small overhang covering the doorway.

She sloshed through the mud and water to the opening before turning to accept Alice in her arms again. "I have you, sweetheart. We are still together."

"Here be the child's bag, ma'am," the man said, looping the string over her shoulder and shoving Elizabeth's crumpled shawl in the hand holding Alice to her. Exhausted and colder than she could ever recall, she turned to enter the inn.

"Give me the child, Elizabeth," Mr. Wickham ordered. "You can barely walk."

"Just require a warm fire," she said as she painfully staggered towards the fireplace. "Permit me to put you down before the fire," she whispered to Alice. Elizabeth bent to place the child down gently; after which, she sank to her knees and stretched out her hands to the heat. Her fingers were numb from the cold or perhaps from holding Alice for so many hours. Tiredness seeped through her limbs, and she longed to close her eyes and sleep. *Yet, not now*, she warned herself. Alice was still in danger.

"Can we not send her and the child from our sight?" Miss Chapman said with a snarl of her nose.

"Not very motherly, my dear," Mr. Wickham warned. "I have asked for a room for Mrs. Darcy and the child. The innkeeper is adding a mattress and setting a fire in the grate. I also ordered bread and cheese for the pair."

"My, you are terribly free with my purse," Miss Chapman accused.

"The room is nothing more than a servant's quarters. Nothing fancy. Yet, neither Mrs. Darcy nor the child can continue without a bit of sleep and food," Mr. Wickham stated in firm tones. "Darcy will not pay if we abuse them. He would rather put a couple of bullets between our eyes. Moreover, I will have the room key. They cannot escape. I have seen to the necessary details. The innkeeper thinks Mrs. Darcy is the child's nursemaid."

Elizabeth was beginning to realize this plan was a combination of greed and revenge. Mr. Wickham, as Elizabeth now knew, always schemed to increase his purse, whereas, Miss Chapman appeared well set with riches. Even with the rain and the mud and the late hour escape from Pemberley, the woman remained immaculately attired. Miss Chapman wanted revenge on Mr. Darcy for unnamed transgressions. Elizabeth and, more importantly, the child, were weapons to use against Mr. Darcy. "How much are you asking for Mr. Darcy's daughter?" she asked.

"I plan to 'negotiate' for the child," Miss Chapman said in confidence. "I might even throw myself into the deal. Darcy always desired me."

"What do you believe Darcy will offer for his daughter? I know there is thirty thousand pounds set aside for Miss Darcy. And how much might he give for you, 'Miss Elizabeth Bennet,'" Mr. Wickham said suggestively.

Elizabeth responded, "I imagine it would depend on the care presented to the merchandise. I have yet to see my husband's rage in order to know its full fury, but I imagine you have an inkling, sir."

"You do not believe Darcy has any need for saving you?" Mr. Wickham asked. His brows had drawn together in disbelief.

"I am of the persuasion, after this escapade, Mr. Darcy will be glad never to view me again," she stated boldly.

"He was always a prude. Always carried about two much pride. It is a shame you chose to accept his hand, but I suppose you were equally as desperate as were the rest of us after so many deaths in Hertfordshire. Sold yourself to the devil himself. How many compromises have you made, Mrs. Darcy, to protect yourself and Miss Mary? How many objections have you swallowed to stay in Darcy's good graces?" Wickham demanded.

Elizabeth saw the real George Wickham for the first time—a man who blamed the rest of the world for his shortcomings. "Mr. Darcy can be as demanding as you say, but he expects no more of those to whom he extends his protection than he does of himself. There were heavy misfortunes, indeed, at Meryton, and great sorrow. Yet, my father was wise to provide me a future, and I will say honestly being the wife of Mr. Darcy also has such extraordinary sources of happiness, that any woman he favors could, upon the whole, have no cause to repine. I do not regret one day of knowing my husband. My only regret is the knowledge those days were numbered by no fault of our own."

"Enough," Miss Chapman declared in obvious irritation. Elizabeth was beginning to know the woman's shallowness. The lady always wished to be the center of attention, something a mother could no longer be while a child lived. The child must always come first. "All this could have been avoided if Darcy would have simply paid me to go away again."

In that moment, Elizabeth realized Mr. Darcy had never met with the woman for a tryst. Even if he chose, in anger, to send her away, Elizabeth would know he had not betrayed her. With that new reason to live, she knew, without a doubt, she must stage some sort of escape for her and Alice.

"The rooms ye requested by ready, sir. Ma'am," the innkeeper said. "I've yer meal in the private room."

Miss Chapman shrugged as if being free of a troublesome ache in her back. "See them up, will you, Wicky. You are in charge of the key. Be certain the room is secure."

Not responding to the woman's attempt at a taunt, Mr. Wickham assisted Elizabeth to her feet and escorted her and Alice to a room set back from the rest. It was small and had a low ceiling, but, thankfully, it was warm. Elizabeth suspected it was over the kitchen and some heat from there kept the room warmer than expected. The fire in the grate was also small, but she and Alice would survive, especially as they were not likely to be at the inn long. When the rain slackened and the toll roads drained, they would be on the road again.

"Reminds me of the quarters I had in the militia," Mr. Wickham said, as he checked the small window to assure it was secure. "Mine and Ruth's quarters are only a few steps away. Do not make me bring harm to you, Miss Elizabeth."

"Mrs. Darcy," she corrected.

"Either way, it would be a shame to bruise up your face, but I will do so if you force my hand," he warned.

"I just want to see the child has eaten, and we both claim a bit of rest," she assured.

"I asked the innkeeper to find you a comb or brush. There is no mirror, but you will manage. You were always quite resourceful." He caressed her cheek, and Elizabeth made herself not pull away from his touch.

"Miss Chapman awaits. The lady does not appear to be the type to share," she cautioned.

With a nod of his head, Mr. Wickham was gone. The key turned in the lock with a loud click. Even so, Elizabeth claimed one of the two chairs in the room and lodged it under the latch to slow down anyone who dared to enter the room. "Come," she told the child, "let us share the bread and cheese and attempt to sleep."

"I no wish to go with them, Lizbet," the child said.

"I know, sweetheart. One step at a time, just like when we were crossing the brook. Eat. Rest. And say a prayer for your papa to come quickly."

※

Darcy stood by the open barn door and watched the rain. It had lessened, but it had not stopped. A steady flow of water snaked its way through the fallow fields. "Do you think they found shelter?" He despised the idea that either Elizabeth or Alice was suffering somewhere, and he was not close enough to protect them.

"Miss Chapman always demanded her comforts," Fitzwilliam said lazily. Darcy's cousin had made himself a bed in the loose straw. "I am surprised she lasted as long as she did in India."

"Ruth would have returned on the next ship to England, but it was the season for bad weather in the Indian Ocean by the time we arrived in the country. Lots of strong storms. We rode out a couple of them after rounding the tip of Africa. Moreover, her father had forbidden her return until after the baby she claimed as mine was born."

"You were good to provide for her under the circumstances," the colonel observed.

Darcy brought the scarf to his nose and sniffed it, hoping the scent of Elizabeth still remained on it. All it smelt of was dampness, or perhaps such was the scent of lost hopes. Meanwhile, he said, "I wanted her as far away from me as possible, but Mr. Bennet had warned I must keep Ruth near to confirm when she delivered the child. It was one of the most distasteful tasks I have ever been called upon to undertake, for I despised every breath the woman expelled from her lungs. Still do. You can likely imagine how she would parade around the quarters half dressed, thinking my lust would convince me to share her bed. The thing was, my hatred for her was stronger than any interest in intimacies. If anything, her willingness to sell her body repulsed me."

"Such was likely what finally carved your character. You were nearly a man when you departed. Possessing of opinions, but yet untested. You have returned with a knowledge of what is important in this world. Men at war learn that lesson quickly. I have always been proud to call you 'cousin,' but I am excessively honored to be a part of your life, now that you recognize what is truly important in this world." Fitzwilliam sighed heavily. "We will wait a bit longer to see if the storm means to kick up again, then we will leave, no matter what we must face," his cousin declared.

"Thank you, Colonel. I am indebted to you."

His cousin's tone softened. "You think I am doing all this for you? I possess my own agenda. George Wickham has warped our dear Georgiana's ability to know right from wrong. She requires a large helping of reality, and I mean to deliver her the truth, whether she wishes to hear it or not. Capturing Wickham and seeing him hanged for kidnapping your daughter will go a long way in bringing Georgiana around."

*

The child had eaten very little. Instead, she curled up on the bed and had gone to sleep. Elizabeth should have joined her, but, first, she meant to have a closer look about the room to determine a means of escape. She worked at the latch, but it would not budge. Next, she looked to the window. It was not so wide, but was tall enough for a possible escape. "Also, not so far down," she commented. "A bit over a storey high. Could we jump?"

AMENDING THE SHADES OF PEMBERLEY

Elizabeth realized she would never be able to convince Alice to leap from this height. "I must carry her down with me if we are to escape. Could we do so without being seen?" The area below appeared to be a short lane of some kind where wagons unloaded supplies for the inn's kitchen. The rain remained steady, but not so heavy as before. "If I do not act soon, Mr. Wickham and Miss Chapman will carry Alice away. I would not doubt they mean to leave me behind when they depart."

She tried to raise the window, but it would not budge. Claiming the fireplace poker, she attempted to pry it open; however, she was unable to wedge the tip of the poker under the window's frame. Next, she began to dig along the seam where the window touched the wood frame. Old paint flaked with each gash she made in the wood. Emboldened, she dug harder until she managed to use the bar to lift the window a mere inch. Now, she did the same for the sides of the window. Yet, to no avail. Frustrated, she struck the window with the bar. The glass cracked and a few pieces fell to the alley below.

Fearing someone heard, Elizabeth stepped back from the window so as not to be seen. "I require something to remove the glass," she reasoned.

Carefully, she lifted Alice from the mattress on the bed to the plain one laid out on the floor. She claimed the sheet and wrapped it about her hands to protect them while she removed chunks of the glass to pile them up along the wall. There were still some small wedges embedded between the pieces of the wooden frame, but the poker made quick work of those. The cool air rushed in, but she had no means other than closing the drapes to keep the chill out.

Next, Elizabeth turned her attention to the sheets. They were a rough cotton and without a hem. Hers was a solution made for a melodrama, such as she often read in a Gothic novel, but today it was real, and, though she did not know whether her plan would work or not, she knew she must make the attempt. With a frenzy driving her response, she began to rip strip after strip off the sheets. At length, she combined several strips, as if braiding them, for strength to form a rope, of sorts. Even so, she knew the rope she created would not be long enough to set them on the ground. It might have reached had she not been required to tie part of it to the bed frame and over the window ledge. As it was, she and Alice would require the courage to drop the remaining six feet or so to the ground.

"Alice will be frightened," she reasoned. "The shawl. It must be the shawl. I must tie Alice to my back. The front would be easier, but the child could be cut on the glass."

She dragged the small bed closer and wedged it beneath the window. If Mr. Wickham and Miss Chapman caught her, Elizabeth held no doubt they would do away with her. Yet, if she and Alice could reach Mr. Bingley, he would protect them until Mr. Darcy could be contacted.

Grabbing the child's bag, she meant to toss it down, but curiosity arrived. Pulling the string wider to open it, she reached inside. The maid, for some ungodly reason, had placed Alice's blue satin dress, lace gloves, slippers, and tiara inside. "Certainly would not keep the child warm," Elizabeth grumbled. "The blind leading the blind, as they say. I suppose Miss Chapman wanted to show off the child." Then Elizabeth's hand fell on the last item in the bag. Pulling it out, she smiled. "Alice's cloak." She shoved all the items back into the bag and placed it on the bed. If worst came to worst, she could sell the dress and gloves and tiara for, perhaps, a few shillings. At a minimum, the pin on her shawl would be worth something to the right merchant. Enough funds to feed them and arrange transportation home.

Kneeling beside the small mattress, she shook the child's arm and whispered, "Come, Alice. Wake for me."

The girl rubbed her eyes. "Must I?" she murmured.

"We are going to escape together," she told the child. "Put on your shoes and fasten the buckles."

"How?" Alice asked, her eyes wide in obvious fear.

"We will climb down," Elizabeth responded in more confidence than she actually felt. "Through the window."

The child's eyes widened. "We will fall," she argued.

AMENDING THE SHADES OF PEMBERLEY

"We will take our time, but if we stumble, it is not so far to the ground. We will be shaken, but still well. We have no choice, Alice. It must be now. We are in Stafford. Mr. Bingley lives in Stafford. You remember him, do you not? He was at my wedding to your father. He will assist us, for he was once married to my sister Jane, and he attended school with your father. They have known each other longer than you have been alive."

"How we find him?" Alice asked, glancing about the room.

"Your cloak, darling. The maid put your cloak in the bag. The pennies in the hem will assist us in reaching Mr. Bingley."

Although she still appeared frightened, the child nodded her head in agreement.

"Your papa will be so proud of you." Elizabeth caressed the girl's cheek. "Come now." She knotted the sheet rope around the bedpost and foot rail and then dropped it out the window. As she predicted, it was still a good six feet or so short, but she would face that danger when she encountered it.

"Hear someone." Alice tugged on Elizabeth's sleeve.

Quickly, Elizabeth pulled the rope back up. They waited as a man with a donkey cart backed it up to what must be the kitchen door. He climbed down from the cart and lifted a barrel from the back and carried it inside.

"It must be now," Elizabeth said, grabbing up the shawl. She lifted Alice to the bed and stood upon its frame to toss down the thin blankets to soften their drop. She placed the shawl under the child's rump. "Your arms are to come around my neck," she ordered. "You must hold on tight, but do not choke me." She bent to permit the child to climb upon her back and brought the ends of the shawl around her front and tied it again and again. "No leaning back, Alice. Understand?"

"Yes, Lizbet."

"Be brave for a few more minutes. I shall not permit you to fall."

Elizabeth tossed the child's bag down to the ground. It landed on the side of the blanket. The child was crying, but she did as Elizabeth asked. It was truly harder for Elizabeth to turn around crawling out the window and to maneuver over the window ledge than she had anticipated, and she was quite winded when her foot found the first knot to brace her weight for the descent.

Wrapping her ankle around the knot to support herself, she grunted, "Here we go. Be brave, sweetheart. Close your eyes if the rope scares you."

"Love you, Lizbet," the child said through her tears.

"I love you also," Elizabeth said and meant the words. Bit by bit, she lowered their combined weight, essentially by sliding from one knot to the next. With a deep breath to brace herself, after each descent, she permitted the cloth to accept her weight. She swung a bit from side to side, but a foot on the side of the building stayed them in place.

Alice gasped each time they dropped, and her grip about Elizabeth's neck and shoulders tightened. Yet, soon, Elizabeth had figured out how best to slide along the makeshift rope, and she became braver. It was difficult for her to ignore the strain on her shoulders, and each time she bumped hard against the side of the inn, she wondered upon the child she suspected she carried. Despite the cold and damp rain, sweat formed on her forehead and above her lips, but there was no means to wipe it away. Knot after knot. The rough cloth slid through her hands, making them raw with a "burn" from the material.

A quick glance down, said in a few more feet, she would be at the end of the rope. They would be required to drop to the ground. She had made a double knot some two feet before the last one as a warning she was nearing the drop.

Her arms ached terribly. The last knot was in her grip, and she was hanging on, her arms stretched high above her head. Any little flex of a muscle had her swinging from side to side and around in circles.

"Here we go, sweetheart," she said and released her hold on the knot before the child could lodge a protest. Elizabeth slammed face first into the frozen ground, and Alice's weight knocked the breath from her lungs, but there was no time to rest. Though she was gasping for air, she forced herself upward to untie the numerous knots holding the child in place. Her fingers were numb and raw; yet, she made herself concentrate on the knots rather than her own pain. There would be time to nurse her injuries, but not yet. Free at last, the child circled Elizabeth and launched herself into Elizabeth's embrace.

"Scared, Lizbet."

"But you . . . were brave," she told the child through another coughing fit. She set Alice from her and caressed the girl's cheek. "We should be prepared when the man comes out of the kitchen. If he will not provide us a ride, we will be required to discover someone who will. We must be quickly from this place before Mr. Wickham and Miss Chapman learn we are missing."

"Is she my mother?" the child asked.

"I am your mother," Elizabeth declared in adamant tones. "A mother takes care of her child. Such is what I do." Hearing noises from the still open door to the kitchen, she backed the child into the shadows and waited. Within less than a minute, a single man exited the kitchen and started for the donkey cart.

Tugging Alice closer, Elizabeth stepped into the man's path. "Pardon, sir," she said, suddenly recalling her appearance. "Do you know the residence of Mr. Charles Bingley."

The man's brows drew together in dismay. "Everyone about knows of the Bingleys. What business have you with him?"

"I know I do not look the role, but Mr. Bingley is my brother-in-marriage. The child and I were on our way to spend time with Mr. Bingley. Unfortunately, during the rain storm, our carriage was washed from the road, and our driver did not escape. A couple stopped to assist us, but I should not have trusted them. Instead of delivering us to Mr. Bingley, they meant to ask for a ransom."

"That be quite a tale, ma'am," he said in skepticism.

"We managed to escape a locked room," she confessed, but did not look back to the cloth rope, clearly on display. "Would you consider taking us to Mr. Bingley? I have five pence in the child's bag. I would

251

happily present you the pence for safe passage to Mr. Bingley's home. I am certain he will be pleased to offer you more upon our arrival."

"Who be the child?" the man asked suspiciously.

"My daughter." Elizabeth edged Alice closer to her side. "I am Mrs. Darcy. You may have heard of my husband. He is the Master of Pemberley in Derbyshire."

"Tell me your name, child," the man demanded in some sort of test. He was still not completely convinced.

"Alice Faith Anne Darcy," Alice said, although her response was not much more than a croak of a whisper.

"You'll be sorry if you mean to bam me, ma'am. I'll turn you over to the sheriff, if'n you do. Get in the back," he ordered.

"Thank you, sir. You are very kind." She lifted Alice to the flat bed of the cart. Even if Mr. Bingley was not at home and the man turned her over to the sheriff, they would be safer than if they had stayed with Miss Chapman. "How far is it to Mr. Bingley's house?"

"Mayhap two miles. Outside the city," he said. "My five pence, ma'am, if you please."

Elizabeth climbed up beside Alice. "I must fetch them from the child's bag," she explained. She covered the child with the seed sacks. Although the cloths were damp, they would conceal Alice from the view of others. Digging the cloak from the bag, she used her nails and her teeth to loosen the stitches of the hem. Within seconds, three pence fell into her hand. "Here are three. I require a minute or two to work two more free, but you can observe they are there." She glanced to the inn, wondering which room held Mr. Wickham and Ruth Chapman. "If we can leave now before we are discovered, I will present you three more, rather than two."

"No cheating me," the fellow warned.

"I would not dare," Elizabeth responded. "You do the child and me a great honor." As the wagon began to roll away, she slipped lower to cover herself, just as she had done with Alice. However, good to her word, she slid three more pence onto the seat beside the man.

AMENDING THE SHADES OF PEMBERLEY

"Stay close," she told Alice. "We will be safe soon."

Chapter Eighteen

"Darcy! Darcy! Wait!" his cousin called.

Darcy's full focus was on discovering his wife and daughter. Certainly, he did not like the possibility his wife might have been a part of Mr. Wickham's plan, but, as he had stood in the barn watching the pouring rain, he had to admit more than a bit of the chaos had arrived at his hands. He had kept too many secrets from Elizabeth, and his wife was a curious sort. Therefore, he had decided if Elizabeth would be willing to return to Pemberley and him, he would rejoice, not criticize.

He pulled up on the reins to wait for his cousin. "Did you take notice of something?" Daylight was just catching hold of the rain-soaked land.

"There is a carriage beside the inn we just passed. I did not have a good look, but I think the crest on the side was that of the Chapman family's business holdings."

"Surely Ruth would not use a family coach to stage a kidnapping," Darcy argued.

"Are we talking about the same Ruth Chapman who claimed to be with child and forced your father to send you away?" the colonel countered. "She would want you to find her, otherwise, how could she demand the ransom. She just might not want to be found so quickly."

Darcy sighed heavily. The colonel's point was perfectly clear: Ruth would do whatever she thought would benefit herself. "Let us have a closer look."

Within a half-minute, Darcy had confirmed the crest. His cousin had been correct. "I will confront the landlord. You come through the back. If Wickham runs, it will be a back door escape."

The colonel nodded his agreement and dismounted. Meanwhile, Darcy rode around to the front. Removing his gun, he entered the establishment and looked around. "Empty," he murmured as the innkeeper, apron over his clothes, rushed forward.

"May I be of service, sir?"

Darcy used the same tone he might with a stubborn tenant. "The carriage outside says you have several guests for whom I have been searching. Two women. One tall and blonde. Finely dressed. One with hair the color of liquid bronze. A small child. And a man. Dark hair."

"I fear I cannot say who occupies me rooms, sir," the innkeeper responded in self-importance.

Immediately, Darcy caught the man by his shirt. "Listen carefully," he hissed. "The woman with the red hair and the child belong to me. I am Fitzwilliam Darcy, and, if I choose to put you out of business, you will be looking for employment tomorrow. My wife and child have been kidnapped and you may hang alongside the perpetrators for your part in this travesty. Now, answer me!"

The innkeeper looked around when he heard the colonel approach, obviously looking for relief. "The man holding you by the collar is quite capable of handling his own disagreements, but, know, as he said, his first name is 'Fitzwilliam,' for he is part of the Fitzwilliam family, better known as those who have inherited the Matlock earldom. Now, I suggest you answer him and then clear from the way."

"The . . . the first room at the top of the stairs."

"All are in the same room?" Darcy questioned. "Such does not sound of Mr. Wickham," he stated.

"No, one of the women be with the child."

Darcy closed his eyes to hide his fury before he asked, "Which woman is with the child and where be their quarters?" For more reasons than he could articulate, he prayed Alice was not with Ruth, but neither did he want Elizabeth in the room with Wickham.

"The red-haired one tends the child, sir," the innkeeper assured.

"Fetch your extra inn keys for both rooms and then remove yourself from my sight."

"Yes, sir."

Darcy released him quickly. As the innkeeper raced away, the colonel said, "I want Wickham. You handle the lady."

"I may strangle her, with Elizabeth's scarf," Darcy remarked as he looked to the stairs.

"Ah, I wondered why you chose to wear that scarf," the colonel said with a smile of knowing. "You wanted your wife close to you in this madness."

Before Darcy could respond, the innkeeper returned. "Here, sir. Here be the keys. The child be in the half room above the kitchen."

"Did you hear, Colonel, my wife and child are housed in the servants' quarters?"

His cousin reminded him, "They are secure for now. First, Wickham and Miss Chapman." His cousin turned to the innkeeper, "Now, go fetch the constable or sheriff or whoever oversees crimes in this part of Staffordshire."

"There truly be a kidnapping?" the man asked.

"I shan't waste time explaining to you the urgency of this situation," the colonel growled.

"Yes, sir." The innkeeper hustled away.

Darcy followed his cousin up the steps to the second storey, though he paused briefly to touch the door behind which his wife and child were being held.

"Come," the colonel whispered.

Darcy nodded and followed. At the top of the stairs, they paused before the only door that was closed while the colonel set the key to the lock. "On three," his cousin whispered. "One. Two. Three." Fitzwilliam turned the key quickly and shoved the door wide.

Wickham, more accustomed to survival-type encounters jumped from the bed he shared with Ruth. Both had, obviously, been in the act of sexual congress. Wickham reached for a small gun on a nearby table, but the colonel was quicker. "Not today, Wickham," Fitzwilliam hissed as his fist sent Wickham spinning in place only to be caught again with another blow to the midsection. Wickham fell backwards across the bed, but the colonel pulled him off the sheets by the hair of Wickham's head to begin his punishment again.

Meanwhile, Ruth had majestically risen to stand draped in the bedding. Enough of her body showed to indicate she, too, was naked. "Look your fill, Darcy," she said and dropped the sheet to expose her breasts as she boldly tucked the bed clothes about her waist. You recall what it was like to see me thusly. We both know how much you always wanted me."

"I remember the advice Elizabeth's father provided me," he snarled. "Even a whore might stir a man's desires, but he does not wish to marry a loose woman. I would advise you to dress before the sheriff arrives to arrest you."

"You would not dare," she declared with a lift of her chin. "If you do so, the whole world will discover your precious daughter is a bastard."

It was then Darcy charged her. With one hand, he caught her about the neck and shoved her backwards, before securing Elizabeth's scarf from where it hung loosely about his shoulders with the other. Within a blink of the eye, he gleefully and purposely wrapped it about Ruth's neck several times. "It would be wonderful to do away with you," he hissed as he tightened his grip on the material. "To view you languishing for a breath of air when there was none to be had." He backed her hard against the wall, adding his weight to his efforts.

"The world would applaud if I squeezed the life from your body. You are the reason my father died without me at his side to provide him comfort. You are the reason Thomas Bennet knew his final breath." Her eyes widened in fear. "Yes, I recognized your hand writing on the letter Mr. Bennet received from his 'business partner.' It was tucked in with Bennet's personal papers which recently arrived at Pemberley." He glanced to where Mr. Wickham had given up the fight, but the colonel was not quite satisfied with rearranging the man's face. "What will Mr. Wickham do when your deeds are made known to him? When he learns your spitefulness cost him Miss Lydia Bennet's dowry? I imagine he will tell the authorities everything he knows of your plans. More importantly, what do you suppose my wife might do when she learns the misery of the last year can all be laid at your feet? She will know, and, trust me, you do not want her angry. In fact, I will furnish her the gun to do away with you and then dig the grave to cover the evidence. There are hundreds of graves in the Peak District for which no one cares to know the truth. And there will be no one to mourn your leave-taking, for the world will learn of your selfish, despicable heart."

"You will be sorry," she growled, as he finally permitted the scarf to drop to the floor and, instead, tightened both hands about her neck.

"You are correct," he countered in cold tones. "I will forever be grieved I did not dump you overboard on our way to India."

"Darcy," his cousin tapped Darcy's shoulder. "The sheriff has arrived below. Permit Miss Chapman to dress. Go retrieve your wife and child. Here is the key."

Reluctantly, Darcy peeled away each of his fingers, one-by-one, from about Ruth's neck. His hold on her had bruised the tender skin of her shoulders and neck, and the scarf had rubbed the flesh raw in parts, but he held no regrets beyond not having done so previously or having finished the deed now. He scooped up the scarf and jammed it into a pocket, took the key and darted from the room as the local sheriff entered and began questioning the colonel.

Skittering down the half flight of stairs, he set the key to the lock. "Elizabeth! Elizabeth!" he called, but there was no answer. "Elizabeth! Alice!"

The lock gave, but the door would only open a fraction. What little he could see and feel sent a dread down his spine, for the room was icy cold. "Dear God!" he prayed as he took a step back to kick at the lock. "Colonel!" he called.

"What is amiss?" his cousin asked as he, too, rushed down the steps.

"A chair is wedged under the lock," Darcy quickly explained.

"Is Mrs. Darcy and the child inside?"

"I pray not. It is bitterly cold within," Darcy kept kicking the area around the latch.

"Together," the colonel ordered. "With your shoulder."

They rushed the door as one, and it gave way. His cousin shoved the chair from the way so they could enter.

"Eliza . . ." Darcy's voice died out in the empty room. "Dear God," he said in stunned disbelief. "Where are they, Colonel?"

His cousin stuck his head out the window. "It appears Mrs. Darcy and the child escaped. Very ingenious," Fitzwilliam remarked.

Darcy looked down at the knotted sheet and the blankets on the ground. "They could have died if they had fallen."

"Although I wish she had waited," the colonel said with a grin, "I would have paid good money to have viewed their escape. Your wife is one of a kind, Darcy. Find her and never allow her to doubt your affection again."

Darcy said dejectedly, "I would do just that if I knew where to look."

"We are here, ma'am," the cart driver announced.

In truth, Elizabeth had nodded off. Finally, she had permitted herself to know a bit of ease. She sat up quickly, wiping at her eyes. "Thank you, sir."

The man climbed down and came around to assist her and Alice to the ground. Evidently, he was still hoping for more compensation.

The house was more modern and less historic in its design than she had expected, but it was a fine looking house. Elizabeth thought Jane would have been pleased to live within. With one final surge of determination, she crossed to the door. She would not be surprised if Mr. Bingley's butler argued with her, but she had come too far to turn back now. She released the knocker, while Alice clung to the side of her leg.

After a brief pause, the door swung wide, and the butler's eyebrows rose in disapproval. "Yes, ma'am."

Elizabeth sighed heavily. "I know my appearance will say otherwise, but I am the late Mrs. Bingley's sister. The child and I have escaped from two who meant to use us to earn a ransom. Please say Mr. Bingley is at home."

The butler looked behind her. "The master is in a meeting and left orders not to be disturbed."

"Could you not tell him Elizabeth Darcy requires his assistance?" she begged.

Before the servant could close the door in her face, a voice called, "What is amiss, Mr. Radcliffe?"

"Mr. Bingley!" Elizabeth called as she darted around the butler.

"Good God, Elizabeth!" Mr. Bingley gasped and rushed down the stairs to catch her up. "What has occurred?"

She glanced to where the man still waited for more money. "Could you pay the man who brought us here? Come, Alice." The child scampered around the men.

"Certainly." Bingley gestured to the butler. "Pay him, Radcliffe. I thank you, sir, for bringing my family home." He then turned Elizabeth's steps towards a nearby sitting room. "Let us see you warm."

"I must look a mess," she said reaching for her hair.

"Such does not matter," he said softly. He instructed the butler, "Bring hot tea and sandwiches." When they were inside the room, he turned to close the door and then seated her before the fire. Kneeling before her, he said in hard tones. "Tell me Darcy has not abused you so."

"Not my husband, but Mr. Wickham," she assured, but exhaustion was claiming her ability even to think straight. "Mr. Wickham stole Alice away from Pemberley. I attempted to stop him, and he forced me into the carriage as well."

"Wickham?" Bingley asked in disbelief. "For what purpose?"

She extended her hands in the direction of fire's warmth. "Money, I suppose. It is a long story, but you likely already know Mr. Wickham is the late Mr. Darcy's godson. He was in league with and likely in the bed of Miss Chapman."

"Oh, my," Bingley shot a glance to Alice, who had sat on the floor at Elizabeth's feet.

"Wanted to ransom the child," she explained as best she could.

"How did you escape?" he asked.

"Climbed down a handmade rope to reach the alley behind the inn where they held us." She showed him her raw hands and knuckles.

"Lizbet be brave and so did me," Alice attempted to tell part of the story.

"Your father will know great pride," she told the child. "I must send word to Mr. Darcy of Alice's safety. I doubt he is at Pemberley, but I must inform the Matlocks, who were staying at the estate for Mary's wedding how we are free and with you." She found herself swaying in place. "Would it be too much to ask to claim a bed? I have not slept for more than a day. I was up several hours before dawn overseeing the last of the details for Mary's wedding. Was that truly only yesterday. It seems so long ago."

"Naturally," Mr. Bingley assured. "I will send word to Darcy. Would you like a hot bath?"

Elizabeth shook her head in the negative. "Maybe later. All my energy has disappeared. Alice, though, might like the sandwiches."

"Go with you, Lizbet," the child announced.

"Apologize to your cook, sir. I simply cannot concentrate further."

"Permit me to support you to a room. Then I will send my housekeeper to attend you." Elizabeth offered him her hand. "My, your fingers are as cold as ice," he declared.

"My toes also," she murmured.

He assisted her to her feet. "Come along, Miss Alice. You may stay in the room with Elizabeth. Would you like sandwiches and cakes?"

Elizabeth heard the timidity in Alice's voice. "Lemon?" she asked softly. Elizabeth thought to smile at the child's singularity regarding cakes, but she could not concentrate enough to lift her lips.

"Lemon, it is," Mr. Bingley assured.

As Elizabeth clumsily climbed the stairs with Mr. Bingley at her side, she murmured. "Tell Mr. Darcy I am grieved. I did not know. I truly did not know what was planned for Alice." It was all she was capable of saying before she collapsed. She could hear Mr. Bingley calling for his footman to assist him and Alice crying, but there was nothing Elizabeth could do to prevent the chaos. The darkness swirled around her, and she permitted it to take her under.

<hr>

"Where can they be?" Darcy asked his cousin yet another time, though he had done so repeatedly without an answer.

Against his first inclinations, the sheriff had finally placed Ruth under arrest. It took the colonel mentioning his father was an earl several times to "convince" the man they would settle for no other outcome.

"Mrs. Darcy is obviously attempting to keep Alice safe," his cousin reminded him. "If you have no objection, I will send for Matlock. Beyond a doubt, Ruth will send for her father. When Chapman arrives, he will demand his daughter's release. We must use Wickham against Ruth. The dastard knows the majority of her secrets."

"You are suggesting we permit Wickham his freedom in order to punish Ruth?" Darcy asked incredulously.

"Heavens, no. I would not want Wickham to earn his freedom so easily. In fact, I am thinking the Canadian frontier or, perhaps, Burma. Both are places his skills would be required to keep him alive. But only if Wickham sends Ruth to a penal colony. If not, they can both hang for kidnapping."

"Where is the innkeeper?" a man asked.

"Attempting to repair the window above," the colonel said with a bit of irritation for being interrupted.

"The one the lady and child climbed out of?" the fellow asked, pleased with himself.

Darcy was on his feet immediately. "You know them. Have you seen them?"

"Yes, sir. I sees them. Delivered them to the Bingley house, I did."

"Bingley? Bingley is here? I had forgotten he had a house in Stafford." Immediately, a bit of jealousy crept in, but Darcy was quick to shove it away, for he had promised himself he wanted Elizabeth's return no matter the terms required to make it happen. "Where is his house?"

"Family's house. His father lived there before him. It be through town and the fork to the left. Gave me a guinea, he did, for bringing the lady to him. Said she be family."

Darcy reached into his pocket and tossed the man another coin. "I, too, am in your debt. They are my family." To his cousin, he said, "I must go."

"I will find you," the colonel assured. "Ask Bingley if he minds housing the earl, as well as me. I do not imagine an inn such as this will . . . Never mind." He gestured towards the door. "Why are you still here?"

Darcy grinned. "Just listening to my much older cousin issuing orders."

"Be gone!" Fitzwilliam barked a laugh. "I am charging all my expenses to you."

"Well worth it. You know where to find me." And with those words, Darcy was gone. Within minutes, he was on the road to Bingley's house. It was the first time he had permitted himself a taste of hope in weeks. At length, he directed his horse onto the drive to Charles Bingley's house. He was exceedingly glad Elizabeth had found assistance, but, if truth be told, he was grieved not to be the one who had rescued her. There was always such ease between his wife and Bingley, he could not quite keep the tendrils of jealousy at bay. Darcy would admit, but only to himself, he and Elizabeth had never developed such easiness between them, and he did not know how to achieve it. It was all very frustrating, for he had thought from the beginning she could not only be his lover, but the one person he could trust above all others. At least, she was safe, and he would finally have the opportunity to confess everything to her and attempt to win her affection.

There was a small black gig before the house when he arrived, but he assumed Bingley had company. Darcy dismounted and handed off his horse to a boy who ran up from the stables. "Thank you," he said as he tossed the youth a coin. "I will be awhile. Rub him down if you would."

"Yes, sir."

Releasing the knocker, Darcy waited for someone to answer the door. Within less than a minute, a proper butler responded. "Pardon the wait, sir. May I be of service?"

"I am Mr. Darcy. I understand my wife and child have taken sanctuary with Mr. Bingley. Might I see them?"

The man glanced to the staircase. "Your family is above, sir, but the surgeon is with Mrs. Darcy."

"My wife? A surgeon? What is amiss?" he demanded as he pushed past the man. "Where is she?"

"Up here," a familiar voice called. "Elizabeth collapsed. I summoned medical care. I did not think an apothecary would do."

Darcy's heart plummeted to his stomach. "I must see her."

"Come up," Bingley ordered and turned to walk away.

Darcy took the stairs two at a time. "How bad is she?" he asked as he closed the distance between him and Bingley.

Bingley rounded on him to say angrily, "Exhausted. Covered in bruises and cuts. Exposed to the weather. The surgeon is concerned about her injuries and her complete collapse, for he suspects Mrs. Darcy is with child. Elizabeth murmured something to that effect. A child, Darcy. Do you know what I would give to be in your shoes? To have a loving wife and children? I pray going forward you will treat Elizabeth better than you have to date. It is not all about the money and the house for her. She would happily live in a cottage and tend the land with you if you loved each other." Bingley paused briefly to swallow his emotions, biting his lip and refocusing his thoughts. "I saw you. At the inn near Yorkshire. With another woman. How could you? Just know, I will not stand aside and permit you to make Elizabeth miserable. I promised Jane I would see to her sisters, and I mean to keep my promise to my late wife."

"There was nothing between Miss Chapman and me," Darcy stated in terms he hoped Mr. Bingley would believe. "I have kept my secrets, but they were to protect Elizabeth, not harm her. She and Alice are my life." He closed his eyes and said a silent prayer of forgiveness. "I did not know Elizabeth was with child. She had not spoken of her suspicions."

"When might she have said those words to you?" Bingley accused. "You have much for which to be grateful, but you did not trust your wife with your secrets, and your pride and conceit could cost you the love Elizabeth offered you, or, worse, her life."

He wanted to lash out against Bingley's judgmental tone, but he knew the man correct. "May I see her? I have sins of which to speak to her and her forgiveness to earn."

Bingley turned to lead the way along a hall and stopped to open a nearby door, before he stepped aside.

From the portal, Darcy could view his wife in the bed. She appeared so small and so helpless, a hard knot formed in his chest. However, before he could step inside, a small voice called, "Papa," as Alice barreled into the side of Darcy's leg. He bent to pick her up, but his eyes remained on the lifeless form of his wife.

He kissed Alice's cheek. "Are you well, sweetheart?"

"Lizbet tected me. She's sick, Papa," his child said with a pout.

"You and I will watch over her. Permit me to speak with the surgeon, then you can tell me what happened." He kissed her again. "We will be here until Elizabeth is well so it is acceptable for you to nap and play. It is my occupation to protect Elizabeth." He turned to Bingley. "That is, if such is acceptable to you, sir."

"I want Elizabeth to recover and to know love. As you are her choice, then such is mine," Bingley said.

"Would it also be acceptable to house my cousin Colonel Fitzwilliam and his father the Earl of Matlock? I will require the influence of both to see those who exercised their will against me and mine are held accountable. Your local sheriff may require persuasion to see this madness through."

"If they mean to know justice for Elizabeth and your daughter, I would be honored," Bingley said. "I will see to appropriate quarters."

"Papa," his child tapped he cheek. "I draw a picture for Lizbeth?"

"Yours is an excellent idea, love." Darcy looked to Bingley. "Might you have paper and pencils the child can use or should I send someone into Stafford for them?"

"I have some in my study. Would you like to come with me?" Darcy placed Alice down between them, and Bingley extended his hand to Darcy's daughter. "I am your Uncle Bingley, and it is time we learned more of each other, for we are family now." Alice looked to Darcy for permission. When he nodded his head in the affirmative, his child tentatively caught Bingley's hand. "Could we have more cakes?"

Bingley smartly asked, "What would Elizabeth say to such a request?"

Alice's lip pouted out at not immediately having her way, but she said, "Lizbet tells me I must eat my soup first."

Bingley leaned down to say, "In all the time I have known Elizabeth, she has been very wise. If you wish to be as wise as her, you must eat your soup before you have cake."

Darcy looked on, realizing, in many ways, God had erred by not providing Bingley a child. By nature, the man was excessively kind, and Darcy finally understood something of Elizabeth's preference for the man.

"Are you the lady's husband?" a man stepped from behind a screen where he had been washing his hands, for he wiped them with a towel.

"I am Mr. Darcy. What can you tell me of my wife's condition?"

The man introduced himself with a bow. "I am Mr. Schneider. In truth, I am more than a bit concerned regarding Mrs. Darcy. It would be natural for her to be exhausted from what Mr. Bingley has described as an ordeal none should endure. However, even exhausted, Mrs. Darcy should still be prepared to respond to simple questions. However, in your wife's case, it is as if when she turned over your child's care to Mr. Bingley, she was 'finished,' if such makes any sense."

"I wish I could say it did not," Darcy reluctantly admitted. "Mrs. Darcy and I have not walked a 'traditional' route to know marriage, but I assure you, sir, I have never raised my hand to her, nor would I ever be tempted to do so. We had an 'arranged' marriage, so to speak, which was surrounded by tragedy on both sides with the death of parents and siblings. Mr. Bingley's late wife being one of them. We have had a great deal to overcome in a short period of time."

Mr. Schneider nodded his head in understanding. "Such may be the source of what my initial examination has revealed. Mrs. Darcy is, I believe, physically strong enough to recover from her injuries and the exposure to the cold; yet, I must offer you a caveat before you take on the notion all will be well."

"What can you mean?" Darcy pressed. "Must I prepare myself to the real possibility Elizabeth will not survive this?" He dared not ask of the child, for he realized, in that moment, he would gladly do without an heir, but not without Elizabeth. Her presence had filled all the gaps in his life and had made him whole again.

"You must convince her to live," Schneider said simply. "Convince her she has a reason to live. Tell her of her worth in your life. Speak to her need to fight for the life you will share together. Tell Mrs. Darcy of what you foresee for your future as man and wife. Of what you wish for your children. Perhaps then, Mrs. Darcy will leave the comfort of languishing in the unknown between life and death and accept the idea of walking into your shared future, hand-in-hand."

Chapter Nineteen

For the next two days, Darcy remained at Elizabeth's side, taking on much of her care, bathing her and adding ointment and salves to each of her cuts and bruises. While he treated her, he spoke of his devotion to her and begged her to remain with him and Alice. When he slept beside her, he wrapped one end of the scarf about her arm and the other about his, connecting them for all time, as well as alerting him if she awoke suddenly or suffered violently. He had no wish other than to see Elizabeth well.

Therefore, when Lord Matlock had again called Darcy back into negotiations with Mr. Chapman, who meant to see his daughter set free, Darcy arrived at the jail already out of sorts.

"A woman cannot be thought to kidnap her own child, and Ruth never actually asked for a ransom," Chapman declared with confidence. "Your request to charge her as such will never hold up in court. None of us wish to parade our private lives before all of London."

Driven by an image of Elizabeth's unresponsive body, Darcy hissed. "In England, a child belongs to its father. Only 'he' determines where a child may travel and with whom." Darcy did not want to play his hand too soon, but he wanted nothing more to do with the Chapmans. They were all alike. Manipulative and caring for none but themselves. "As to Ruth claiming she is the child's mother, such a statement would not hold up in court. Beyond her claims otherwise, Ruth is not Alice's mother."

"How can that be?" Chapman protested. "I am not best happy to know Ruth chose to lay with Captain Meachem, especially as he was a married man . . ."

"Especially," Darcy interrupted. "You would have preferred for your daughter to seduce someone richer and less worldly. Such would certainly have described me when I stepped onto the ship to India with your daughter. I imagine you knew Ruth was not with child then, but you recognized how I once favored her, and you suspected my father would do anything to keep scandal from his door, even going so far as to banish his son to a life neither of them ever fully comprehended. My father thought I would write of his grandchild's birth, and he would welcome me home. All would be forgiven. Yet, when no grandchild was produced, George Darcy realized it was he, rather than his son, who had created the uproar which was my banishment."

Darcy recognized as he provided an excuse for his father's actions, he was more than likely speaking the truth. "I imagine your daughter was not a virgin when we departed England, but you assumed I lusted after her and would eventually succumb to her so-called 'charms.' I presume my not doing so was equally as troubling to you as it proved to be for Ruth. After all, according to those who knew her, your daughter had several lovers that first year or so we were in India, but none of them was I. In fact, I gave Ruth enough money to return to England or to stay, and I moved inland to look for some sort of employment. It was not until Meachem contacted me nearly a year after I had last seen Ruth regarding her being with child, did I return to oversee her care. She was some six to seven months along, at the time. Did you or your wife instruct her to become with child? Did you think people in England cannot count the days it takes to deliver a child? Did you think there was no one to stand witness to the fact your daughter and I had been several hundred miles apart for some ten months?"

Ignoring Darcy's questions, Chapman took up another round of objections. "Ruth says you changed the child's birthday, and Alice is actually younger than you tell others," Chapman accused. "I 'am guessing,'" he said mockingly, "you thought it would be easier to claim Ruth's child as yours in that manner."

AMENDING THE SHADES OF PEMBERLEY

Darcy avoided the question for the time being. "Did she also tell you, I presented her three thousand pounds to leave the child with me, rather than to carry Alice across India, chasing after Meachem, a man who left Ruth within six months of his wife discovering something of his infidelity. Your daughter forgot how some younger sons marry into a rich and powerful family, but they must walk a thin line in fear the wife's family will destroy him if he abuses her. Meachem is one such man. I would be surprised to learn that Captain Meachem thought it would advance his career or his marriage to swear in court something of his affair with your daughter. All of society would be there to witness what the good captain would have to say of Miss Ruth Chapman. My bet is on a denial. What of yours? Moreover, Meachem will be quite angry to have his family name dragged through the mud of scandal."

"Such does not mean the child belongs to you," Chapman argued. "Ruth gave birth to her. She belongs to Ruth. I have seen your wife, Darcy. No one would believe the child belongs to Mrs. Darcy, if such is what you intend to profess."

Darcy said with a smirk, "Mrs. Darcy is currently recovering from the abuse put on her by your daughter and Mr. Wickham at the home of Mr. Charles Bingley. Do you know Mr. Bingley, Chapman?"

"Not personally, but I am aware of his influence in the area. His father was apparently part of the *nouveau riche* we find much in society today. What does all this have to do with Ruth and Alice?"

"It might have been better if Ruth bothered more with those not of the gentry. If she did, she would have realized when she, Wickham, and my family stopped in Stafford, my Elizabeth would not permit the chance to escape pass her by. You see, Mr. Bingley's late wife was Miss Jane Bennet, a woman tall and statuesque and blonde, and Elizabeth's eldest sister. In fact, of Mr. Thomas Bennet's five daughters, no two had the exact same shade of hair. Mr. Ericks's wife, the former Mary Bennet, has a mossy brown shade of hair. I understand Miss Lydia Bennet and Miss Katherine Bennet also differed from the others. Ask Mr. Wickham if you do not believe me. He was to marry the youngest daughter. The fool learned of my allegiance to Mr. Bennet and attempted to wedge himself into my life again by claiming one of

Elizabeth's sisters. So, Mrs. Darcy could be Alice's mother. Then again, my mother was blonde, not so tall, but my sister is both blonde and tall. Who says Alice does not favor Lady Anne Darcy?"

"Yet, people will never believe Mrs. Darcy is Alice's mother," Chapman insisted. "You may protest all you want, but people believe what they see."

"People believe what the master of one of the largest estates in England tells them to believe," Darcy corrected. "Moreover, if any be so foolish as to ask, I possess a baptismal certificate provided by the Church of England which states Elizabeth and I are Alice's parents. Tell me you are smart enough not to press me further, Chapman, for you will become the laughing stock of your little corner of the gentry. Or should I say your wife's corner of the gentry?."

Surprisingly, or perhaps not so surprisingly, the man still did not back down. Darcy was beginning to recognize the source of Ruth's tenacity and lack of listening carefully to warnings. "You would not dare to embarrass your wife with such a falsehood." Chapman puffed himself up in importance. "I know you did not marry your lady until you arrived in England this last September past."

"And I have a marriage certificate which says Elizabeth and I have been married for more than five years, actually, shortly after I confirmed Ruth's ploy to be false. My wife and I married in the Church of England in India's capital."

"How could you marry in India? The woman was in England." Chapman pointed an accusing finger at Darcy.

"It was a proxy marriage, which is legal in England and Wales, as long as it is conducted in and by a member of the clergy from the Church of England. Such is the reason we had a second marriage in Hertfordshire, so our joining would be legal in all of King George's kingdom. I explained it all to Mr. Williamson, the vicar in my wife's former community. He thought the union in Mrs. Darcy's former home a splendid homage to her father, whose letter I showed the vicar regarding his permission for Elizabeth and I to marry. She was not of age for the first ceremony, but was when we recently wed. You will discover it was all quite legal."

"Even if you did marry the woman by proxy, no means exist for her to deliver a child in India," Chapman countered.

"Such is the thing with a baptismal certificate, many people wait a few months or even years before the child is brought before the clergy, what with the rate of early deaths and all. The English in India are often slow to bring their children before the clergy in India. Sort of snobbery with thinking their children will not be accepted in British society, even though the clergy are part of the Church of England. Likely, such explains one of the reasons the British church has not known the dominance we living in England and elsewhere within the British Empire would prefer. Yet, 'Alice' has her name on such a certificate, which both her father and mother signed."

"Mrs. Darcy has never been in India," Chapman declared in triumph.

"Do you know, from the beginning, Ruth despised how I stared, sometimes for hours upon end, at the miniature of Miss Elizabeth Bennet, which Mr. Bennet left behind on the dock when he saw me off to India. For me, Elizabeth became the only woman I could consider taking to wife. From her father's letters, I learned more about her preferences and dislikes and character than most men of our station discover in a decade of marriage. When I knew for certain your daughter had fabricated her tale of carrying a child, though I already knew she did not carry my child, for we had never lain together, I decided Miss Elizabeth would be my wife. No matter how often your daughter flaunted her 'wares' before me, and, believe me, such was often, I could not and would not be tempted."

"So, you presented the Bennet girl your heart early on," Chapman growled in frustration, "but your doing so does not make Mrs. Darcy Alice's mother."

The tension in Darcy's shoulders came down a notch. He would expose how he had trapped Ruth in a corner. Mr. Bennet's plan had been as complete as one designed by the greatest of masterminds. He hoped his wife woke soon so he could explain it all to her and permit her to marvel at the "lovely" deviousness of her father. Darcy suspected, despite the absurdities practiced, Elizabeth would be impressed.

"Ask any in Elizabeth's former Hertfordshire neighborhood, and he or she will tell you something of how my sweet Elizabeth left her home for an extended period a few years back to tend her ailing grandparents. Such coincided with not only Alice's birth, but also with my traveling to the English side of Africa to secure the purchase of the mine I came to own in India. Would any who knew me to have lusted after your daughter for a few short months all those years removed think me devious enough to concoct such a plan while Ruth was in labor? After all, you and your daughter had the whole world thinking I was the most 'gullible' man ever to claim a breath, so 'gullible' I would marry a woman of Ruth Chapman's reputation and consider myself blessed by her desire for my family's fortune," Darcy hissed. "Tell your daughter to agree to Lord Matlock's offer or prepare herself for a public trial where all of England will recognize her depravity. After all, each day she is incarcerated here is another day for the gossip to spread to the neighboring shires. We all know how hard it is to contain gossip or quash it once it begins. God only knows there are still men like Mr. Benson who think I pine after a woman any man with a purse of more than a thousand pounds could claim. Hell, Ruth was in bed and in the act of intimacies when Colonel Fitzwilliam and I found her at the local inn, and Wickham rarely has more than a few pence in his pockets."

"I ought to . . ." Chapman stood toe-to-toe with Darcy.

"Please do," Darcy said in cold calmness, knowing he had won. "For years, I have wanted to beat you into a pulp."

Matlock stepped between them. "Head back to Mrs. Darcy, my boy. Chapman and I will come to terms without you. I told your father on his death bed, you would be the best of the Darcys for you possessed a large dollop of George Darcy's dogged determination, but a larger scoop of Lady Anne Darcy's cleverness. My youngest sister was quite tenacious and clever when outside forces meant to destroy her family. The idea of your success pleased your father greatly, for he laughed easily. With tears in his eyes, he said, 'Anne would find my observation wonderfully delightful. I will tell her when I see her.' Then he took his last breath.

⌘

Elizabeth worked hard to pierce the darkness and to reach the point of light dangling like a carrot on a stick before a stubborn donkey. She wanted the light. Wished to learn if Alice was well and if Fitzwilliam had arrived. Would he turn from her? Would he believe she had no knowledge of Mr. Wickham's plans?

She had been so cold, even her bones felt as if they had been formed of ice. Yet, there was no time to seek warmth. Alice had depended on her. The child was so frightened, just as had been she.

Easily, Elizabeth recalled the sound of her husband's voice—his calling her name in desperation—but, also, in some other emotion—something which spoke of betrayal, but was the betrayal his or hers? Would he forgive her? Did she require Mr. Darcy's forgiveness? Should he not require hers?

Her husband had kept so many secrets regarding Alice and the child's mother, and those secrets had placed Alice and her in danger. "*And my own child*," Elizabeth's mind announced, and, behind her closed lids, she saw herself reach to place a protective hand across her abdomen as she turned on her side to protect the babe from harm.

Like it or not, she began to drift back into the darkness, but a noise alerted her of someone's presence nearby, and, for a moment, she thought she and Alice had been discovered. She still clung to a rough cloth, and, for the briefest of moments, Elizabeth thought she was remained hidden under the dirty seed sacks with Alice. Yet, the cloth did not smell of horses or of manure: The cloth smelled of clear air on a sunny day and a most familiar scent, but one she could not name.

A tug upon the cloth had her reaching to protect Alice, but the only child she could find was the one she carried. Her hand remained upon her abdomen, too heavy to lift it, but still protective, nevertheless. She remained still. Wherever she rested shifted from a heavier weight, and she expected Mr. Wickham to snatch away the cloth which covered her and to strike her. He had warned her he would do so if she attempted an escape. Yet, she could not move, though her mind begged her to return to the darkness.

Someone or something tugged her hand free of where she cuddled her child. She wanted to protest, but a warm whiff of air crossed her knuckles and a tender brush of flesh had her wanting more. "Stay with me, Elizabeth," a voice sounding very much of her husband spoke softly to her. "I cannot do any of this without you. Please, darling, Alice and I desperately require your guidance. Your father promised me you would make me a better man. I still require your hands to mold me into a man of whom you may be proud."

Sometime recently, but not a time she could name, Elizabeth had briefly caught a glimpse of her father and had thought to rush into the comfort of his arms, but he had waved her away—motioned her back the way she had come—before he disappeared again.

"Your father chose me for you long before his passing. Wake and permit me finally to speak to the brilliance of Thomas Bennet's plan for his favorite daughter."

Elizabeth desperately wanted to know it all. She could not leave this earth without knowing. Her eyelids were nearly too heavy to lift; however, almost of their own will, her eyes flickered open, and she saw Fitzwilliam's face, pale and grief stricken, then the image dissolved into darkness once more, and she spun backwards into the abyss. Yet, a tug of his hand over hers begged her to remain.

⁂

Within a little over a half hour, Darcy entered his wife quarters in Bingley's household. His host was reportedly away overnight, and both Lord Matlock and the colonel remained in town. He glanced to where Alice was curled up and asleep on a small mattress. A large trunk sat open along the wall. A note in Sheffield's handwriting said he and Hannah had chosen several changes of clothing for Alice, Elizabeth, and him. A mention of how his servants were offering daily prayers for

Elizabeth's recovery had Darcy looking to the bed. Somehow, Elizabeth had turned on her side, but her face was still flushed and she appeared still to be unconscious. Reaching down to claim Miss Cassandra from the trunk, he tucked the doll under Alice's arm. His daughter had, of late, not been so dependent on the doll, but he suspected Alice would again require reassurances.

Sitting in a nearby chair, he removed his boots, the ones he customarily wore in the fields—those he had forced upon his feet when he departed Pemberley. Standing again, he deposited his jacket on the back of the chair, along with his waistcoat. Quietly, he lifted the bed clothes and slid in beside his wife. Capturing her hand, the one about which he had tied the scarf, he brought it to his lips for a kiss. "Stay with me, Elizabeth. I cannot do any of this without you. Please, darling, Alice and I desperately require your guidance. Your father promised me you would make me a better man. I still require your hands to mold me into a man of whom you may be proud. Your father chose me for you long before his passing. Wake and permit me finally to speak to the brilliance of Thomas Bennet's plan for his favorite daughter." He tugged on her fingers a second time.

Yet, his wife did not respond, and so, with a sigh of defeat, Darcy caught hold of his end of the scarf and closed his eyes, setting his mind once again to remembering all which had transpired between them. This business with Ruth was not yet over, although he held no doubt Lord Matlock would prevail. Darcy knew his uncle was considered a most excellent negotiator.

He brought forth the sweet image of Elizabeth at sixteen, captured on the miniature. He had studied it extensively—knew every line of the artist's brushstroke—had imagined how she might have grown into the woman she was—had wondered, if he had courted her properly, would she have accepted him. Somehow, he feared she would have refused him, especially as he possessed too much pride in those early days of his acquaintance with Mr. Bennet. The son of an earl's daughter and one of the richest men in all of England had a right to his pride, or so he had thought. As fiery as he now knew her to be, Darcy could easily imagine what his Elizabeth would have said to his very "constipated" proposal.

"From the very beginning, I may almost say, of my acquaintance with you, your manners impressing me with the fullest belief of your arrogance, your conceit, and your selfish disdain of the feelings of others, formed the groundwork on which I built so immovable a dislike I can say I felt you were the last man in the world whom I could ever be prevailed upon to marry."

It had taken him years of working side-by-side with those less fortunate than any could have imagined to open his mind and his heart to a woman willing to do the hard work a truly successful marriage required. His image of such a marriage had been honed in the little discussions conducted, first, over several cups of strong coffee at the inn table he and Bennet had shared that fateful night, as well as by long-distance mail—letters so thick they would have cost the average laborer several month's wages.

From the beginning, Darcy had learned how Thomas Bennet's marriage to Miss Frances Gardiner had started well, or so the gentleman believed, but Mr. Bennet admitted to a less than pleasing painting of conjugal felicity and domestic comfort. "Captivated by youth and beauty," Elizabeth's father had told Darcy as they drank and talked together in honest conversation, "and the appearance of good humor which youth and beauty generally give, much as you have previously looked upon Miss Chapman, I married a woman whose weak understanding and illiberal mind, I am sorry to say, very early in our marriage put an end to any chance of real affection—real understanding between us. You must, boy, not permit this to happen to you. Respect, esteem, and confidence will vanish quickly. They can each die a quick death. Any hopes of domestic happiness will be lost forever, for marriage is exactly that: Forever."

Darcy was soon to understand Mr. Bennet was not of a disposition to seek comfort for the disappointment his own imprudence had brought him in those pleasures, which too often console the unfortunate for their folly. "I am fond of the country, actually despise London, and am very fond of books. This is not the sort of happiness which a man would, in general, wish to owe to his wife . . ." Bennet had shrugged off any disappointment he felt. "Yet, where other powers of entertainment are wanting, the true philosopher will derive benefit from such as are given.

"I worry some on the younger two of my daughters, for they follow their mother's ill-advised ideas. Mary will name her own way once she discovers her voice." Darcy had stood witness to Miss Mary claiming her happiness. The idea Elizabeth's father had been correct would have pleased the man's ego greatly.

"My Jane will do well. She is a beauty of both countenance and spirit. She will choose a man whose tempers are by no means unlike her own. I expect them to be so complying, nothing will ever be resolved. So easy, every servant will cheat them and be so generous they will always exceed their income." The idea of Charles Bingley fitting Mr. Bennet's description before Bennet had even taken Bingley's acquaintance brought a smile to Darcy's lips. "And for Elizabeth . . . "

Soft fingers touched his mouth. "You smile," a raspy voice said.

His eyes sprang open to view Elizabeth's hazel ones looking upon him. Darcy reached for her, but made himself not jerk her into his embrace. "My darling girl," he said as his hands searched her face. "I feared I had lost you."

"Feared I had lost you, as well," she said with some apparent difficulty in forming the words.

"Never," he said adamantly. "Never will you lose me. I love you, Elizabeth. Most ardently. I loved you before I ever actually knew you."

Tears filled her eyes. "How?"

"It is a long story, too long for this moment, but I promise you will know it all as quickly as you are well enough to hear it."

"Alice?" she asked.

"Asleep on the mattress on the floor. She will be ecstatic to learn her 'Lizbeth' has awakened," he assured.

"Miss Chapman? Mr. Wickham?" A frown formed on her forehead in disapproval.

"In jail. Lord Matlock and the colonel are overseeing an agreement to send Wickham to either the Canadian wilderness to serve with British forces there or to Burma, and Miss Chapman back to India. Neither will have an option to return to England, unless they wish to face kidnapping charges and transportation to Australia. I have told Mr. Chapman I do not fear the scandal Ruth believes will result for Alice. Years past, your blessed father concocted a plan to protect me and Alice."

"Why did you never tell me?" she asked, and, again, Darcy noted the doubt crossing her countenance.

"I feared you would not believe me, but I will speak honestly of the events. Moreover, my trunk from India is at Pemberley. I will offer you a full accounting and then you may read it all in your dear father's handwriting. Just say you will provide us a chance to begin again. Say you might learn to love me in return."

"I do so most ardently."

Unable to control his ardor, Darcy leaned over her to claim her lips for what he hoped was a kiss of renewal. He had just felt Elizabeth relax when a small voice said, "Papa, why you eat Lizbet's lips?"

Elizabeth froze, turned her head to bury it in the pillow, and shook with giggles.

Darcy said under his breath, "Remind me to add small bells to the hem of her dresses." To his child, he said, "I was simply delighted with joy to have my wife awake, at last."

"I delight joy also," Alice said. "See Miss Cassandra finds me. Finds you too, Lizbet."

"So, she did," Elizabeth said with a genuine smile for his daughter. "Would you like to join us in the bed?"

"Yes, peas. Miss Cassie, too, Papa."

"Absolutely," Darcy said as he rose to lift Alice to the bed to sit close to Elizabeth. He looked on as his wife caressed Alice's cheek in obvious affection.

"Did you tell Miss Cassandra how brave you were?" his wife asked.

"You brave, Lizbet," his child said with a slight quiver of her bottom lip.

"'We' were brave together," Elizabeth corrected. "I could not have known courage without you assisting me."

"I could not be brave without you holder me," the child responded, and Darcy's eyes filled with quick tears.

"Did you teach Alice to say that?" he questioned quietly.

His wife's eyes were also misted with tears, but a quick shake of her head in the negative was her response. Instead, she took Alice's little hand in hers. "When I was small, my papa, who was a very learned man, told me if I shared my fear with my doll, it would be cut in half. I imagine Miss Cassandra would be willing to hear your secrets. Has she not always kept your secrets for you?"

Alice nodded quickly in the affirmative.

"Then tonight, before you fall asleep, tell Miss Cassandra your secrets," Elizabeth whispered.

"Kin I tell Miss Cassie how papa ate your lips?" the child asked in earnest.

Elizabeth again hid her humor, while Darcy scooped the child from the bed. "Why do you not find the drawings you made for Elizabeth, while I ask someone to fetch a bath for her? Our sweet Elizabeth has spent more than four days in these same clothes. She will feel more like herself with a bath and something to eat and then more rest."

"I draw you a flower," Alice said as she darted away to secure the drawing.

Elizabeth said softly. "I always wanted a flower drawing from you."

Darcy glanced to his wife to note how she looked after the child with such softness, it nearly broke his heart. He prayed her words of a possible child to the surgeon had not been part of Elizabeth's delirium.

His wife should be surrounded by children. Their children. However, first, he must convince her to stay the course he and her father had set in motion years past.

Chapter Twenty

It was another four days before Elizabeth was able to stand on her own, but each day she had been awake for longer and longer periods of time. He had told her parts of his story when she was up to learning more. He had insisted on being brutally honest: It was important she knew it all.

"So, my father suggested you wait until you and Miss Chapman reached India before you married the lady?" Elizabeth sat on the end of a settee with Alice's head resting in Elizabeth's lap and the child asleep. His wife aimlessly stroked Alice's hair in a loving gesture.

"Your father reasoned, as I claimed never having lain with Ruth, she was either lying about being with child or, if she had conceived, the babe belonged to another. He wisely surmised I should not marry Alice in London, as my father had instructed. I was to call on my godfather the morning before the ship was to leave and secure a special license, just as I did for us, and marry Ruth without fanfare at a small church, any we could find where the clergy was willing to conduct the service. However, your father had reasoned, a marriage in India would be as legal as would be one in England, as long as it was conducted by a clergy of the Church of England. Mr. Bennet reminded me a woman generally does not know of the child's existence until she feels the quickening, which, as I understand it correctly, is customarily in the fourth month." Darcy watched his wife carefully, for she had yet to speak of the possibility of their own child. "The fact four months earlier, actually more than four months earlier, I had been in Scotland at the Fitzwilliam property located there, had held no sway in the argument with my father regarding whether I had done the deed or not.

"Mr. Bennet had cautioned me not to succumb to Ruth's so-called 'charms' during the journey to India and, instead, demand I become Ruth's 'guard' to assure she did not permit any among those upon the ship access to her before we reached India."

"I suppose my father's logic made sense," Elizabeth mused, "as the journey to India is, customarily, believed to be eight to twelve weeks. If Miss Chapman had been far enough along to recognize herself as being with child, she would be between six and seven months, enough for her to be increasing in girth by the time you stepped off the ship in India."

"Such was as Mr. Bennet so cautioned," Darcy assured. "Obviously, with five daughters, he knew something of a woman's time before her actual lying in."

"I still do not understand why your father did not suggest something similar," his wife said softly. "Surely, he did not want to send you away. From what I have heard from Mrs. Reynolds and Mr. Nathan, George Darcy was never quite the same after his hasty decision."

"You know me well enough to recognize I ranted and raved against the storm. Perhaps my father thought to force my hand. I was nearly five and twenty at the time, and, truthfully, quite awkward in public. In hindsight, I suspect he recognized his own mortality and wished to view his grandchildren. Unfortunately, he held no idea of the depth of Ruth Chapman's duplicity. He was familiar with her family. Wealthy on the father's side. Good blood, and all that, in respect to her mother. And then, it was Mr. Wickham who brought the Chapmans to my father's notice. George Darcy always trusted his godson to speak the truth. At the time, Wickham was set to marry the Hartis girl over near the Nottinghamshire border. I had thought, with the elder Wickham's passing, the younger was long removed from Pemberley. I did not learn until I was some years in India of how Mr. Hartis ended negotiations with Mr. Wickham when he learned of Wickham assisting Mr. Chapman with this business. Hartis's son warned his father away from a joining with Wickham, for Young Hartis had been at Cambridge and had witnessed for himself Mr. Wickham's propensity for gambling and loose women."

"And Mr. Wickham, as we have discovered since returning to Pemberley, wished to have you from the estate. Mrs. Reynolds believes Mr. Wickham meant to convince your father to set you aside in the inheritance," Elizabeth shared. "The lady had thought surely Mr. Wickham would leave soon, for he was supposedly engaged, but your explanation ties up those ends."

"I could not think on the extent of the betrayal, just the betrayal itself," he explained. "After all, Mr. Wickham, at one time, was my childhood friend. Naturally, I knew of his propensity for selfishness and spending beyond his means, but I never considered the idea of being set aside. There is an entail. The only means for it to end would have been my death. A fact of which your father often reminded me. He said all I had to do to prevail was to live. Perhaps Mr. Wickham thought I would perish on my journey or even in my daily life. India is a 'hard' country, especially for those not willing to bend. Englishmen have an unspoken code of considering anything not 'British' as not civilized. Mayhap once Ruth was Mrs. Darcy, she meant to do away with me herself and return to England as the grieving widow. What neither of them considered is my father's cousin Samuel Darcy would have inherited Pemberley. He is a renowned archaeologist and often away from England, but he is still the heir and could not be displaced by a grieving widow. "

Elizabeth glanced to Alice. Lowering her voice, she asked. "Alice belongs to the woman. When did Miss Chapman conceive? In the carriage, she said you played God and changed Alice's birthday."

Darcy did not wish to explain the compromises he had made in those first few years in India, but Elizabeth deserved to know it all. "After confirming Miss Chapman did not carry my child or any child, for that matter, I presented her half the funds her father had entrusted with me. Naturally, she argued for it all, but I told her she could have the other half when she departed India. In the meantime, I moved out of the quarters we shared."

"You lived in the same house with her?" Elizabeth hissed in protest.

"My doing so was necessary so I might make certain Ruth was not one of those women who did not 'show' the child she carried. I know the arrangement was not proper, but I kept thinking my trials were far from over, especially when I wrote to my father to inform him Ruth had tricked him, but I continued to receive no response."

Elizabeth kept her eyes downcast when she softly asked, "Is such when you sired Alice?"

"Look at me, Elizabeth," he demanded. When his wife did as he asked, he said, "I have never lain with Ruth Chapman. Never touched her in such a manner. I kissed her briefly in the garden at Sir Anthony Lewis's home at a garden party. It was the only time I touched her beyond holding her hand during a dance set."

Her eyes swept downward again, but this time to Alice, before returning to meet his steady gaze. "How is such possible? Who then is Alice's mother?"

He sucked in a quick breath to steady his voice when he told her this next part. How Elizabeth responded would determine their future. "When Ruth finally admitted no child existed between us, as I said earlier, I presented her half of her father's purse. She was to book passage as quickly as possible. Having not heard a word from my father, I was determined to earn a fortune and prove to the world I was more than just George Darcy's heir. How Ruth survived, I did not know and did not much care, especially as I was working side-by-side with the men I had employed for the mine I had leased with an option to purchase. My days were long and exhausting, but, for the first time in my life, I felt proud—not the type of pride one has from a place such as Pemberley, but proud of what I accomplished with no leg up from my father or uncle or any of my family's lofty connections. I was looked upon by those men who worked beside me shoulder to shoulder deep into the earth to do my part for us to know success, and I did my best to meet those expectations.

"I was inland, away from the coast where Ruth and I had lived among those of the British East India Company, some ten months when I received an urgent message from Captain Lord Stanley Meachem. His lordship had written to say Ruth was truly with child. Meachem's child. He asked that I come to oversee her care, especially as it was I who held control of the last of her funds. In truth, I had placed her so far from my mind, I did not consider she had yet to claim the remainder of the money her father provided for her. Before I traveled to the site of the mine, I made arrangements for her to claim the money when she booked departure for England. I was to receive a notice of her claiming her small fortune, but my signature was not required for her to do so. Whether she understood the process, I cannot say. Your father said Ruth reminded him of your sister Lydia, though Ruth was obviously more mature than was your youngest sister. Mr. Bennet often said Miss Lydia possessed 'selective hearing.'"

Elizabeth chuckled. "He said the same of Mama."

Darcy would not share some of Mr. Bennet's less than flattering words regarding Mrs. Bennet. Instead, he said, "When I arrived back in Calcutta, Ruth was more than five months along. No friends. No one to tend her. As much as I despised her, I had begun to see what your father had said of my banishment. He had claimed my journey to India would mold me into a man who appreciated life more than many of our class. A man who would learn to love the land upon which his destiny was tied. I can say honestly, although my father was not a lazy man, he would not have lasted even a few hours in the mine I worked every day for more than four years. The heat. The filth. The stink was nearly unbearable. Not a place an English gentleman can call home, but I did just that, for the mine was my future, and, later, also Alice's future."

The child must have recognized the sound of his voice, for she rolled to her back and then settled in sleep once more. At length, Elizabeth asked, "You tended Ruth those last few months then? Did she give you Alice?"

Darcy snorted his contempt. "Sold me the child. Three thousand pounds. I took out a loan against the mine to save the child. Ruth meant to be as far away from her responsibilities as possible. I hired a wet nurse, packed up Alice's few belongings, and returned to my mine and my existence. I could not, in good conscience, permit Ruth to carry the babe across India, as she rejoined the English 'society' surrounding the British East India Company and the other military stationed there."

Elizabeth appeared more sad than any other emotion. "In that manner, you played God, just as Miss Chapman said. You claimed Alice and presented her a different birthday so those other British citizens would not know she was Lord Meachem's daughter, which means she is actually four, not five. Such explains much. Alice is tall enough to be five, but her pronunciations are a bit delayed. Fortunately, her mind is quick, and I am excessively proud of how much she has learned since she came to me and Mary." She caressed Alice's cheek. "You should know women prefer to be younger, not older," Elizabeth half teased, but that slight turn of her lips quickly reversed, and she frowned. "How will we protect her? What if others discover she does not belong to you? Worse yet, whose name is on Alice's baptismal certificate as her mother? Society can be so cruel. Oh, Fitzwilliam, I could not bear to see Alice shunned."

At last, they had reached the crux of the matter. What happened in the next few minutes would spell disaster or happiness. He rose briefly to kneel before his wife. Claiming her free hand, Darcy presented it a gentle squeeze of reassurance. "Alice's baptismal certificate contains my name as her father and Elizabeth Bennet Darcy as her mother."

He knew Elizabeth's first instinct had been to jump to her feet in protest, but Alice had snuggled into his wife's side, so she held herself in place. She whispered in harsh tones, "Such cannot be. We have only known each other for a matter of months, not years. How may I claim Alice as my child? I have never even been outside of Great Britain."

"Yet, you were away in Wales for nearly a year with your paternal great-grandparents. Ironically, I was 'reportedly' on the western coast of Africa at about the same time—in the Cape Colony learning more of gold and diamond mining. No one knows we were not together. Paperwork of our booking passage exists, as does an agreement for a small let house between me and a British naval captain stationed there to oversee British interest in the area since the Battle of Blaauwberg.

No one knows we had never met to consummate our marriage. No records exist which would prove otherwise. One thing you must understand in such situations is if a man throws enough money at something, it will happen. I was actually inland opening a second mine, but only a few knew of my whereabouts, and none of those were English. However, your father knew."

"My father refused to permit my return to Longbourn even though Great-Grandmother Bennet had recovered from her fall," she murmured in obvious recollection. She looked at him and frowned. "Yet, we were not 'actually' married when Alice was conceived. She would still be called a 'bastard.'"

"We married by proxy in Calcutta in the Church of England before we celebrated our marriage in the African protectorate, where we conceived our daughter. I took the child back to India with me, for we initially planned for you to join me there. You and I had agreed you would face censure if you returned to Hertfordshire with a child and a 'supposed' husband you married by proxy in a country few of your neighbors could even imagine."

"Yet, no one would have believed me to have left my child behind," she argued.

"They might if you reminded them, I am very wealthy man, who is descended from the Earls of Matlock and a noble family from the time of the Normans and my estate rivals that of many dukes. To many of your neighbors, ours would have been a brilliant, though perhaps eccentric, match. Add to the story the idea of how we initially planned to have our marriage sanctioned by your local vicar and to host a large wedding breakfast to introduce your new family to Meryton and the story becomes more believable. As long as we speak the same story to all who ask, no one can challenge us. Even if they doubt us, the proof of what we say will win out. All will be legally justified, even if we are both termed to be a bit unconventional."

"In your tale, we did more than 'sanction' our joining," she whispered. "Was such your plan when you arrived in Hertfordshire—to claim the foolhardy Elizabeth Bennet and make her your wife to provide your child legitimacy?"

"It was not," he said adamantly. "Having my ship set in off the Norfolk coast, I was on my way to London to settle my father's affairs when I saw the notice of your father's passing and the auctioning off of Longbourn. I never expected to involve you in all this unless it was Mr. Bennet's wish. Yet, when I realized the magnitude of what had occurred, I thought perhaps your family might require my presence in your life, as much as I had once required yours. The advert did not tell me who had passed other than your father. When I arrived at Longbourn that day, despite your obvious despair, I was excessively glad to find you. You see, in India, I carried your miniature about with me. Everywhere I went."

"Miss Chapman said something similar, but I did not believe her."

"Ruth hated it. The miniature represented all her lost hopes and my aspirations for a future. It was of the nature of a two-headed coin. I studied it all hours of the day and often well into the night. It will sound absurd to say how I constructed a life for us, even though I had never met you. I knew much about you, for your father's letters spoke often and long of his Elizabeth. I learned more of you from those pages than I could have if we had courted, in reality, all those years."

"Such is not fair, for I knew nothing of you. Why do you think my father would not tell me of you? Beyond Mr. Wickham's tales of woe, I had never even heard your name," she remarked. "Even when you introduced yourself, I did not make the connection until long after we married. There is a small village in Hertfordshire named 'Kimpton,' and, for the longest time, I thought Mr. Wickham meant the Hertfordshire village, rather than the living at Kympton, of which Mr. Morgan Harris is the curate."

"I would sometimes ask Mr. Bennet if he had told you anything of me, and he would say I was easier to lead than you," he shared with a grin in remembrance. "Though we agreed neither you nor I was obliged to follow through with a courtship or a marriage, it was all Mr. Bennet's plan. When I wrote of Ruth's condition with Meachem's child and my choice to take the child from Ruth, he wrote back immediately to suggest the proxy marriage and to add your name to Alice's baptismal record, as well as specific instructions to change the date of Alice's birth. After I sold the mine and returned to England with his profits, he was to explain it all to you and determine if you would agree to marry me. He seemed to think, despite your claiming wanting to marry for the deepest love, he could convince you we would do well together."

"Yet, I never heard my father's arguments. I would have liked to have known his reasons," she said in obvious sadness.

"The letters will explain some of it," he assured. "Yet, I must admit, I would have enjoyed being a spectator when Mr. Bennet explained the presence of your husband and daughter waiting for you in your mother's favorite sitting room."

"The sight of Pemberley would have struck Frances Bennet silent," she said with a giggle. "Mama always thought Jane would marry the wealthiest suitor and the rest of us would be thankful to be introduced to other eligible gentlemen."

"Your first sight of Pemberley did not have you stumbling with fear," he remarked.

"No, it was you, my husband, who did not want to leave the coach."

He shook his head in resignation. "Once we were there, I knew I must confess it all to you, and I feared it might be too much for both of us, and, as odd as it might sound, I did not want to lose you."

"You have not lost me," she said softly.

The fact Elizabeth had not edged Alice to the side and stormed away provided Darcy a bit of encouragement. He leaned in. "May I kiss you, Mrs. Darcy?"

Her eyes widened, but she nodded quickly in the affirmative. Darcy kissed her then, beginning slowly, with a series of small, sweet kisses. When she sighed, he deepened the kiss, attempting to convince Elizabeth of his devotion to her. He was just beginning to relax into the kiss when his wife shoved him backwards.

Blinking away his dismay, a frown began to form, but her fingertips on his lips prevented his protest. "Shush," she warned and reached for his hand. She tugged it to her and splayed his fingers across her abdomen. He thought she meant finally to tell him of her suspicions regarding a child. He opened his mouth to tell her she had spoken her fears to the surgeon, but she leaned forward to place her lips against his mouth. "Did you feel it? Tell me I am not imagining this." He concentrated on where his hand rested against her, but felt nothing unusual. Elizabeth began to nibble on his ear. Then he felt it. A "ku-thump" against the palm of his hand.

Darcy's expelled his breath quickly. "Tell me such is true," he whispered, never removing his eyes from where his hand rested on her body.

"Do you wish it?" she asked close to his ear.

"With all my heart," he admitted. Saying the words aloud presented what was once a possibility firmer ground.

"I have been feeling this for perhaps a fortnight," she continued to speak in soft tones, as if she feared hexing this bit of happiness, "yet, I could not know with any assurance if I imagined it."

The babe made his presence known again, as if in protest of her words.

"He has quite a kick," he murmured in amazement.

"The child could be a 'she,'" she reminded him in sweet opposition.

He looked lovingly upon her. "I do not care," he declared. "If I have you and our children—even if they are five daughters, I will know satisfaction. The question is are we to be united not only in marriage, but also in the tale we share with the world regarding our coming together and Alice's birth? Only our united insistence will allow people to believe us."

She reached across him to caress Alice's hair. "If they do not, you will still be my husband and the father of my children?" She smiled on his daughter. "Alice will make an excellent elder sister, do you not think?"

"Superb. Just as strong and as intelligent and as beautiful and as tenacious as her mother, Mrs. Elizabeth Darcy."

"I still must memorize the actual dates of our time in Africa and the other details, and it would not hurt for you to speak to what you know of the area and the nautical miles and such," she said with a devious smile. "I would not want the world to think our courtship and marriage not worthy of my recall. What type of wife would you consider me then, sir?"

"The only one for me," he declared as he kissed her again.

"Papa," a sleepy voice said from close by. "You like to kiss Lizbet."

"I do," he declared with a smile. "Very much so." He turned to his child. "I like to kiss you too." He scooped Alice up and planted several quick kisses on her cheek.

"Me as well," Elizabeth said as she kissed Alice's other cheek.

His daughter giggled sweetly, a magical sound for a man who had just been presented a world he never thought possible. "Top! No more kisses!"

"Our affection is not required, Mrs. Darcy," he teased. A genuine smile had claimed his lips, and he would be sorry to know regret again.

"No, Papa." Alice grabbed his face to turn his head to her. "Love you," the child said and kissed his cheek before leaning towards Elizabeth to do likewise. "Papa and Mama," Alice said tentatively.

Elizabeth caught Alice to her. "Thank you, sweetheart. I am honored you wish me to be your mother, for I have been so all your life."

⁂

Two days later, using Bingley's small coach, Colonel Fitzwilliam had escorted her and Alice to Pemberley.

"Neither Alice nor I wish to leave," she had told Darcy as they stood together in the drive.

"Knowing you are waiting for me at Pemberley will hurry my return," he had told her.

"I cannot believe Mr. Chapman thinks he will prevail against Lord Matlock," she had said softly.

Her husband's countenance had hardened. "The man is a fool to think Ruth does not deserve punishment. He stills believes I will relent. I might have agreed to a compromise if she had not staged Alice's kidnapping and a threat to your life, but never again will I present the woman the time of day. Lord Matlock and I will follow them to London and have assurances Ruth is not released by the authorities until she steps on the next ship to India."

"Permitting her to live a life of pleasure in another country rather than to suffer transportation or hanging is compromise enough," Elizabeth had emphasized. "With your permission," she lowered her voice, "I shall ask Mr Sheffield to fetch Papa's letters from your trunk. I should become familiar with it all sooner, rather than later."

"I agree," he had said. However, a bit of sadness marked his features. "I wished for a different future for us, but when Alice arrived, I could not leave her to Ruth's neglect. You deserved better than what I have presented you."

"I deserve the husband I have accepted. I would have acted as Alice's mother whether you required it of me or not." She lowered her voice further. "Once I have read my father's letters, we must craft a tale for Mary. Likely something to the effect Mr. Bennet spoke to me of a gentleman of whom he wished me to approve. The issue of Alice is more problematic."

"Tell her what you think proper. We will stand together."

A brief kiss had sent her on her way. Now, as Colonel Fitzwilliam set her down before Pemberley, an upward glance to its façade announced she was "home." When she was uncertain of her future with Mr. Darcy, Elizabeth had desired a return to Longbourn. However, only where her husband dwelled would do.

"Mrs. Darcy," Mrs. Reynolds said with a large smile and a curtsey. "Welcome home, ma'am. You were sorely missed."

"I feel as if I have been away for a lifetime," Elizabeth observed.

"Welcome home, ma'am," Hannah said as she darted around Elizabeth to direct the footmen regarding the trunks.

"Thank you, Hannah. I have missed your tender care."

Lady Matlock appeared in the still open door. "Come in out of the cold," she ordered. "I asked Mr. Nathan to fetch us tea." Her ladyship turned to lead them all inside. Elizabeth would have preferred to report to her own quarters, but she hid her sigh of regret and followed the countess inside.

"I will apprise my mother regarding what occurred in Stafford while you inform her of the possibility of a child," Colonel Fitzwilliam instructed. "Both will please her greatly. Tomorrow, I will escort her to Matlock, where I plan to 'enlighten' Georgiana with an accounting of all which has occurred, especially Mr. Wickham's culpability. She has too long believed the scoundrel and requires a hard taskmaster to set her aright."

"You have been very good to Mr. Darcy," she remarked as the colonel lifted Alice into his arms to carry the child inside.

"Darcy deserved better than what occurred with Miss Chapman. I am glad he finally took the earl into his confidence when George Darcy did not respond to Darcy's letters. It was also excellent how your father took time to advise him again and again. Not many men would be so gracious to a stranger. Darcy was very fortunate to have taken Mr. Bennet's acquaintance. Otherwise, things would never have found a course to happiness."

The countess had been ecstatic with the news of a possible child, but Elizabeth had cautioned her ladyship not to discuss hers and Darcy's hopes with others, especially with Miss Darcy, until Elizabeth could confirm her condition with the local midwife.

When Alice became sleepy, Elizabeth took the child upstairs with her and left the colonel to discuss matters of the chaos in Staffordshire with his mother.

"Until we choose new quarters for you, you may stay with me. I thought you might prefer if we move you closer and choose a new maid for you." Alice was very quiet, and Elizabeth realized the child was still quite frightened. "I shall permit you to assist me in choosing a new maid, and, later this evening, after supper, we will take your papa's big map, and I will show you how far away your father means to send both Miss Chapman and Mr. Wickham. You already possess a good idea, for you have traveled to England from India."

"Long time," Alice said as her features screwed up in distaste. "Lots of water."

"Exactly," Elizabeth said. "Your father means to put an ocean between you and those who took you away from us."

Alice appeared satisfied with her answer and permitted Elizabeth to put her down for a nap. Meanwhile, stepping into the sitting room so as not to awake the child, Elizabeth rang for both Mrs. Reynolds and Mr. Sheffield. The housekeeper arrived first.

"Yes, ma'am. How might I be of assistance?"

Elizabeth asked, "What has been done with the maid who assisted Mr. Wickham?"

"She is still locked in the attic," Mrs. Reynolds explained.

Elizabeth admitted, "I should have spoken to Mr. Darcy regarding what he wished to do with the girl before I returned to Pemberley, but we did not have the opportunity to do so. However, I do not want Alice to encounter the woman. The child has had several nightmares since the events in Staffordshire."

"I shall see to it, ma'am," the housekeeper assured. "What say you to sending her away? Appears only appropriate. No letter of character. No pay for this quarter. Require her to travel to Wales or Scotland or the Americas. If not, she will be jailed and transported."

Elizabeth was not happy to see all involved permitted to live out their lives elsewhere, but she would tolerate it to keep Alice safe. "For now, let us keep her locked up in one of the worker's cottages, away from the manor house until I contact Mr. Darcy for an opinion. Someone should guard her day and night."

"Yes, ma'am. I will make the necessary arrangements."

Elizabeth continued, "I have told Alice she may choose new quarters closer to me and her father. I thought you might make several appropriate choices, and we will permit the child some say in the matter. I believe she must choose the room and some of the decor to allay her fears. I wish for Alice also to have a say in which maid assists her."

"I understand, ma'am," Mrs. Reynolds said. "The poor thing shall have special attention, Mrs. Darcy."

Elizabeth chuckled, "No spoiling our Alice."

"No, ma'am, just a bit of care and affection."

Elizabeth smiled easily. "A small bit." She straightened her shoulders. "Now, for something more personal. I would like to speak to the local midwife sometime after Lady Matlock leaves tomorrow. Would you make the necessary arrangements?"

"Oh, ma'am, is it possible?" the housekeeper gushed.

"Possible," Elizabeth assured, but with a gesture to remain calm. "However, Mr. Darcy and I would prefer to confirm our suspicions before we announce such to the rest of the household. I expect you to keep this to yourself until that time. I have not yet informed Hannah of my needs, and she would be devastated if she knew I had not taken her into my confidence."

"I shall carry the message to Mrs. Skidmore myself," Mrs. Reynolds assured.

"Very good. I will also require a message delivered to Mrs. Ericks. Assure my sister I am safely at Pemberley and ask her to call on me at her leisure tomorrow. Tell her I am claiming a bit of rest in my own bed this evening, but will welcome her with open arms then."

"Yes, ma'am. Anything else?"

However, before Elizabeth could respond, Mr. Sheffield knocked and entered the sitting room from the hall. "Pardon, Mrs. Darcy," he said with a bow. "I did not realize you were meeting with Mrs. Reynolds. I will step away until you are prepared for me." He backed towards the door.

"No, wait," Elizabeth said before he could escape. "I simply wished you to fetch the stack of letters from my father to Mr. Darcy from the trunk which recently arrived from India. Mr. Darcy is aware of your giving them to me and has extended his permission."

"Certainly, ma'am. I shan't be long. I know exactly where they are." As he passed Mrs. Reynolds on his way to the door to Mr. Darcy's dressing room, he asked the housekeeper, "Did you share the other letters we discovered with Mrs. Darcy?"

Mrs. Reynolds pulled herself up royally. "I have yet to have the opportunity." The woman's eyes pointedly landed on the dressing room door, through which Mr. Sheffield quickly disappeared. Clearing her throat, the lady explained, "Much to my chagrin, I must report Mr. Wickham evidently has been hiding in the north wing of the house. The maid who assisted him reportedly has been sneaking him food and the like. She even warned him of when you and I were to examine the rooms there so he would hide his things away."

Elizabeth remarked, "Hiding in plain sight. Mr. Darcy has searched high and low for his former companion, but never did he search his own house. My husband was beginning to think my encountering Mr. Wickham several times over the last few months was my imagination. No wonder he disappeared so quickly after striking Jasper." Such was not the truth, but the housekeeper had no business knowing of Mr. Darcy's accusations of infidelity.

"We discovered a variety of items Mr. Wickham had pilfered from several of the other rooms which are not currently in use," Mrs. Reynolds explained. "We imagine he meant to sell them to earn a bit of money. He told the maid he would take her to Bath." The housekeeper paused before saying, "We also discovered something I believe Master Fitzwilliam will wish to have: A stack of letters from Mr. George Darcy to his son."

Elizabeth reached out a hand for the back of the chair to brace herself. "Hidden away?"

"Yes, ma'am. Apparently, Mr. Wickham has used the rooms often since returning to Derbyshire. We do not, obviously, know Mr. Wickham's motives. Why did he not rid himself of them as the late Mr. Darcy wrote them? Did he think to sell them to Master Fitzwilliam or do something more nefarious to bring harm to the young master? Did Mr. Wickham also intercept Master Fitzwilliam's letters to his father? It is as if Mr. Wickham wished Mr. Darcy to discover them, years from now, and realize what Mr. Wickham had done—what he had executed against Master Fitzwilliam." Tears ran down the housekeeper's cheeks. "My former master often lamented not hearing from his son."

"And my husband is tormented with the idea of his father abandoning him," Elizabeth whispered into the stillness.

"Should we send the letters to Mr. Darcy?" the housekeeper asked.

"No," Elizabeth said quickly. "If Mr. Darcy knows of Mr. Wickham's betrayal, he might strangle the life from Mr. Wickham's body. Then our dearest Fitzwilliam would be charged with murder and taken from us when we require him desperately to be among us. We will return them to him when this business of Alice's kidnapping is settled. Such will provide him the calmness and love with which we may all surround him in coming to forgive his father for an ill-advised decision which tormented both of them."

Chapter Twenty-One

"There you are."

Elizabeth looked up to view her beloved sister. She rose quickly to cross to where Mary tossed her cape across the back of a chair to catch Mary up in her embrace. "I have missed you terribly."

"I was so worried for you," Mary said with a deep sigh. "I hear you were as daring as our Lydia, escaping out a window and all." She set Elizabeth from her and smiled. "I imagine you displayed more initiative than did our Lydia. Remember how she slid down the bed clothes right into one of Mama's prized rose bushes. We said those in Meryton could have heard her yelps, for she screamed so loudly."

Elizabeth permitted herself a bit of amusement to displace her tears. She had been reading letters her father had written and was missing him terribly. "I tied knots every few feet in the cloth, which I had already torn into long strips and tied together so it would support our weight. No roses bushes below. Just an inn's back door. And I used my shawl to harness Alice to my back."

"Oh my. You are so brave," Mary gushed.

"I had few choices," Elizabeth explained as she tugged Mary down beside her on the settee. "Fortunately, God had other plans for Alice and me, for, weeks before I required his assistance, our dear Lord sent Mr. Bingley to Pemberley to bring you news of your pianoforte. In all he shared with us that day, the bit of information I required most was he planned to return to his father's home in Stafford after celebrating Mr. and Mrs. Hurst's anniversary with them and his aunt. When I realized the inn in which we stopped because of the storm was in Stafford, I knew Alice and I must reach Mr. Bingley before Miss Chapman and Mr. Wickham could take Alice from me to 'sell' her to my husband."

"It is difficult for me to think upon Mr. Wickham as being so cruel," Mary admitted. She caught Elizabeth's hand and studied the bruises and cuts as she spoke. "How could he hide his true self for so long? So easily? He initially sought your attention, but I thought he held real affection for Lydia. They seemed so easy together. It is very sad to realize he duped us all."

"I have come to believe Mr. Wickham purposely came to Hertfordshire because he had intercepted the letters Mr. Darcy sent to his father in which Fitzwilliam spoke of his relationship with our father and of Mr. Bennet's involvement in Mr. Darcy's mine. I also think he singled me out, at least in the beginning, for our father wrote often of me to Mr. Darcy where he promoted a possible joining between us two."

"I thought you did not know anything of Mr. Darcy prior to his appearance at the household auction," Mary questioned.

"Obviously, Mr. Bennet had his own reason for not discussing his aspirations with me," Elizabeth said with a shrug. "I understand how he could not speak to our mother of his communications with Mr. Darcy. Perhaps he feared telling any of us would reach mama's ears and her 'nerves' would be overwhelmed with the idea I could some day be the mistress of such a grand estate. Such also explains how Papa had more than his dislike of Mr. Collins in mind when he refused Mama's pleas to force my hand in accepting the man. In truth, I have spent the morning reading papa's letters to Mr. Darcy, and he often extols my few so-called 'attractions' to my now husband. I suppose our father knew I would not be happy for him to play matchmaker. We had all suffered our mother's attempts often enough."

"Not me," Mary said quietly.

Elizabeth caught Mary to her. "We all loved our mother, but she could often be cruel, unless she was speaking to either Jane or Lydia.

Such did not mean she did not love each of us." She grinned. "Just think, if mama had any inclination of Mr. Ericks's interest in you, you might have been the first of us married. He told me he had thought of you since you were fifteen."

"Really?" Mary asked. "He has not told me that tale. Such would have been marvelous to have been chosen first, but, in all honesty, I doubt I would have been a very good wife to him at that young age. I had no voice of my own. I would have been more his 'child' than his 'partner.'"

Elizabeth patted Mary's hand. "Your very wise husband said something similar also. I am excessively pleased you have found such a good man."

"I have." Mary said with a sigh of obvious satisfaction. "Finish your tale, Lizzy. What about our father's letters?"

"Yes, as I was saying, I believe Mr. Wickham learned of the fortune Mr. Darcy had earned in India, as well as Mr. Darcy's intention to pay our father ten thousand pounds to increase our dowries. Since learning all this, I have come to believe, not only did Mr. Wickham wish my shares of the dowry money, but his attention to me was meant to thwart Mr. Bennet's obvious wish for me to marry Mr. Darcy. Do you not recall how quickly Lieutenant Wickham told me of his poor treatment by the Darcys? We now know such was not true, at least not on George Darcy's part. The late Mr. Darcy presented his godson a position of honor in his household and one thousand pounds."

"Yet, not the position for which Mr. Wickham wished. He wanted to be his godfather's heir," Mary whispered into the quietness between them. "It was easier to convince Lydia—sweet, but naïve, Lydia—daring Lydia—who would risk her own reputation to claim a man in a red coat, just as mama had taught her. A minor officer in the militia with no money and, apparently, no morals. Kitty did much better with Captain Denny. He was to inherit a small estate in Yorkshire, and he had family, but Lydia thought herself more fortunate, for Mr. Wickham was fair of face." Mary paused as if to consider all she had just learned. "Lydia was to receive the same dowry as Jane or you or, even, me and was much easier to seduce, so Mr. Wickham set his sights on Lydia. By marrying Lydia, the lieutenant would have been 'brother' to Mr. Darcy if father's plans for a joining between you two succeeded. He would still make claims on the Darcy fortune."

"Such is my opinion," Elizabeth reluctantly admitted. "I should also tell you Mr. Wickham has been hiding in one of the unused wings of Pemberley, likely for many weeks. Alice's maid assisted him. Worse yet, he had the letters the late Mr. Darcy had written to Fitzwilliam hidden away there. Mrs. Reynolds and I agreed not to tell my husband of this turn of events until his return to Pemberley."

"How shocking!" Mary gasped. "Both the late Mr. Darcy and your husband have spent years without knowing each other's love and respect, and now it is too late for them to recover what they lost."

They two remained silent for a good minute or more before Elizabeth spoke again. "Something else has occurred in all this sadness, and I will require your cooperation, for you may be called upon to speak a lie to protect me, Alice, Mr. Darcy, Mr. Ericks, yourself, your future children, as well as the child I carry."

"You are with child? How wonderful! Mr. Darcy must be beside himself with happiness," Mary gushed.

"Although my husband knows my suspicions, I have only confirmed my condition on this day," Elizabeth said with more calmness than she actually felt. She wished to be dancing around the room in triumph, but such would not be very ladylike. Her future, as well as Mr. Darcy's and Alice's rested in Mary's capable hands and likely in those of Mr. Ericks. Mary was not the type to keep a secret from her new husband. "However, Alice's future is not so sound as is this child's." Her hand caressed her midsection before she continued. "Would you permit me to explain what our father and Mr. Darcy designed to save Alice? I have agreed to what they have enacted in order to save our dearest child. Obviously, if Miss Chapman is still alive, Alice already has a mother, but the woman sold her child to Mr. Darcy for three thousand pounds."

Mary's countenance screwed up in confusion. "Why would Mr. Darcy pay the woman for his own child? As a man, even in India, Mr. Darcy had the legal rights to the child."

"My husband did not sire Alice," Elizabeth declared.

Mary leaned back into the cushions. "I suppose you must explain it all, for I am thoroughly befuddled."

Elizabeth reached for the letters from their father to Mr. Darcy, which she had set aside earlier, for they spoke directly to the situation. "This will take some time to unwind the story before it is clear enough for you to make a decision. Please bear with me while I summarize how our father and Mr. Darcy came to be in each other's pockets." Mary nodded her encouragement. "It all began . . ."

Three-quarters of an hour later, they sat in silence, each considering how to respond. "It is all very convoluted," Mary whispered. "Our father obviously thought Mr. Darcy would make you a good husband before he chose to aid Mr. Darcy in saving Alice."

"Mr. Darcy has been a good husband. We both know our journey to this point has not been the easiest, and I often wondered if we would survive. For a good while, I considered leaving Fitzwilliam without telling him of the child I carried, which was very wrong of me. For more than a few weeks, I thought he meant again to take up with Miss Chapman. Mr. Ericks can attest to my dismay, for he was with me when I first viewed Mr. Darcy with the woman. Although my husband promised me an explanation, one never came, and, after a while, I feared asking because what would I do if he displaced me for the woman."

Mary sighed heavily. "You feared Mr. Ericks might turn from me? You stayed to protect me."

"How could I not? Mr. Ericks's living is at Mr. Darcy's pleasure," Elizabeth said through tears. "Moreover, you had a chance at happiness, while I would have been considered a fallen woman. I held no knowledge Miss Chapman was not still Fitzwilliam's wife. I considered her to be Alice's mother."

"We must protect the child," Mary said in determination.

"It is not likely we will ever be called upon to repeat the tale of my arranged marriage to Mr. Darcy. In fact, you can honestly say you knew nothing of it until recently, after Mr. Darcy appeared in Hertfordshire and after our father's passing, as well as to confirm I was gone to our great-grandparents for nearly a year."

"Does Alice favor Miss Chapman?" Mary asked.

"Yes, but the child could just as easily be described as favoring Jane. Mr. Bingley has commented in the last few days of how Alice reminds him of Jane. Equally as important, Miss Darcy is tall and blonde," Elizabeth reminded Mary. "Lady Anne Darcy was not so tall, but she, too, was blonde. Traits often skip generations. Alice could justifiably belong to Fitzwilliam and me. As to the entailment, she will not remove my first son from his rightful claim to Pemberley, and my husband has previously set aside equal dowries for any daughters we might have, including Alice, as well as endowments for any minor sons."

"Very good of him to act honorably for the child," Mary observed. "I cannot think upon tormenting an innocent child, especially as you and Mr. Darcy mean to treat her with equal love and care. Such is what God would wish for Alice. If asked, I shall play my part. I do not think God would judge me as evil. As *Isaiah* tells us, 'For I will contend with him who contends with you. And I will defend your children.'"

"And you may always count on me to defend yours," Elizabeth responded with thanks.

Before more could be said, Alice burst into the room. "Aunt Mary!" The child rushed into Mary's embrace. "You come and see my new room. Biss Raynolds say I kin have blue bed dapes with stars sewed on. Bewteaful!"

The child tugged on Mary's arm. Elizabeth's sister rose with a smile. "If you require me, Elizabeth, I shall be judging the possibility of blue drapes with stars for all our children."

AMENDING THE SHADES OF PEMBERLEY

"I shall order tea and sandwiches and cakes for after your tour." Elizabeth chuckled and gave them a shooing motion as she rose to pull the cord.

"Lemon, mama," Alice said as she tugged Mary towards the door.

"Yes, *mama*," Mary emphasized with a grin. "Lemon cakes for Miss Alice."

───※───

Tomorrow, he and Matlock would depart Bingley's company and travel to London, along with Chapman and the man's daughter. They would oversee Ruth being placed on a ship to India. No return.

"The post, sir," Mr. Bingley's butler said.

Bingley glanced down to the salver and nodded to Darcy and the earl. "Leave mine by my setting, Radcliffe."

The butler did as instructed, then paused before Lord Matlock. "My lord."

"Ahh," the earl said with a smile. "The countess."

"I am surprised her ladyship did not send the missive with the colonel," Darcy remarked, "when my cousin returned from Derbyshire yesterday." Darcy had actually hoped for a letter from Elizabeth, though he knew the colonel had not called upon Pemberley again after escorting his mother back to Matlock. "Your son should be in Liverpool now and seeing Mr. Wickham off to America. Mr. Wickham has always carried around a healthy, or not so healthy, fear of the colonel. The dastard always thought me his equal, but never did he consider your son as such. I imagine he will also be glad to be free of Miss Chapman when he departs England," Darcy remarked.

The earl ignored Darcy's observations, for the matters had been thoroughly discussed repeatedly over the last few days. Rather, his lordship observed, "The countess and I have an arrangement. We correspond, with some degree of regiment, once weekly when I am away from home, no matter the reason for my absence. Little things, Darcy. Despite what your cronies at your club may say, it is the little things which allow a man to know a bit of happiness. Marriage is not a business arrangement, as some may think. It cannot simply be like any other business deal to which a man places his signature on a line or else his soul will shrivel up and fall into an abyss."

Darcy stared at his uncle in both dismay and admiration. For a moment, he did not realize the butler now extended the tray to him. He hurried to claim two pieces of correspondence from the tray. He smiled easily. "Mrs. Darcy."

"Little things," Lord Matlock said with satisfaction. "Your soul just lifted, did it not, boy."

"Yes, sir." Darcy repeated, "Yes, it did. When I was in India, my heart lightened when I heard from Mr. Bennet. It was as if I still mattered in this world. I have often admitted, if I had not taken the acquaintance of Elizabeth's father on that fateful night, I likely would have been at the bottom of the Atlantic Ocean not long after Miss Chapman and I set sail."

Matlock's gaze spoke of pride. "Then I am extremely pleased for God's intervention in the matter," his uncle said softly.

Bingley laughed. "Look what I have, Darcy." The man held up a crayon drawing of a field of blue with white circles. "I also have a letter from Pemberley from Miss Alice. She wrote, or I should say, she attempted to write 'Uncle Bingley.'"

For a split second, Darcy was jealous, but the earl pointed to a similarly folded page beside Darcy's plate. He picked it up and broke the seal to unfold the creased paper, and, an instant later, a large smile claimed his lips. "Elizabeth permitted Alice to choose her new room and decoration, according to the notation written by my wife. The drawing is of the bed drape Alice wanted. A sky and stars above her head. It says, 'Love you, Papa. My new bed.'"

Bingley grinned. "Mine says, 'Tars and ski.' This is going in a frame and hung in my office."

"The child is claiming family," the earl said before Darcy could comment on Bingley's desire to frame Alice's drawing. Elizabeth and

AMENDING THE SHADES OF PEMBERLEY

Mary still claimed Bingley as family, and so Darcy would set his mind to doing so, as well. He must forgive Bingley for telling Elizabeth of his meeting Ruth at the inn near Yorkshire.

"I am glad Alice's art pleases you, Bingley. Elizabeth has been teaching the child something of shapes and of nature and to read and write." Saying the words aloud was important, for, in such matters, he knew Elizabeth had the right of it, and his wife had agreed to both drawings. To his uncle and Bingley, he said, "Would it be rude of me to read Mrs. Darcy's letter at the table? I wish to know how things are progressing at home."

The earl decided for all of them. "I believe we each could take a few minutes to read what is enclosed. Is such acceptable to you, Bingley?"

Bingley shuffled through his stack. "I have a couple from my man of business, one from my youngest sister and another from Mrs. Ericks." He paused before saying, "Caroline likely wishes an extension of her allowance. I will read the one from Mrs. Ericks. I wish to hear more of her wedding and whether the pianoforte fit her parlor."

Darcy picked up the one from Elizabeth. It was actually the first from her he had ever received, and he instinctively knew it was not a letter expressing his wife's affection, although he could wish for such. It was a letter detailing how things had transpired with Mary and . . .

"My dearest, Fitzwilliam," it began. "Although the days at Pemberley have proved themselves to our liking, the house feels exceedingly empty without you within its wall. Alice and I are carrying on, just as you asked us to do; yet, your return to our home is greatly desired by those who love you completely, including the child I carry. Yes, the midwife has confirmed what we suspected. Soon we will number four."

Darcy squeezed his eyes shut and said a silent prayer of thanksgiving.

"Is something amiss, boy?" his uncle asked in concern.

Darcy shook off the question. "Just offering my gratitude to our dear Lord. The midwife has confirmed Mrs. Darcy is with child." He glanced to Bingley who purposely did not raise his head. Darcy should temper his happiness, but it would be hard to contain after waiting so long to name his future.

"Very good," the earl declared. "Soon an heir for Pemberley. Secure your line."

Again, Bingley did not look up from his letter from Mary. Darcy had sympathy for the man, though the earl's words were not meant to be cruel.

Returning to his own letter, Darcy read of what the midwife had suggested and what they were to expect over the next few months. In reality, he was aware of some of what Elizabeth described, at least the changes for the last three months of her carrying his child, only because he had tended Ruth. Naturally, he did not expect Elizabeth to be as demanding as had been Miss Chapman, but he enjoyed the idea of observing his first child growing in Elizabeth's womb.

Next, Elizabeth explained which of the rooms Alice had chosen and which maid would be assigned to the child's daily care. "Mrs. Reynolds agreed to have a new bed drape made for Alice's bed. You would have laughed Fitzwilliam to view how your long-time housekeeper expertly diverted Alice from a bed with black drapes. Instead, our daughter will have light blue bed clothes and a darker blue drape overhead, with white stars sewed on it. Alice is skipping through the house in happy anticipation. I am pleased she has accepted the possibility of her own room; yet, we must, realistically, expect her occasionally to know bad dreams. She will know more courage when you return to us. We both depend upon you."

Without Elizabeth, Ruth could have succeeded in her plans to use Alice against him.

Elizabeth then chronicled her conversation with Mrs. Ericks. "I told Mary the truth of it all, for there were too many variables to trust everything to Fate. I also shared the letters from our father where Mr.

Bennet instructed you to 'create' a marriage between us and to have Alice named our child. Like us, Mary will protect Alice.

"Finally, I have troubled over this decision. Originally, I thought to wait until your return to Pemberley, but, like Alice, in my heart, I believe you still require a bit of courage—a bit of affirmation." Darcy wondered to what she referred. "In this packet, I have enclosed a letter from Mr. George Darcy to his beloved son. It was among a stack of like letters hidden in the room Mr. Wickham used for his personal pleasure. Yes, with the assistance of Alice's maid, who, by the way, I have had locked away in one of the shepherd huts until you return home and we decide what to do with her, Mr. Wickham has been hiding in the north wing of Pemberley."

Darcy swallowed the growl of anger rushing to his lips. He would not alert either the earl or Bingley.

"Although I have been made aware of Wickham's deceit, I did not send this information to you until I knew Wickham was well away from England, not because I wished to protect him, but rather to prevent you from committing a heinous crime of your own. I have read none of the letters Mr. Wickham secreted away, but I am confident George Darcy knew instant regret for being persuaded to send his only son away. I chose as best as I could, based on the handwritten dates on the outside of the letters, one of the first, if not the first letter, sent to you. If I am in error about what is inside, send word and I will burn the rest. If I am correct, it is time you healed, my love. You cannot be whole until you know the truth, no matter what words were spoken by your father."

"Bad news?" the earl asked with a hint of concern. "Your hands shake, boy."

Darcy swallowed hard to drive the bile back down his throat. "Elizabeth and Mrs. Reynolds have discovered my father's letters to me. They were hidden away at Pemberley. Obviously never sent upon their way. Mrs. Darcy believes I will find peace within these pages." He reverently fingered the folded over paper. "They are the last vestiges of my father; yet, I do not know whether I wish to read them. My wife seems to think this was the first of those he wrote to me."

Matlock said, "You have a decision before you, Darcy. Eventually, you must read the letters you thought were never sent. Yet, is today the day? Does your father's opinions of you still control your identity?"

"If you each will pardon me," Darcy said as he rose. "I mean to return to my quarters." Gathering both Alice's and Elizabeth's letters, as well as the unopened one from his father, Darcy rushed towards the rooms he had recently shared with his wife and child. Before him, he saw nothing but an image of his father's countenance as George Darcy closed the main door to Pemberley, leaving Darcy standing beside the coach which was to carry him and Ruth Chapman away from his beloved Pemberley. Had it been anger, as he first thought, or remorse on his father's expression? Darcy had not known then nor did he know now.

Three-quarters of an hour later, his uncle found him still sitting in a chair pulled up before the fire, staring into the flames, the letter unopened on his lap. Matlock pulled a chair closer, and they sat in silence for several minutes. At length, his uncle spoke, "Although you did not ask my advice on this matter, I would tell you not to miss your destiny, Fitzwilliam, simply because you are concerned with what others say of you. Even if those others included your earthly father. My countess says, though we sometimes go through disappointments, such is how God sees us, which is important. Not man's view, but God's. I would remind you to look at how much you have achieved on your own. Your Alice would have died in India, if not for you. Pemberley's future and all who depend upon it would suffer without your guidance and your compassion. You spend too much time giving consideration to the life you were, in your mind, born to live. I am calling out the man you have become not to focus entirely on the man you once thought to be. Did you not always despise how people looked only on you for the wealth of Pemberley? Is such not what Miss Chapman saw in her hopes of marrying you? Was such the reason Mrs. Darcy agreed to accept your hand?"

Darcy shook his head in the negative. "Though she was looking at greatly reduced means, Elizabeth initially refused me. She only accepted me when I agreed also to protect Mary and after she was assured Mr. Bennet had been my dear friend. She trusted me to do my best by her, and I trusted her to execute her best by Alice, who now calls my wife 'mama.' In only a few short months, Elizabeth has changed Alice's life for the better. My child has a future money could not purchase. Elizabeth fought to save Alice, a child not of her flesh, even though she suspected she carried a child of her own. Most women would not have thought to act in such a violent matter: They would have simply cried out for assistance." Darcy paused briefly and smiled. "My wife will likely be the quick death of me, a prediction of which Mr. Bennet warned me. Truthfully, at the time, I thought the man foolish, but he was correct: My Elizabeth is fearless. I could not ask for a better wife or a better life. Elizabeth has confessed her affection for me. For me, not for Pemberley. Is such not remarkable?"

"Earning such a woman's devotion speaks to your character, Darcy. Now, you must stop running from your life—rather, run towards it. Although each man wishes his father's affirmation, it cannot truly make him a better or a worse man unless he chooses to believe the labels life has thrust upon him. Surely you know I am a kinder, more loving man than those in the House of Lords believe me to be. The only 'true' opinions are those from whom I show the real Lord Matlock and, naturally, that of our dearest God. God made you and me as His masterpieces. In doing so, He has presented you his affirmation. Such should be enough."

Tears formed in Darcy's eyes. "Elizabeth and Alice view me as the center of their world. The colonel and you and her ladyship and Mr. Bennet presented me direction when I stumbled. Although I often thought it, I am not alone in this world, and soon another will reach for me. Thank you, Uncle. Perhaps some day I will read my father's letters; yet, a bit more time must pass. The wound is still too fresh. Like Elijah hiding beneath the broom bush in the wilderness, I may 'Rise up and eat,' while still requiring a bit more time to name the path God has designed for me. Yet, I will reach it. My dear wife reminded me recently, if I had not gone to India, I would not have taken her father's acquaintance and we would have never met. If I had not gone, Alice would have likely died from neglect. If I had not gone to India, I would not have learned of other farming techniques nor would I have developed connections which have already served my tenants and the family coffers. Pemberley suffered badly in my absence, especially in the last two years. Yet, even if I had been at home, I might have simply accepted the status quo if I had not viewed the extremes of land use in India. You are correct, Uncle: Without the trials of my banishment, my future and that of my family and my land would not be as bright."

Chapter Twenty-Two

It was another fortnight before he and Matlock had viewed Ruth Chapman on a ship to the African coast, where she was to meet a different vessel to take her around the tip of Africa and on to India. Mrs. Chapman had dressed down both Darcy and his uncle, but they had stood firm. Before the colonel had escorted Mr. Wickham to Liverpool, they had secured a written and notarized confession of all, well, as far as Wickham's dealings with the Chapmans and with Ruth's manipulations. In return, a lieutenancy in the British Army Regulars had been purchased for the dastard, with the understanding Mr. Wickham was to build himself a new life somewhere in British Canada or in the United States. He was never to be permitted to return to England. In addition, Darcy presented the man five hundred pounds, meaning to be rid of the scoundrel forever. All in all, Darcy laid out nearly one thousand pounds. As the war in North America was winding down, Wickham had the opportunity to change his destiny. Even so, Colonel Fitzwilliam bet someone would put a bullet between Wickham's eyes within a month of Darcy's former companion being on the frontier.

Darcy held a different opinion. "Mr. Wickham will seek out the most eligible heiress in British Canada and woo the woman. She might shoot him for his infidelity; yet, I doubt it. More likely, he will run through all her money and leave her alone and destitute."

Finally, after four days on the road, he rode his mount into the circle before Pemberley House. Two boys ran up from the stable to take his horse as Darcy dismounted. "Welcome home, sir," they chorused as he stepped down.

"Glad to be in Derbyshire," Darcy responded as the knot in his stomach eased, but it unfurled completely as the main door to the house opened, and Elizabeth scampered into his arms, pulling his head down to kiss him before God and all his servants. Not very "ladylike," but Darcy did not give a farthing for what others thought. His wife greeted him in affection, and he enjoyed their kiss.

In less than a minute, he heard Alice calling, "Papa! Papa!" as she bounded out the front door to barrel into the side of his leg.

Darcy released his wife with a whispered, "More later," before bending to gather the child into his arms. He placed a kiss on Alice's forehead. "What a wonderful greeting. Thank you, sweetheart, but let us remove into Pemberley's warmth." Darcy carried Alice as Elizabeth snuggled into his side. "Your father is saddle-sore and cold; however, I am eternally grateful to be with you and Elizabeth at last."

"Welcome home, sir," Mr. Nathan said with a bow.

"No place better than Pemberley, Mr. Nathan," Darcy responded in greeting.

"Most assuredly not, sir." The man closed the door to shut out the cold, and Darcy's heart left the chaos of the last month behind.

"Should you care to join me in the green sitting room?" Elizabeth asked. "I was just constructing a letter to Aunt Gardiner, but it can wait. There is a warm fire and hot tea awaiting us. We should have you warm quick enough."

Darcy claimed her hand. "Your and Alice's welcome was all I required to know contentment."

"Then you do not desire another display of my regard?" she asked with a teasing smile.

"Trust me, Mrs. Darcy, no man alive would dare to present you such an asinine response."

"So, I am to assume you have missed more than a warm bed in your ancestral home?" she asked under her breath as he seated her on a settle before the fireplace.

"As long as you are in said bed," he whispered as he leaned over her, "I would not care if we were floating on an iceberg."

His wife burst into laughter, and Darcy thought the sound the most delightful one he had ever heard. When he sat beside her, his child climbed up beside him to chatter away about her new quarters, the lessons Elizabeth had designed for her, and how his cook had taught Alice to stir a batter without knocking the flour upon the work table. "Cook shown me the harbs and let me pick one."

"Parsley," Elizabeth explained.

"Did you eat it?" Darcy asked, simply enjoying the pleasure of being with his wife and child.

A smile of anticipation marked his child's response before Alice's little face screwed up in distaste. "Not like pars until it cooked in the soup." Unexpectedly, but very welcomed, Alice's arms came about his neck. "You home. No more mean people."

"Your papa and Lord Matlock sent them both far, far away," Darcy assured.

Elizabeth added softly, "I showed Alice the map in your study, permitting her to see where we live and where Mr. Wickham and Miss Chapman now live."

Darcy nodded his gratitude for the information. "Remember how long we were on the ship?" he asked Alice.

"Ll--oo--nn-g time," Alice exaggerated the word as she spread her little arms wide.

"Yes, exactly. A very long way. No one can hurt you again. Neither Elizabeth nor I will tolerate it. You are our dearest child."

Alice leaned across him to plant a kiss on Elizabeth's cheek. "Mama brave."

"Brave and beautiful," Darcy said softly. For several weeks, he had been considering reclaiming his wife. They had been separated by lies and suspicions, and he wished to demonstrate to Elizabeth how much he desired and admired her.

"I go draw a picture for you and mama," Alice announced just as Mr. Nathan delivered additional tea.

"Mr. Nathan," Elizabeth instructed. "Would you have someone escort Miss Alice to her quarters and send Lucy to assist her?"

"Right away, Mrs. Darcy," the man repeated.

"Bring the tea and cakes?" Alice asked.

"Nursery tea and one cake," Elizabeth instructed. "Our midday meal is not so long removed."

Alice's little lip stuck out in disappointment, but she said politely, "Yes, mama."

With the child's removal and that of his servant, Darcy quickly gathered Elizabeth in his arms to kiss her thoroughly. "I have missed you desperately," he murmured against her mouth when they broke for air.

Her arms tightened about him as she closed her eyes and sighed, "And I you, sir. Pemberley has been excessively empty without you in residence."

Elizabeth's words filled his heart with joy. "You do realize we are sharing a bed this evening and every evening to follow," he said as he looked upon her loving countenance.

His wife blushed prettily, but she did not pull away. "Let us have our tea," she instructed in a bashful manner. "You may change your mind. After all, I am rounder in places than I was previously. Hannah has adjusted my day dresses twice already."

Darcy knew he frowned, but he could not quash the gesture. "As you carry my child, why would I object?"

"How am I to know?" she said defensively.

He nearly responded with equal zest, but he paused before he spoke, just as his uncle had suggested while they were dealing with Mr. Chapman. Elizabeth deserved to know he would never desert her. "Then permit me to assure you, I desire you with every thread of my being. I will know pride in your sharing yourself with me and know the joy of watching our child grow within you. Over the last few weeks, I have counseled with my uncle upon multiple occasions." Darcy accepted the cup of tea she handed him. "I have come to understand, despite what I lost, I have gained so much more, for the losses led me to you. I would have to be quite stubborn, one might say irrational, not to claim with all my heart what you offer to a man as tainted as I. Naturally, I wish to share your bed and your life, Elizabeth. Completely. Until we take our last breath."

Tears misted his wife's eyes, and for a moment, Darcy thought he had said something to upset her. "Being with child has me teary-eyed at the oddest moments," she admitted with another blush to her skin. "Lady Matlock named these tears the result of the 'baby blue devils.'"

Darcy permitted himself to relax, sitting back into the settle's cushions. "Why do you not tell me something of the things I have missed regarding my child? I do not want to be ignorant of any part of this journey."

"Some of it is a bit embarrassing," she admitted.

"Yet, I should be made aware," he emphasized, but not demanded. He must learn another way of speaking to Elizabeth. She was his wife, not someone he employed to do a particular job. With her, he could not be simply the master of Pemberley. "It is my child you carry. My first child. I wish to cherish all the memories of this venture. Please trust me, Elizabeth."

"I trust you," she was quick to say. "It is just . . . some things are so intimate." Her eyes dropped rather than to meet his.

He set the tea cup and saucer on the low table. "Sweetheart," he said softly, but encouragingly, as he recaptured her hand, "there is nothing more intimate than what we executed to conceive this child. Just as our dear Lord prescribed, we gave ourselves to each other. I want no more secrets between us. We may not always agree, but we must be honest with each other."

She nodded quickly in acceptance of his words and swallowed hard, but, thankfully, she began to chronicle all the things she had shared with the midwife and how the woman had examined her. His wife's tale proved to be a real education. Although Darcy had overseen the care Ruth had received the last three months of Miss Chapman carrying Alice, he had never touched Ruth beyond assisting her from room to room. He had paid others to tend her. Yet, with Elizabeth and her eventual lying in, Darcy intended to be more than her husband. He had set his mind to assisting her—to being with her through each marker in his child's life.

Although somewhat shocked by her revelations, Darcy listened carefully, asked some questions, and tucked away the information for future reference.

"Did the midwife provide you an estimation of when we should expect the child?" He had done his own calculations based on when they had first shared intimacies to when Elizabeth had forbidden him entrance to her quarters. The difference could be a month or more."

"Mrs. Skidmore thinks from the swell of my abdomen I am nearly five months along. She based much of her estimation on when I was experiencing my dizziness and my dislike of certain scents. Many believe such happens in the fourth month or thereabouts, and I was one of those people, but the lady assures me such reactions are when a woman's body begins to change. I thought it was my hunger from being so worn weary that first month or so of being at Pemberley, but Mrs. Skidmore says the nausea can come at any time. It is simply God's plan for a woman's body to begin its change to nourish a child."

Darcy rolled his eyes and chuckled. "Thankfully, I missed those marks with Alice and Ruth. However, Meachem chronicled some of Ruth's antics in his letter, with a declaration such was a woman's occupation."

"But he sent for you?" Elizabeth argued.

"I suspect he knew I was not susceptible to the woman's demands, but such is not the subject of this conversation. I wish to know all there is worth knowing about this child and any others with which we are to be blessed. Even the smallest of details.

I pray never to be absent again for any of my children."

"You can be satisfied with our marriage?" she asked tentatively.

Darcy knew instant remorse when he realized his actions had caused Elizabeth to doubt his affections for her. "What I thought I had lost with my father's banishment faded quickly when I heard Mr. Thomas Bennet speak of his jewel of a daughter. Of his Elizabeth. You have no idea how much pleasure I took when a letter arrived from your father, for I knew it would include more tales of you somewhere within. Elizabeth Bennet was the woman I coveted for years before I had the right to hold her hand and to kiss her. I do not want to consider what might have happened to me, if Mr. Bennet had written to me of your having accepted another. I realize what I say sounds preposterous; yet, it is true. People who knew me previously would not recognize the man I am today, and it is all because the idea of you had taken root in my soul. When I worked the mines, I did it for you and for Alice. My former friends praised my name based on my family's wealth and history. However, their accolades proved false, for they were someone else's standards. They were the pitfalls of the man I had thought to be.

"Yet, what is important—what makes me happy—makes me satisfied with my lot, is not the false glory from their lips, but the sweet taste of yours when I return to Pemberley each night. You are here at Pemberley, and, hopefully, some day, our children will be here. You are for whom all my efforts in India and in Hertfordshire were executed. I mean no longer to wait for tomorrow to begin. Instead, our life and our love freely starts tonight."

A light tap on the door drew their attention from the moment. "Pardon, Mr. Darcy," Sheffield said. "I have taken the liberty of ordering you a bath and have laid out clean clothes when you are of the mind for them."

Darcy squeezed the back of Elizabeth's hand as he stood. "Sheffield has reminded me I have subjected my fair wife to the powerful scent of my favorite horse on my clothes. Would you walk with me, Mrs. Darcy?"

Elizabeth rose to lace her arm through his. "I was never one offended by the various odors of the home farm."

He leaned down to kiss her forehead. "Mrs. Darcy is one in a million, Sheffield," Darcy announced.

"You will hear no argument from me, sir," his valet confirmed. "Nor from any others at Pemberley." With a quick bow, Sheffield darted through the servants' door, while Darcy led his wife on a slow, but steady stroll towards their quarters.

"I should tell you," he said, as they climbed the main staircase, "I called upon your Uncle and Aunt Gardiner while I was in London. I enjoyed taking their acquaintance. They asked me to dine with them, so, naturally, I did. Your aunt remembered my mother. I suppose I should have realized Mrs. Gardiner had grown up in Lambton, but it, honestly, did not occur to me until your aunt mentioned how much I had the build not only of my father and paternal grandfather, but also the look of my maternal grandfather, the previous Lord Matlock."

Elizabeth stopped to look at him as if he had grown another head. "You called upon my aunt and uncle in Cheapside?"

"Should have I not?" he asked in amusement.

"My relatives live in Cheapside," she said as if speaking to someone who had been kicked in the head by a mule.

"I took note of that fact," he said, enjoying how he had caught his ever-efficient wife unaware. "A very nice town house. I was humbly surprised. I asked them to join us this summer and to bring their children along. I thought Alice would enjoy the company. Their youngest is only a little older than our Alice. Moreover, I thought, as you would be close to your lying-in, having your aunt near would permit you a confidante and make it easier on you. I know you will grieve not having your mother and father at Pemberley when you deliver our first child. Did I act against your wishes?"

"I . . . I . . . I do not know what to say, Fitzwilliam." She spontaneously pulled his head down for a quick kiss. "I am so grateful for your continued kindness, despite how our journey has often been blinded by the darkness of others. Both Mary and I shall thoroughly enjoy having our aunt close. Aunt Gardiner has always been a favorite for Jane, Mary, and me."

He smiled at her. "Your uncle and I decided we might partake of the fishing in the lake before Pemberley and the other streams. It has been years since I have spent an afternoon in such quiet pleasure." He turned their steps again towards their quarters. "I am excessively happy to have pleased you."

"You did, sir. Very much." His wife became teary-eyed again. "You answered a prayer I had not yet sent out into the world."

⁂

Elizabeth had changed quickly and called in on Alice to see how the child's drawing had progressed. "Ah, sweetheart, you have the soul of an artist," she had told Alice, "but you should dress for our first meal with your papa in weeks."

The drawing was a nice mix of crooked lines and circles; however, the girl had a good eye for color arrangement on the page, a skill well above her tender years. Elizabeth would tell Fitzwilliam to add to Alice's praise when he joined them at the table.

"Pardon, Mrs. Darcy," Mr. Nathan said when Elizabeth entered the morning room. She had become accustomed to eating all her meals in the smaller room.

"Yes, Mr. Nathan?"

"A letter, ma'am." The butler extended the salver to her.

"For me?" she asked, oddly concerned whether to reach for the letter or not.

"From Miss Darcy, ma'am. Addressed to the master."

Elizabeth nodded her understanding. "Place the letter beside my setting. I shall see Mr. Darcy receives it this day." She felt a twinge of guilt for not immediately sending the letter up to her husband, but Fitzwilliam had finally come home, and they had a chance at true happiness. What if Miss Darcy spit out more maliciousness? Elizabeth would see her husband read the letter, but, she quickly decided it would be later, when they were alone again. When Mr. Nathan slipped from the room, she slid the letter into the pocket of her overdress.

Within minutes, Darcy strolled into the room with Alice holding one of his hands and Miss Cassandra occupying his other. Instinctively, Elizabeth's hand came to rest on her midsection, caressing the swell of her stomach. It was a habit she ought to break, but the presence of the child within kept her calmer. Moreover, her husband noted her gesture, and a smile broke across his lips. The man was extraordinarily handsome when he smiled, and Elizabeth's heart swelled with longing, for she wished to see a smile on his lips with some regularity. He had known enough sadness.

Jasper led Alice to the child's chair, lifted her upward onto the wooden box-like seat Elizabeth had ordered made for the girl. Then the footman placed the doll in the chair next to Alice.

"What have we here?" Mr. Darcy asked as he paused to kiss Elizabeth's temple on his way to his chair at the head of the table.

"Mama made for me," Alice explained.

Elizabeth blushed before her explanation. "Naturally, I did not make the seat, but I did draw a sketch of what I envisioned and then asked Mr. Waterboro to design this block to boost Alice in her seat. Mrs. Reynolds asked one of the seamstresses to create a cushion from a discarded pillow. Such means Alice is not required to perch on her knees to enjoy her meal. I always worried she would slip out of the chair or it would tip over with her. The seat is not exactly how I saw it in my head, but it is an improvement Alice has embraced to enjoy her meals."

"Very creative," her husband remarked with a seriousness which surprised Elizabeth. "What did you envision?"

Elizabeth was a bit embarrassed to respond. "I am not criticizing Mr. Waterboro's work. Not in any means," she assured. "The height is perfect for Alice, but the wood is still a bit rough, and she occasionally scrapes her knee. Perhaps I should again ask one of our seamstresses to add a cover with more padding. Something similar to an upholstered chair."

Her husband studied the seat with great interest. "An upholstered half chair for children beyond high chairs or something of that nature." He nodded his head in apparent approval. "I have been pursuing ideas for products which could provide our people occupations when I set the land to fallow to allow parts of it to recover from overuse. Lace making. Conserves. Those sort of things. I had not considered furniture making, but, perhaps I should. Do you think Mr. Gardiner might assist in such sales?"

"Uncle has a substantial business in furniture sales," Elizabeth confided. "His furniture can be found in some of the best houses in London, as well as at grand estates in the countryside. I am certain he would be interested in corresponding on any of your ideas," she assured. "There is also Mr. Bingley. His warehouses are not yet as large as Uncle Gardiner's, but he caters to many of the gentry, as well as wealthy businessmen."

"I spoke briefly to Bingley while Uncle Matlock and I were in residence in Stafford, but the negotiations with Mr. Chapman provided me little time to expound on my ideas," Mr. Darcy admitted.

"Despite Jane's untimely passing, Mary and I still consider Mr. Bingley as part of our Bennet family. He is our brother-in-marriage. I would not object if he has a role in our Darcy family, as well," she said with caution.

"Mr. Bingjoy likes my drawing," Alice remarked as Mr. Nathan set a plate of food before the child.

"Mr. Bingley has excellent taste," her husband assured his daughter, "and I am excessively indebted to him for his kindness to you and Elizabeth." He turned to her. "I will write to Bingley of my suggestions for items and services we might produce for him and assure him we expect to see him often at Pemberley."

"Perhaps a sketch of Pemberley on the label, for the items will have other purchasing a bit of the 'aristocracy' for their own tables," Elizabeth suggested.

"Perhaps so," her husband responded. "My father would not have approved, but we live in a different time. When this war ends, there will be thousands of unemployed soldiers, mark my words, seeking work. We must be creative if we wish to save my family's heritage and those to whom we owe much for their loyalty to Pemberley and this land."

And so, they spent the remainder of the day—the three of them laughing and talking and enjoying Alice's antics—as a family, at last. They had had glimpses of happiness previously, but now true hope lodged in Elizabeth's heart. Yet, as they returned to their quarters that evening, she feared another heartbreak would result with Miss Darcy's letter. Even so, Elizabeth could no longer delay speaking of her husband's sister. "Would you step into our sitting room with me?" she asked. "I have a confession to make which I do not wish either Mr. Sheffield or Hannah to overhear."

"Something very serious?" her husband asked.

"I pray it is not 'serious,'" she assured. "Yet, you must be made aware of my actions."

He opened the door for her to precede him into the room. Mustering her courage quickly, Elizabeth said, "After returning to Derbyshire from Stafford, I have worried extensively regarding how all these events would take their toll on you. When you wrote to say you had chosen not to read your father's letter, I was distraught. I wanted you happy, Fitzwilliam, and I feared you would never know peace until you could repair your family's history.

"Therefore, I took it on myself to write to Miss Darcy and provide your sister my point of view on all which has occurred and the 'truth' of Mr. Wickham's manipulations from my perspective. I know the colonel recently has done his part, but I want Miss Darcy to hear from another who had once thought Mr. Wickham's fine countenance meant he was a man of honor. I spoke to her of his sudden appearance in Hertfordshire, his initial overtures towards me, his intended marriage to Lydia, his demands on Mr. Bennet's accounts, even after my father's passing, the debts he left behind in Meryton, his hiding in Pemberley, and Mrs. Reynolds's finding your father's letters to his beloved son hidden in the north wing chamber Mr. Wickham had occupied. I also spoke of my suspicion of us someday discovering your letters to George Darcy also tucked away. I prayed my confession would permit Miss Darcy to forgive your so-called 'abandonment' of her person."

Elizabeth reached in her pocket for the letter she had secreted away. "This arrived today. I should have presented it to you immediately, but I chose a day with your wife and child over your sister's insecurity. I pray you will forgive me for presuming to know you better than you do yourself. I shall be waiting for you in my quarters if you are of a mind to pardon the audacity I have practiced against you and your family once you have read Miss Darcy's response to my letter. Please know my intentions were meant to assist you. I could not bear to view you in sadness for the remainder of your days for something not of your making if there was any chance I could better your way." With that, she hurried to her quarters, leaving her husband staring in wonderment at the letter in his hand.

※

Darcy knew Elizabeth had departed the room before he could tell her he was thankful for his wife's, as well as the colonel's, attempts to resolve the rift between him and Georgiana. Yet, he had stood dumbfounded—the letter between his fingers—holding it as if it was a vial of poison.

The click of the door Elizabeth once had kept locked between them brought him from his stupor. Instinctively, he waited to hear the lock slide into place: Thankfully, the click did not come. She had promised not to turn from him again, and his wife was a person of her word, just as was he. They were now in a much better place, and it would be foolish of him to ruin their future by reading Georgiana's letter. Yet, he caught up a candle in its holder, lit the waxed string in the fireplace and set it on a table as he sat heavily in a nearby chair. He broke the wax seal with his finger and threw the pieces into the fireplace to watch them spark and melt there. Even then, he did not unfold the multiple pages. It was one thing to ignore his father's letters. After all, it was too late for him and George Darcy to know forgiveness. It was another thing to ignore Georgiana, for, in many ways, she had suffered as he did and, to a greater extent, still suffered. Although he was as prepared as any man to permit his sister her to leave his care for that of another, Darcy knew he would eventually feel as if he had lost a limb when she was no longer in his life. He would permit Georgiana freedom, if such made her happy; yet, he would know regret at her leaving him behind.

With a deep sigh of resignation, he unfolded the pages and began to read Georgiana's tightly written script.

Twenty minutes later, he sat staring at the fire in the hearth. He had read through the letter three times, unconvinced he had read it correctly the first two times. He looked up when the door to Elizabeth's quarters opened. She paused, waiting for his response, until he reached a hand to her; then, his wife scampered across the room to kneel at his feet.

"I am grieved," she said as she rose to her knees to dab at his cheeks with a handkerchief she produced from her sleeve. "I never meant . . ." she began.

However, Darcy placed a finger on her lips. "You brought me no harm, my love. On the contrary, there is hope. Georgiana writes she is promised to Lady Matlock for the Short Season, but she asks to come to us afterwards. She wishes me to write to her at Matlock House in London. Evidently, the colonel told her some of what you shared. Hearing the truth from two sources has provided her cause to repine. Georgiana begs my forgiveness and yours, as well."

"You will not speak to her of the truth of Alice's birth?" Elizabeth asked softly as she rested her head against his knee.

"I will not." He aimlessly stroked her hair. "There already exists a half-dozen people who know of Alice's lineage. Such is enough. As far as the rest of the world is concerned, I initially married Miss

AMENDING THE SHADES OF PEMBERLEY

Elizabeth Bennet by proxy while I was still in India. We met for a brief period of time, and such is when we conceived Alice. You were called home, but we planned for me to follow shortly with our child. However, the mine did not sell as quickly as we thought, and so I returned to India to set our future on its legs, thinking it would not take as long as it did. When I arrived in Hertfordshire, we were to announce our marriage to the world, but your father's passing placed everything in jeopardy. I have our Indian marriage certificate and Alice's baptismal records. They are, though not truthful, legitimate in the eyes of the law. They cannot be overturned and will withstand any legal challenge, though I do not expect one. We simply must repeat the same story. The children we share will be Pemberley's future. Your father was quite wise in proclaiming you the perfect woman for me."

Chapter Twenty-Three

(Mixed with a Bit of Epilogue)

First Week of August 1815

Darcy tapped on the door of a suite in a nearby wing. He glanced to the way he had come. Tapped a second time. This time a bit harder. Elizabeth had presented him specific orders. Twice, in fact. In impatience, he raised his hand a third time, but the door opened slightly, and Mr. Gardiner looked out at him. "Elizabeth requires Mrs. Gardiner immediately," he said in a voice he hoped did not sound as frightened as he felt.

"It is time?" Elizabeth's uncle asked.

"Yes, she woke me to fetch Mrs. Gardiner. I must also send for the midwife," Darcy explained. He attempted to recall the list of items his wife had insisted he address. Did she not realize all reason had abandoned him as quickly as he realized her night-rail was soaked, as was their bed?

Mr. Gardiner smiled knowingly. "I'll fetch Madeline. You send for the midwife and tell the kitchen to heat plenty of water. Send Hannah to assist my niece into dry clothes, and remind Mrs. Reynolds the midwife will require plenty of clean rags and Alice's maid must keep the child from being underfoot." Darcy nodded his gratitude, for Elizabeth's uncle had just reiterated all those items on Elizabeth's list Darcy could not recall. Some day he would ask how the man knew all going on in Elizabeth's mind, but not today. "I will dress and oversee Alice and my children."

Mrs. Gardiner's voice was heard from within the suite. "Did Elizabeth ask for Mary?"

"No, ma'am," Darcy assured.

"Send someone to inform Mary of what has happened. Assure Mrs. Ericks it will be hours before Elizabeth delivers, but if Mary wishes to be here, Mrs. Darcy believes her sister's good sense an admirable attribute."

Darcy frowned. "I believe Elizabeth thought it inappropriate for Mary to be here during the child's birth," he protested.

The door opened a fraction wider. "Elizabeth has always taken on the role of protecting everyone else, just as she has with you and Alice. Today, she will require the protection. Send for Mary. It is not necessary for Mary to witness the actual birth, but she can hold Elizabeth's hand and remind my niece how essential she is to all our lives."

Darcy swallowed hard. "Could I lose Elizabeth today?" Images of his mother's decline after giving birth to Georgiana flashed through his memory.

Mrs. Gardiner widened the door's opening to take an effective stance before him. "Childbirth holds its risks, but Elizabeth is strong, and she will not wish to leave you and Alice alone again. My niece loves you both dearly."

"My wife is quite incomparable," Darcy admitted.

"Be about it, then," Mrs. Gardiner instructed. "Hurry now. Elizabeth is alone and frightened, although she will never admit so to you. I will be there in less than a quarter hour."

Darcy nodded and started away, but Mrs. Gardiner called him back. "Grab your watch. We must know how much time passes between each of the pains Elizabeth experiences. The shorter the time, the closer to when my niece will deliver your child."

AMENDING THE SHADES OF PEMBERLEY

Although the midwife had not approved of Darcy's presence in Elizabeth's quarters, he had ignored Mrs. Skidmore's admonishments. Only Mrs. Reynolds knew his personal fear of losing yet another woman of importance in his life. Childbed fever had claimed Lady Anne Darcy, just as it had done Elizabeth's sister, and neither he nor his father nor Pemberley had been the same afterwards. Life had returned to him and the estate with Elizabeth's arrival, and Darcy did not believe he could go through such decline again. Therefore, he sat dutifully by Elizabeth, facing away from what Mrs. Skidmore did to his wife. Instead, he wiped Elizabeth's face with a cool cloth and permitted her to squeeze his hand through each of her birthing pains and took note of how the time between the spasms had progressively shortened, just as her aunt had predicted.

They were some nine hours into their journey when Mrs. Skidmore instructed, "Mr. Darcy, please, if'n you would, sir, place Mrs. Darcy in the chair. Then you must leave."

Darcy wished to protest against his exile from his wife's bedroom, but Elizabeth caught his hand to say, "Aunt Gardiner . . . and Mrs. Reynolds . . . will not permit . . . any harm . . . to come to me. You must assure . . . the others . . . I am well."

"I love you," he declared before all present.

"And I . . . adore you," she had whispered against his mouth as she held his head where she could see him. "Now, assist me . . . as Mrs. Skidmore . . . has instructed."

Darcy nodded his agreement, bent to lift his wife from the bed, and carried her to the odd-looking chair, supposedly designed to make the child's delivery easier on the woman. As he set Elizabeth down, her aunt hiked up his wife's gown, exposing Elizabeth to the eyes of all in the room. Although he understood the necessity of the move, he still wished to protect her from any shame. The chair had the center cut away to permit the baby an easier passage; yet, he feared Elizabeth too weak to balance her own weight on the piece of furniture. Mrs.

Gardiner presented him a gentle shove. "I will be outside the door if you require me," he told his wife.

Mrs. Skidmore nudged him from the way before Elizabeth could respond. "Mrs. Darcy, when next you feel the pain, I needs you to hold your breath and bear down until I tells you to breathe."

Elizabeth nodded her understanding, but he noted the fear in his wife's eyes as he backed away.

"Go, Mr. Darcy," her aunt ordered, presenting him a not-so-gentle shove this time.

"Save Elizabeth," he said softly to Mrs. Gardiner as she slowly shoved the door in his face. "If a choice must be made, save Elizabeth."

"All will be well," her aunt said. "Now go, Elizabeth must concentrate on herself and the baby, and my niece will not do so if she fears your disappointment."

Reluctantly, he stepped back into the hall outside the room. He mouthed the words, "I love you," before the door closed in his face. His breath came heavy as he realized he was shut away from her. He knew he should have sought out Mr. Gardiner and Mary and Mr. Ericks, who Darcy knew waited for news somewhere below, but he could not leave Elizabeth so easily. Instead, he leaned with his back against the wall and slid down it to sit on the floor outside the room, where he offered up another round of prayers, while, on the other side of the door, Elizabeth expelled a blood-curdling scream, which made him shudder in fear. The last time he had heard such a cry, a support beam cracked and a cave-in took the lives of two of his workers in the mine.

As the room repeatedly drew silent, except for mumbled orders, followed by the excruciating screams of his poor, sweet Elizabeth, Darcy covered his ears with his hands. Closing his eyes, he could see himself as an untested youth of twelve hiding behind a suit of armor in the passageway outside his mother's quarters, as she, too, screamed in childbirth.

AMENDING THE SHADES OF PEMBERLEY

Lady Anne had been so excited for a new child, for his parents had lost two others of which he was aware and, supposedly, a third while he was but a babe of one year.

However, Lady Anne's fifth attempt to produce another child held hope, for his mother had insisted on complete rest. Darcy easily recalled how he would sneak into her room several times each day. He would bring her a treat he had pilfered from the kitchen or they would play chess or he would read to her from his current lessons. Sometimes they would simply talk of the world outside her rooms. Lady Anne would always ask about his day, his studies, or the games he had played with the other boys, and he had gloried in her attention, too foolish to realize the danger she was in. He should have been protecting her, when all he had done was to be as selfish as the rest of the household.

The world as he knew it ended: His mother had screamed as Elizabeth now screamed, and he could do nothing for Lady Anne but to hide behind a suit of armor. Nor was there much he could do for Elizabeth but pray, which he did with all his heart.

Although he adored Georgiana and would not wish for her never to have been born, not a day, since he was twelve, had he not regretted his mother's passing. Lady Anne, most assuredly, would never have permitted George Darcy to send her son away. His mother would have executed what Mr. Bennet had suggested. She would have brought Ruth Chapman to Pemberley and kept the woman under supervised lock and key to determine whether Ruth was truly with child.

"My mother would have presented Chapman a promise of marriage if Ruth's tale proved true," he whispered to the "ghosts" of Pemberley. "If Chapman thought Lord Matlock impossible with which to deal, the man would have known instant regret if he had encountered the earl's youngest sister, Lady Anne Darcy. Where my father would not dare to make such an accusation regarding an unmarried woman of supposedly 'good' family, Lady Anne would have called a spade a spade and said 'to Hell' with the consequences. She would not have stood by quietly and permitted George Darcy to send me away. My father thought to protect the family's name from scandal, but scandal still found us all."

With a heavy sigh for what might have been, Darcy removed his hands from his ears to wipe away the tears, he, initially, did not recognize had formed, upon his sleeve. It was only then he realized Elizabeth's screaming had ceased. Scrambling to his feet, he charged the door only to discover it locked. "Let me in," he ordered as he pounded on the door. "Let me in or I'll break it down."

"One minute, Master," he heard Mrs. Reynolds call, which was followed by a shuffling of feet, and, at last, a whimper and then a wail of complaint.

"The child," he whispered, as his knees became suddenly weak. He leaned against the door frame. "Elizabeth!" he called. "Elizabeth!" Fear rushed to his chest. "Please God," he murmured as Mrs. Gardiner opened the door. Ahead, Elizabeth slumped in exhaustion against the side of the chair. A bowl of blood and other body fluids he did not recognize stood beneath the opening in the contraption. Darcy felt everything go black, but just as he grabbed at the framework to prevent his fall, Elizabeth raised her weary head and smiled at him.

"It is over," she announced weakly.

"Not completely," Mrs. Skidmore corrected, "but yer lady, sir, done well."

Darcy still clung to the door frame as Mrs. Reynolds approached carrying a squirming and fussing wrapped bundle. "You have a son, Mr. Darcy," the housekeeper announced with pride. "An heir for Pemberley and a time to rejoice." She placed the child in his arms, arranging his hands better to support the baby's weight. "I imagine Mrs. Darcy would enjoy viewing the literal 'fruit of her labor,'" she hinted.

His eyes darted between the red-faced damp, dark-haired child in his arms and the woman who had become essential to his existence. With a nod of his head in gratitude, he stepped around the chaos of the room to where Elizabeth rested in what surely was an uncomfortable position. Kneeling beside her, he rose up on his knees to kiss his wife's sweat-soaked hair. "We have a son, Elizabeth," he whispered near her ear. "Bennet Thomas George Darcy wishes the pleasure of his mother's kiss." They had previously discussed names for their child, choosing both male and female possibilities. They had agreed a son should be named "Bennet" so her family name would not end with her father's passing.

"Is he well?" she asked in obvious concern.

He turned back the blanket to reveal the child to her. "Appears so," he assured. "Legs and hands and arms and feet all attached."

His wife's smile was weak, but genuine and announced her tease before it arrived. "Hopefully, the feet are attached to the legs and the hands to the arms," she murmured. She leaned closer to have her first look at their son. "He has your look, Fitzwilliam."

"He does, love," he whispered. "And here I was hoping for a bronze-haired beauty."

"You want more than one of my temperament under your feet?" she asked as Bennet's fingers wrapped around the tip of her index finger.

"Your temperament suits me best," he assured her. "If I have not told you so today, you are quite magnificent, Elizabeth Darcy." Worried for how she slumped against the chair, he implored, "Should I move you back to the bed so you might rest, love?"

"Must still pass the sack," she murmured. "Then I may rest. You must tend Bennet. You might start with showing off your heir to my uncle and Mary as well as informing the staff."

"As you well know, I am quite capable of handling a baby," he assured. Darcy kissed her temple. "I love you more than words can express. You have presented me and Pemberley a new world, one full of possibilities."

She raised her head to look him in the eyes. "Remember, we agreed: There is no future for those who live in the past."

A Bit of an Epilogue (for those who always want to know what happens next)

Shortly before Bennet was born, England learned the British forces under Wellington had defeated Napoleon Bonaparte at a place called Waterloo. A great celebration swept across the United Kingdom, but, naturally, he and Elizabeth had their own private "celebration" at home, for Elizabeth was close to her lying in, and Darcy would not chance her traveling under those conditions. Instead, he had arranged for fireworks to be shot off from Pemberley, so all those at and around his estate could recognize their country's great achievement and enjoy the day together.

Unfortunately, for Pemberley and the rest of the nation, when the hordes of soldiers returned to what they had left behind to serve their country, they were met with what was later called "The Year Without Summer." At the time, no one truly knew what had caused the unusually wet year of 1816, but everyone across the country suffered. No one from King to peasant escaped being touched in some manner by the chaos caused by this phenomenon. Crops rotted in the ground. The few alternative income sources Darcy had put in place softened the losses at Pemberley, but not enough to keep all his tenants in place.

One of the more joyous parts of the early months of 1816 had been Georgiana's marriage to Captain Sir Robert Spurlock, a baronet who had served as one of Wellington's junior officers. Darcy's sister had never returned to Pemberley as she had promised, though she did come for short visits, but Darcy had to accept Georgiana had carved out a different life while she was with the Matlocks. Even so, he was proud to view her well settled, although he knew Lord and Lady Matlock's influence had proven more beneficial than had his. The stain of scandal had not been rinsed away by the days and months of torrential rains.

It was well into 1817 before the newspapers suggested the source of the nation's misery was a volcano in a place of which none of them had ever heard. All they knew was it was somewhere south of China. Many thought the tales of soot traveling on the trade winds to be preposterous; yet, those were men and women who had spent their entire lives in Lambton.

"If they had ever viewed what is called the 'Silk Roads,'—the trade routes for the silks and spices they covet—then they would realize how we are all connected," he had told Elizabeth.

"You believe this is true? Trade winds carrying soot to block out the sun?" his wife had asked in amazement.

"I have friends and business acquaintances who crisscross Asia in camel caravans to trade for goods of all kinds. There sea captains in places such as Calcutta and Bombay who bring those goods to Europe and England and on to America. The world becomes smaller and smaller by the day."

"But what of these trade winds carrying soot and such?" she repeated her question.

"Those same sea captains I mentioned before speak of how pumice stone washed up on the coast of India for months on end, as well as strong storms with waves ten feet high."

"A hurricane?" Elizabeth asked.

"Those types of storms are generally called 'cyclones' in India," he explained. "I have heard those along the islands off the coast of China call them '*tsu*' meaning '*harbor*' and '*nami*' meaning '*water.*' *Tsunami,*" he pronounced. "One learns lots of names for the same phenomenon when he travels." He shrugged with a bit of embarrassment about going on and on. "Anyway, when I was recently in London, I dined with two sea captains who travel to India often—the ones I have been courting to take some of Pemberley's products to other parts of the world. Neither spoke of a cyclone, but they did describe a 'churning' of the ocean floor which made sailing impossible, for the waves were so high they were glad to be in dock at the time of the occurrence rather out on a rough sea. Said it reminded them of the story of the parting of the Red Sea in the Bible."

"I do not think I could travel so far from home," Elizabeth admitted.

"Of course you could, my love," he teased. "After all, you were brave enough to join me in Africa, where our Alice was conceived."

She swatted at his chest in protest, as she snuggled closer to his side. "You will never permit me to forget how impetuous I once was."

"Once?" he corrected. "Who scampered across the stream earlier today to retrieve Alice's bonnet?"

His lovely wife elbowed him this time. "Alice was in tears, and you would have done the same."

"Exactly," Darcy said in triumph. "I sailed to India, and you would also, if necessary."

"'Necessary' is the keyword. It was 'necessary' for me to join my husband in Africa. Nowadays, I am satisfied with Derbyshire. Like my father before me, even London holds no great draw."

<hr />

It was in the later part of 1817, when he heard from his Aunt Catherine. "I was not aware you held my aunt's acquaintance," Darcy said as they sat to supper alone for a change, for Alice was spending the night with the Erickses and Bennet was down for the evening in the nursery. "Lady Matlock told her of you, and Lady Catherine recognized your name immediately. Her rector's wife was a friend of yours or something to that effect."

"Do I?" Elizabeth asked. "Not of which I am aware. The only daughter of an earl I have ever encountered was Lady Catherine deBourgh."

"One and the same," Darcy admitted with a smile. "Yet, how did you take her ladyship's acquaintance?"

His wife sipped her soup. "You must have heard my father speak of his heir to Longbourn," she said with a slight shiver from the cold.

Darcy rose to add another log to the fire and sent Mr. Nathan to fetch the shawl Elizabeth had left in the small sitting room. "Mr. Collins, was it not?" he asked as he returned to his seat.

"Yes, Mr. Collins. He came to Longbourn in November 1812 to make amends to the rift between Mr. Collins's father and mine. In reality, your aunt had sent him to Longbourn to claim a wife. He was Lady Catherine's rector, and your aunt decided he required a wife. He thought to propose to Jane, but Mrs. Bennet assured him Jane was expecting a proposal from Mr. Bingley, but I was of equal beauty and kindness, which had the man foolishly making me an offer of his hand. He quickly realized I had only a dollop of Jane's kindness coursing through my veins. I refused, though my mother attempted to convince my father to order me to do so."

"Mr. Bennet knew we were already married by that time, and we shared a child," Darcy said with a teasing lift of his brows.

"A fact both you and Mr. Bennet neglected to share with those who should have been made cognizant of the facts," she said with a matching teasing tone.

Mr. Nathan returned with her shawl, and they paused for a couple of minutes while she fastened it about her shoulders and thanked the servant.

"You refused Mr. Collins . . ." he prompted her to share the rest of her story.

"The fool dined with the Lucases that same evening and proposed to my friend Charlotte, who readily accepted him, for she had had no other offers." His wife sighed heavily. "I could not understand Charlotte's urgency when she told me of her choice. She was customarily quite intelligent, but she feared being a financial burden on her family. Moreover, with Mr. Collins, she would have a home of her own and respectability in the world. I thought her quite insensible, but I, essentially, did the same thing with you. I suppose what goes around comes around."

She shrugged away her revelation. "I visited with the Collinses for a bit the spring after they married. Such is when I took Lady Catherine's acquaintance." She stopped to sip her wine. "Her ladyship found me quite rude for I was not one to toad to her edicts. I felt terribly sorry for Miss de Bourgh, for she was the sickly type." Elizabeth blushed. "I should not have spoken of your cousin in such a manner, Fitzwilliam. I offer my apologies."

"Anne was always ill," he confirmed. "Or so we all thought. My aunt wished me to marry her, but my banishment changed her mind."

"Oh!!" Elizabeth gasped. "You were the cousin meant for Miss de Bourgh. What a small world in which we live," she observed. "I heard something of you from Charlotte Collins, not from Lady Catherine. There was a young gentlemen calling on Miss de Bourgh while I was there. Very green behind the ears, if my opinion means anything in such matters."

"Likely, her ladyship chose him specifically for that reason." He leaned closer to Elizabeth to say. "It will be such a pleasure to inform my aunt the reason you were not in a position to accept Mr. Collins was you were already married to me and had delivered our first child."

"Fitzwilliam, you would not," she begged.

"I would. After all, she turned from me when my days in England were numbered. I was no longer her 'favorite' nephew. Today, she asked me to call upon her, but, I have the perfect excuse: We cannot be available until well after your third lying in. Is such not correct, my love?"

Elizabeth patted the back of his hand. "You may use me as your excuse in Kent, my husband, for I often use you to avoid unpleasantries here in Derbyshire."

Laughing easily at her teasing, he leaned closer still and stole a kiss before they returned to their meal. Neither of them much required the affirmation of others to know happiness.

In November 1817, Elizabeth delivered a second son, who they named "Edward," after the colonel. Edward Louis Samuel Darcy was the "spare" many men required to secure their estates, but to Darcy and Elizabeth he was simply a son in which they knew great pride.

It was in the spring after their sweet-natured Edward was born that Elizabeth asked to see Longbourn again. They were on their way to London for part of the Short Season and for Darcy to conduct business affairs. They had all three children and a nurse maid in tow, when she asked, "If it would not be inconvenient, might we stop at Longbourn and view the cemetery? I fear no one has attended it. I promise not to be overlong."

"You may stay as long as you like," Darcy had said. "I have asked you previously if you wished to do so."

"I know," she was quick to say. "You have been most kind in these matters, but I believe I would like to introduce Bennet to his namesake. Likely, he will not recall any of what I say, though he is as studious as his father," Elizabeth added with a quick smile. "Yet, I do want him to know something of my father and of where I lived."

Darcy simply nodded his agreement, tapped on the roof of the carriage, and presented Mr. Farrin with orders to call at Longbourn and to take the hill up to the cemetery. He watched as Elizabeth slid closer to the window to catch sight of, once, very familiar places. "When we leave," he said, "you should point out Oakham Mount and Netherfield and the like to Alice and Bennet. They will wish to hear your stories of when you were a little girl."

She did not answer, for she was taking it all in, as was customary with her, but Elizabeth nodded her agreement. Finally, the arch above the gates of Longbourn came into view. "Mary and I clung to each other when we left here with you and Alice. Neither of us held any assurance of our future. It all seems so long ago, but, in reality, not fully four years. We were both blessed the day you walked into Longbourn to save us. I thank you most generously, my husband."

At length, the coach stopped, and Darcy stepped down to lift her to the ground. "Take Alice up with you. I will bring the boys."

"Do not give Bennet a lecture about behaving himself," she warned. "He is not yet three and has been in a small carriage for several hours. Permit him to run about if such is his nature."

Darcy smiled at her. "Yes, ma'am." As he walked in the direction of the smaller carriage, he called over his shoulder, "You sound a great deal of the nature of Lady Anne Darcy. She said the same to her

343

husband when they traveled with their son." He passed his daughter as Alice scampered towards where Elizabeth waited.

"Mama, where are we?"

The child accepted Elizabeth's hand as they started up the hill. "This is where I used to live," he could hear her say to their daughter. "Remember. This is where your papa and I were married in my parents' house."

Alice looked around and spotted Longbourn off in the distance. "I see it, Mama."

"Do you remember when Papa showed you where his parents were buried at Pemberley?" The child was quiet, but attentive. "This area is where my mother and father and sisters are buried. Surely you recall how Mary told you of Lydia and Kitty? How silly they were at times and how we miss them terribly. And Mr. Bingley spoke of our sweet Jane and how much he loved her?" Darcy waited at a distance as Elizabeth tugged Alice closer and bent to speak the child. "There is no need for you to look so sullen. This is a happy place, for it is where I began and you began." She touched her heart and then the child's. "Without each of the people who came before us, then we could not be here in this moment together. So, if you wish to run about and pick flowers or just sit quietly and enjoy the sunshine and being outside the carriage after such a long ride, it is permissible to do so. There is no need for you to whisper or to cry or to be anything but yourself. My father wanted your father and me to be married and to give birth to you and your brothers. He planned it long before he spoke of it to me. In fact, he designed a means for your father and me to claim each other and then you. Therefore, he wanted you to be my daughter, and he wanted Bennet and Edward to be my sons and your brothers. This is not a scary place, but one in which joy lives."

In that moment Darcy recognized the pure beauty in the woman he had married, for his Elizabeth was not like any other woman in the world. Carrying Edward in his arms and watching as Bennet scurried to be close to his mother, Darcy heard what she had said to Alice and now watched as she bent to whisper something similar to their son. Holding the boy's hand they walked together to where Thomas Bennet was buried. She guided the child's hand over the word "Bennet" and told him how he was a part of all the land spread out before them. Elizabeth pointed to the house off in the distance and spoke of how it was where she lived as a small girl and how she had loved being a part of the Bennet family and was so proud their son carried her family name. She hugged Bennet then and sent him on his way to trail Alice about the gravestones, looking for flowers and pebbles and whatever else interested them, as Elizabeth returned to his side. "Thank you, Fitzwilliam," she said softly. "As my father predicted, you have made me completely and perfectly and incandescently happy with all you have given me." He bent to kiss her upturned lips, and, in that moment, Darcy made a silent promise somehow to bring Longbourn back to his Elizabeth.

Early 1818 brought another update. This time it arrived in a newsy letter from Mr. Bingley to Elizabeth.

"Listen to this, Fitzwilliam," his wife said. She had been curled up in the chair before the fire while he read from a book which did not hold his attention as powerfully as did his wife. *"I pray you will not be upset to learn I have extended my hand to Miss Evelyn Sumner. I admit I do not love her as I did our Jane, but I am quite fond of the lady, and, in truth, I am not built to live alone. Moreover, I owe my family name the duty of children. When you are next in Town, I would be proud to introduce you and Mary as my dearest sisters."*

"I was wondering when Bingley would claim another wife. He grieved a respectable time for your sister," Darcy remarked. "It may surprise you, but I thought Bingley might pursue Georgiana," he admitted. "The countess said they danced together at several events, and they got along well."

Elizabeth remarked, "I imagine Mr. Bingley did so out of a sense of duty to our family. I doubt he would choose someone who might remind him of Jane. Without meeting Miss Sumner, I suspect the lady is dark of head."

"Perhaps you are correct," he commented and then returned to his page. For nearly two minutes, his wife was lost in the letter, but she sat up straighter and leaned forward. "*You must pay attention to this part, as well, Fitzwilliam.*" She lifted the letter to catch the light. "*I have more news to relate, specific to your Darcy family. I was at the docks today, for I had two ships bringing in goods from Madras. While there, I espied Mr. Chapman and made certain to eavesdrop upon the man's conversation with the captain of one of my ships, for you know we all love a bit of gossip, and, in truth, I thought perhaps Miss Chapman was attempting to sneak back into England.*

"Evidently, the man did not notice my presence on the dock. Anyway, the captain and Chapman argued over expected payment for delivering Chapman's grandson, a boy of perhaps two years, to England, along with the child's manservant. After Chapman left with the child and the Indian servant, I questioned the captain on what had occurred. He said Chapman's daughter had married a textile merchant—a man who was Catholic. Supposedly, according to the captain, both Miss Chapman and her husband died in the aftermath of the volcano's explosion, thus requiring the boy being brought to England.

"It seems within weeks after the explosion in April 1815, the temperature in Madras dipped to freezing. Darcy will tell you, Sister Elizabeth, Madras has but one temperature: Hot! Apparently, the clouds of soot also blocked the sun in India, just as it did here in England. Now, whether this part is true, I cannot say with any certainty, for there is no record of such in any papers from the East India Company colonial masters I have searched; yet the captain, who I trust implicitly, claims what I mean to impart as such.

"Ironically, where the ash brought rain to England and much of Europe, in India, there was no annual monsoon. Therefore, crops failed. Famine spread, which was followed by widespread cholera. According to the captain who met with those overseeing the boy, both Miss Chapman and the woman's husband contracted the disease from some of the men with whom the merchant did business."

"My goodness," Elizabeth gasped.

"It is hard to believe," Darcy said, "but such means we no longer face fears from Ruth's corner."

Elizabeth glanced back to the letter. "Yet, what a terrible way to die." She lifted the letter again. "There is one more point of reference Mr. Bingley made." She read, "*I should not say this; however, I thought the child greatly favored Mr. Wickham, but I am certain he could easily belong to another dark-haired man.*"

Darcy remarked, "I suspect if there is a chance Wickham is the child's father, Chapman learned from my maneuvers. He has likely purchased a copy of Ruth's marriage certificate, the one by the Church of England; otherwise, a Catholic marriage would not be considered legal. The statute of 1746 clearly states a marriage between a Papist and a Protestant is null and void for all intents and purposes. Other than Jews or Quakers, everyone who is English, including Catholics, must be married in the local parish church by a Church of England clergyman. If not married in the Protestant church, their children would be considered illegitimate under the law of the land."

Elizabeth observed, "Chapman would want his grandson to be legitimate." She sighed heavily. "Perhaps Miss Chapman wished for the boy to be brought up as a Catholic or her husband insisted as such. As she was not permitted to return to England, for all we know, her husband might not have been an Englishman. Surely a place such as Madras has many nationalities streaming through the streets."

"But then the child would not resemble Wickham," Darcy summarized.

"I never wished the woman to die," Elizabeth stated. "I simply wished her as far away from us as possible and for her to find her own happiness where none was to be had in England. We will likely never know for certain what she intended for her son. Like us, she obviously meant to protect her child. At least Miss Chapman is no longer to be feared for Alice's future."

In February 1820, they welcomed their first daughter, Jane Mary Elizabeth Darcy, so named for Elizabeth's two sisters. A third son, William Alexander Joseph Darcy, with a shortened version of his father's name, made his appearance in June 1823, and their youngest, Anne Frances Edith Darcy, called as such to honor both their mothers, joined the family in January 1826. By then, Elizabeth was in her mid-thirties and Darcy in his early forties. Three daughters and three sons filled the halls of Pemberley, and for Darcy it was everything for which he had ever wanted.

Meanwhile, Mary and Samuel Ericks had been blessed with three children of their own—two sons and a daughter. Thomas Lucas Martin Ericks came into the world in January 1816, named for both Mary's father and Mr. Ericks's older brother. Samuel Marcus John Ericks, named for his father, made his first appearance in June 1818. Finally, their daughter Frances Cora Alice Ericks, which Darcy's oldest assisted in naming after herself, arrived in May 1820. The Bennet sisters had claimed a bit of Derbyshire for their own children, and both Elizabeth and Mary never took their good luck for granted. They were together, a mere five miles apart, and their children knew a shared family history many did not.

In 1820, good to the silent promise he had made that day at Longbourn, Darcy petitioned to reclaim Longbourn for the Bennet family through common recovery. As no male heirs could be located, the property had sat empty for nearly five years. Unfortunately, it was another three years and more than a thousand pounds in legal fees and taxes before the Bennet family estate was turned over to Elizabeth Bennet Darcy. He had never viewed his wife cry such tears of thanksgiving. "Longbourn can be an estate for Edward or William or for one of Mary's children," she had declared as he held her to offer his support. "You are one of the most generous men our dear Lord ever created."

For the time being, they had agreed to let the estate to John Lucas and the young man's new wife, who were looking for a place of their own in an over-crowded Lucas Lodge, which the pair would inherit after Sir William Lucas's passing. At John Lucas's request and Mr. Darcy's most whole-hearted approval, the contract between the Lucases and her husband said John and the new Mrs. Lucas could not use Longbourn to house any of their family members beyond Mrs. Lucas's widowed mother, if such should occur before John inherited Lucas lodge, as well as any children of their own loins. As Sir William and Lady Lucas had nine children, with seven of them still at home, the temptation to send a few to live with John would be natural.

"Mama always said Lady Lucas was jealous of Longbourn's size," Mary had said one day over afternoon tea when she learned of the stipulations.

To which, Elizabeth responded, "The Lucases were good friends, but Sir William was still a merchant, not of the gentry. Mama knew Lady Lucas was jealous not to have caught Thomas Bennet's eye." She sighed heavily. "Would Mama not have been silenced by Pemberley? I might have replaced Jane and Lydia as her favorite."

Mary laughed easily. "She would expect you to find rich husbands for the rest of us. Yet, as for me, I am satisfied with my lot. I could find no better man than Mr. Ericks."

✑

"She is too young to marry," Elizabeth had protested again and again after Alice accepted the proposal of Lord Nathaniel Barber, a baron from Northumberland. Now, it was the girl's wedding day, and Mr. Ericks was to perform the ceremony.

"It is a spectacular match for a girl whose life started under less-than-ideal conditions," Darcy reminded his wife. "You are only upset because once Alice leaves us, then the others will soon follow."

"They cannot leave, Fitzwilliam. I forbid it," she proclaimed.

"I have already presented Lord Barber my permission," he countered, "and our Alice makes an absolutely stunning bride."

Elizabeth ignored his reasons. "You must tell his lordship you have changed your mind. I cannot bear it, Fitzwilliam. Alice was the first to call me 'mama.'"

"And you have been an exemplary mother for the child. Alice will be a competent mistress of Barber's households and a good influence on the baron. I have not regretted even one day of taking Mr. Thomas Bennet's advice and claiming his second daughter to wife," Darcy assured as he brought the back of Elizabeth's hand to his lips for a kiss.

"Fitzwilliam," she said softy as he meant to step away to fetch Alice for the ceremony.

"Yes, love."

"I wanted to thank you for always holding my hand," she admitted. "I feel stronger when you do so, and also very protected. I required your protection all those years removed when we stood before Mr. Williamson at Longbourn. I knew then, when we faced the world together, any fears I held were shared by you. Shoulder by you. My insecurity drained away, and my fear subsided because of your tender gesture of taking my hand in yours. My father was truly a wise man: He bargained for a husband who most assuredly best suited me."

"And a wife who encouraged me to be the best man possible." he countered. "Thomas Bennet was truly a forward-looking man. Brilliant in more ways than one." He kissed the back of Elizabeth's hand. "The most fulfilling moments in my life happened because your father suggested you would fill my life with love and a solemn promise and a future. Such moments occurred because of you, Elizabeth Bennet Darcy. Because you saw something in me I did not know existed. You embody my 'reason,' my 'hopes,' and my 'dreams.' No matter what what happens to us in the future, every single day we are together will be the greatest day of my life. I love the sound of your voice. The warmth of your smile. The joy you bring to all our lives. And I love that you permit me to hold your hand as we do now. Connected. Together. Forever."

~ Finis ~

Meet the Author

With nearly 60 books to her credit, Regina Jeffers is an award-winning author of historical cozy mysteries, Austenesque sequels and retellings, as well as Regency era-based romantic suspense and historical romances. A teacher for thirty-nine years, Jeffers often serves as a consultant for Language Arts and Media Literacy programs. With multiple degrees, Regina has been a Time Warner Star Teacher, Columbus (OH) Teacher of the Year, and a Martha Holden Jennings Scholar, as well as a Smithsonian presenter. Her stories have been acknowledged by the Daphne du Maurier Award for Excellence in Mystery/Suspense, the Frank Yerby Award for Fiction, the coveted Derby Award for Fiction, the International Digital Awards, and the Chanticleer International Book Award, among her many accolades.

Other Novels from Regina Jeffers

Jane Austen-Inspired Novels

Darcy's Passions: Pride and Prejudice Retold Through His Eyes

Darcy's Temptation: A Pride and Prejudice Sequel

Captain Frederick Wentworth's Persuasion: Jane Austen's Classic Retold

Vampire Darcy's Desire: A Pride and Prejudice Paranormal Adventure

The Phantom of Pemberley: A Pride and Prejudice Mystery

Christmas at Pemberley: A Pride and Prejudice Holiday Sequel

The Disappearance of Georgiana Darcy: A Pride and Prejudice Mystery

REGINA JEFFERS

The Mysterious Death of Mr. Darcy: A Pride and Prejudice Mystery

The Prosecution of Mr. Darcy's Cousin: A Pride and Prejudice Mystery

Mr. Darcy's Fault: A Pride and Prejudice Vagary

Mr. Darcy's Bargain: A Pride and Prejudice Vagary

Mr. Darcy's Present: A Pride and Prejudice Holiday Vagary

Mr. Darcy's Brides: A Pride and Prejudice Vagary

Mr. Darcy's Bet: A Pride and Prejudice Vagary

Mr. Darcy's Inadvertent Bride: A Pride and Prejudice Vagary

Elizabeth Bennet's Deception: A Pride and Prejudice Vagary

Elizabeth Bennet's Excellent Adventure: A Pride and Prejudice Vagary

Elizabeth Bennet's Gallant Suitor: A Pride and Prejudice Vagary

The Pemberley Ball: A Pride and Prejudice Vagary

A Dance with Mr. Darcy: A Pride and Prejudice Vagary

The Road to Understanding: A Pride and Prejudice Vagary

Pride and Prejudice and a Shakespearean Scholar: A Pride and Prejudice Vagary

Where There's a FitzWILLiam Darcy, There's a Way: A Pride and Prejudice Vagary

In Want of a Wife: A Pride and Prejudice Vagary

Losing Lizzy: A Pride and Prejudice Vagary

The Mistress of Rosings Park: A Pride and Prejudice Vagary

Pemberley's Christmas Governess: A Pride and Prejudice Vagary

Amending the Shades of Pemberley: A Pride and Prejudice Vagary

Honor and Hope: A Contemporary Pride and Prejudice

Regency and Contemporary Novels

The Scandal of Lady Eleanor: Book 1 of the Realm Series (aka A Touch of Scandal)

AMENDING THE SHADES OF PEMBERLEY

A Touch of Velvet: Book 2 of the Realm Series
A Touch of Cashémere: Book 3 of the Realm Series
A Touch of Grace: Book 4 of the Realm Series
A Touch of Mercy: Book 5 of the Realm Series
A Touch of Love: Book 6 of the Realm Series
A Touch of Honor: Book 7 of the Realm Series
A Touch of Emerald: Book 8 of the Realm Series
His American Heartsong: A Companion Novel to the Realm Series
His Irish Eve
Angel Comes to the Devil's Keep: Book 1 of the Twins' Trilogy
The Earl Claims His Comfort: Book 2 of the Twins' Trilogy
Lady Chandler's Sister: Book 3 of the Twins' Trilogy
The Heartless Earl: A Common Elements Romance Novel
I Shot the Sheriff: A Tragic Heroes in Classic Lit Series Novel
Captain Stanwick's Bride: A Tragic Heroes in Classic Lit Series Novel
Lady Joy and the Earl: A Second-Chance Regency Romance
Letters from Home: A Regency Romance
Courting Lord Whitmore: A Regency May-December Romance
Last Woman Standing: A Regency Christmas Romance
The Courtship of Lord Blackhurst: A Regency Romance
Lord Radcliffe's Best Friend: A Regency Friends to Lovers Romance
The Jewel Thief and the Earl: A Regency Romance
His Christmas Violet: A Regency Second Chance Romance
The Earl's English Rose: A Regency Summer Romance
Bell, Book and Wardrobe: A Regency Romance
Beautified by Love
Something in the Air

REGINA JEFFERS

Escape to Love

Second Chances: The Courtship Wars

One Minute Past Christmas, a Holiday Short Story

Coming Soon . . .

Indentured Love: A Persuasion Vagary

Obsession: The One Where the Princess Saves Herself

Lady Glynis and the Earl

Loving Lord Lindmore

You May Connect with Regina on: Facebook, Twitter, Pinterest, Amazon Author Page, BookBub, Instagram, and YouTube,

as well as on either her

Every Woman Dreams blog

or the Always Austen blog

or her Website (which contains all the links you require).

AMENDING THE SHADES OF PEMBERLEY

Enjoy an Excerpt from "Lady Glynis and the Earl"

Chapter One

Late September, 1819

Glynis watched as the English white cliffs gave way to the shoreline leading to the Thames's estuary. She had departed Italy as quickly as arrangements could be made. Her Aunt Althea had argued the journey was too dangerous for a young lady not quite old enough to claim her majority, but Uncle George had reminded his wife, "Since she was fifteen, our Glynis has managed to charm half the diplomats in Europe. Surely, she can travel to England with a male servant and her maid in tow."

She had been but a babe in swaddling clothes when her aunt and uncle had arrived at Padon Hall to claim her. Lord and Lady Millard were related through the maternal line, as Lady Althea was sister to Glynis's mother, Lady Magdaline Padon, née Reiker, who had passed during childbirth.

As a child, Glynis could remember exactly when she realized she had neither father nor mother. Her governess at the time, Mrs. Lanard, had punished Glynis for creating a mess of her letters because a left-handed person tended to drag his or her knuckles through the ink before it dried. In her anger, Mrs. Lanard had lashed out, declaring, "You have no mother, and your father does not want you. Why would he wish to know such a messy child?"

Afterwards, her uncle had held Glynis for hours, making his explanations. "Your Aunt Althea and I were not in England when you were born, my girl. By the time we arrived, you were nearly three months old. My Althea was so sad not to have been near when your mother, Lady Magdaline Padon, passed into the hands of our Heavenly Father, she was quite beside herself with grief.

"Moreover, your father was so distraught he was near exhaustion. He begged your aunt to take you until he could again set his estate and his life aright, as well as spend time grieving properly for Magdaline. As we already had Lucinda and Jonathon, you were no trouble to us. At the time, we were on our way to Denmark, but Padon said we could send you back any time we wished, but, you see, we did not wish. You were our Glynis, the third of our children. Then your father married Lady Caroline Hexham."

Uncle George never said the words aloud, but, eventually, Glynis understood: Her father had remarried and wanted no reminder of his first marriage, or, perhaps, it was Lady Caroline who did not want the responsibility of another woman's child. From what Glynis had heard of the woman, and, in truth, such was not extensive, her ladyship had not proven much of a mother to her own son, Glynis's half-brother, a child now twelve years of age, Robert, or "Robbie," the 10th Earl Padon.

"Thank you for meeting my ship, Spencer," Glynis said as her cousin extended his hand to assist her steps from the wooden plank between the ship and the wharf.

"Glad to, my girl," he said. "You are aware I have a vested interest in this matter. Papa is cousin to your Uncle George."

Glynis accepted his proffered arm and permitted him to escort her to his waiting coach. Once they were settled in and her trunks were secured, she asked softly, "When did he pass?" Although she had never lived with her father, actually had only encountered him once, some four years removed, she had known a loss when the letter from Spencer's father had reached her in Italy, where Lord Millard now served as a British diplomat. He had been thus employed for more years than she could remember, long before she was born. Spencer, too, had spent some of his childhood in the Millard household, and Glynis looked at him more as a brother than a cousin.

"Not quite three months. Father attended the funeral. And the boy, of course. Poor child. Left alone so early."

"I will travel to Hertfordshire as quickly as arrangements can be made. I pray the boy has someone with him during this time." She wondered briefly on whether Lady Caroline had assisted the child to an understanding of what had occurred. She frowned when thinking upon the reception she was likely to receive; yet, such could not be helped. She was a "Padon," and, as such, the proper thing to do was for her to call upon her family's estate, although she had never seen it in all her twenty years. "I pray you will consider accompanying me, Spencer. That is, if I can convince you to be away from Lady Theodora," she teased. Lord Bond had written to Uncle Millard of the continuing "romance" between his son and a woman referred to as "Lady Theodora." Glynis was happy to tease her cousin regarding this relationship, for Spencer had always taken great delight in commenting on her many suitors.

"I suppose father wrote to your Uncle Millard of my courting Lady Theodora," Spencer grumbled. "This was the Season I had planned to extend my hand in marriage to the lady."

"There was just a mention in his last letter to Uncle Millard," she admitted. "Nothing of the progress of your efforts."

"My progress and my prospects are both dim," Spencer confessed, a deep frown marking his forehead. "Dora left London with her family some weeks back, and I have no idea of when she will return."

Glynis could not quite fathom such a situation. "Is not the Short Season already in progress in London Society? In your father's letter, I thought things might be settled with the lady before I arrived. I had hoped for the opportunity to welcome her to the family. In truth, I half expected to arrive and find you already married. You were always one to act upon your decisions once they were made."

Spencer shrugged as if he did not care about the girl, but Glynis knew differently. Since her cousin had taken the mysterious Lady Theodora's acquaintance nearly four years removed, Spencer had planned to make the girl his wife. "Her guardians were called away. No explanations. And, as we are not engaged, we could not correspond."

"Does your father not know how to reach the girl's parents or guardians? I cannot imagine Lord Bond would permit you to court someone whose parents he held no knowledge."

"Father says they are from an obscure Irish title," Spencer revealed.

Something was definitely odd, but Glynis made no other comment. However, while she was in England, she hoped to learn more of Spencer's "lady love."

"Then you are free to serve as my escort and, I suppose, chaperone. England is quite antiquated in such matters compared to Europe. There, I can travel alone."

"We will see what father has to say to the matter," he said as the carriage turned onto a fashionable street. She had left with hopes of many family issues being resolved now that her father had passed, but she had already hit a wall if Spencer did not accompany her. If he chose not to travel with her, then she would be required to hire someone, which would delay her arrival in Hertfordshire, for she had sent Uncle Millard's servants back to Italy when the ship upon which she traveled set out across the English Channel from Calais to Dover. As silly as it would sound to another, although being treated as their child, Aunt and Uncle Millard were not her parents. Now, both her mother and father were no longer alive, but her half-brother was now Lord Padon, and, as she approached her majority within a matter of weeks, Glynis meant to have a say in the boy's upbringing. She was not the child's guardian, but, in her opinion, he required someone in his life with whom he shared blood and history.

<hr>

"I do not approve of all this nonsense," Lord Bond said as they shared supper that evening. "However, George and Althea say it is time you claim your rightful family, and I agree, as you are the daughter of an earl, you should know something of your place in English society. Therefore, I suppose my cousin correct. Yet, I must warn you, you will likely not be readily welcomed by those at Padon Hall. They have had things their own way for some time and will not be ready to relinquish their power to you. All that being said, you are the eldest and have the right to displace the interlopers occupying your father's estate."

"Interlopers?" Glynis questioned, her first doubts of something less than success arriving with his choice of words.

"Just the sister of Lord Padon and the woman's son, but you will have the right of all that has transpired soon enough. Such is not to say they will not attempt to sway you otherwise. I have previously placed the necessary legal papers in the hands of Lord Warwick," Lord Bond said.

"Lord Warwick?" she asked.

"Padon's nearest neighbor," Bond explained.

"Should we be exposing Glynis to Warwick?" Spencer asked.

"Why ever not?" Glynis's curiosity demanded.

Spencer blushed thoroughly. "Fellow does not possess the most pristine reputation," he confided.

Glynis smiled. "There is more than one man in Italy without a 'pristine' reputation, but we prefer to speak to their honesty and dependability when it is required. Can Lord Warwick be considered honest and dependable? Does he possess a smidgeon of honor?"

Spencer shrugged his shoulders in obvious uncomfortableness. "I have not had many dealings with the man. Affable enough."

Glynis's attention returned to Lord Bond. "Well, my lord?"

"You should make your own judgements, my girl, but, in my opinion, Warwick will serve you well."

"Then I will be happy for the gentleman's acquaintance," she said. She glanced to his lordship. "And Spencer may accompany me, my lord?"

The baron looked upon his son. "As I am not best pleased to have him moping about here in London, I suppose an escape into the countryside might do him well. At least, doing so is likely to present Spencer a true eye-opening experience."

Lord Bond refused to elaborate, despite both Glynis and Spencer pleading for more information, but it was obvious to both her and Spencer that Lord Bond knew more of the situation at Padon Hall than he was sharing.

༺༻

Although they had taken the Bond's smaller coach, Spencer had chosen to ride beside the carriage rather than to join her inside. She supposed he was still brooding over Lady Theodora or perhaps he was ruminating on the "mystery" his father had dumped in their laps. Despite the well-sprung carriage, Glynis, too, was as restless as her cousin. The scenery outside the coach's window reflected the change of the seasons, but the beauty of England in autumn was lost on her.

The chaise and four, however, had made good time, and they traveled the final leg of the journey from London to the market town of Hitchin and then on to the village of Walsworth, some two miles to the north. At length, the coachman turned the team from the main road onto a narrow lane that sloped gradually upward. She watched for her first glimpse of the house in which she had been born.

Glynis wondered what would await her at her family estate. In truth, in contradiction to her customary bravado, Glynis knew something of fear as the coach turned onto the gravel drive before the house. She was half tempted to instruct the driver to turn around. She knew her Aunt and Uncle Millard would welcome her with open arms, but she was seriously exhausted from being ignored by her father's family. It was not as if she was a "bastard," at least she prayed she was not, although she supposed anything might be possible.

Within a few minutes, Spencer was handing her down. "Prepared, my girl?" he asked.

"Not in half," she admitted.

AMENDING THE SHADES OF PEMBERLEY

"Perhaps with your half and mine combined, we might make a whole," Spencer suggested in an obvious attempt to shore up her qualms.

She looked up at the formidable door and swallowed hard. "Do me the favor and release the knocker. I do not think I am capable of raising my hand."

He did as she asked, and they waited and waited. After what felt forever, the door swung wide, and a very proper-looking butler asked, "May I be of service, sir? Ma'am?"

"You may step aside," Spencer ordered in an authoritative voice, reminding her of his father. "Lady Glynis wishes admittance."

"Without offense, sir, I do not know Lady Glynis. The mistress spoke nothing of visitors. The household is in mourning with the loss of the master."

"I would speak to your mistress," Glynis said in sharp tones. "I am Lady Glynis Padon. Lord Padon was my father." She darted past the man, and Spencer followed, nudging the servant to the side with his shoulder, but her cousin froze in place when his eyes fell upon a woman on the stairs.

"Mr. Bond, why are you at Padon Hall?" the girl asked in the softest of voices.

The lady was quite lovely with reddish-blonde hair and deep chestnut-colored eyes, and Spencer's expression announced her name before his lips formed the words. "Lady Theodora," Spencer said. "I could ask the same of you."

The young woman's eyes drifted to where Glynis stood. "You have brought another with you." She swallowed hard, silently announcing she was not as immune to Spencer's charms as her cousin assumed. "Might you provide me an introduction?" She reached for the railing, obviously requiring support to remain standing.

Spencer frowned, but he was always a gentleman. "Lady Glynis, may I present . . ." He paused in momentary awkwardness, unable to continue. Glynis had no doubt his suspicions had been raised as easily as had been hers. He glanced to the girl on the stairs and then to Glynis. It took several such searching looks for him to come to the same conclusion as had she. Spencer stood stiffer, but he managed to say, "Forgive me, Lady Theodora, but I thought your parents were the Kanhaways. You responded to their family name when we first were acquainted."

"My aunt and uncle," she said simply. "They raised me. From—"

Glynis overrode the girl's explanation. "From the time of your mother's death."

"Yes," the girl said simply. She looked as confused as Spencer was but a moment earlier. "I did not know my real name until we arrived at Padon Hall," she admitted.

The girl swayed in place as if this new realization was too much for her. Immediately, Spencer was by the young woman's side offering her his comfort. He turned to Glynis. "How is this possible? Your aunt has always said Lady Padon passed after giving birth to you."

Glynis nodded to her cousin. "Yes, she has. She has also, upon occasion, mentioned Lord and Lady Kanhaway, my father's sister and the lady's husband, who reside in Ireland. Is that not correct?"

Lady Theodora glanced to Spencer before nodding her agreement.

Spencer argued, "Cousin Glynis, you were always told you were Lord Padon's first born and, afterwards, your mother passed. How is such possible if Lady Theodora is also Lord Padon's child?"

"Aunt Millard did not come for me until I was nearly three months of age," Glynis reminded him. "We do not know what arrangements were made between the sisters of my parents. Perhaps you should ask Lady Theodora something of her birthday," Glynis suggested.

The girl responded when Spencer nodded his encouragement. "The eighteenth of October."

Glynis supplied the answer to the remaining part of the question. "1798. I am assuming Lady Theodora and I are twins."

They were not to have a response from the young lady, for a maid appeared at the top of the stairs. "Pardon, my lady. The young master is asking for you. He appears poorly."

"I have not fetched his milk," Lady Theodora said. She swayed in place again, and Spencer steadied her as best he could, while keeping proprieties.

Glynis glanced to the butler. "Your name, sir?" she demanded.

"Merrick, miss. I mean, my lady."

Glynis was accustomed to knowing when to take control and when to permit others to lead, for she often assisted her Uncle Millard during his negotiations with the representatives of other countries. "Mr. Merrick, Lady Theodora appears to be under the weather. My cousin, Mr. Bond, will see she is returned to her room without incident. I expect you to send up Master Robert's milk and an ale and, perhaps, some bread and honey, as well as Lady Theodora's maid to attend her." She glanced to the waiting maid. "Your name, girl?"

"Sophie, miss."

"Sophie, you will direct me to Master Robert's quarters, and then please send the housekeeper to me. My cousin and I will require appropriate quarters."

"Yes, miss. This way, miss. I mean, my lady." The maid gestured toward the way she had arrived.

As she passed Spencer, Glynis said, "See to Theodora. You and I will speak later."

At the top of the stairs, Glynis paused for a quick assessment of the condition of Padon Hall. It had been let go for some time. Her Aunt Millard would be livid if she viewed it. With a nod of her head for the maid to lead, she followed the girl through first one hall and then another until they reached what was obviously the nursery.

"Master Robert does not have quarters in the family wing?" she asked the girl.

"No, my lady."

"Ridiculous. Despite his age, Robert is the new Lord Padon."

The maid did not respond. She simply led the way into the boy's quarters, but they both came up short for the child was not alone. "Oh, my lord," the girl gasped. "I thought you had departed."

"I would not leave the boy alone," he said. However, his eyes remained on Glynis, assessing her appearance.

She knew her own eyes widened in appreciation. Before her stood one of the handsomest men Glynis had ever beheld, and living the majority of her years in Italy, she was familiar with the adage of "tall, dark, and mysterious." His lordship's hair, which he wore a bit too long, was the color of a raven's wing. His shoulders broad. His waist trim. And his eyes were a honey umber. He stood a full eight or nine inches taller than her. She felt rather petite and delicate, but she did not allow him to think he had mastery over her. His height, however, demanded she look up to view his countenance. High, well-carved cheekbones spoke of his lineage. She knew the type: Italy was polluted with them. Unfortunately, such did not keep her heart from skipping a beat or two. Tall and confident, he was taking in her appearance, as she was his. Glynis resisted the urge to straighten her pelisse and her jaunty hat.

"Who is there, my lord?" a weak voice coming from the bed called.

"Cannot say, my lord." To her dismay, his lordship's expression deepened and intensified as he watched her, as well as adding to his all too pleasing features. "It is a lady not of my acquaintance," the gentleman pronounced with a humorless smile, which said he intended to make it his business to learn her identity.

Glynis stepped around him. The crisp, masculine scent of sandalwood clung to him and invaded her senses. She spoke to the boy, not to the gentleman. "I fear, Lord Padon, you will also not recognize me." She came to stand beside the bed, and fear struck her. Glynis had thought the boy might have suffered from a cold in the head or some such minor illness. However, the boy's face was white and far too pale to think he would recover quickly. The idea saddened her, for she might lose him before she came to know him. "I am your sister. I have traveled from my home in Italy when I received word of our father's passing."

AMENDING THE SHADES OF PEMBERLEY

The man she noted earlier came to stand on the other side of the bed, which she wished he had not, for her visceral response to him was something of which she had no control. Glynis had difficulty drawing her eyes away from his face. It was one which warned men away while drawing women like flies to honey.

His lordship repeated her family history to the boy. "My father always said Lady Magdaline had more than one child. One lived with the Kanhaways. We have learned such is Lady Theodora. The other went to live with Lady Magdaline's sister; however, I cannot recall the name of the other girl."

"Lord Robert might believe your lack of memory, my lord, but I do not." She sat on the edge of the boy's bed. "I am Glynis. I have lived with my aunt and uncle, the Millards, all my life. Lord Millard is a baron and a British diplomat. He has been so employed for more than five and twenty years. I grew up with their children, Lucinda and Jonathon. I was nearly seven years of age before I learned I was not their youngest child. Unfortunately, I only encountered our father once. It was after the last war. Our family came to England as part of an English delegation. At a supper at the palace, our father was there, as were we."

The boy responded in a weak voice, "He told me . . . of the supper . . . but not . . . of you."

"I am sorry he denied you family. My aunt and uncle say Lord Padon was quite distraught at the death of my mother," she explained. Off to the side, the gentleman snorted in apparent disbelief, but Glynis ignored him. "With your permission, my lord, I would like to stay at Padon Hall and make myself useful to you and Lady Theodora."

"My permission?" the boy asked weakly.

"You are Lord Padon," she declared. "This house and all in it are yours."

"Do not feel . . . much like . . . an earl," the boy admitted.

"I would be honored to assume your care. Whatever ails you also appears to be affecting Theodora."

"Dora's ill too?" the boy asked.

"I am afraid so. My cousin, Mr. Bond, has seen her to her quarters."

The gentleman asked, "Mr. Spencer Bond?"

"Yes, Lord Bond's son," she supplied.

The gentleman turned to her brother. "Robert, my lad, what the lady says is true. Your father's first wife delivered twin girls. Theodora, as you know, went to live with Lord Padon's sister and Lord Kanhaway in Ireland, while the elder was to live with Lady Magdaline's sister in Europe."

"Another sister?" the boy asked.

The gentleman said, "You are surrounded by beautiful women, lad. Enjoy it while you may." His lordship bowed to Glynis. "It is time for me to depart. Therefore, I will take my leave, Lady Glynis."

"Thank you, Lord Warwick," she said with a challenging lift of her brows.

"You know me?" he asked.

"Lord Bond told me your estate marches along with this one," she shared. "He also said he forwarded certain legal papers to you which I might require during my stay at Padon Hall."

"Yes to all accounts, my lady." With a bow of farewell and a fond squeeze of the back of Robert's hand, he headed toward the door.

Glynis quickly said to the boy, "Permit me to learn where the maid is with your milk. I will return in a moment."

She followed Lord Warwick into the hall. "My lord, might I have a word with you?"

He halted his steps. "Yes, my lady. How might I be of assistance?" He presented her a generous smile, one which melted all her most feminine parts.

"Can you tell me how long Robert has been in such a state?"

His lordship's expression screwed up in seriousness. "Longer than I would like. Lady Kanhaway has assumed charge of the house in Lady Caroline's absence."

"Lady Caroline is not in residence?" Glynis asked.

"You have not heard?" he said with a frown of disapproval. "Three weeks after Lord Padon's interment and shortly after the arrival of the Kanhaways, Lady Caroline married Mr. Conrad Chambers. At least, we all assume she married the man, for they left for the Scottish border together. I am surprised Lord Bond did not inform you of the change in the lady's marital status."

Glynis listened carefully to what Lord Warwick shared, but also to what he did not say. "About two months prior," she surmised. "I am guessing such was about the same time as Robert took ill."

"I cannot prove it," the gentleman admitted. "Lady Kanhaway says the boy is grieving over his father's passing."

"Yet, you do not believe it," Glynis surmised.

"My disbelief is the reason I call daily on the young lord. I want this household to know someone is watching. I had hoped Theodora's appearance would change things for young Padon. Unfortunately, the girl was brought up with a milquetoast personality by her relations. She will be an obedient wife, but not her brother's savior."

"A very harsh portrait you paint of my family, my lord."

"View it for yourself, my lady, and draw your own conclusions. Just know, whatever goes on here, I will not stand by and permit Robert Padon to pay for the sins of his father with his young life." With that, he was gone.

Printed in Great Britain
by Amazon